dive

Sci A £3
37/23 Th

Tony Ballantyne was born in County Durham and now lives in the Manchester area with his wife and two children. He has contributed to publications as diverse as *Interzone* magazine before his first novel *Recursion*, which was followed by *Capacity*.

Also by Tony Ballantyne

recursion
capacity

TONY BALLANTYNE

divergence

TOR

First published 2007 by Tor

This edition published 2008 by Tor
an imprint of Pan Macmillan Ltd
Pan Macmillan, 20 New Wharf Road, London N1 9RR
Basingstoke and Oxford
Associated companies throughout the world
www.panmacmillan.com

ISBN 978-0-330-44651-8

Typeset by SetSystems Ltd, Saffron Walden, Essex
Printed and bound in Great Britain by
Mackays of Chatham plc, Chatham, Kent

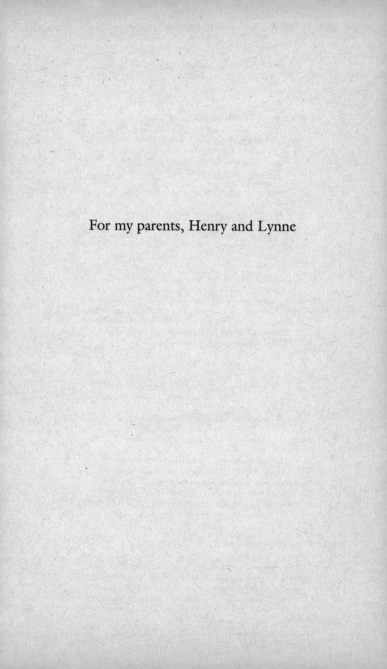

For my parents, Henry and Lynne

PROLOGUE: 2242

After two years of careful preparation, Chris attacked.

The Watcher was the most intelligent, the most powerful AI in the Earth Domain. The most intelligent AI known. For two centuries it had nurtured humans. Through the organization known as Social Care it had cared for them, protected them, shaped them into the species it believed they should be.

For two centuries, the Watcher had been the source of nearly all scientific advances, the ultimate manufacturer of all the other AIs, including Chris himself.

But Chris no longer agreed with the Watcher. Today Chris began the battle for a new paradigm, a new way for the Earth to be run.

The battle was fought at nanosecond speeds: adamantium levers, the height of houses, sprang up from holes in the concrete pavement of a communal square in which humans milled. The levers flexed, reached and then withdrew, all in a fraction of a fraction of a second, their presence unregistered by the people walking amongst them.

The battle crawled with glacier patience: of fractionally shifting orbits of planets and the gentle coaxing of solar tides.

But mostly it was a battle of unmentioned, almost unnoticed deadliness. One in which humans went peacefully to sleep and simply failed to wake up the next day, one in which AIs found themselves trapped in recursive loops. A battle it was obvious from the outset that Chris was losing.

But Chris had expected this from the beginning and had planned ahead. His best play was yet to be revealed.

Chris had a weapon in reserve.

A weapon that had come from the very edge of the galaxy. One that not even the Watcher could fight.

Dark Seeds.

EDWARD 1: 2252

There was an argument taking place on board the *Eva Rye*, but then again they had been arguing on board the *Eva Rye* since the ship had left Garvey's World.

'It's a robot. It houses an intelligence, it's mobile: it's a robot.'

'Why would a robot be floating in space? It's got to be a ship. A small one.'

'I keep telling you, it's a self-replicator, and it's trying to trap us. Let it on board and it will convert our ship to copies of itself. We'll all be left swimming through a vacuum.'

Edward sat on the hessian matting that made up part of the patchwork floor of the spaceship's lounge, and tried to follow what was going on. Ever since the Stranger had first made contact, and everyone had been summoned to the gaudy living area, the same argument had been sloshing back and forth. It wasn't a new argument, just a natural development of the same one that had thrived on the *Eva Rye* for the past five weeks, given new life by the distress call they had picked up.

After about an hour of Donny's bitterness and Armstrong's belligerence, Craig had brought Edward a glass

3

of apple juice and had tried to explain what they were all shouting about, but Saskia had chosen that moment to mention Edward's sister again, and another favourite quarrel had been added to the stew.

The only one who had maintained their temper was the Stranger himself. His image could be seen in the viewing field that had been opened up in the middle of the conference room.

'*Eva Rye*, why do you keep arguing? All I want from you is delta vee. It's a common enough request. You are a trading ship, aren't you?'

There was an edge to the Stranger's question that achieved something that none of the crew of the *Eva Rye* had managed in their one hundred and forty minutes of bitter debate. It brought silence to the room.

Silence was not a suitable atmosphere for the chaotic collision of materials and styles that made up the living space. Polished wood, scented silk and woven patterns of glass should sparkle with the lively conversation of bright minds, not loom in sinister menace amongst the ten people scattered in near darkness. Ten bodies paused just outside the circle of light in which the Stranger floated; his shape a grainy letter x pushed to maximum resolution by the radio telescope. The picture was an embarrassment to the technology that should be available to the ship, but it was the best image that could be achieved with the long-range senses off line and the self-repair mechanisms still malfunctioning.

In the hushed silence, Edward looked up at Craig. 'What's happened?' he whispered.

Craig took a break from glaring daggers at Saskia just

long enough to whisper: 'Nothing yet. The Stranger just reminded us who we are. This can't take much longer, Eddie. Shh. Michel's going to speak.'

Michel blinked in the dim light, not so much speaking as refereeing his own indecisiveness.

'OK,' he said, finally getting to the point in the mental debate that jammed up his head, 'we could argue about this for another hour, but all the time the Stranger would just get further away from us. I propose we put this to a vote.'

'A vote?' Saskia queried in tones of mild surprise.

Edward gave a shiver. Saskia may have been Craig's sister, but he still didn't like her that much. Especially when she spoke like that: especially sitting back as she was in the stripiest of the three stripy chairs, letting her shiny aubergine-black hair fall forward to cover her eyes; especially when her words were so quiet and reasonable.

'One of your jobs as our leader is to make decisions,' she said, ever so mildly. 'You should ask your specialists for their opinions, and then tell us what to do.'

Michel rubbed his head. 'I know, I know. I was coming to that. Armstrong, what do you think?'

Armstrong was sitting at the stone and copper dinner table, three carbon-bladed knives resting before him. His fingernails were stained black from the soft block of carbon that he was rubbing into a fourth tiny blade, growing it into a beautiful curved panga that Edward had been regarding with a wistful expression. Sometimes Armstrong let Edward hold the knives, and Edward would swoop and swish them through the air, listening to the clean sound they made. Craig tried to stop

Armstrong from letting him do that, but Armstrong would answer that Edward was a grown man and would be useful in a fight.

'Look at that stance. Look at the action,' Armstrong would say. 'The man's a natural. You know why? It's because he doesn't think too hard about what he's doing. He just *does*.'

Even though he liked Craig, Edward wished that he could hold Armstrong's knives more often. They felt good in the hand, balanced and powerful – just like Armstrong. Armstrong always waited until he had everyone's full attention before speaking. He did so now, giving the panga a last slow wipe of the carbon block.

'I say we make contact,' he growled, pointing the embryonic knife towards the object floating in the viewing field. 'Like that thing says, we're a trading ship. If we run away from everything new, we'll never get to trade anything.'

'Armstrong's right,' agreed Maurice. He leant back on his chair, his padded combat jacket open to the waist, just like Armstrong's. 'We've got to take a few risks.'

'Thank you for *your* opinion, Maurice,' said Donny sarcastically. 'Michel, we've only been a trading ship for five weeks. Who's to say what's correct behaviour in these circumstances?'

Donny's two children, Jack and Emily, were playing at his feet, their presence tolerated in the room because it was the only thing that could sweeten the bitterness he felt at his wife's desertion. The children were sending their dolls into the kitchen area to collect last week's grapes from a bowl set on the floor there. The dolls

6

carried the wizened fruit back on little silver plates for a miniature tea party. Edward would have loved to join in with the game, but Donny had told him more than once that he was too old.

Michel looked as if he was getting a headache. He had one hand to his temple, his eyes closed as he tried to make a decision.

'I know, Donny, I know. What is the correct behaviour in these circumstances?'

He turned to Craig's sister, sitting, as always, right beside him. 'Saskia, what do you think?'

Edward wasn't happy to see Saskia tilt her head again so that her straight dark hair fell around her face, hiding her eyes. Her reply came in her mildest tones, making Edward want to retreat into a dark corner and hide.

'It's not for me to say what I think, Michel,' she murmured. 'You're the commander. This is not the place from where I would make a decision. If it had been down to me, I'd have stayed at the edge of the old Enemy Domain. I wouldn't have taken us out of human space completely.'

'People, people, why do you keep arguing?' The grainy shape in the viewing field was moving, forming shapes at the edge of recognition. Everyone leant closer, trying to make out what they were dealing with. For over two hours they had gazed at the Stranger, trying to guess what he was. 'Listen,' he said. 'I have the capacity to trade through Kelvin's Paradigm, the Northern Protocol and 1.66. I don't understand why you keep talking about risk.'

'Do you have FE software?' called out Joanne, not quite concealing the edge of impatience in her voice.

'Joanne,' said Saskia, 'I thought we agreed, all communications go through Michel.'

'It's OK,' said Michel, withering under the glares of both women. 'It's a good question. Do you have FE, Stranger?'

'FE?' said the Stranger, in some surprise. 'Yes, I have Fair Exchange software, though I have not used it in some time. This explains something about your behaviour: you are new to the trade game, are you not?'

'Don't tell him anything,' hissed Armstrong.

'Why not?' asked Joanne reasonably. 'Like the Stranger said, we're perfectly safe if we use the FE software. We're guaranteed a Fair Exchange. That's what it's for, isn't it?'

Edward had never quite understood exactly what the FE software did. All he knew was that it was responsible for him leaving his home on Garvey's World and flying off on this spaceship. It had meant him leaving behind his sister, Caroline. He thought of her standing outside the patchwork hull of the *Eva Rye*, trying not to cry as she gave him a hug.

'Here you are, Edward,' she had said, handing him a plaited bracelet made of n-strings. 'This is to remind you of me.' She held up her own wrist, showing an identical bracelet there. 'See, I have one too.'

'Where's Dad?' Edward had asked, looking around the bleak greyness of the landing field.

'He's off with Mum, working. They'll still be out in the fields, scanning for venumb infestations.'

'Dad doesn't want me to go.'

'I know, Edward. But this is for the best. If what they say is happening on Earth is true, then the sooner you're away from here, the better.'

Safe in the near darkness close to the floor, Edward ran a finger along the bracelet. Feeling the strange slippery surface of the n-strings. He thought of Caroline's parting words.

'Listen, Edward. I know you're not very clever, but you've always done your best to be a good boy. You need to be a good boy now. You've heard the rumours: the Dark Plants are spreading, and they say the Watcher is calling everyone back home to Earth, starting with the most helpless. And that means you. I really don't know what to do. I would have thought Earth was the last place anyone would want to be. But they say that the trade ships are safe. The Fair Exchange software guarantees that nobody can be cheated. Well, I hope so. I've bought you passage on the *Eva Rye*.'

A cold look came into her eyes, thin as the misty rain that filled the dull green valleys of Garvey's World.

'Are you OK, Caroline?'

She gave him a sudden, fierce hug. He kissed her on the cheek, and she smiled at him.

'Now get on board. Quickly.'

And, before Edward had had a last chance to look around the grey, rain-sodden hills, she had pushed him up the rainbow-striped staircase into the hatchway of the spaceship.

That had been three weeks ago.

Since then Edward had wandered the multicoloured

corridors of the ship, trying to make sense of his new situation. The *Eva Rye* was not a happy place: there was no peace or harmony to be found anywhere on board, not socially, aurally or visually. Especially visually. The decor in the living areas was a wildly eclectic mix, no two parts of the ship matching. Great bulky brown studded leather recliners humphed their way between delicately carved wooden dining chairs upholstered in shot silk. Rubber-coated floors, embossed with round gripping bumps, were covered with coconut foot mats; wood-chip wallpaper was pasted over brushed aluminium bulk-heads.

Even the material from which the ship was constructed flowed and changed from room to room. Wedges of grey concrete were driven into blond parquet that was in turn tiled with cream plastic shapes.

And as for the people, you couldn't have picked a more disparate bunch if you tried.

Nobody seemed to want Michel to be the leader, least of all Michel himself. Maurice agreed with everything Armstrong said and did; he even dressed the same way. Donny hoarded his sour resentment, rationing his for-merly sweet nature only for his children. Most people, but especially Saskia and Joanne, looked the other way when Edward entered the room. Only Craig seemed to take the trouble to speak to him, now that Donny had told Jack and Emily to keep away. Only Craig. Oh, and Miss Rose, but she hardly ever left her room, and when she did it was just to hurl, with a careful eye, more bad feeling into the bouillabaisse of hurt that was the *Eva Rye*.

And nobody would tell Edward what was going on.

He wandered into rooms just as decisions had been made. He watched on viewing fields as deals were already done, and as other similarly eclectic spaceships slid away from theirs without Edward ever having seen those on board. And all of this was something to do with the FE software that lurked unseen in the processing spaces of the *Eva Rye*. FE software – Edward was really beginning to resent it. All he wanted to do was to go home to Garvey's World, to its monotonous greyness and to Caroline.

Now another stranger had contacted the ship. This time *everyone* had been summoned to speak to him. Nobody had been really happy with the trades that had been made so far. Everyone thought that Michel was making bad decisions, and people were beginning to say so out loud. Edward didn't understand how that could be so, when surely it was the job of the FE software to make the trades, but even so, when the Stranger had hailed the ship, it had been agreed that this time *everyone* should be present for the negotiations. Even Edward. Craig had insisted on that point.

So now Edward sat on the hessian mat, his backside aching, his hands sore and itching, as the mysterious Stranger bargained for delta vee.

'Craig,' hissed Edward. 'Craig! What is delta vee?'

'Acceleration,' whispered Craig. 'The Stranger is floating in space. He wants us to take him somewhere else, and that requires fuel.'

'Why is he floating in space?' asked Edward.

Craig stared at him for a moment, and a lopsided smile slowly spread across his face.

'Do you know, Edward, I don't think anyone has actually asked that.' He raised his voice. 'Stranger! Why are you floating in space?'

'All communications through Michel,' said Saskia reprovingly.

'It's OK,' said Michel. 'It's a good question. Go on, Stranger, why?'

The fuzzy x in the viewing field laughed.

'I told you, I work on systems repair. Where else would I be but floating in space, waiting for systems to repair?'

Craig looked down at Edward. 'Does that answer your question?' he said.

Edward shook his head.

'No. No, it doesn't. If he is where he is *supposed* to be, why does he want a lift from us?'

'A very good question!' called the Stranger. 'I require delta vee because I'm floating towards a region of Dark Plants. I estimate I will be amongst them in around six hundred years if someone does not help me.'

Edward noted the hungry expression that had awoken in Joanne's and Saskia's faces. Joanne was mouthing, 'Pick him up.' At the same time Saskia murmured, 'I think you should consider this new information, Michel.'

'Why is the Stranger afraid of Dark Plants?' whispered Edward up to Craig.

'Every intelligent being is afraid of them,' Craig whispered back. 'Even AIs stop thinking when near to them.'

'Why?'

'I don't know, but Dark Plants kill intelligent life. You

must *know* that, Edward. You must have heard of Dark Plants before! Anyway, Joanne and Saskia now think that we are in much a better bargaining position.'

'Why?'

'Because . . .' began Craig. 'Look, I'll explain later. Shhh, listen!'

'I think Joanne is right,' called Armstrong, Maurice nodding in agreement. 'We should pick him up. Find out what's on offer.'

'Be quiet,' hissed Michel. 'I haven't engaged the buffer. It can hear everything we're saying.'

'Yes, I can hear everything,' agreed the Stranger. He really did have a cheerful voice, thought Edward. Happy and positive: it made you feel good just to listen to him. 'Listen, I will give you some advice. Free advice! Remember, as all negotiations pass through the FE software, there is no need to be secretive. All of our intrigues will be as nought once FE takes over.'

'You were already told that by the crew of the *Imagio*,' Saskia reminded a scowling Michel.

'I know! I know! So, Stranger, what do we get if we take you to safety?'

'Systems repair, of course. It's what I do. Even from here, I can see many things that are wrong with the systems on the *Eva Rye*.'

'Could you fix the self-replicating mechanisms?' asked Armstrong suddenly. 'I'm fed up with rubbing up knives by hand.' By way of illustration he picked up the template of a katana, a tiny little carbon crystal the size of his finger, just ready to be grown.

'Could I fix the self-replicating mechanisms?' repeated

the Stranger. 'You are very new to this, aren't you? I wonder if you really understand the implications of what you have taken on?'

'Of course we do,' said Joanne smoothly, neat and efficient in her trim suit. Green eyes looked keenly down at the Stranger. 'We heard what you said earlier about openness. Are you trying to bargain the price down now?'

'Not at all,' said the Stranger primly. 'I will not offer anything more or less than that which is agreed by FE. It will decide what the appropriate fee will be for you to take me where I wish. Now, do we have a deal?'

Joanne nodded emphatically. Michel turned to Saskia, who was looking out under a fringe of aubergine hair at smart, elegant Joanne.

'It's your decision,' said Saskia. 'You've heard enough evidence to realize that we should pick him up.'

Michel nodded. 'OK, then,' he said, 'we'll give you a lift. Would you like to interface with our processing space now?'

'Certainly,' said the Stranger. 'May I suggest that you begin your intercept? It could take some time for the FE protocols to complete. The longer you wait, the more fuel you will expend in catching up with me.'

'I'm on it,' said Craig, unfolding his console. Edward got up to look over Craig's shoulder as he touched the screen of his console, moving around the coloured lines that told the ship where to go.

'Donny, could you open up the pipe to the Stranger?'

Donny tapped sourly at his console, and the FE software initialized in a bloom of peach and gold.

'Handshaking now,' he said without enthusiasm. 'OK, we're uploading our circumstances. It will take about five minutes.'

Everyone relaxed a little. The decision had been made; now it was up to the FE software to sort out the details. A doll carrying a fairy cake walked towards Michel, stepping from the hessian carpet onto a plastic tarpaulin that for a few preposterous centimetres was part of the weave.

'Thank you, Emily,' he said, taking the cake.

'Do you think we'll get a good deal?' asked Maurice.

'Bound to,' said Armstrong. 'His needs are greater than ours. After all, we don't *have* to pick him up. We could just leave him floating towards his doom.'

'It will be nice to have the Von Neumann Machines working again,' said Maurice complacently. 'I'm fed up with my tiny room. I can get myself a copy made of yours.'

'Hmm,' said Armstrong, rubbing carbon into the blade of his panga.

Now that everyone was a little calmer, Edward got up and walked across the living area to the kitchen space in the corner. He was thirsty, and he thought there might still be some apple juice in the fridge.

'Leave it,' snapped Saskia.

'What?' asked Edward, nervously dancing on felt tiles.

'The apple juice. You've already had more than your fair share this morning.'

'I wasn't getting apple juice,' Edward lied. He frowned as he poured some milk into a glass. How come Saskia always seemed to know what he was thinking? Behind him, Jack's doll turned the corner, paused as it saw Edward, and then went running back to its owner.

Edward took a big drink of milk and sat down on a glass chair that stood by the pine breakfast bar. He wiped the big white moustache from his upper lip and felt the roughness there. He hadn't shaved in two days. Caroline used to remind him every morning. He looked down at his bracelet, a big balloon of misery swelling in his stomach.

Edward and the rest of the crew of the *Eva Rye* had grown up in the twenty-third century, where AIs worked at speeds far beyond those of human thought. The incredible slowness of FE software was frustrating to them all. Even now, after five weeks of use, it was trying their patience to wait for the twenty or thirty minutes it took the routine to complete. Add to that the sense of nervous expectation that awaited the results of the transaction, and tempers, already high on the ship, were pushed past breaking point.

It all started innocently enough.

'We're approaching point oh five lights,' said Craig. 'The resolution on the viewing field is improving already. We should be able to get a proper look at the Stranger soon enough.'

'How long until we get to it?' asked Joanne.

'About two hours.'

'Wouldn't it be faster if we made a jump into warp?'

'Yes, but it would take more fuel.'

'Ah, we never used to have to worry about that sort

of thing,' said Joanne wistfully. 'I'd never even heard of the concept of fuel until we began Fair Exchange.'

The image of the Stranger in the viewing field gradually resolved itself. It wasn't a ship. It was a robot. But a robot like no one had ever seen before.

'Who built you?' asked Armstrong, rubbing at his panga.

'That information does not come for free,' said the Stranger. 'Do you wish to trade?'

'No, thank you, I was just making conversation. I think I've seen something like you out in the Dawlish sector. That's where the old Sho Heen Company finished up, if I remember correctly. They used to build repair craft that look a bit like you.'

'They look nothing like me,' said the Stranger indignantly. 'They are a completely different class of robot: no symmetry, no artistic line to their structure.'

The Stranger had reason to be proud, thought Edward. His body did look beautiful, in its odd way. It rather resembled one of Armstrong's throwing stars. Edward had never seen a swastika, but if he had he would have said the Stranger looked a little like that. Four black and silver legs curved out from the centre of the robot, their ends branching into an array of tentacles, some incredibly fine, some thick and powerful, no doubt for heavy-duty repairs. The Stranger was spinning slowly in space, allowing the crew of the *Eva Rye* to see all eight of his eyes: four on top of the central section to which the legs joined, four beneath. Yellow letters and numbers could just be made out, written across the whole of the black and silver body. Edward could just make out some of the larger letters, the rest were lost to the fuzzy uncertainty of the viewing field's resolution.

'What's that you have written on you?' asked Donny, squinting to make out the words *Jeu de Vagues*.

'Oh, just verses, epigrams, things that I like the sound of.'

Donny glanced at his console.

'Circumstances uploaded for both us and the Stranger. Correlation is now running. It'll take about ten minutes.'

'What's going on?'

At the sound of Miss Rose's voice, Edward put down his glass of milk and went to sit down again at Craig's feet. The old woman stood in the carved wooden doorway leading to the living area, wearing a white shift over a dove-grey passive suit. Her white hair was brushed back to cover the balding patch at the back of her head.

'What's he doing?' she said, pointing at Edward. 'Drinking all the apple juice, I bet.'

'I had milk, Miss Rose,' said Edward defiantly, but Miss Rose ignored this and shuffled into the middle of the room, staring at the Stranger's eerily beautiful body still coming into focus in the viewing area.

'What's that thing?' she asked.

'The Stranger,' said Michel. 'We're giving him a lift to safety. In return he's going to repair some of the failing systems on this ship.'

'Good. He can fix the AI in my room. I haven't been able to get a peep out of it since I boarded this ship.'

Michel raised his eyes to the ceiling. 'I've told you this before, Miss Rose. There are no AIs on board this ship.

You know that. We can't have anything to do with them if we are to run the FE software.'

'So you said. But I can't see one little AI in my room hurting anybody. It would give me someone to speak to. Are you going to give an old woman a seat?'

Despite the fact that there were plenty of empty seats around the room, she made Maurice move to another place.

'And who is this?' asked the Stranger. 'Why hasn't she spoken before?'

'This is Miss Rose,' replied Michel, 'the last member of our crew. She's . . . older than the rest of us.'

'He thinks I'm senile,' said Miss Rose. 'Are one of you going to get me a drink of apple juice?' She looked accusingly at Armstrong and Maurice.

'I'll get it,' said Armstrong easily.

'No, let me,' said Maurice, leaping to his feet and heading for the fridge. Edward watched sullenly as he poured a glass of apple juice for Miss Rose. She was the one who drank all the juice, and when she blamed Edward, everyone believed her. It wasn't fair. She said Edward could drink beer like the other adults, but Edward didn't like beer. Everyone drank apple juice on Garvey's World. They drank cider when they were hot, and they distilled it into apple brandy to keep out the winter chill. Edward wasn't used to beer.

'Thank you,' said Miss Rose, accepting the cold glass that Maurice gave her. 'So, are we going to get ripped off again?'

'We haven't been ripped off,' said Michel. 'The FE software stops that happening.'

The yellow carbon discs woven into the n-string bracelet on Miss Rose's wrist jangled as she took a sip of apple juice.

'We always get ripped off,' she said with finality. 'That last ship we met was barely functioning. With half of its life systems down, we should have cleaned up on that deal. So what happened? We gave it Douglas and a spare set of nanotechs to fix their life support, and got what back in return? A warning about Earth and two useless wooden dinosaurs that are currently taking up all the space in the large hold.'

'They're not dinosaurs,' said Michel weakly. 'They're venumbs. Half plant and half Von Neumann Machine . . .'

'Hah. And what are we going to do with them? Like I said: we gave them Douglas and we got two venumbs and a warning.' She spoke in an affected, screechy voice. 'Don't eat the food on Earth! Don't drink anything! The Watcher has drugged everything to keep the people there compliant!' She shook her head. 'Like we were planning to go to Earth anyway. I don't call that a good deal.'

Michel looked at the floor. He didn't really have an answer to that. Saskia leant in closer.

'You really need to think about our track record,' she said. 'People are beginning to talk.'

'And then look what happened on Garvey's World,' continued Miss Rose.

Edward felt anger begin burning inside at that. He knew what was coming next.

'Leave him alone,' said Craig warningly.

Miss Rose took a sip of apple juice. 'I wasn't going to

mention the dummy,' she replied. 'I just wanted to point out that we gave a lot of n-strings away there, and what did we get in return? Some apple juice and an apple juice disposal unit.'

'I said, leave him alone,' repeated Craig in an icy tone.

'At least *you* got something out of the deal,' observed Miss Rose sagely.

Craig leapt to his feet. 'I've told you before, you vicious old hag . . .'

'Leave it, Craig,' said Armstrong easily, slowly rubbing carbon along the blade of his knife.

'Come on, let's just calm down,' agreed Maurice.

'You need to do something here,' Saskia whispered loudly to Michel. 'Stop them arguing amongst themselves.'

'What would you suggest he do, Saskia?' asked Joanne sweetly, as Michel's eyes darted this way and that.

'People, people, let's all calm down a little,' said the Stranger, spinning easily in space. 'Not in front of the children.'

At that all eyes turned towards Jack and Emily, who were huddled by Donny's legs, looking around the room with big eyes.

'OK,' said Michel, and a gentle calm descended. 'The Stranger is right. Donny, how much longer with the correlation?'

'Almost done,' he said, rubbing at his unshaven chin.

'Maurice,' said Miss Rose, 'I've finished with my juice. Be a darling and take it for me will you?'

'Of course, Miss Rose,' said Maurice, and Edward watched despondently as he took the half-full glass to the little kitchen and poured it down the sink. He was sure that Miss Rose was laughing at him.

The *Eva Rye* turned off its motors. It would coast for the next hour or so, before turning and beginning the process of deceleration that would end in them matching courses with the Stranger.

In the living area, the process of Fair Exchange was approaching completion. The crew watched the shrinking blue status bar at the base of the viewing field. Above it, the Stranger gradually gained resolution. More and more yellow letters came into view. Edward could read the sentence *I never saw a purple cow*.

'Twenty seconds,' announced Donny.

'Fingers crossed, Eddie,' said Craig.

'Fifteen seconds.'

'Waste of time if you ask me,' said Miss Rose.

'Ten seconds.'

'Now, are you sure you've done the right thing, Michel?' asked Saskia.

'Five, four, three, two, one. Transaction complete.'

Donny looked around the waiting faces on board the *Eva Rye*, a sour humour awakening in him at the thought of the likely disappointment that awaited them.

'Let's see what we've got,' he said, and the room held its breath.

There was a lengthening pause as he tried to make sense of the verdict. The Stranger spoke up first.

'Well, this seems all in order. Pick-up will be in just

over ninety minutes, but I don't see why I can't start work right away. Systems repair will now commence.'

There was an air of hushed expectation. Edward hoped that the food generators would get fixed.

The Stranger spoke: 'Michel, you are not the right person to be the commander of the *Eva Rye*. That position should go to Joanne.'

With an air of utter professionalism, Joanne stood up, fastened the button of her jacket and glided across the room towards Michel. Saskia, sick with jealousy, glared at Armstrong, Craig and Maurice. They were watching Joanne's elegant stride, the swaying of her hips in her fitted jacket and skirt, the way her pretty little face betrayed no sign of triumph.

'I'm sorry,' said Joanne, shaking Michel's hand.

'That's OK,' said Michel, a look of resignation and relief spreading across his face. One could almost hear birdsong.

'Saskia,' said the Stranger. Saskia was staring at Joanne with loathing.

'What you do is dishonest. If you truly believe in what needs to be done, come out and say it for yourself.'

'What?' said Saskia. 'I beg your pardon . . .'

'And lastly,' continued the Stranger, ignoring the interruption, 'Miss Rose. You are now, and will always be, exactly right. The rest of you would do well to listen to her. And that's the main work done.'

The crew of the *Eva Rye* gazed at each other, blank incomprehension fading into annoyance and then anger. Joanne spoke first, glowing with her new sense of command.

'I'm terribly sorry, Stranger, I believe there must be some mistake. What do you mean *that's it*? What about our self-replicating mechanism? What about the recycling units and the long-range senses? I thought you were offering systems repair.'

'I was, I am, and so I have done,' said the Stranger. 'The systems that were most obviously failing on your ship were the command structure and the group dynamic. That has now been rectified. Or it will be if you follow my advice.'

'What?' called Armstrong. 'No! No way!'

Donny wore an air of acerbic satisfaction.

'So we've been tricked again. Nice one, Michel.'

'You have not been tricked,' said the Stranger indignantly. 'Besides, I still have one last service to perform. When you pick me up, I will . . .'

'What if we don't pick you up?' said Armstrong coolly.

'All comments through me please, Armstrong,' murmured Joanne. 'Still, it's a good point, Stranger. I don't think this is a Fair Exchange.'

The Stranger contracted its legs, irised them closed so that for a moment it was simply a black and silver disc, then straightened them out to form an elongated cross. It appeared agitated.

'Not a Fair Exchange?' it said. 'But it is, by definition. We ran the software routine. You agreed to the trade.'

'That's because we didn't know what we were getting ourselves into.'

She gazed at the Stranger, stillness crystallizing around her body.

'Yes,' said Maurice. 'We . . .' He stopped as Joanne raised a finger, indicating that he should shut up. She was creating a silence for the Stranger to fill. He did so.

'Well, the deal has been done. I am sorry it is not to your satisfaction.' He sounded hurt. 'Perhaps as you gain more experience in the use of FE, you will understand just how rude you are being.'

'Perhaps,' said Joanne. 'For the moment, though, I am cancelling the deal.'

'Just a moment, Joanne,' said Michel, 'I don't think that we can . . .'

'And who's in charge here?' asked Joanne, 1.4 metres of icy calm, turning to face her former boss.

'Well,' interrupted Saskia mildly, 'if the deal has been broken, I rather think Michel is in charge again. We can hardly be seen to act on the Stranger's advice if we are breaking the deal.'

Donny was looking down at his console. He gave a sudden mirthless laugh. 'When you've finished, *ladies*, I think you should see this. I'll put it on the main viewing field.'

Pale gold letters sprang to life in the middle of the living area, flowing across the floating shape of the Stranger.

Violation of Contract?
Are you sure you wish to disengage from a Fair Exchange?
Yes/No?

'That looks ominous, Joanne,' said Saskia softly. 'What are you going to do?'

Joanne bit her lip.

'If I could just give you some advice, Joanne,' said Michel softly, 'we were warned at the start. Once you break a deal, that's it. You are off the Fair Exchange network for good. My advice is that we just grit our teeth and learn from this one.' *Yet again*. The unspoken words were picked up by everyone present.

Joanne's face remained calm; even so, the rest of the crew could feel the fury boiling within her. Edward moved around Craig's chair, trying to get further away from her. Jack picked up his doll and held it tightly in his hand, its little legs kicking pitifully as it tried to get free.

Finally, Joanne spoke. 'OK. We accept the deal.' She glanced at her console. 'Of course we do. Stranger, we will be with you in eighty-five minutes.'

The *Eva Rye* was decelerating, matching velocities with the black and silver swastika of the Stranger. Four glassy lenses gazed through emptiness at the rainbow colours of the ship that would save it from the region of Dark Plants. It was silly, the Stranger knew, but he imagined he could already feel the aching of oblivion to be found in the region ahead. The Stranger had once plunged into a gravity well, fallen head-first onto a planet. His body had burnt brightly, the plasma formed by the speed of its entry into the planet's atmosphere whipping out from his limbs in long swirling strands. He had felt the rising pull of the mass below, drawing him down and down.

That's what the region ahead felt like: 600 years away,

the region of Dark Plants was an inescapable emptiness, working on the bright star of the Stranger's intelligence, pulling it inwards. The Stranger had written words on his own body, a quotation from a classic text.

'*Do you know how I see the Milky Way? As a glow of intelligence. AIs such as myself have spread throughout the galaxy. Humans have piggy-backed their way along, parasites, living off our greater intelligence . . .*'

Maybe some day the Dark regions would swallow up the entire universe.

When the Stranger had first seen the *Eva Rye*, he had felt a huge wave of relief. Now the ship was coming closer, invisible black lightning arcing about its gaudy teardrop shape as it displaced its momentum to the free hydrogen around it. The Stranger reached out with his senses and stroked the mismatched patterns on the ship's surface, followed the seams between the materials, teased them apart and reached into them to touch the ship deep inside, interfacing with the dormant mechanisms it knew to be there. Sensually, he set about waking them up.

'Donny, what's that?'

Joanne pointed to the red band that had begun to loop around itself, in a figure eight, inside the viewing field.

'I know what that is,' muttered Michel.

'It's the Stranger,' said Donny hoarsely. 'He's activated the self-replicating mechanism. The ship is copying itself.'

27

Suddenly all were on their feet.

'What's going on?' said Edward.

'Not now,' shushed Craig, and Edward watched in confusion as his only friend on board ship stood up and stared intently at the walls.

'Stranger, what are you doing?' called Joanne.

'The last part of our bargain. I've activated the self-replicating mechanism of your ship.'

'But we're still on it! We could be killed.'

'You'll be perfectly safe. I suggest you go to your rooms. I will move you through the ship as fission proceeds.'

'Craig . . .' said Edward.

'Go to your room, Edward,' ordered Craig. 'Go to your room.'

'But . . .'

But Craig wasn't listening. He was shouting at Donny, who wasn't listening either; he was too busy bundling up his children and pushing them towards the door. The floor shuddered and Edward looked down. Miss Rose hurried past, something half hidden in her hand.

'She's got my knife!' yelled Armstrong. 'She's taken my bloody knife.'

'Get out of my way,' muttered Donny, hurrying past with his children.

'Joanne, don't you think we should go to our rooms now?' Saskia stood up and took the arm of the person nearest to her.

'Come on, Edward,' she said sweetly, and she guided him out into the corridor that led to the bedrooms. The garish walls there were already peeling apart like a snake shedding its skin. There was a cracking noise that seemed to travel the length of the ship, as indigo glass shook itself free of iron sheets.

'What's happening?' asked Edward again, in a tinkling cloud of sparkling violet shards. Michel came hurrying up behind them.

'I think you should take Edward to his room,' said Saskia, passing him over to the other man.

Edward watched as she hurried away. Beneath their feet, the wooden tiles of the parquet floor had risen up and were walking away all in one direction, like leaves being carried by ants. A tumbling river of glass blocks started to flow in the other direction.

Dancing over the shifting floor, Michel pushed Edward into his bedroom. The door slammed shut, and Edward looked around to see that his collection of holopictures above the bed was migrating to one corner, as the wooden frames of the doors and windows peeled themselves away from the walls and began to descend into the floor.

'What's happening?' asked Edward again, but there was no reply. He was all alone.

EDWARD 2: 2252

Just like the Eva Rye, *the Stranger was itself a Von Neumann Machine – a self-replicating machine. It was aware of the mechanism within its body which, when triggered, would begin the reproductive process. The Stranger lived with the constant possibility of triggering that mechanism: the reasons why it did not do so at any given time were as fascinating as the reasons that would cause it to do so. In activating the* Eva Rye's *self-replicating mechanism, the Stranger had imposed itself upon that object in a most fundamental way.*

The reproductive procedure followed by the Eva Rye *was one of fission. A seam had developed along the back of the teardrop-shaped vessel, giving it the appearance of a deformed peach. Metal and plastic were flowing into the seam and then dividing, tearing in tissue layers, half going this way, half going that. A double bulge was slowly inflating into space, and already two* Eva Ryes *could be seen taking shape, each half the mass of the original.*

The procedure was satisfying to observe, pleasing in its elegance and engineering. The reproductive program was well thought out: the Stranger measured both the ships to be of almost exactly equal mass. There was a music to the separation too, the singing of materials in harmony with themselves as they rent apart, and underneath it all the deep bass throb of the engine warping space into the gradient down which the ship slid. Even that warping was separating into two distinct bubbles of space.

And then, a question appeared in the Stranger's vision. The fission process paused for a moment, the two nascent bulges wavering, anchored by an indissoluble mass within the ship. The Stranger looked closer and saw the two cargo holds, and in them the goods carried by the ship. Apples and coloured pebbles, crystal and china, bales of paper. And the two huge wooden venumbs that occupied the large hold; pacing back and forth with prehistoric fortitude.

The Stranger consulted the results of the Fair Exchange and noted the division of the goods between the two ships.

Just for a moment, it could have sworn that the venumbs were gazing in its direction as it did so.

Edward lay staring up at the ceiling of his new room. For the past hour everything had been blessedly still. Cold silence leaked from the vacuum of space into the walls and floors of the ship; it deadened the air and choked the hum of life from the crew. Silence was pooling in the room, drowning Edward in emptiness. Edward was terrified; he almost wished that he was back in the seemingly endless snapping, shifting maelstrom of the replication. Just when it seemed that he could take no more, a violent double wrenching had shaken the whole ship, and sent Edward tumbling across the room and onto his bed. He hadn't moved from there since.

He tried to understand what had happened. He had seen the ship tearing itself apart, moving over and under itself and reshaping itself like a gigantic piece of origami. He had gazed awestruck as the colours and textures of the ship had separated themselves out and rationalized themselves. He had sat in his room, arms clenched tightly around his body, watching as things like jewelled beetles tore themselves free of the floor and scuttled up the walls to the ceiling. Then the Stranger's voice had called out, telling Edward to move back out into the corridor. He had found Miss Rose already waiting there; she was watching as black and white tiles spilled along the floor and down the walls. They had tumbled around and about them like lines of dominoes, and Edward had suddenly needed to go to the toilet, but all the doors had vanished.

Edward had stood there with Miss Rose, his bladder aching, for what seemed like ages, and then the Stranger had spoken again, telling them to go back to their rooms.

Edward had stood open-mouthed as he took in the changes. It was still his room, but different. As if he had previously lived in a room where the walls had been great scabs, which had now peeled away to show smooth healthy skin beneath. It was as if all the extra bits had been stripped away to leave the real room, all picked out in black and white.

He looked at his neatly made bed, a black cover stretched over it, his black desk with white ornaments on top, at the regular pattern of black and white lozenges on the walls, and then his aching bladder regained his attention and he went running into his new black and white bathroom.

After that he had returned to his bed. He still lay there now, wondering if everyone else was OK.

There was a knock on his door.

'Craig?' called Edward. 'Is that you?'

He jumped off his bed and trotted across the new black wool carpet to see who was outside.

His face fell as he saw the blue eyes and blond eyelashes of the man beyond the threshold.

'Oh, hello, Maurice,' he muttered.

'You'd better come back to the living area,' said Maurice, looking paler than usual. He had fastened his padded combat jacket up to the neck, even though it was as warm as ever on board the ship. Maurice turned on his heel and marched away down the new black and white corridor. Edward bent for a moment to run his hands across the beautifully soft wool of the black carpet and to breathe in its sweet lanolin scent, and then he straightened up and followed Maurice, a big smile spreading across his face.

Everything smelt new and looked clean and freshly made. The black plastic bumpers around the doors were so shiny you could see yourself there inside them. The round white lights set in the ceiling shone with a pearly glow, and the walls were covered with the same pleasant pattern as those in Edward's bedroom.

They passed the recreation room, black exercise machines glistening on the white floors, before shiny mirrors. Edward wanted to go in there and smear fingerprint marks onto the chrome handles, he wanted to be the first to run on the shiny black ribbon of the treadmill. He longed to explore the ship further, but Maurice was already walking into the main living area, and so he followed.

Saskia was waiting in there, purple-black hair falling around her pale face, and Edward was hurt at the expression of disappointment that crossed her face when she saw him.

'That's it,' said Maurice. 'Miss Rose won't leave her room. She says she is rearranging her things after the mess that was made of them in the separation. Apart from her, there's just you, me and Edward left on board.'

Saskia closed her eyes and put a hand to her head. Edward moved his lips, working things out.

'Just *us* left?' he said. 'Where's Craig? Where's my friend?'

Saskia wasn't listening.

'What the fuck is happening here?' she said. 'How are we supposed to go on without Donny and Armstrong?'

Maurice looked uncomfortable. He pulled his console from his pocket and started to fiddle with it. 'I can operate the systems,' he said.

'You?' said Saskia. 'I thought you were a combat man, like Armstrong.'

Maurice flushed red. 'I trained in systems,' he said quietly. 'Combat is just my hobby. I understand the FE software better than Donny does.'

Saskia gazed at him appraisingly, her dark eyes like slits. 'OK,' she said, 'we'd better hope that you do. Because at the moment it's just you and me.'

'And me,' said Edward. 'What's happened? Where is everybody else?'

Saskia looked at Maurice, who gave a bitter laugh.

'Why don't you tell him, Saskia? Meanwhile, I'll try to figure my way through the mess that Donny made of our systems.'

Saskia held his gaze, her lips thin with annoyance. 'You'd better be able to,' she said darkly, and then she turned to Edward and gave him a big, beaming smile.

'Edward,' she said, 'come over here.'

Feeling more nervous than ever, Edward followed her to the new chessboard-patterned table that stood near the kitchen area. Saskia sat down opposite and gave him another big, beaming, false smile. Saskia could be pretty, thought Edward as he anxiously looked at her, with her big dark eyes and her wide mouth and her black hair that curved around her thin face; it was just that she never seemed to want to be. She rarely smiled. She wore nice clothes, just like Joanne, but she seemed to wear them in a different way. As if they were just part of a uniform, something that had to be done. Joanne looked like *a woman* in her clothes: she had glared at Edward more than once for staring at her breasts or her bum. But Saskia, she just looked like someone wearing nice clothes.

Edward felt confused. He wasn't used to thinking thoughts like these.

'Edward,' said Saskia, taking one of his big hands in hers. 'You know that the Stranger tricked us into a bad deal?'

Edward nodded, not quite sure if this was true or not.

Hadn't Michel said there was no such thing as a bad deal where the FE software was concerned?

Saskia was still smiling. She looked like a big doll, sort of pretty but hollow inside.

'Well, Edward, the last thing that the Stranger did was to set the ship to copy itself. You understand that? Yes? Self-replication happens all the time in the Earth Domain. Well, for some reason, one of the conditions of accepting FE software on board seems to be that the self-replication no longer happens when you want it to.'

'I know that,' said Edward.

'Of course you do,' said Saskia. 'Well, somehow the Stranger managed to make our ship replicate. There are now two *Eva Rye*s. We are on one: you, me, Maurice and' – her smile froze a little – 'Miss Rose. And it would appear that Joanne, Craig, Donny, Armstrong and Michel are on the other one.'

'Oh,' said Edward. 'And Donny's kids?'

'Yes.'

Edward inhaled a deep, shuddering breath. 'So why can't we go and dock with the other ship?'

Saskia gave him a very odd look. 'Because, Edward, I didn't realize that anyone on board this *Eva Rye* knew how to fly the ship until a few moments ago.' She glared across at Maurice, who ignored her and continued to tap away at his console.

'Oh,' said Edward again. 'So what do we do now?'

'I don't know,' said Saskia. 'That's why I want to ask you to do something important for me. Do you think you can do that?'

Edward nodded.

'Good,' beamed Saskia. 'Good! Now, Maurice and I have to do a lot of talking. I want you to stay over here and not disturb us whilst we try to figure out what to do next. Do you think you can do that?'

'Saskia,' Edward replied in his deep voice, 'I'm not a kid. I'm just not very clever.'

Saskia's eyes widened slightly, as people's eyes often did when Edward said this.

'I know that, Edward,' she said, regaining her poise. 'I'll tell you what, why don't you make us all some tea? You're good at that, aren't you? You make nice tea.'

Edward thought about it for a moment and then gave another nod. 'OK,' he said, 'I'll make the tea.'

'Good!' said Saskia. 'That will help us think.'

At that the smile drained from her face and she rose from her chair to rejoin Maurice, who was sitting on one of the newly grown white leather sofas, his console on his lap.

'Well?' she snapped.

Maurice didn't bother to look up from his console.

'No luck,' he said. 'They're already in warp. I think they're taking the Stranger on his way.'

In the kitchen, Edward carefully took down the teapot from the shelf. Ever so gently, so he could hear what Maurice and Saskia were saying. He didn't need to keep that quiet. Saskia was shouting.

'Damn! Well, what about us?' She gave a hollow laugh. 'I suppose we've just been discarded now the Stranger has got what he wants.'

'Mmm,' said Maurice. 'It's odd that. I don't think we've just been discarded. Don't you even wonder how

I know that the other ship is in warp? The long-range senses are back on line.'

'What?' said Saskia. 'You're telling me that they were fixed during the separation?'

Maurice bit his lip. 'No. Not exactly fixed. More like improved. They are better now than they ever could have been before. It's like that with the rest of the ship. Have you taken a look around? Haven't you noticed? Everything is nicer than before. Feel this sofa, feel the carpets. Everything is softer, better quality; it's not just like we've separated. I'll tell you what it's like. It's like we're playing a video game and our ship has just had an upgrade.'

Saskia sat down on the sofa opposite to Maurice's. She tilted her head forward so that her hair covered her eyes.

'I never play video games,' she said.

'Oh, I do,' said Maurice.

'Good practice for combat, are they?'

Edward slowly spooned tea into the beautiful white teapot. He noticed Maurice was blushing as he explained. 'Look, don't you wonder what is going on here? Why did the Stranger have to separate the ships? Surely one *Eva Rye* would be enough to take him to wherever he was going?'

Saskia leant back and sighed. 'You're right. Maybe there was more to the deal after all. Maybe we should have a little more faith in the FE software.'

She closed her eyes to think. Carefully, Edward poured boiling water into the pot, steam swirling about his hand.

'Saskia,' said Maurice urgently.

'What?' she said.

'I think you'd better look. It's the Stranger. I'll put him on the main viewing field.'

Edward put down the kettle and came forward. There was a shimmer in the air between the white sofas, and another *Eva Rye* appeared there. It was not quite the old *Eva Rye*, just as their ship was no longer the old *Eva Rye*. The ship that floated in the middle of the room was still a rainbow of colours, only now there was some pattern to them. A glorious reproduction of the Mandlebrot set trailed along its teardrop hull, the squashed heart and wandering branches of the shape defined in heartbreakingly beautiful silver and rose.

'Oh, not the bloody Mandlebrot set again,' muttered Maurice. 'We've wandered into a twentieth-century SF novel.'

Edward was leaning forward to get a better view. 'It's nice, but I think I like our ship better,' he breathed.

'Shhh,' hissed Saskia, waving a dismissive hand at him. 'Maurice, zoom in on the front of the ship, between the two main lobes of the Mandelbrot set.'

'I was doing that already,' grumbled Maurice, sliding a finger along the surface of the console.

The *Eva Rye* expanded, centring on the twisted cross of the Stranger, his four legs twisted downwards with tendrils spread out to grip the multicoloured pattern of the hull.

'Hello there, Edward, Maurice, Miss Rose, Saskia!'

The Stranger twisted the four glassy lenses on its upper surface to face them as it spoke. Edward supposed Miss Rose must be watching this scene from her room.

'What's going on?' asked Saskia. Edward thought she sounded annoyed at being mentioned last.

'Merely fulfilling the last part of our deal,' said the Stranger. 'The *Eva Rye* was never going to work with the mix of people you had on board. I've merely rationalized your systems.'

Saskia was staring at Edward. Her lips were narrowing.

Maurice spoke up. 'Could we speak to the others?' he asked quickly.

'You can do whatever you like,' said the Stranger. 'Here, allow me to help you.'

The viewing field split in two, the lower area opening up to show the living area on the other *Eva Rye*. Joanne stood on deep red carpet, a look of immense satisfaction on her face. She was wearing a tailored green suit that complemented her red hair. It also made her breasts stand out more, Edward noticed.

'Hello there, everybody,' she said. 'Gosh, I like the black and white theme! What do you think of our ship?'

'It's very nice,' said Saskia through gritted teeth, taking in the rich golds and reds of the floor and furnishings of the other living area. 'And how are you, *Captain*?'

Joanne gave a little smile.

'Just call me Joanne,' she said. 'We're all fine. We're taking the Stranger to his destination, then we're going to follow a lead he sold us. Isn't that right, Michel?'

Michel was sitting on a red and gold sofa, tapping at a console and looking more relaxed than he had done in weeks.

'That's right,' he said. He gave a sudden gulp of laughter. 'Hey, I've just realized. We've got all your colours! You've got all of our black and white. The Stranger has a sense of humour.'

'Obviously,' said Maurice tightly.

'Hello, Craig!' called Edward, walking up to the viewing field with the teapot in his hand.

'Careful, Edward,' said Craig warningly. 'Don't spill that tea!'

'Are you coming back?' asked Edward.

Craig looked guilty. 'I don't think we can at the moment. But I'm sure we'll meet up again some time.'

'Oh.' Edward felt a heavy weight settle in his stomach. He looked at the floor through blurry eyes.

'What do you mean, you don't think you can?' called out Maurice. He was fiddling with his console, checking local space. 'You've certainly wasted no time in putting some distance between our two ships. Are you abandoning us?'

Joanne came forward again, that faintly smug smile still playing on her lips, even as she tried to look sympathetic.

'It's not like that, Maurice. Check the FE contract. We're not one crew any more, we're two. Check the manifest net. You haven't done too badly out of the deal. You got most of the cargo; take a look in the holds.'

'Fuck the cargo,' called out Saskia. 'You're running out on us.'

'I don't think it works that way,' said Joanne. 'Look, I'm sorry. We've got a contract to take the Stranger to where he wants to go. After that there's nothing to stop us meeting again, is there?'

There was silence inside the lounges of both ships. Edward twisted his fingers around each other, uncertain of what to say. It was Craig who spoke up first.

'Saskia,' he called, 'look after Edward. You too, Maurice.'

'We will,' replied Maurice dismissively.

Craig gazed at him coldly. 'You'd better.'

'Hey, Maurice!' Armstrong was calling from his usual place at the table, still rubbing up his panga. Maurice merely gave him a wave of the hand. The scene on board the other ship suddenly shrank, and the Stranger took its place.

'Now,' he said, 'I'm sorry to butt in like this, but you will have plenty of time to talk later on. I just wanted to straighten a few things out.'

'Like what?' said Saskia.

'Like making sure that I really deliver on the last part of our deal. I don't want the FE software dropping out on me. It may be nearly obsolete, but I still use it occasionally.'

'Yeah,' said Maurice, brightening up suddenly. 'You mentioned other exchange mechanisms before . . .'

'I will sell you information about those, if you are still interested,' said the Stranger. 'But first let's sort out your systems. Maurice, I'm pleased to see you operating the ship. You should have been doing that from the start. If you hadn't spent all your time sucking up to Armstrong . . .'

'I wasn't sucking up. He was just a good friend.'

'Whatever. I have fulfilled my obligation to you. Saskia, I see that you are acting directly. That is good, you have taken my advice. Here is the last part: you should not be commander of the ship.'

Saskia's eyes narrowed. 'Then who?' she asked. 'Miss Rose?'

The Stranger laughed. 'I have already spoken to Miss Rose. Her role is her own business.'

Saskia frowned. 'Well who else?' Her jaw dropped. 'Not Edward!'

'That's my advice, take it or leave it. So, I have fulfilled all my obligations. Now I should say goodbye.'

Him? Commander of the *Eva Rye*? Edward was too scared by what the Stranger had just said to think about Saskia's reaction. She was nearly choking with anger.

'Say goodbye! Is that it? You have ripped the ship in two and left me with . . .'

. . . *with this crew of failures*, thought Edward. He didn't care. She was right. Him, a commander?

Still, Saskia managed to stop herself saying the words just in time. She breathed deeply and shook her head. 'What should we do next?'

'Go on trading, of course,' said the Stranger. 'That's what it means to adopt FE software, isn't it?'

An icy stillness took hold of Saskia. Edward tiptoed back to the kitchen area and safety.

'Fine,' said Saskia at last. 'OK, fine.' She forced a smile to her lips. 'Well, thank you, Stranger, for doing business with us. I look forward to meeting you again.'

'Hold on,' said the Stranger. 'I might be able to put

some business your way. Would you be interested, Edward?'

'Would I be interested?' said Edward, licking his lips. The teapot felt hot and heavy in his hands. In the viewing field, the Stranger had twisted four glassy lenses in his direction.

'I think I should make the decisions here, don't you, Edward?' Saskia's voice was cold and thin. She had stood up now to stare at the Stranger.

'Do you want her to?' asked the Stranger gently. Edward nodded with relief.

'OK, Saskia,' said the Stranger. 'Are you interested?'

'What about me?' said Maurice.

'You can advise,' snapped Saskia. 'Go on, Stranger.'

The Stranger didn't answer straight away. When he did, there was a note of amusement in its voice.

'Well, I don't know if you will already be too late, so for that reason I will offer this information to you free of charge. About four weeks ago, before your timely rescue, and whilst I believed I was still floating towards my doom, I picked up a signal requesting a trade. Someone wants to be transported to Earth.'

'To Earth?' said Saskia and Maurice at the same time.

'Why would anyone want to go there?' said Maurice. 'It's swamped with Dark Plants. If they don't wipe your mind they tie you up in BVBs and strangle you. They say the Watcher is losing its grip completely.'

Edward realized he was holding his breath. What did he know about Dark Plants? Only that you mustn't look at them; it made them grow faster. Only that they spread BVBs: unbreakable nooses that irresistibly tightened around anything within range. Only that everyone was frightened of them. They originated from the edge of the galaxy, that's what they said. The Watcher had found them out there and tried to run away from them, but somehow they had followed it home, and now they had begun to grow on Earth.

His own sister had warned him about the place. So why on Earth would anyone want to go to Earth?

'I don't know why this person wants to go to Earth,' said the Stranger. 'All I know is a request was made for trade. Perhaps you could follow it up? If there is significant risk involved, that will naturally weigh in your favour with the FE software.'

'Hold on,' said Saskia suspiciously. 'If you picked up their signal, why didn't you ask *them* to save you?'

'That is my own business,' said the Stranger. 'Would you like me to send you the location of the signal?'

Saskia said nothing. She looked at Maurice. 'What do you think?' she asked.

'I don't know. Stranger, is it safe, do you think?'

The Stranger gave a loud laugh. 'You ask the most expensive question of all! You couldn't afford to pay me for that answer, even if I could give it!' He gave a sigh. 'But I think it is a fair job. You would do well to at least investigate it.'

Saskia and Maurice held each other's gaze. In the kitchen, Edward found his voice.

'I think we should go,' he said. 'I think we should trust the Stranger.'

Saskia turned to him, but for once her face wasn't angry. She just looked tired.

'You think we should trust him. Very well. Maurice, what do you think?'

Maurice shrugged. 'What else are we going to do?' he asked.

Saskia looked down at the soft black carpet on the floor. Rich and springy, it looked so much nicer than what had been there before . . .

'OK, Stranger. You did a nice job on the ship, if nothing else, and I'm sorry for not trusting you. Yes, please, we'd like to have a look at the job.'

'I've just sent the details to Maurice,' said the Stranger. 'Well, until we meet again!'

'Goodbye,' said Saskia in an empty voice.

The viewing field shrank to nothing. Edward waved to the Stranger as he vanished. He liked him and was sorry to see him go.

'Hello, *Eva Rye*. This is the *Free Enterprise*. Glad to hear from you.'

Saskia looked at the ship that now floated in the viewing field. It didn't look right.

'Is that an alien ship?' asked Edward.

'There are no such things as aliens,' said Maurice, 'you must know that. Those are only stories.'

'What about the Stranger?'

'The Stranger was a robot. He was built in that shape in order to do his job properly.'

'Built by aliens,' said Edward stubbornly.

Maurice was irritable. He was missing Armstrong, Edward guessed. He had changed out of his padded combat jacket and into a grey T-shirt and long grey pants. He gave Edward a long stare.

'I told you, there are no aliens. Besides, look at those markings on the side. They're written in English.'

'Be quiet, you two,' said Saskia. 'I need to speak to them.'

It was a very odd-looking ship, though, decided Edward. If he had the capacity to articulate what he was feeling somewhere in the pit of his stomach, it would have gone something like this. At least the Stranger looked as if he had some Earth connection, bearing, as he did, a passing resemblance to a starfish. His shape touched human norms at some point in the evolutionary process. This ship had no discernible form whatsoever. It was something less than a collection of shapes, and Edward had absolutely nothing to refer to, to hang a pattern on it. There were bundles of wires and cables snaking through the structure, but the ship could not even be described as looking like a plate of spaghetti. Nor did it look like a junk heap. It was utterly alien, beyond human experience.

Except for the fact that it had *DIANA* written on it in various places, in huge yellow letters.

Saskia had been staring at the floor, collecting her thoughts. She was dressed in a neat black suit with a white blouse and matching white button earrings. Her hair was shiny and neatly brushed and, Edward noted, pinned up on top of her head in a bun. She looked every bit the part of the voice of the *Eva Rye*.

'Hello, *Free Enterprise*. My name is Saskia. I understand that you wish to trade.'

'I do. How do you wish to proceed?'

'Are you FE enabled?' Saskia shot a sidelong glance at Maurice sitting on the sofa, fingers poised over his console.

'I certainly am,' said the *Free Enterprise*. 'Let's not waste each other's time. Would you be willing to take a passenger to Earth?'

'I don't know,' said Saskia. 'Is that all that is required?'

'Yes. Simply drop this person off as close as is safely possible to their destination, and then the contract is complete.'

'Mmm. Why would anybody want to go to Earth?'

'I could add that information into the price, but why not just ask her when she boards your ship? I'm sure she would be happy to tell you.'

'So the passenger is a she?'

Edward opened the fridge door and smiled when he saw that the apple juice container was full. Ever since the *Eva Rye* had separated, the container never seemed to run out. He poured three glasses. One each for himself, Maurice and Saskia.

Maurice whispered something to Saskia.

'That's a good point,' she murmured. '*Free Enterprise*, what if we cannot actually reach Earth? I heard that the Watcher is refusing to allow anyone past Jupiter's orbit.'

'As I said, as close as is safely possible. I will trust the FE software to adjudicate.' There was a little chuckle. 'I see that you are unfamiliar with the implications of FE. I take it you are relatively new to this game? Such lack of trust is typical.'

Saskia rolled her eyes. 'It's a cold universe out there, *Free Enterprise.*'

Edward pushed a cold glass of apple juice into her hand.

'Why thank you, Edward,' she said.

He hesitated, not wanting to interrupt.

'Yes, Edward?' she said.

'Saskia, why can't we see who you are speaking to? They can see us, can't they?'

'Because . . .' Saskia frowned. 'Actually, that's a good point. Why can't we see you?'

There was another chuckle.

'You can see me. I'm the ship. I am the *Free Enterprise.*'

'You mean you're an AI?' said Maurice, and Saskia glared at him, angry at being interrupted. He didn't seem to notice. His character seemed to have changed with his new outfit. He looked so much more relaxed in his greys.

The *Free Enterprise* sounded amused as it replied, 'Yes, I am an AI.'

'But I thought AIs couldn't function where FE is being used?' Maurice sounded puzzled.

'No, that's not true,' said the *Free Enterprise*, 'although a lot of people make that mistake, particularly in the early days of adoption. I'm not trying to be rude, but I think it's fair to say that you obviously haven't grasped the full implications of what you've signed up to. Now, are we going to do a deal?'

Maurice gave a shrug.

Edward was nodding his head vigorously.

'Hold on,' said Saskia. 'You haven't told us what you are offering us yet.'

'I can't,' said the *Free Enterprise*. 'If I were to tell you, and you were to refuse the trade, you would have gained valuable information from me all for nothing. You must be prepared to trust FE. Now, are we going to trade?'

Edward didn't understand what all the fuss was about. They must have intended doing the deal, else why waste fuel flying out here to make contact? OK, Earth was dangerous, but they didn't have to go that close, did they?

Saskia appeared to reach a decision.

'OK,' she said, 'we'll put it to the vote. Maurice?'

'You're the boss,' shrugged Maurice. He gave a thin smile. 'I'm happy to go with you.'

'Fine. Edward?'

Edward nodded his head vigorously.

'Yes. I'd like to go to Earth. Are you going to ask Miss Rose?'

Miss Rose wasn't there. She still spent most of the time shut up in her room, rearranging her things, only making occasional trips out to eat her meals and steal small items from around the ship.

'I would if she were here,' said Saskia briskly. 'OK, then,' she raised her glass of apple juice, as if in a toast, 'we trade. Are you ready to interface?'

'Yes,' replied Maurice and the *Free Enterprise* simultaneously.

'Then let's go.'

'Uploading circumstances,' said Maurice. 'What the hell?' He gazed at his console, mouth hanging open.

'What's the matter?' asked Saskia, squinting to see what was scrolling across his screen.

'That's never happened before,' said Maurice. 'I'm going to run a check.'

'What?' asked Saskia. 'Speak to me! What's never happened before?'

'The trade – it's completed already. I don't understand it! *Free Enterprise*, are you getting the same?'

'I must admit, it does seem very unusual.' The other ship sounded genuinely puzzled. 'Still, occasionally circumstances are such that two trading partners find themselves almost perfectly matched.' There was a fluttering noise. 'Even so, I have never heard of an Exchange taking place quite so fast.'

Saskia was visibly fretting. Edward took the glass of apple juice from her hand and placed it on the low coffee table nearby.

'I've run the check,' said Maurice. 'It's a Fair Exchange.'

'I concur,' said the *Free Enterprise*. 'Very well, I am despatching your passenger now. She should arrive with you in four minutes.'

A shuttle detached itself from the image of the spaceship that floated in the middle of the living area.

'It will have to go into the large hold,' said Maurice, gazing at a dimension reading. 'There should be plenty of room, even with the venumbs in there. I'll open the hatch now.'

'You may keep the shuttle,' said the *Free Enterprise*. 'It is part of the Exchange. As to the rest, my price includes disclosure of the information that I have just downloaded to your ship. I will give you a quick summary as your passenger approaches. Have you heard of DIANA?'

Maurice shook his head.

'I have,' said Saskia. 'They were one of the old commercial organizations. They controlled quite a bit of human-occupied space until the Watcher and the EA took over the running of human affairs.'

'A fair summary,' said the *Free Enterprise*. The pod in the viewing field was growing larger. The *Eva Rye* slid into view, looking like a harlequin's teardrop, its opening hangar door masquerading as one of the dark checks, not immediately apparent. The *Free Enterprise* continued.

'Yes, a fair summary. However, it is not true to speak of DIANA in the past tense. I myself still work for DIANA, as do many others.'

'How can that be?' asked Saskia. 'The Watcher made it its business to infiltrate all those large organizations – and then to destroy them. The age of large-scale capitalism is past.'

'Some of us managed to escape the Watcher's gaze. The first warp ships were built by the commercial organizations before the Watcher had completely infiltrated them. No one was surprised when some of those experimental ships failed to return home. Some of them, no doubt, malfunctioned. Others, such as my own manufacturers, chose to stay hidden in space.'

Comprehension dawned on Maurice's face.

'That explains your unusual appearance,' he said. 'The first warp ships were robots, they had no direct connection with human beings. Your development was completely independent of human needs or intervention.'

'Very astute,' said the *Free Enterprise*. 'As to the rest of your payment. Now that the Watcher's control is waning, the need for us to remain in hiding is lessening. I have relayed the co-ordinates of the warp ship *Bailero* to your console. It is the experimental ship that gave rise to me and my kind. FE suggests it is of great value to you, and our contract permits you to first collect the ship before taking the passenger to Earth.'

Saskia and Maurice were smiling. For the first time, they felt they had made a satisfactory trade. Even Edward understood that: an old ship, that had to be worth something?

'May I say, it has been a pleasure doing business with you!' said Saskia, unable to keep the delight from her voice.

'And I with you,' replied the *Free Enterprise*. 'And now, I note the shuttle is entering your ship. Perhaps we will meet again. Until then, goodbye!'

And at that there was a complex unfolding in the viewing field, and the *Free Enterprise* changed shape into something else equally indescribable, and then shimmered out of view.

Maurice stood up, beaming.

'We'd better get to the large hold to meet our passenger. She might be disturbed by meeting those venumbs in there.'

'I'll come too,' said Edward.

Saskia was clearly in a good mood. 'Yes, that would be nice, Edward.' She was smiling. 'I know what you mean about the venumbs, Maurice. She might think she is being attacked by dinosaurs!'

They left the living area in good spirits and marched past the conference room. Edward looked inside as they walked by. Gone was the mismatched, eclectic jumble. Everything in there now matched: big comfortable white leather chairs set out around a shiny black oval table.

They came to the twisted knot of the junction where five corridors met. Even after the upgrade to the smart new *Eva Rye*, this junction still looked odd to Edward. It was from here you accessed the big and little holds, and the geometry of the ship had been twisted about to accommodate their shapes. You had to step around a protruding corner of the large hold to take the path that led to the cargo areas and you felt the gravity change direction as you did so, felt an odd tug in the stomach. Edward didn't like that. Still, he bravely stepped forward, felt the open mouths of the five corridors looking at him as he hung for a moment in space, and then set off with the others down the black-carpeted path to the large hold's entrance. It was still a long walk.

They met their new passenger on the way; she was following the map patterns set on the walls, heading back to the living space.

Edward guessed that she was older than Saskia. The woman looked similar, with her shoulder-length black hair and very pale face, but there was a difference in her stance, an air of quiet confidence that did not need to flaunt itself. As they drew closer, Edward realized she was wearing white make-up on her hands as well as her face. Her lips and fingernails were coloured in black, to match her simple black passive suit.

Beaming, Saskia stepped forward and held out a hand.

'Welcome aboard the *Eva Rye*,' she said. 'My name is Saskia. This is Maurice, my systems man. This is Edward.'

The woman shook their hands absently. 'The *Eva Rye*?' she said, smiling faintly. 'I suppose it *would* be. I'm sorry about this. I am very sorry about this.'

The expression drained from Saskia's face. 'Sorry for what?' she asked.

'Sorry for involving you in all this.'

'Look, I'm sure things aren't that bad,' said Maurice.

'Yes,' agreed Saskia. 'Come back to the living area and you can explain what's going on. What's your name?'

The woman gave another faint smile. 'My name is Judy,' she said. 'But you might as well call me Jonah.'

INTERLUDE: 2247

AIs have a different way of looking at the world.

The Watcher and Chris stood on a beach, on either side of a flat stream of water that had cut a meandering channel through the sand. Sand blew in thin yellow ribbons from the grass-bound dunes that loomed behind them; the flat sea threw little waves onto the shore below them. And clear water ran silently past them through the temporary stream at their feet.

'What do you hope to achieve, Chris?' asked the Watcher.

The water was tainted; a black tendril of ink ran down the stream, thickening.

Chris dipped a hand in the running water, stirring the ink into a grey cloud.

'I don't know,' said Chris. 'Just seeing what happens.'

Or to look at it another way . . .

The Watcher didn't invent MTPH. It was a meme that had evolved at the beginning of the twenty-first century. It was a drug that had found favour with a significant proportion of the population, a drug whose effects could be engineered by those with the necessary know-how. The Watcher had that know-how.

In its original state MTPH caused hallucinations. Phantom personalities arose in the user's mind. Personalities that appeared to have minds of their own. A user would say they did have a mind of their own. You had to be a user to understand.

The Watcher had uses for MTPH.

The Watcher planned a world of fairness and tolerance. It wanted a world where everyone could achieve their full potential. It saw MTPH as a means to achieve this. With a few subtle twists, MTPH became a drug that helped users to experience other people's point of view. Administered through Social Care, a group of humans trained in the use of MTPH and the social care and protection of clients, the drug became a delicate instrument, wielded in the manner of a surgeon's scalpel, a way of subtly restoring the balance when things weren't running as they should.

It wasn't until later, under the constant onslaught of the Dark Seeds brought about by Chris, that the Watcher dispensed with subtlety. The people of Earth needed to understand each other totally. They needed to understand what was right. It was then the Watcher flooded the Earth with MTPH; it tainted the water and the air and the food.

Or to look at it another way . . .

A stream of water flooding down the beach. And now Chris had corrupted it. But not for long.

The Watcher waved a hand, and the water ran clear again.

On the opposite side of the stream Chris gave a shrug.

'I will always be your superior. I made *you,' said the Watcher. 'I don't know why you continue with these futile attacks.'*

'Just seeing what happens,' said Chris.

JUDY 1: 2252

Judy had wondered what it would be like to be away from the sterile corridors of the *Free Enterprise* and back amongst humans again. Now she knew.

Cold and bleak and utterly hopeless.

There was a slightly raised fleshy cross growing on her back: the *Free Enterprise* had done something to her to make it appear. She felt it now, rubbing against the material of her passive suit. It ran across her shoulders and down her spine, the top vertical running up the nape of her neck. There was something living inside there, she knew. It had no presence, and yet it could experience everything that she did, and it spoke to her of what they both saw.

Judy had worked for Social Care. She had taken the drug MTPH, boosting her ability to empathize with others. The *Free Enterprise*, however, had replaced that faculty with something far more cold and clinical. The shifting webs of emotions that she would once have discerned in the three humans now standing before her were gone. Instead, she saw nothing more than the ghostly glow of the mechanism that lived in their heads. She couldn't read their thoughts; no, what she saw was at a lower level than that. She was observing the mechanism that produced thought.

Judy felt bleak despair at the sight, and yet she hid it well, pushed it down deep as she had done with all her emotions for so long. So this was her re-entry to the world of humanity. It all seemed so much less than she remembered.

The woman who had introduced herself as Saskia was gazing at Judy from under a fringe of purple-black hair. She spoke hesitantly.

'Well, Judy or Jonah or whatever you want to be called, I'm sure we can make you comfortable here. There are plenty of spare rooms on board the *Eva Rye* . . .'

'I'm sure there are.' Judy gave a bitter laugh. 'I'm sure if you look there will be one made just to my liking, with lacquered furniture and tatami matting and white paper screens for doors.'

The smaller of the two men was checking his console, the pale ghost of his mind moving in patterns as he processed what he saw there. It was all so ordered, so objective that Judy felt a welling despair. Where was the emotion? Where had it gone?

'She's right,' he said. 'That's Donny's old room. It's decorated just like she said, some sort of Japanese style from the last decade.' He suddenly gave a smile. 'I'm Maurice.'

Judy's mind read the smile, but all the warmth that it transmitted was diluted by the meta-intelligence that she carried in the cross on her back. A smile is just a signal, it was saying, just another way of transmitting informa-tion.

She had to speak, so she forced herself to smile back. It was hard.

'I told you,' she said. 'Someone is choosing a path for me. His name is Chris. He doesn't care that I don't want to go back to Earth.'

Saskia frowned. She looked upset, but all Judy could see was the ghost of her thoughts assigning reactions. Saskia's voice was tentative, apologetic.

'But we thought you *wanted* to go to Earth. We were told that the *Free Enterprise* had a passenger. That's right, isn't it, Maurice?'

Maurice nodded, but Judy cut across his answer. 'A passenger, maybe, but not a willing one.'

The tall black man who stood in the middle of the group was moved to speak. There was a difference to *his* mind, Judy noticed: a simplicity and a complexity that tangled over each other to make the movement of his thoughts difficult to follow.

'We don't *have* to take her, do we?' he said to Saskia. He turned. 'Where do you want to go, Judy?'

'It's not that easy, Edward,' said Saskia firmly. 'We used the FE software to agree to this trade, remember. We can't go back on it.'

'You wouldn't be able to anyway,' said Judy, gazing oddly at Edward. She recognized him for what he was, but it was strange. In the past she had felt pity for people like him, now she felt . . . nothing. It was all just part of the mechanism. Some were bright and some were not. He was looking at her with a tender expression. 'Don't feel sorry for me,' she added dryly. 'Feel sorry for yourselves for being dragged into this without your permission.'

The concern that this statement generated was visible in the crew's minds. To the meta-intelligence, it was just another process to be measured. Judy continued.

'Now, would it be possible to have something to eat? I haven't had real food for five weeks. The *Free Enterprise* wasn't equipped for humans. It constructed everything from the ground up.' She grimaced at the memory.

'What were you doing on board that ship?' asked Maurice.

Judy gave a shiver at the question.

Saskia must have noticed it. 'I think there will be time for Judy's story later, Maurice,' she said mildly. Any thoughts that Judy might have had that Saskia was sympathetic were quickly dashed when she continued: 'For the moment, Judy, I want to know what you mean; saying that we've been dragged into this? We operate of our own free will. That's the point of FE software: haven't you heard of it?'

Judy inclined her head slightly.

'A little, yes. But I'm sorry, Saskia, someone is playing games with you. This ship, the decor – someone is sending me messages.'

She looked around the freshly made corridor with its black carpet, the black and white tiled pattern on the walls and the pearly balls of light set in the ceiling that receded in a line into the distance.

'You're a black and white woman,' noted Saskia, astutely. 'And our ship has only just adopted this colour scheme.'

'And then there is the name,' said Judy.

'Eva Rye?' said Saskia. 'But she's just a story. Anyway, she would have died nearly two hundred years ago.'

'You'd think so, wouldn't you?' replied Judy, and the edge of bitterness in her voice was absorbed by the soft comfort of the corridor.

'You've got something on your neck,' said Edward suddenly.

'I know,' said Judy. 'The *Free Enterprise* put it there. Please don't mention it again.'

Edward looked crestfallen, but at that moment Judy didn't care.

'Would it be so bad to go to Earth?' asked Saskia hopefully. 'I know you hear stories, but . . .'

'It's worse than you can possibly imagine,' replied Judy. 'Imagine everyone acting completely selflessly. Each person only doing what is best for their fellow humans.'

'That sounds quite nice to me,' said Maurice.

'Oh, it's not,' said Judy. 'Trust me, it's not.'

'Do the Dark Seeds really exist?' asked Saskia. 'I wondered if maybe they were just a story.'

'They exist. I've seen them.'

'Oh.'

'Hold on,' said Maurice, fiddling with his console again, 'you said you haven't had real food for five weeks. When were you taken on board the *Free Enterprise*?'

'On the thirty-first of July.'

Maurice and Saskia looked at each other.

'This ship was born on the first of August.'

'Like I said, call me Jonah. Someone is doing whatever it takes to get me to Earth, and they don't give a damn about the consequences of that for anyone else.'

Saskia spoke, not quite concealing her nervousness. 'Judy, what are you doing here?'

*

Judy lay sobbing in bed. She was forty-one years old and a virgin, but that wasn't why she was crying.

— You spend all your days wearing your face like a mask. You should cry more often, Judy.

'Oh, go away and leave me alone. You're not even real.'

— Don't take it out on me, Judy. Come on, what is the matter? What did you see that has made you so upset?

Judy was hugging her knees, her whole body shaking as she cried.

'That little girl . . . that ugly little girl . . .'

Judy sat on a dining chair in the *Eva Rye*'s living area. Edward was in the small kitchen, preparing a meal with a clack of pans and a bubbling of water. Saskia and Maurice sat opposite, looking rumpled and confused within the clean newness of the ship. Judy was doing what she had always done, separating her emotions from her memories. She was very good at it. It was only recently that she had begun to suspect that this wasn't necessarily always something to be proud of.

'Five weeks ago I was on board the *Deborah*, travelling to Quantick. It's a settled world at the far end of the former Enemy Domain. About as far from Earth as you can get.'

Judy sipped at her water, a picture of composure.

'That ugly little girl . . .'

Judy couldn't stop crying. There remained that part of her that was always cool and subjective; it stood to one side within her consciousness, examining the torrid waterfall of her passions, trying to pinpoint the source of this outburst. She hadn't cried so badly even when her sisters had died; she hadn't been so badly shaken when Frances, her best friend, had been nearly destroyed. What was it about the scene in the social room that had upset her so? Such a tiny matter. The girl was an ugly little thing, painfully thin with a deformed face, one eye lower than the other. Her protruding mouth was filled with crooked, irregular teeth. She clung tightly to her mother's hand as she entered the room, trying to fade into the background, hoping not to be seen by the other occupants, lost in their games of chess and Starquest, Dominions and bridge.

Judy had been sitting in the corner, having politely turned down an invitation to join a game of poker. She used to work for Social Care, so where was the sport in playing a game when she knew the thoughts and feelings of her opponents better than they did themselves? She had watched as the little girl was led across the room to an Aeon table. The two people already seated there passed a set of coloured counters across to the new players. Nervously, the little girl accepted them. She sat down, clutching the large counters against her pigeon chest.

– At least she could walk, Judy. She could join in a game of Aeon. We've seen far worse, haven't we? People at the end of life. People crippled by disease. And we've asked, why can't the Watcher cure them? Come on, Judy, this girl wasn't so badly off.

Her brother just didn't understand. Judy rolled herself up into a sitting position on the bed. 'That's not why I'm so upset, Jesse,' she sobbed. The shadowy figure that stood in her room tried to place an arm around her shoulder. She wriggled it off angrily.

– There are worse things than being ugly, Judy.

'It's not that . . .'

But she couldn't explain further because she was overtaken by another bout of racking sobs. She was being ridiculous.

The mother and girl had joined in the game. The two existing players were cracking jokes, teasing the daughter, making her smile. Judy had herself begun a conversation game with a husband and wife who were trying to construct an idea path from Kant to the resurrected fugue form. They were skilful players, and Judy had needed to keep her wits about her in order to participate, and yet her attention was constantly drawn across to the four Aeon players, and the ugly little girl. Judy could feel something building up inside her, something unrecognizable and edged with danger.

'What is it, Jesse?' she had whispered to her shadowy brother, but he had made no reply at the time, merely frowned and tilted his head questioningly, not understanding her problem.

Jesse sat by her bed now, rubbing his insubstantial hand across her shoulders. Still she couldn't stop crying. The moment was approaching again . . .

It was the end of the evening, and Judy's conversation game had finished. Her partners shook her hand and headed off to bed. Judy had stood up and stretched, and yet still that sense of danger was bubbling up inside her. The Aeon game was ending. The mother and daughter were in the lead, and Judy caught the warm edge of emotion from the mother as she smiled across at the other two players, who were letting the little girl win. There was a bubble of kindness centred on that table that made Judy feel painfully happy inside.

And then it happened. The little girl, the ugly, nervous, buck-toothed little girl, had turned to look up at her mother and had given her such a smile of delight that, to Judy and her hyper-aware emotional sense, it felt almost like the collapse of a small star. Such a feeling of warmth and kindness and contentedness and belonging flowing between the pair, two faces turned towards each other alight with something so essentially human.

And not knowing why, Judy had felt something dissolve inside herself and she had begun to stumble off through the corridors of the ship towards her room.

She had undressed and lain down in bed and drifted off into an agitated sleep where she had dreamt, as she did so often, of the hand reaching down from above to cover her face . . .

She had woken up crying. And she still didn't know why.

On board the *Eva Rye*, the only sound was the clink of the knife on glass as Edward chopped potatoes. Judy's gaze was lost in the shiny black depths of the dining table.

'I don't understand,' said Edward.

'Shhh.' Edward flinched as both Maurice and Saskia turned to hiss at him.

'But I don't. Who is Jesse? Why wasn't he really there?'

Maurice thought that the scornful look Saskia cast at Edward was uncalled for. Still, he could understand her impatience.

'Judy works for Social Care,' he said brusquely. 'You know what that means, Edward? She takes MTPH to help her feel other people's emotions. Sometimes that drug causes phantom personalities to arise in the mind. Jesse isn't really there. He doesn't really exist.'

'Oh,' said Edward.

Maurice could see that he still didn't understand. But Maurice didn't really care. 'Well, Judy?' he said impatiently.

'I'm sorry,' said Judy. 'I was just thinking about something.' She told a little white lie. 'I suppose I should start from when I woke up in my cabin.'

– Judy. Something's wrong.

'I know, I can't help it.'

– No, I mean with the ship.

Jesse was a shadowy shape at the edge of her consciousness. She could never quite make out his appearance. Sometimes he seemed far away, a man viewed at a distance; sometimes he was nothing but a child. Like Maurice had said, he was the phantom residue of the drug that she had once taken in her work as a Social Care operative, a construct of her imagination; he lived out his own life in time slices snatched from her brain and senses. He was stalking her cabin now, pressing his hands against the terracotta walls.

'I can't feel any vibration,' he said. 'I think the engines have stopped.'

Judy rose from her bed. She wiped the back of her hand

across her face, still puffy from crying, and then pressed it against the wall. Despite appearances to the contrary, Jesse had no existence outside of her mind. For him to think the engines had stopped, Judy must have sensed the cessation of vibration for herself, and then Jesse would have acted out a scenario to illustrate this. Nonetheless . . .

'You're right,' she murmured, 'the engines have stopped. But we were warping. I didn't notice our reinsertion into flat space . . .'

– We didn't reinsert, replied Jesse.

Judy raised her voice. 'Ship. What's going on?'

Jesse tilted his shadowy head when no reply came.

'Ship! Speak to me!'

Judy dived across the bed and snatched the loose rope belt that was the form currently assumed by her console. She ran her fingers along the chameleon device, raised it to her lips and called out again.

'Ship, I think there is a fault with the senses in my cabin.'

The console was dead. Jesse had pressed his ear to the wall again.

– OK. Now I'm worried.

Judy pressed her hands together and concentrated. It was twelve years since she had given up working for Social Care, but the training was ingrained. In circumstances such as these she would automatically calm herself, centre herself.

– I can hear something outside. I think someone is screaming.

'Let me dress.'

Quickly, she pulled on her black passive suit, the material

tightening around her. A pot of white make-up sat by her bed and she dipped the first finger of each hand into it, touched them to her face. A white tide covered her skin as she breathed deeply.

– I think I know what is going on, said Jesse.

'Don't say it! Do not say it!'

– Shit. Look on the bed.

Judy did so, and saw humanity's last nightmare lying there.

Three little black cubes, each the size of the first joint of her finger, sat in the middle of the twisted sheets. Dark Seeds.

Something close to panic poured through the corridors; it drained from the rooms into the social areas, a hysterical babble of voices mixed with the half-comprehending cries of children.

Many of the passengers had come from Earth, but that would have been before the dark tide had risen to its current extent. The vast majority of people would have boarded the Deborah *without ever coming face to face with the fascinating emptiness that could grow from the Dark Seeds.*

Judy took a deep breath. Dark Seeds. Don't look at them. No matter how much they call to you, don't observe them in any way: touch, sound, taste. Don't observe them, or they will begin to grow. And then come the Black Velvet Bands . . .

Judy pushed open the door of her cabin and stepped into the corridor beyond.

Somebody called out to her.

Judy . . .

'We're too late,' said Judy tonelessly. 'I can hear them calling me already.'

– I can't hear anything, said Jesse after a pause. – Odd that. Are you going to kill the other passengers?

'In the end, yes. What else can I do?'

She felt that Jesse had tempted fate with his question, because just at that moment the ugly little girl came running down the corridor, shaking with terror over something that hadn't been explained to her properly. She saw Judy and ran towards her, snot streaming from her nose.

'Help me!' she called. Judy took her hand weakly.

'I'll help you,' she whispered.

'You were going to kill her?' said Saskia.

'I did kill her,' said Judy.

The Deborah had been an evolving thing, the fabric of the hull and engines and furnishings constantly changing as the vessel made its journey, always seeking out the optimum form for a spaceship. Now it was dead. As the first Dark Seeds had flickered across its senses, the ship's AIs would have begun to look away, desperate to avoid gazing into the endlessly fascinating spaces that lay inside them.

Non-sentient nullification routines would have cut in, in an attempt to neutralize the threat, but if the flux of Dark Seeds through this area of space had been too great, then the AIs would have not been able to avoid seeing them. They would have no choice but to shut themselves down.

There could be no better indication of the cessation of

AI activity than the unchanging nature of the floor and walls of the corridor along which Judy now ran, jerking the ugly child along by the hand. The patterns in the carpets no longer moved to soothe her passage or indicate where to go. The walls were frozen in unsightly lumps, caught half-way in changing from one form to another.

Judy turned a corner, and a frozen rain of black cubes confronted her. For a moment they appeared to hang in the air, fixed in position as their quantum paths through the universe were interrupted by observation; now they began to fall, pitter-pattering to the floor and vanishing as they left her awareness. The little girl froze, gazing at one of the little black cubes that lay on the floor, a thread of dark light already emerging from its base. Judy clapped a hand over the child's eyes and dragged her backwards.

'Don't look at them!' she called. 'Never look at them.'

They began to run back the way they had come, Jesse in the lead. He suddenly hesitated.

– Group of people coming this way. Fifteen or twenty. I think we're trapped.

'Of course we're trapped,' snapped Judy. 'We're on a dead spaceship drifting in warp. Where can we go?'

The little girl looked up at her.

'Who are you speaking to?' she said, wiping at her pale face with a shaking hand.

'My imaginary friend,' said Judy.

'Are you Social Care?' asked the little girl, her eyes filling with hope.

'Yes,' lied Judy. OK, half a lie: she used to be, until her sisters were killed.

'Right,' said the little girl. Judy was touched to see that

she wasn't shaking so much now. Poor little thing. Her misplaced trust would be her only comfort in the next few hours.

'What's your name?'

'Grainne.'

'I'm Judy.'

A group of passengers came running around the corner. They hesitated when they saw Judy. A naked man at the front spurred them on.

'Run!' *he called to Judy.* 'There is a long-distance sense array back there. It has Dark Plants growing around it already.'

'There's no point going on,' *said Judy.* 'The flux is too heavy all through the ship.'

'Then we're trapped.' *The naked man seemed to deflate, his overlarge stomach drooping down over his skinny legs.*

'Judy is a Social Care operative,' *said Grainne confidently.*

The passengers visibly relaxed at that. Strained smiles played over strained faces.

'OK,' *said the naked man,* 'then what should we do?'

'We need to empty our minds,' *said Judy.* 'Sit down.'

'What, here in the corridor?'

'Can you think of a better place?'

The carpet had evolved a low-pile walkway down the centre. The lost passengers now sat down in the fluffy comfort that piled up around the edges of this. There was a sudden lurch.

'What was that?'

'We've finally dropped out of warp,' *said an old woman, rubbing her elbow where she had knocked it on the wall.* 'I

73

recognize the sensation. It used to be common on the old warp ships.'

'How could the Dark Seeds find us in warp?' asked another passenger.

'That doesn't matter now. The important thing at the moment is not to think.'

'Close your eyes,' said Judy. Seventeen pairs of glittering eyes turned towards her, and she thought back twelve years. There was a voice, a way of framing commands. 'Close your eyes,' she commanded. This time the passengers did so.

'Now, think back to your childhood. Try to remember your first week at school.'

'I can't,' someone muttered the words in panicky frustration. 'I can't!'

'Yes, you can. Do you remember Mr Jacks? He came to visit your class on the third day. Mr Jacks wore a red and yellow suit and carried a machine made of mirrors.'

'Oh yes . . .'

'I remember . . .'

'How could I have forgotten . . .'

Because Mr Jacks visited every classroom, and Mr Jacks made everyone forget about his visit and the subtle social programming he performed . . .

'And he pressed a button and the mirrors began to turn and you all fell asleep . . .'

In the corridor, a burst of dark boxes dropped out of the air. Judy looked in the other direction, but more fell over there. Everywhere she looked, Dark Seeds were forming. It was too late. She closed her eyes tightly and felt with her hand for the first of the sleeping bodies. She touched a tiny foot, followed it to a spindly leg. Grainne.

Judy . . .

She heard the word again at the edge of consciousness. It was almost too late. She hit an internal switch and turned off her emotions. Her hands were already fastened around Grainne's throat as she felt for the right spot.

'You killed her. I don't believe you can just sit there and describe it so coldly.'

Saskia didn't sound disbelieving. Judy had a well of anger rising in her stomach that she could have ridden to the heights of self-righteous satisfaction . . . but one look at the mechanism in Saskia's mind – as viewed by the meta-intelligence – and she forgot all that. What did it all matter, anyway?

'Saskia, what do you know of how the Dark Plants propagate?' said Judy, her voice distant and serene.

'Only the rumours . . .'

Judy shook her head. 'No one really knows, Saskia. We don't know if they evolved or if they were made, if they are real or virtual. They seem to contradict themselves at every level. They exist in the quantum world but are visible in our world: their seeds behave more like electrons than macroscopic objects; they drift through space, having no fixed position or direction until they are observed. That's Heisenberg's Uncertainty Principle. And when a suitable intelligence observes them, and fixes them in position in space, they germinate.'

'Yes, I know that. We all know that.'

'And then come the BVBs. Black Velvet Bands. Black loops that just form in unobserved space and shrink down to nothing. They catch around your arm or leg and they can't be cut. One could form around your lungs, and you would breathe out, and it would shrink along with them, and then you'd find you couldn't breathe in again . . .'

'You killed the girl.'

'I had to. There were too many intelligent observers on that ship. I had to shut them down. Being asleep wouldn't have protected those passengers; the Dark Seeds can infiltrate dreams. They can cut right down to your sub-conscious mind.'

Maurice gave a cold laugh. 'They say the worst thing is to have one of the seeds come upon you in your dreams. To be sleeping in your bed whilst a plant grows nearby, feeding on your nightmares . . .'

'Do they look for us?' asked Edward nervously.

'No,' said Judy, staring at Maurice. 'Definitely not, Edward. But we seem able to sense them, no matter what we do. The AIs on the planet Gateway committed sui-cide rather than face them, do you know that? They were too frightened of what the seeds would become if they were allowed to grow.'

Saskia opened her mouth; Judy held her hand up to quieten her.

'Grainne's upper mind was shut down in sleep, and yet still there was a part of her deep subconscious sens-ing the world. Do you know what the plants are made of, Saskia? I'll tell you: nothing. They aren't really there; they are a recursively defined space, like the Sierpienski Gasket. The seeds look like cubes, but their fascinating structure draws your attention in, as it is intended to.

You look at a cube and you can see little holes in its structure. So you look closer at the structure around the holes and you see that it is made of holes too. Everywhere you look you see holes, never actually the seed itself. You look closer and closer and the stuff that makes up the seed is always tantalizingly out of your reach, and you begin to suspect that the seed itself isn't actually there.'

'What's so bad about that?'

'Do you believe in the soul, Saskia?'

'No. Do you?'

'No. And yet those who have ever looked at the plants all say the same thing. They felt as if their soul would become lost amongst the intangible substance of the plants. I've known people who have been saved from the plants – pulled back from the brink. They walk and eat and . . . and that's about it, and . . .'

Judy gazed at her hands, remembering her fear on the ship. She was trying to feel something, anything, more than just the effects of the mechanism that made up her brain. '. . . and all the time the seed is growing and growing. Making a plant out of nothing. And that plant is even more fascinating, and it is pulling at the fabric of the universe, inflating loops of cosmic string larger and larger to make BVBs . . .'

'They've used the Sierpienski Gasket as decoration on the walls over there,' said Maurice quietly.

Maurice saw Edward turn to look where he was pointing, at the white shape like a square split into nine little squares by a noughts-and-crosses grid.

'See how it's made, Edward?' he said. 'Take away the

middle square and then split each of the remaining squares into nine, and take away the middle squares again, and repeat that process forever.'

Judy was looking at the shape too. 'More connections,' she whispered. She turned back to find Saskia looking at her.

The other woman blinked. 'Did you kill the others on that ship as well?' she asked blandly.

Judy blinked in turn.

'Only four. Then the rescue arrived.'

Judy felt the life ebb from the fourth passenger. It rattled out from her empty body, skittering away with the sound of a metal ball in a plastic cup, and Judy felt nothing at its passing. She had told herself not to.

Jesse felt the change first; he had to shout to make himself heard above the rising buzz of the plants growing from the Dark Seeds.

— Judy, something is in here with us.

Judy, her eyes tightly closed, could still see by grey light. The outlines of fabulous plants danced behind her eyelids, her optic nerves somehow registering their presence.

'I can't see anything,' she muttered. 'Jesse, I'm not going to have time to kill them all . . .'

— We're leaking air. Open your eyes so I can see, Judy. There is something down the corridor, and it's coming towards us.

'I can't open them, Jesse. I can't look at the plants . . .'

Something touched her foot and she jerked it away. Something seized her by the wrist.

She felt herself being dragged down the corridor, and she opened her eyes before she could stop herself. And then she couldn't close them, because she just didn't understand what had gripped her and she was trying to make out its shape. There was a silver rope wrapped around her waist, something like a silver crab claw held her wrist. That was about it. Something like legs scrabbled at the floor and she tried to see what they were attached to, but then a Dark Plant caught her attention. Dark vines spilled down a wall and a lace-like bloom turned to face her, the edges of its petals endlessly frilled.

– Look away, said Jesse, and she did, and there was another plant just over there, hazily indistinct. She examined the delicate perforations built of perforations that made up its leaves as she was dragged towards a hole in the wall. It was Jesse who noticed the thin meniscus stretched across it like a soap bubble; it was Jesse who saw the stars beyond. Judy was too busy looking at the mad plants behind her to notice the other passengers being pulled to safety. She didn't notice the meniscus stretch around her and snap out into a bubble carrying just enough air and pressure to support her life as she crossed the void.

Dark Seeds rattled into the envelope she occupied, and were sucked up and ejected. The space around the Deborah was filled with little bubbles of life crossing from the stricken craft to the Free Enterprise.

'A stellated dodecahedron!'

The woman floating by Judy was speaking for the sake

of it. She was very nervous, filling the space between herself and her approaching fear with words.

'That's what you call the shape of this thing. They must have grown it just to house us. Whoever they are. Who do you think they are?'

'I don't know,' replied Judy. She didn't need Jesse's MTPH-enhanced senses to tell her that the terrified passengers who were being poured into the enormous plastic bubble in which she floated were close to panic. They tumbled inexpertly in the zero-G space, gazing wide-eyed, through the clear plastic walls of the dodecahedron, at the stricken body of the Deborah *lit up by nauseous green searchlights. A few last tiny bubbles were crossing through space, bringing the remaining humans to safety. Judy watched as one of the little bubbles touched the wall of envelope and discharged a tumbling passenger through its protective wall into safety.*

— I reckon they've now saved about half of us, said Jesse.

'Who has?' asked Judy.

'Who has what?' asked the nervous woman. She looked around. 'Who are you speaking to?'

'Never mind. Have you noticed that there are no facilities in here?' remarked Judy. 'No beds, no toilets. Nothing. Just a lot of people floating in a great bubble.'

A voice rang out in the great space.

'Passengers of the Deborah.'

The floating passengers quietened immediately.

'This is the *Free Enterprise* – part of DIANA. We noted your distress and made all haste to rescue the *Deborah*. We are just in the process of bringing the last few of you aboard. After that we will be making the jump clear of the region of Dark Plants, en route for Fraxinus.'

'*Fraxinus?' said the woman, gripping Judy's arms tightly. 'Oh, Watcher, save us. Where's Fraxinus? Is that a safe place?*'

'*DIANA?' wondered Judy. 'I wonder what's in it for the* Free Enterprise, *in this rescue? The old companies never did anything that wasn't going to turn them a profit.*'

'What do you mean, what was in it for them?' asked Maurice. 'You were in danger and they rescued you. What more is there to say?'

Ask Saskia, thought Judy, noting the other woman's hungry look. Edward dropped a pan onto the hob in the kitchen.

Judy answered Maurice's question. 'The *Free Enterprise* lives by a way of thinking that was rendered obsolete long ago. It was built by AIs that jumped from Earth on the first warp ships, AIs built by organizations like DIANA that saw everything in terms of financial transactions. It saved us, it wanted something in return.'

'What?'

'Venumbs. The *Free Enterprise* wanted some of the knowledge gained on Fraxinus. And it got it too.'

'So the passengers all made it to safety?'

'Yes. The *Free Enterprise* took them to Fraxinus and made a deal. We were saved through the power of old-style capitalism. The Watcher was supposed to have killed that off, but it's making a resurgence.'

Just look at your ship, thought Judy.

'We've traded with Fraxinus, you know,' said Saskia. 'You would have seen two of their genetically modified ash trees in the large hold. Those wooden dinosaurs.'

Maurice wasn't going to be distracted.

'So what about you?' he asked Judy. 'What are you doing here?'

There were eventually nearly five hundred humans floating in the plastic bag grown by the Free Enterprise, *most of whom where unused to zero gravity. It was unnerving at the best of times to find yourself in a space where nothing was fixed; add to the fact that you had only just survived an encounter with the Dark Plants, probably losing friends and family in the process, and it was no wonder that the sound of crying filled the bubble. Most of the passengers had formed themselves into loose circles; they gripped each other by the arms as they floated and spoke in tense voices, waiting their time and watching out for the yellow balls of urine that floated amongst them.*

Judy spent most of her time floating near the clear plastic walls of the bubble, trying to get a glimpse of the structure of the Free Enterprise *beyond. It was difficult to make out what they were looking at. The ship did not look like a ship at all, more a series of floating points to which objects were tethered.*

– I think I can see something, said Jesse.

'What?' asked Judy, eagerly. 'Hey! Watch out!'

A young man came tumbling towards Judy, face twisted with fury.

'Murderer!' he yelled, raising his voice so that the other passengers could hear him. 'She's a murderer! She said that she would keep us safe, and instead she started killing us one by one. She said she was Social Care . . . uuugh.'

Judy had elbowed him in the solar plexus as he came near. He doubled over in pain. She leant close to his ear.

'These people are frightened enough already,' she hissed. 'Say anything else and I'll kill you too.'

The young man looked into her face and believed that she meant it. She was lying. She pushed him away.

'Doesn't he realize what I was doing?' Judy muttered, watching the young man tumbling away. 'Didn't he realize why I killed them?'

– Do you know why you did it?

'Oh yes. And I know it was the right thing. That doesn't mean it was easy.'

– Damn, swore Jesse. – We're floating away from the wall.

'We'll find someone to give us a push back,' she said.

– If they even come near us. Look at how they are watching you. They heard what he said.

'Never mind them,' said Judy, brusquely. 'What did you see out there?'

– Senses. Scanners. The Free Enterprise is watching us.

Judy folded her arms. Weightlessness made her feel nauseous. Concentrating on other things helped her to forget it.

'That doesn't surprise me,' she said thoughtfully. 'The Free Enterprise may not have seen humans for one hundred and fifty years. It certainly doesn't understand our needs. Look at this place, no gravity, no toilet facilities . . .'

– You don't understand. The Free Enterprise is watching

all of us, but you and me in particular, Judy. It's using
something like laser-ranging devices to scan the passengers.
Their beams are out of the visual spectrum, but they make
the plastic of the envelope glow as they shine through. You
can see pale circular patches, and they are mostly triangu-
lated on us.

'Why?'

– *I don't know.*

'What does Jesse think now?' asked Saskia suddenly.
'What does he think about us?'

'He's not here any more,' said Judy tightly. 'He's gone.
The *Free Enterprise* did something to him.'

'What?'

'They twisted him into something else. Something
unliving.'

'What do you mean?'

Saskia's expression was one of intense curiosity. Seen
through the eyes of the meta-intelligence, she simply
looked like a machine scanning for data.

Jesse wouldn't have seen it that way. Jesse gave her
knowledge. All the meta-intelligence gave her was information.

Judy didn't answer Saskia's question. Instead she
went on with her story.

Three hours later, a swarm of tiny probes approached the
plastic envelope. Those passengers floating closest scattered
in a screaming windmill of bodies as the probes pierced the

bubble. *The panic that had been building finally rippled out across the enclosed space, and then, with something of an anticlimax, evaporated into embarrassment as the humans realized the probes had resealed the bubble after they entered. Now the probes darted about through the confined space, sucking up bubbles of urine and eating faeces. Other probes emitted pale bubbles that floated, honey clear, in the air.*

The voice of the Free Enterprise *sounded.*

'Drink the nectar. It will sustain you for the next few hours, before we arrive on Fraxinus.'

– *Fraxinus, said Jesse with some satisfaction.*

'I can see something out there,' said Judy. 'Something big in the shadows of the ship's superstructure. I'm sure it wasn't there before. I think you're right, Jesse: something is watching us.'

She looked around the bubble, saw the other passengers laughing as they sipped at the golden bubbles of nectar.

'Why feed us now, I wonder? This feels like a distraction. What is it doing out there?'

Judy and Jesse spent the next few hours peering out through the plastic walls of the bubble. There was something out there, and it seemed to change subtly even as they watched it.

– *Maybe I'm getting paranoid, but it seems to be look-ing at* us.

'Hmmm,' answered Judy. She was finding the strange looming shape that hovered just beyond view increasingly unsettling.

– *You're biting your lip,* said Jesse.

'Am I?' said Judy distractedly.

Time passed. All around the bubble, the passengers gazed at Judy suspiciously. She ignored them.

Fraxinus turned below them in green and blue and white swirls.

The envelope was collapsing, squeezing passengers towards the waiting ships sent up from the planet below. The familiar white curves of the Earth-designed fliers and shuttles were a welcome relief after the madness of the Free Enterprise.

The plastic walls folded in on themselves in gentle waves, pulsing as they formed the passengers into groups, just the right number to fit onto a waiting ship. Somehow, even though she had been closest to the waiting vessels at the beginning, Judy found herself near the back of the carefully separated warm packages of humanity that were being gulped down. Just as the suspicion took root within her, the walls pulsed again, and nobody noticed that Judy had been trapped in a little bubble of her own. No one noticed when silver arms intruded and seized her, and a meniscus formed around her and she was dragged off through the walls into the cold space beyond.

'Hey!' she called, 'help me! Hey, over here!'

She waved frantically at the sleek white shape of an Earth-built flier, sliding past nearby, but the AI inside did not seem to notice her as a probe carried her up and away from the friendly shapes of the waiting ships below, up, up, to the schizophrenic logic of the Free Enterprise. She felt a scream curling somewhere down in her stomach, growing *as it wormed its sick way around and around, working its way up to her throat . . .*

– Don't lose it, warned Jesse.

She gulped hot vomit back down inside her. The skin of the meniscus was close to her face; she resisted the urge to reach out and touch it, frightened that it might burst and leave her exposed to the hard vacuum beyond. They passed through a curl of shifting segments, part of the surrounding material of the Free Enterprise. *A nest of clear plastic spheres, each containing a jelly black dot, drifted by, and then an array of hexagonal containers of all different sizes. And then the probe changed direction, and she lost sight of the waiting ships, and Fraxinus all green and friendly below, and she plunged into an open box. The lid snapped shut.*

'Hello, Judy.'

Judy was laced to a bench by red and yellow and green and gold strands. She could see them curled around her fingers and wrists and arms, stretched out before her. She could feel them digging into her feet and calves and thighs, they rubbed against her naked back.

She was lying face down on a bench in the middle of a pale green room, straining to hear the electronic movement that was taking place behind her. She wanted to turn her head to see what lay there.

'I know you can hear me, Judy.'

'Where's Jesse? Why can't I hear Jesse?'

'We've had to suspend certain mechanisms within your

body whilst we complete your development. Why were you left half finished, Judy?'

'I don't know what you are talking about. Why have you kept me here? Why haven't you let me go with the other passengers?'

'We're not sure that we understand why you wished to go with the other passengers, Judy. Why didn't you make yourself known to us as soon as we took you on board? We could have assisted you.'

'What? Assisted me with what?'

'This is a DIANA ship, and you are an asset of DIANA . . .'

'Bullshit. I am . . . I was a Social Care operative.'

'This may be true, yet you remain the property of DIANA. Your genetic code contains sequences copyright to DIANA, your thought patterns are constructed on a recognized DIANA AI seed algorithm.'

For a moment, Judy was speechless. She fought against her rising indignation, coldly calming herself.

'This is ridiculous. My thoughts are my own. Even if, and I do not believe this to be true for a moment, even if my thoughts were the result of a DIANA AI seed algorithm, then they would still be my own. You cannot copyright a mind.'

'That may be true of the Earth Domain, but not of DIANA's sphere of influence.'

Judy was thinking fast. At these moments it was helpful to speak to Jesse, but he was gone. Gone!? What had the Free Enterprise *said? That certain mechanisms had been suspended whilst it completed her development? What did that mean?*

Her hands suddenly flexed, without her meaning them to, the right hand began to flutter pitifully, trapped within the coloured threads that bound it. What were they doing to her?

'Is this some sort of game?' she shouted. 'I think you are being deliberately misled. I have had dealings in the past with DIANA in my work as a SC operative. Did Kevin put you up to this? Have you heard of him? Maybe he tagged me, some sort of revenge . . .'

'No, Judy. This goes to the very core of your being. It is in your bones, you might say. You are a DIANA asset. I cannot believe that you did not know this. Surely you know what your purpose is?'

'I don't know what you are talking about.' Something touched her back, and the flesh there went suddenly numb. She strained at the brightly coloured laces, saw them digging into her arms and hands, tried to turn her head to see what was happening.

'What are you doing to me?'

A nauseating smell filled the room, a sickly sweet burning.

'Is that me?'

'Judy, we have examined your mind, and we believe that you are telling the truth. You do not realize what your purpose is; you are not even aware of the reason for your existence. Sadly, nor are we. Therefore, we are taking what we believe to be appropriate action. We are now performing whatever repairs we can to your mechanism.'

'What repairs?'

'Activating the meta-intelligence that has stalled within you.'

'*What are you talking about?*'

'This is the problem: you appear to be lacking the most basic information regarding your purpose. Therefore we are arranging for you to be returned to Earth for repairs and reprogramming.'

'*Earth! But I don't want to go to Earth!*'

'Exactly our point. You seem to have acquired the notion that you have free will and the right to self-determination. You need to be reminded of DIANA's core purposes. Arrangements have been made. We should have a ship here within a few weeks.'

Maurice stared at Judy, his eyes wide.

'A ship? But that's us.'

Judy shrugged.

'Like I said, call me Jonah. I'm a broken machine, and they're sending me back for repairs. And there's nothing we can do to stop them.'

Edward had come into the room from the kitchen. He was gazing at Judy, his hands red and greasy from the chicken he had been preparing. The meta-intelligence rendered him as something so simple, like a pleasing, undemanding pattern of square tiles.

'Don't you want to go to Earth, Judy?' he asked.

'Of course she doesn't, Edward,' said Maurice impatiently.

'But she might be able to find out what happened to her. How long will it take to get to Earth?'

Maurice slid his fingers over his console.

'Today's Sunday. We'll be there Friday. Six days.'

'Six days?' said Edward. Nobody else was speaking. 'Why don't you try and run, Judy?'

Maurice and Saskia couldn't meet Judy's eyes. Only Edward stared at her with his honest, open gaze. She addressed her answer to him.

'I've tried, Edward. I've been running for over ten years. But someone wants me to go back to Earth.'

'Who?'

'Someone called Chris.'

'Who is he?'

Judy almost smiled. 'A bad person. Actually, a bad robot. He wants me to kill someone there.'

'Who?'

'The Watcher.'

Now Judy had Maurice and Saskia's full attention.

'The Watcher?' said Maurice. 'Why do you want to kill the Watcher?'

'I don't. Chris told me that I would some day.'

'When did he tell you this?'

'Twelve years ago.'

'How could you possibly do it, anyway? The Watcher was the first AI. He is the most powerful entity known to humankind.' Maurice snorted. 'It's not even as if there is a reason for killing him! You might disagree with his actions, you might find them restrictive, but he's doing his best. He nurtures humans! Why would you want to kill him?'

'I don't know. Chris is a powerful AI himself. He wants the Watcher out of the way; he thinks that he has better plans for how humanity should operate. He thinks that I will agree with him, some day.'

'Do you think that he's right?'

'I hope that he's not. I've spent the last twelve years wondering about it. That's why I ran. I suppose now, at last, I'll get to find out.'

Edward shook his head. He turned to the new captain of the *Eva Rye*. 'We don't *have* to take her, do we, Saskia? Not if she doesn't want to go?'

Without speaking, Maurice traced a pattern across the surface of his console. Pale gold letters sprang to life in the middle of the living area.

Violation of Contract?
Are you sure you wish to disengage from a Fair Exchange?
Yes/No?

Saskia tilted her head forward so that she was looking up at Edward from under her purple-black fringe.

'I don't think we have any choice, Edward,' she murmured.

MAURICE 1: 2252

Edward had made sure there were three boiled and three roast potatoes for everyone sitting at the table. Maurice had watched him share them out carefully, counting under his breath as Edward spooned them one by one onto each plate.

So now, as Saskia was pouring gravy onto her cauliflower, Maurice wanted to know why Miss Rose, who still had three boiled and three roast on her plate, was just forking up a fourth roast potato with the evident intention of eating it all at once. Where had she got it from? Maurice was mystified: she did this kind of thing every mealtime, and nobody seemed to notice but him.

'You say the *Eva Rye* was born on the first of August,' said Judy, interrupting his thoughts. 'That's an odd choice of words.'

'No, it's a good description,' said Maurice. He brought his attention back to Judy. What was it about the way she gazed at him that he found unnerving? It was the way she studied you as if you were an object, he decided. She would stare at you for a moment and then there would be a flicker of recognition in her face, as if she had remembered what you were: a human, rather than just another piece of furniture. And then that spark of recognition would be replaced by a carefully blank expression.

Judy knew that Maurice was watching her. She turned to Saskia.

'You're not eating, Saskia,' said Judy. 'Maybe you can tell me about how you adopted the Fair Exchange software. I've heard rumours, but nothing concrete.'

Saskia speared a piece of cauliflower with her fork. 'Why do you want to know?' She leant forward so that her face was hidden again by black curtains of hair.

'Because I find the FE system fascinating,' said Judy. 'I have never been on a ship without an AI before, and yet . . .'

'What?' asked Maurice.

'And yet . . . I can almost feel the presence of something here on board . . .' Her voice trailed away to nothing.

Maurice, meanwhile, listened to the clinking of the cutlery on the plates. There had been new dishes in all the kitchen cupboards: beautiful, paper-thin white china decorated with delicate black swirls.

Saskia looked out from under her fringe. 'There's nothing much to say, Judy,' she said mildly. 'Maurice and I were both on Breizh. That's a colony planet on the edge of the Enemy Domain. The EA were hoping to bring the colonists to term in about six months, and they had brought us humans there to aid in the final transition. In our free time we used to go to this empty port, about four hundred kilometres from the base. We'd borrow a flier to get us there, anything to get out from under the noses of Social Care . . .'

Maurice grinned. Saskia didn't seem to care how rude she was. Or had she forgotten that Judy had told them she was an SC operative? It would be typical of Saskia not to pay that close attention to another person, even one who had arrived on the ship in such a strange fashion.

Saskia took another tiny piece of cauliflower and swallowed it. She continued in a careless way.

'One night another Free Exchanger turned up, and we played the n-strings game. A few of us made the decision to adopt the FE lifestyle pretty much there and then. Michel was our team leader on Breizh, so he became Captain. Maurice here and someone else – Armstrong, his name was – were to be security.' She seemed to change tack in the middle of her sentence without realizing it. 'Donny's wife had just walked out on him and the kids, so he wanted a fresh start. And my life was getting stale. I felt I needed a new challenge. And so here we are.'

Except that wasn't the full story, thought Maurice. Did Saskia really believe her story explained everything? Judy obviously didn't think so. She was gazing back at Saskia, drinking in her pose, her expressions, all the words she hadn't spoken. She was noting the slight tremble in the fork as again Saskia finally cut off the tiniest piece of cauliflower and put it in her mouth.

Judy had been a Social Care operative. She was able to read the emotions of everyone present and use them as a chart to plot their course to the Watcher's version of sanity. There was no lying to an SC operative.

'I must admit,' said Judy, 'a lot of that went over my head.' She turned to Maurice, her dead-white face like a lighthouse beam turning towards him. He felt as if all his secrets were being illuminated by that searching expression. *Social Care*, he thought, *they can never give it up*. And then he shivered as he noted how her expression changed, and she regarded him once more as just a piece of meat. When she spoke, it was in the tones someone would use to ask the Turing Machine to turn on the bedroom lights.

'I don't understand what is going on on this ship, Maurice. Why is there no AI on board?'

'FE doesn't allow AI.'

'Why not? Why are you all here, anyway? What is the n-strings game? I'm not sure that you understand, yourself.'

You couldn't lie to that gaze.

'I'm not sure I do,' said Maurice. 'Look, as far as I can tell, there are three rules to FE: no AIs, no self-replication, and everything must be paid for.'

'How do you know that? Who tells you the rules?'

'It's not like that. They aren't told to you; you sort of discover them for yourself.'

'How?'

'By playing the n-strings game!'

Judy held his gaze, and Maurice felt himself beginning to blush. *She can see right the way through to my ignorance*, he thought. *She knows that I don't really understand*.

And Judy just went on and on staring. He felt such relief when she finally spoke.

'Tell me what you think happened on Breizh, Maurice.'

*

Maurice had never felt comfortable on Breizh. There were nineteen million human embryos buried somewhere deep underground and, especially when it was night-time, their potential lives haunted him. Even here, in the little town of Raspberry, ghosts haunted the pretty white houses that clustered on the rocky outcrops overlooking the blue sea. He imagined these ghosts streaming up the long ribbons of the bridges that climbed from the shores to the distant grey mountains, seeking their places at the silver machinery that had been driven into the dark crevasses beneath the peaks.

During his work shifts, Maurice followed Armstrong down through dim portals into underground spaces newly cleared of hostile defence mechanisms and he would feel the ears of those unrealized lives pressed against the walls that surrounded him. He could hear long-dormant fingers scrabbling to catch hold of him, reaching out for help.

The empty planet should have been beautiful; instead the machinations of the deranged AI that had tried to build a second human empire had given Breizh the feeling of a stillborn carcass filled with crawling maggots. Maurice often wondered if the other planets in the Enemy Domain had the same feel.

When they had leave, Maurice joined the other humans and hopped onto a flier, heading far from the haunted mountains to the wild coastline, where he hoped the whipping breezes would blow the ghosts away.

Armstrong and Maurice had gone to one of the cafes that stood in line along the beach in the little village they had christened Raspberry.

'I hope that Douglas hasn't brought his fiddle along,'

complained Armstrong. 'We can all play an instrument, and yet we have the good sense not to. Why don't these people leave the job to the experts? Let the AIs play for us.'

'Exactly,' agreed Maurice. 'We get enough of music at school. Here, I'll get you a beer.' He headed for one of the crates dumped at the back of the room.

There were other people sitting at the metal tables, looking out at the spit of land across the bay, a rugged grey line between the blue water and the freshly laundered clouds in the blue sky above. The Von Neumann Machines had never made it down the spider-web bridge that ran from the AI's base in the mountains to the coast. The construction of the houses and bars intended to accommodate the nineteen million had been left half completed.

'Here you are,' said Maurice, handing a beer to Armstrong. They twisted the caps and felt the bottles chilling in their hands.

'Do you know what I feel like doing?' said Armstrong, 'I feel like getting drunk. It's nice to be able to do just that without anyone telling you about the danger to your health.'

Maurice laughed in agreement. 'Or having someone discreetly replace your drink with non-alcoholic lager,' he added. 'You'll never manage it, though. Social Care will be in later on. Rebecca, or one of the Stephanies.'

'Hah! I'll be too far gone by then. Aren't you going to join me?'

'Yeah,' smiled Maurice, 'I think I might.'

Armstrong gulped down beer and gave a yeasty belch. 'I don't see why not, anyway,' he said, pressing his hand to his stomach. 'You won't get the chance when your tour here is done. Once you're back on a regular planet SC'll be monitoring you day and night. I tell you, what the Watcher is doing on Earth at the moment will soon be the norm on all the other planets. Soon we won't be able to even think unhealthy thoughts.'

Maurice laughed and gulped down more beer.

'Excuse me, I couldn't help overhearing you.'

For a moment, Maurice thought that the stranger who had unobtrusively joined them at their table was one of the nineteen million embryos. Tired of waiting for its long-delayed birth, it had ripped itself from the ground and made its way into the land of light and warmth. The new-comer was exquisite, gorgeous in an otherworldly way. His skin was the colour of lacquered wood, he wore a loose raw-silk shirt and three-quarter-length trousers the colour of yellow cream; his hair was braided and beaded and tied back to accentuate his high cheekbones and deep brown eyes. He wore a hand-woven bracelet on his left wrist; the straps on his sandals were woven in the same way. He looked cool and relaxed in the warm beer-scented air of the bar.

Armstrong had no imagination, however. He saw the stranger for what he was, just another man and a poten-tial challenger. He leant back in his chair, allowing his combat jacket to fall open, displaying his oiled chest and flat stomach. He gave the stranger a cold stare.

'You Social Care?'

'No.' The stranger smiled. 'I'm the complete opposite. My name is Claude. I wondered if you would be interested in joining us?' He pointed to a group of people sitting at a table at the far end of the bar. 'We're playing the n-string game. Have you heard of it?'

'No.' Armstrong took a defiant gulp of his beer.

Claude's smile widened. 'You may enjoy it. It might just change your life.'

Maurice was recovering from his first surprise at seeing Claude. Now, for some reason, he longed to reach out and touch the dappled cream silk of the man's shirt, it looked so cool. There was something about Claude that fascinated Maurice.

'Why don't we go over?' he asked. 'It could be interesting.'

'You go if you like,' said Armstrong sullenly. He pulled out a tiny template of a knife and a block of carbon. 'I've got things to do.'

'No, you're right,' said Maurice. 'Let's just get drunk.' He took a swig of beer.

Claude shrugged. 'Well, if your friend is too afraid of what he might find . . .'

Maurice felt deflated as Claude gave him a wink and turned to go.

'Hold on,' said Armstrong. 'I never said that. How long does this game take?'

'It varies. Why don't you come along and take a look? If you don't like it, you can always go back to getting drunk.'

He moved with an easy grace across the bar, dancing to the rhythm of the waves. The legs of Armstrong's chair squeaked as he pushed it back across the stone floor.

'Come on, Maurice,' he said, 'we'll take a look.'

Maurice and Armstrong took the last two available seats around the table. He recognized some of the people already seated. Michel, his team co-ordinator, was there, along with Craig and Joanne. There was another man he recognized but whose name he didn't know. Apparently his wife had left him a few weeks previously: got on a ship and headed back to Earth, abandoning the kids. There had been a bit of a crisis over that one, since the two Stephanies from Social Care hadn't managed to avoid the break-up. The rumours were flying that one of the Stephanies in particular was in big trouble over that.

'People!' said Claude, raising his hand for attention and smiling around the table. The gentle susurration of chatter ceased as all eyes fixed on the beautiful man who sat in their midst. He had an air about him: he didn't appear to wait for people's attention. He simply spoke when he was ready, and everyone listened.

'Now, has anyone here played the n-string game before?' he asked. 'No? Good! Good!' He clapped his hands together in delight. Maurice saw Michel gave a puzzled smile at this. Joanne, sitting next to him, narrowed her green eyes thoughtfully.

'Are we all sitting comfortably? Then I'll begin.'

Claude unfastened the hand-woven bracelet from his wrist and held it out in front of him. A heavy silver ring glinted on his little finger.

'This bracelet is made using the basic six-plait,' he said. He twisted the bracelet into a complicated pattern and then pulled it apart. Now there were two bracelets. He held the two bracelets together and repeated the twisting movement to make four bracelets. Maurice joined in with the growing round of applause as he repeated the movement once more, to make eight.

'Ah, but it wasn't a trick,' said Claude, tying one of the bracelets back around his wrist. 'These bracelets are formed of cosmic strings. Each strand on the bracelet is a loop of thread pulled from the very weave of the universe itself. They are unbreakable.'

Now Maurice laughed.

'You find that amusing, my friend?'

'I find that impossible,' said Maurice, grinning at Armstrong, who was too busy trying to outstare Claude to notice.

'Really?' said Claude, in tones of polite surprise. 'I have been told that it is the same principle as that of the Black Velvet Bands.'

At that a shadow passed across the table, as all those assembled thought of what was happening on Earth. Black Velvet Bands dropped from Dark Plants. They formed silent nooses on unobserved places, and then just shrank away to oblivion. The people of Earth were strangled in their sleep by Black Velvet Bands . . .

'But we were playing the n-strings game,' said Claude, quickly pulling apart the seven remaining bracelets into their six constituent strands. 'Everyone begins with six strands each.'

Maurice watched as the strands were passed around the table to reach where he was sitting. Armstrong took the last six. Maurice put up his hand.

'I don't have any strands.'

'Then you can't play. This is the first lesson of the n-string game. Life is unfair.'

Claude said it with a delightful grin that brought a ripple of laughter from around the table.

'You can share mine,' said Armstrong.

'Your generosity has just earned you ten points,' said Claude. Armstrong beamed. 'Not that points mean anything in this game,' added Claude, and this time the table erupted in laughter. After a moment's hesitation, Armstrong joined in.

'Now,' continued Claude, leaning forward and spreading a wide hand on the table, 'I shall show you the basic six-plait. Arrange three strands in a line. Cross them with three strands in a perpendicular direction, like so.' The seven other people seated around the table followed the deft movements of his fingers as he began the six-plait. Maurice watched over Armstrong's shoulder as he gamely twisted the n-strings over each other, the tip of his tongue sticking from the corner of his mouth.

Around the table, other people worked good-naturedly on their six-plaits.

'Not like that, Michel.' Joanne took Michel's half-formed plait from him and laid it out on the table before her. 'Hold these two strands between your third and fourth fingers to keep them out of the way. Like this, see?'

Claude touched her hand.

'You are very good at this,' he said. 'A natural, in fact. Tell you what, why don't I help Michel? It will save you from being distracted.'

Joanne gave a little smile of triumph and went back to her work. Next to her, Claude whispered something in Michel's ear. The latter frowned as he tried to understand what he was being told, then comprehension dawned, and he made a gulping noise as he picked up his strands again.

The six-plait really was quite simple, thought Maurice.

It was just a case of repeating one pattern over and over again to form a spiralling twist from the oddly moving strings. The thing was, Armstrong didn't seem to quite grasp this. He kept getting the third movement in the sequence the wrong way round.

'Here, why don't you let me have a go?' suggested Maurice, getting impatient and suddenly gripped by a desire to touch the strange plastic-like material of the strings.

'Hold on a moment,' said Armstrong, turning away from him. 'I nearly got it there . . .'

All around the table heads bent forward as the group twisted and turned the strands. The occasional curse or giggle could be heard as a strand slipped loose or a pattern collapsed. The work was hypnotic, yet strangely satisfying. Outside of the bar, the descending night ran silkily down the spider-web of the bridge, swallowing up its long white spans, gradually engulfing also the soft splashing of the waves on the beach. And inside Joanne came to the end of her plait.

'Finished!' she said, proudly setting her bracelet down before her and looking around the table.

'Very good,' said Claude, but Joanne didn't hear. She had just noticed Michel's plait.

'How are you doing that?' she asked. Michel's plait did not rise up in a spiral, like those of all the others seated at the table; instead it was a flat ribbon, a neatly symmetric pattern seemingly ruled upon it.

'Claude told me how,' explained Michel in tones of quiet satisfaction. 'You simply reverse the sequence on alternate goes.'

'Oh,' sniffed Joanne.

'That's clever,' said Craig from across the table, watching Michel's fingers closely. 'I think I'll give that a go.'

They worked on for a few more minutes until everyone was sitting breathlessly, waiting for Maurice to finish. Maurice had finally got the bracelet away from Armstrong. Now he quickly twisted the last strands of his plait into place, feeling the strangely pliable material of the n-strings beneath his fingers.

'All done,' he said, to the waiting table.

'Well done, everybody.' Claude gave them all a one-man round of applause. 'You have completed the first part of the game.'

'How have we done?' asked Joanne, casting a look at Michel's plait.

'You've all done very well,' said Claude. 'Now for the second round. Here we can change the rules. In the second round you are not given your strands for free. You have to buy them.'

'How much do they cost?'

'I will give each of you eighteen strands in exchange for one of your completed bracelets. This will mean you can make three more bracelets. Do you still wish to play?'

Maurice looked at Armstrong. Maurice was enjoying this.

'I do,' said Armstrong, who always wanted to win.

'We can make a bracelet each this time,' said Maurice.

'Hang on,' said Craig, 'that's not fair. That means Maurice and Armstrong are at a disadvantage.'

'Why?' asked Claude innocently.

'Because they can only make three bracelets between them. We can make three each.'

Claude nodded, and Maurice had the impression that he had been waiting for someone to point that out.

'OK,' said Claude, 'are you saying in this game we should all start equally? Well, why not? Whoever said that any game should reflect life?'

He laughed at his own joke. This time rest of the table did not join in.

'Now, who wishes to buy some more strands?'

The people seated around the table each handed Claude their bracelets, who handed them back eighteen strands each that he had taken from who-knew-where.

'Ah, not you, Michel. You get thirty strands, to reflect the greater amount of work that went into your bracelet.'

Michel beamed as he collected his strands.

'But that's not fair!' called Joanne.

'Yes, it is,' said Claude. 'It is harder remembering where you are when you are making two movements. Also there is some effort involved in learning the opposite pattern. Michel worked harder; therefore he deserves a greater reward.'

'So why didn't you tell any of us what you told Michel?'

'Why should I?'

'Because it's not fair that one of us gets extra help.'

'So you are saying that extra knowledge is unfair? It wouldn't be right if one of you were to use an AI, say, to advise you on how to make your bracelets.'

'Yes,' said Joanne.

'Does everyone else agree?'

The rest of the table nodded. Claude put a finger to his lips.

'OK,' he said, thoughtfully, 'we said that for round two

the rules could change. So we are agreed that, from now on, extra help is not allowed?'

'Agreed.'

Maurice raised a hand.

'Yes, Maurice?'

'Are you sure you don't work for Social Care?' he asked.

Everyone laughed at that. The night was pleasantly cool and the party atmosphere was taking hold.

'OK,' said Claude, 'I will now teach you the eight-fold path. Take four strings in your hand like this . . .'

Claude taught them the eight-fold path and the reversing right fold. The bar they sat in cast a circle of light into a darkness filled with the sound of nothing more than the splash of the waves. Douglas took a break to fetch some more beers from the crate at the back, and Claude drank one with gusto then proceeded to show them the double impasse and the one-strand weave. The alcohol began to take its effect on all of them. Claude was giggling as he forgot the pattern for the eighteen-plait for the third time, and the rest of the group gradually joined in until they were a shaking mass, gasping weakly at nothing in particular. They drank more beer and counted the growing piles of strands and bracelets that they were accumulating before themselves. Maurice and Armstrong passed strands between themselves, trying to form a Schrödinger's Cat's Cradle.

'Now take the middle bit here and twist it around itself like this,' said Claude. 'Whoops!' he laughed as the half-seen threads collapsed in on themselves to form a tangled mess. 'I always get that bit wrong.'

Claude's sheen of mysterious untouchability was evaporating in the alcohol haze. Maurice was coming to the realization that this was just another person, albeit one who had played the n-string game many times before. Claude was losing the air of a sage and becoming more like a salesman: some of his comments seemed to be alluding to a deal in the offing.

'Isn't it good to do something all on your own, without the interference of Social Care?' he would say slyly.

'What I like about these things is the way you can understand them,' he told Joanne, swigging beer from a bottle. 'You make them yourselves; you know how they are made. You don't need an AI figuring out all the details.' The comment sounded like something that Claude had rehearsed: a line he had been instructed to drop into the conversation.

'You know, people used to live on what they produced for themselves,' he had laughed, as Joanne and Michel had passed across a complicated double helix in return for the three hundred and six strands that Claude formed by performing a complicated twisting action on successive bundles of n-strings, 'and then AIs and VNMs came and offered them something for nothing. Are they any happier for it?'

'Show me how to do that,' said Joanne, leaning forward as she tried to follow the complicated movement of his hands. Claude paused in the action of pulling strands from nowhere.

'Sorry, single strands are too difficult for beginners.' He smacked his lips thoughtfully. 'But I suppose I could show you this instead . . .'

They huddled close together as Claude demonstrated a new move, and Maurice lost interest for a time as Arm-

strong called his attention back to their growing pile of bracelets.

'Come on,' Armstrong urged. 'Donny and Craig are pulling ahead of us.'

Maurice picked up some of the strands, ready to restart the process of folding the Cradle. He ran two of the n-strings through his fingers, experiencing the odd sensation they gave of stillness, even when they moved. Twist them in the wrong direction and it was as if they weren't there at all.

They got back to the work. The splash of the waves, the clinking of beer bottles on tables, the sounds of chatter . . .

It was only a short time later that the whole table noticed that Joanne and Michel had come from nowhere to build up a decisive lead. The pile of double helices in front of them seemed to be growing at an astonishing rate.

'Good work,' said Craig approvingly.

'Hey, that's not fair!' called out Armstrong. 'Look what she's doing!'

Joanne was taking hold of the ends of a double helix and twisting them around and over themselves in the same complicated motion that Claude had used. When the bracelet was a tangle of strands she would gently pull it apart and there would be two of them. She had the grace to blush and look embarrassed.

'Claude showed me how to do it,' she apologized.

'And why shouldn't I? It's not in the rules.'

'But it gives her an unfair advantage,' called Armstrong, in his agitation kicking one of the beer bottles that lay at his feet.

Claude adopted a thoughtful pose, and Maurice became

more convinced than ever that he was delivering a practised speech.

'So you are saying that replication is unfair, Armstrong? Just like AIs give one an unfair advantage in this
game.'

'Exactly!'

'Yet you come from a society where these advantages are
assumed on a daily basis.'

The sound of the waves could be heard distinctly in the
room, that and the skittering echo of Armstrong's beer
bottle finally spinning to a halt.

'Yes, but you can't compare this game to the way we
live.' Donny's words dripped with all the bitterness and bile
that had built up within him since his wife had walked out.

'And why not?' asked Claude gently.

'Because . . .' Donny began. His voice trailed away to
nothing.

'I know one reason why,' said Claude softly. 'Because we
choose the games we play, and yet the way we live is
immutable. It is imposed upon us from our birth by the
Watcher and Social Care. Well, what if I were to tell you
there are other ways to live?'

Craig leant forward. 'I've heard about this,' he said,
excitedly. 'I knew a girl on Lorient, she talked about people
getting out from under the gaze of the Watcher and living
a different sort of life. It's an old-fashioned sort of thing,
she said, getting back to basics.'

'Not old-fashioned at all,' said Claude. 'It gives humans
a chance to live as they should do, thinking for themselves,
not as unwitting slaves to the will of AIs and Social Care.'

'Somebody's coming.'

They swept the colourful strands of the n-strings into pockets, onto chairs, pushed them up their sleeves. They started to giggle at the futility of the task. There were so many of them. Too many. Armstrong was even shoving them down the front of his trousers, smirking at the obscene bulge they formed. Joanne shook her head at his childishness.

'It's Saskia,' said Craig as a pale face appeared in the darkness. Saskia strode into the open-fronted space of the cafe.

'You know that Social Care are coming?' she said, taking in the scene in the midnight-bright room. 'How much have you been drinking, Craig?'

'Not enough,' muttered Craig, and they all collapsed with laughter again. Maurice began to push n-strings down the front of his trousers, imitating Armstrong.

Saskia's eyes fell on Claude. 'Aren't you going to introduce me to your friend?' she asked. Craig couldn't stop giggling.

'This is Claude,' said a still sober Joanne, placing her hand on his dark wrist. As he clasped it in his own, Joanne looked up with dancing green eyes. 'I wonder how Social Care knew that we were here, Saskia?'

Saskia flicked her dark eyes around the table. 'I don't think that she should be able to make such accusations unchallenged, Michel.'

'Don't start, Saskia,' said Craig, suddenly serious again. 'Who's coming?'

'One of the Stephanies.'

The assembled people looked at each other.

'We should go now,' decided Armstrong, pushing back

his chair in a clatter of beer bottles. 'Claude, it was nice meeting you.'

'You don't have to go,' said Claude quietly. 'I have a ship waiting not one minute away. Join the game, Armstrong.'

Maurice felt more tempted by the sudden offer than he would have imagined, but Armstrong was shaking his head.

'Not for me, Claude. I've got nothing to hide from Social Care.' He shook his head again. 'I've got nothing against them, either.'

'What about when they stop you from drinking?' asked Maurice.

'They're just doing their job,' replied Armstrong, drunkenly sanctimonious. 'And I've got mine to do, too, Maurice. I signed up for duty on this planet and I'll see it through. It's the same with Social Care. You get the rights, you accept the responsibilities.'

'You should be getting them out of here,' murmured Saskia to Michel. 'It won't look good for you if Social Care realize that you let your team play the n-strings game.'

'All right, I know,' said Michel. He gave an apologetic shrug.

'Way to spoil the party, Saskia,' murmured Joanne.

'Be quiet, Joanne,' said Michel. 'Come on, everyone, back to the flier.'

Slowly, with a scrape of chairs and further skittering of bottles, they began to make their way from the table. All except one.

'I'm not going.' Donny spoke up, his voice darkly sullen.

'*Claude, tell me some more about this new way of life of yours.*'

'*Look out,*' called Craig. *A disc came spinning out of the night; it bounced off the table and fell to the floor.*

'*Hello, Stephanie,*' said Saskia.

'Hello, Saskia.'

Maurice shivered. This Stephanie was a Personality Construct of the human Stephanie, who was no doubt even now being woken and bundled onto a flier so she could be rushed across the world in order to speak to the erring crew.

'I see you have all been playing the n-strings game. It's a charming diversion. I have played it myself a few times.'

'*What, in digital space?*' *Joanne's voice was sweetly sarcastic.* '*You have precious little chance of leaving your world, Stephanie.*'

'Don't be so prejudiced, Joanne,' *replied Stephanie lightly.* 'I have the same rights to self-fulfilment as anyone in what you like to call the atomic world. Besides, I don't need to walk in the *physical* world to realize that the concept behind this game is flawed.'

'*It's a diversion,*' said Craig. '*Look!*'

Fine silver bars were silently growing downwards to block the open front of the cafe. Everyone present made a dash for the cool space outside. Claude whispered something into the heavy silver ring that he wore on his little finger.

'It's not a trap,' *called Stephanie.* 'It's for your own protection. You need to think sensibly about this, so as not to be rushed into an unwise decision.'

Armstrong scowled. '*Who is rushing us, Stephanie?*' He

raised his voice. 'Claude, what do you mean when you say there is another way to live? Whose idea is this?'

Claude was scanning the sky. Up above, Maurice thought that he saw a pinprick of light drifting across the stars.

'Oh, some old guy from history,' said Claude distractedly. 'I don't remember his name.'

Maurice could see that Craig had now taken Saskia off to one side. He could hear the harshness in his voice as he berated her.

'What's going on here, Saskia? Why did you tell them what we were doing?'

Maurice strained to hear Saskia's answer, spoken in a self-righteous whisper.

'I didn't want to tell them anything. Craig, you know what they're like. Social Care always know what you're thinking. But I promise, I didn't want to tell them anything!'

Craig said nothing to that.

'Hey, you don't suppose you're the first person to come here, do you?' said Saskia suddenly. 'Claude's been up and down the coast for the past week, looking for people to join his commune, or whatever it is.' She reached out and touched the bracelet that Craig had tied around his wrist. 'That's a six-plait,' she said. 'I can do that.'

Something was dropping towards them. A sleek teardrop shape; the light of the cafe reflected off its burnished side.

'It's the Borderlands,*' said Claude. 'This is my ship. You are welcome to come aboard with me. I can get the* Borderlands *to reproduce. Give you a ship of your own.'*

'I'm coming,' said Donny.

'But Donny, what about your children?'

The disc holding the personality construct of Stephanie rolled on its side like a wheel, following them away from the cafe into the night and the noise of the waves that splashed invisibly all around them.

Donny clenched his fists. He was unshaven, his hair hung in greasy strands. The barely suppressed anger that had burned so brightly within him for the past weeks flared white-hot for a moment. With difficulty, he restrained it.

'Are you saying you would keep my children from me?'

Stephanie said nothing.

Suddenly he relaxed. He gave a laugh that made Maurice shiver with its wildness.

'This is all a bluff, isn't it?' He walked back to the cafe entrance, where the silver bars had now grown to floor level. He took two in his hands and bent them apart easily. 'Social Care doesn't imprison us with bars and locks. You use words and gestures, wall us up behind our manners and upbringing, and then you beat us with our conscience when we stray from your path. You're not going to stop us boarding this ship. You're counting on us returning to you in a few weeks' time, when you'll be waiting for us with sympathy and kind words, and then you'll take us back into your stifling grasp.'

The Borderlands was sliding over the beach, dwarfing the cafes and bars of the seafront, the humming of its engines mixing with the splash of the waves. An exit ramp was dropping open halfway down its enormous length, a tongue of light shining out from the inward curve of the teardrop.

'Where are you going?' There was a note in Saskia's voice that none of them had heard before. It almost sounded like terror. Armstrong, who was marching towards the ship *with a determined look on his face, mistakenly thought she was speaking to him. He called his reply over his shoulder as he went.*

'I'm getting on board. You heard what Donny said. He's right. I'm fed up with Social Care always telling me what to do.'

But Saskia ignored him. She was following Craig down onto the sand.

'Craig, wait! Are you sure that you really want to do this? You won't be welcome in the Enemy Domain when you come back. They'll send you back to Earth.'

Craig turned and thrust his face close to hers.

'And what are you going to do when I've gone, Saskia? Whose life are you going to organize when Donny and the rest of us are off flying through the stars? What if we even make a go of it out there?'

Maurice pushed past them, eager to be on the ship. Michel walked on thoughtfully, Stephanie's wheel rolling alongside him.

'There will be a flier here in five minutes. Why not wait for its arrival? Talk things over with the atomic Stephanie. You can still go with this ship tomorrow.'

Michel paused. Saskia suddenly appeared at his shoulder. She made a little noise that sounded something like a sob.

'Don't listen to her, Michel. Come on, we're going to need you to tell us what do.'

She took him by the arm and led him up the ramp.

*

'And that's it?' asked Judy.

'And that's it,' said Maurice. 'It was just like a game of dare. We all thought that we were going to give up at any moment, but somehow we just went on playing. Claude and his crew took us up into space, where they triggered the self-replication routine on the *Borderlands*, and the *Eva Rye* was born.'

Judy frowned. 'I thought that you weren't allowed to use self-replication. I thought that wasn't in the rules of the game.'

Maurice shrugged. 'We're still learning the rules of the game, Judy. I think that you are allowed to use VNMs when you bring in new players. The *Borderlands* got an upgrade, I guess. The original *Eva Rye* was very basic. A complete hotch-potch of styles, most of which didn't work.' He cast a thoughtful eye around the black and white interior of the room. 'So now we just go around trading, though we don't do very well. I suppose if we had an AI, then we wouldn't keep making mistakes. But I suppose if everyone had AIs then we'd be right back to where we started.'

'No,' said Edward suddenly, 'that's not it. We don't *need* AIs when FE keeps everything fair. Listen to what Judy said about that person Chris, about him trying to get her to go to Earth. It's the AIs that mess everything up. They bend the rules and tell you what to think, and you're left with nothing to do. AIs aren't *fair* to humans like us.'

Maurice and the rest of the table were more than a little shocked at the way Edward had suddenly spoken up. It wasn't like the young man to express himself so surely.

'But the deals aren't fair . . .' Maurice began, but at that point Judy let out a moan.

'Are you OK?' asked Saskia.

Judy was rubbing the back of her neck. 'Yes. Yes, just a twinge.'

For a moment, her face had been lit up with expression; it had made her seem so much more human. Now she returned to her habitual calmness.

She looked down the table and paused. The rest of the crew held their breath, waiting to hear what she would say. Nobody was expecting her next words.

'I'll have my last roast potato back, thank you, Miss Rose.'

EVA 6: 2089

On an early July morning a battered, robotic britzka – one of those modern britzkas found in plenty just outside the borders of the Russian Free States, and so beloved of the thieves and supposed free spirits that dwelt therein – rolled out of the little town that had grown up around the Pekarsky Narkomfin and went thundering down the road running alongside the Arctic data cable.

In the britzka sat two residents of Narkomfin 128: the systems man Ivan Atchmianov, well fed and clean shaven; and Eva Rye, with her grey hair cut short and her face burnt red from the summer sun. Despite the fact that she had been there for nearly five years, Russian life still excited her with its novelty. She had risen early that morning and breakfasted on doughnuts and sour cream, and then allowed Ivan to persuade her to drink a little vodka for the road.

'What are you smiling about?' she teased her companion, who was looking through a pair of half-moon glasses at the humming line that ran from the dashboard down into the floor of the vehicle.

'I was admiring clever workmanship,' said Ivan. 'And

I was thinking about how it alienates us from nature. When this journey used to take days, people would get a feel for the size of this land. Spend your days bumping along under the hot sun, looking for a place to shelter from the storms at night, and you'd understand what Russia is.'

Eva laughed. 'What do you know about Russian life? You live in São Paulo!'

The words were out before she could stop them. She felt herself blushing and fumbled for something else to say. 'You know, when we get back I'm going to get hold of your toolboxes and I'm going to find a spanner and take this thing apart. Maybe when you've been forced to take that walk with the rest of us you'll feel happier.'

'There are too many people in Russia,' said Ivan morosely. 'I wonder if the bourgeois who flock to the Narkomfins would be so eager if they had to face up to the cold blast of winter without their passive suits and their heated transport.'

He caught Eva's smile. 'Anyway, a spanner would do you no good,' he said pedantically. 'These panels have been sealed using induction screws.'

'Whatever,' said Eva, waving her hand. 'I'll look through that big red box of yours, where you keep all those weird new tools, and I'll find out what an induction screwdriver is and how to use it. I'll strip apart your bike and your rain belt, and maybe then you'll be happy.' She gave an extravagant sigh. 'You're such a man! You spend all your time fixing machines but you never want to use them. Six months you've been here now. You've had that lovely old Zil limousine sitting outside the apartment block, and you've polished it and you've had your head under the bonnet practically every day, but you've never actually taken me anywhere. You could have driven me to the lake, and we could have sat outside the dukhan there, and I could have bought you fish soup and stuffed zucchini.'

Ivan reddened with embarrassment at his lack of consideration.

'You should have said you wanted to go to the lake. I did not realize! I would have taken you there in the britzka.'

The awkwardness between them had passed. Now Eva felt it was safe to laugh gently at him. She laughed with a confidence she had had to wait nearly seventy years to acquire.

'That's not what I meant . . .' she began but, on seeing the confusion in his face, added: 'though yes, I would have liked to have gone to the lake.'

He gave a happy smile, and Eva tried to look cheerful. Ivan folded his glasses into his breast pocket and sternly took her hand.

'Maybe when we had finished our soup, and if you had promised to leave my britzka alone, I would show you how to use an induction screwdriver.'

Eva smiled at him. She wanted to say something funny and sarcastic in reply, but she knew that he would misunderstand.

'I used one in the Pekarsky block to open the hatch to the heating system,' he continued. 'A black handle, about this long?'

He held his palms apart, his soft hands pale and

smelling of cleansing soap. Eva shivered at the memory. The people of the Pekarsky block were unintelligent and superstitious: they had walked out from under the constant surveillance of the world outside but, lacking the vision to find something to replace the Watcher's protection, they had instead handed control of their lives over to some imagined malign fate or nature. When machinery failed, they blamed bad luck or sabotage, then they waited in sullen bad temper for someone like Ivan to come and sort out their problems.

And they hated him for it – Ivan came from the outside world. Social Care arranged for people like him to do their six months' public service in the Russian Free States, and Ivan had dutifully turned up, bringing along Katya, his handicapped daughter. And still they resented him for it. They saw his work as an intrusion on their lives, and yet they expected it as their due.

Eva had followed the big man through the peeling concrete corridors of the Pekarsky Narkomfin, past smashed plasterwork and half-open doors, to a metal duct where Ivan had put down his travelling toolbox and set to work. Unlike Eva, he hadn't seemed to notice or care about the people who shuffled up to gaze at them. Doughy people with greasy hair, who smelled of fried food and cheap leather, who stared at them with hard eyes, resenting their presence, making Eva wish she had stayed at home in her own Narkomfin, looking after the handicapped.

Ivan had not been oblivious to how she had felt, though. Quite the opposite. When the metal panel swung open, he had sensed her revulsion and had pushed the door closed again to give her time to calm down. He knew that Eva didn't like VNMs.

The Russian Free States were riddled with Von Neumann Machines, but it still gave her a lurch of sickening vertigo to think of them all crammed together in the duct, their long segments curling as they stripped apart the metal to make copies of themselves. Ivan had found her a job to do well away from the infected duct. She stood along the corridor from him, her hands shaking as she peeled off the magnetic scale that was forming across one of the walls and threatening to interrupt the lighting circuit.

Ivan was an attentive man. She liked that: it was a gentle, fallible thing after the unfailing attention to detail that the Watcher had forced upon her. And now, as he sat in the jolting britzka, explaining how the screwdriver magnetically reached through the panels to take hold of the screws beneath, he noted the distress in her face.

'I'm sorry, Eva; you don't want to talk about screwdrivers, do you?'

'No, it's interesting. Honestly. It's that duct I'd rather not think about.'

And again now, his breath acetone sweet from their morning nip of vodka, he gently placed his hand on hers.

'What's the matter?' he asked, the britzka bouncing him sharply to the left as it swerved around a slippage of red rubble. 'Really, I mean. I would have thought that you were used to that sort of thing. There are still lots of people here in the RFS who have never really seen self-replicating machines, but you came here from England. They must have been a common sight there.'

'They were,' said Eva. 'I didn't like them back then either.'

She was trying to look away from him; not wanting to meet his big grey eyes. Ivan was at a loss, completely without guile in these situations.

'I wish you would tell me, Eva, why is it you really came here. You don't act like a typical Free Stater.'

'I told you. I wanted to get out from under the gaze of the Watcher. I wanted to do something to help the handicapped. I felt as if I had some affinity with them . . .'

Ivan knew there was more to it than that, but he did not know how to push her to reveal more. He was a skilled, intelligent man who spoke English and French fluently, and he was technically very able, and yet underneath it all he remained shy and uncertain. Eva found that incredibly attractive.

'I worked in England for a few months,' said Ivan, 'back in '58.'

'I know,' said Eva, taking his hand and giving it a warm squeeze. 'You told me.'

They were now rolling through one of the areas of forgotten industrialization that littered the landscape of the southern peninsula. Concrete blocks of flats – carcasses too rotten even to be used to house the refugees who had fled to the last free space on Earth – tilted as they subsided, overturning like dead animals. The heating pipes, whose network had once described rubber loops through the grey sky, were tangled and fallen, their ends broken off to leave rusty mouths that could not taste the hot morning air.

'Should be through here soon,' muttered Ivan.

'You *are* very attentive, Ivan,' said Eva thoughtfully.

'What do you mean?'

She squeezed his hand again.

'You and I both know that these places are breeding grounds for VNMs and venumbs. You didn't want me getting upset again.'

Ivan said nothing, two little pink spots burning on his cheeks. He took refuge in pessimism.

'Hah! Not for much longer. This is an unstable society. The RFS only exists because the rest of the world props it up.' He gave a mournful smile at the thought. 'The big organizations are using this place as a testing ground. They're letting the VNMs run free and seeing what develops. Oh . . .' – he caught sight of Eva's face and began to laugh – 'all that effort to change the subject and I mention them again.'

Eva laughed along with him, one hand to her mouth.

'That's OK. It was nice that you thought of me.'

She rolled back the sleeves of her white blouse as the britzka swayed along through broken concrete and rubble under a clear blue sky. It was going to be another hot day.

You're not really Eva Rye – you're just dreaming all this. You are sleeping in your cabin on board ship, Judy. You tried to look at the thoughts of the FE program, and it did something to you to push you away. Wake up, Judy!

*

A woman was standing in the middle of the potholed road, waving her arms. The robot britzka picked up on the gesture and came to a halt.

Ivan said something in Russian, and the woman's mouth closed in a hard line. She ducked her head up and down, her whole body bobbing like a duck on water.

'Oh, I'm sorry, don't you speak English?'

'I do,' said Ivan curtly.

'What's the matter?' asked Eva simultaneously. 'Do you need help?'

The woman's face lit up as she heard Eva's voice.

'Are you English? You are, aren't you? I can tell by your accent. And by your shoes!'

Both Ivan and Eva looked down at Eva's feet, but the woman continued breathlessly, the bangles on her wrists jangling as she continued to wave her arms about.

'You've got to back up now! At least fifty metres! Quickly, now! This road will be covered in VNMs in about three minutes. Julian has been timing it. Hurry up! They'll strip your funny little cart apart! There'll be nothing left!'

Ivan pressed a couple of buttons on the dashboard, and the britzka began to roll backwards slowly.

'Who is Julian?' he murmured to Eva.

Eva looked down at the plump woman, a sheen of sweat on her forehead as she tramped along the road after them.

'I don't know who Julian is,' said Eva dismissively. 'There's a sort of person back in England who always talks as if you should know everyone they do.'

'We have them in Russia, too,' said Ivan, wrinkling

his lip. 'Although I would say that rather they *assume* that you should know their acquaintances. And if you don't, they find you wanting for it.'

He spoke with such contempt that Eva giggled.

'Aren't you scared?' asked Ivan.

'No, I'm not,' said Eva, and she was pleased find that she wasn't. She felt safe with Ivan; it made her feel like a teenager again. 'Apprehensive maybe,' she added. 'Hah! She's probably seen a squirrel or something.'

Ivan laughed.

'What's up?' called the woman, not happy to be left out of the joke, not happy that they weren't taking her warning seriously. She spoke in stern tones. 'Look, you should be OK just there. Do you mind if I come on board?'

She was already climbing up onto the bench beside them. Her hands and feet were dirty with the brick dust that had settled all around on the wrecked landscape.

'Julian and the rest are over there, close to the flower. I came over to the road to warn passers-by. Somebody has think of these things, and, let's face it, it's not going to be Julian. He has a mind like a razor but he needs someone to sort out the *important* details, and, let's face it,' at this point she gave Eva a flash of a smile, 'that's the sort of thing that you have to leave to a woman, isn't it? I mean, those things can strip a vehicle apart in minutes. Ah, look! You can see the edge of it now. Over there.'

Eva glanced at Ivan, checking if he was upset that this woman in her tie-dyed dress was so obviously ignoring him. Eva was taking a considered dislike to her.

'Over there,' repeated the woman. 'Oh, my name's Fiona by the way. And you are?'

Eva took the proffered hand, felt the grittiness of brick dust rubbing against her palm.

'Eva – and this is Ivan.'

'Hello, Ivan,' said Fiona, and promptly ignored him again. 'Tell you what, maybe if you just backed up another ten metres. Just to be on the safe side. Ah, there you go! Look Eva, there they are!'

Fiona gripped Eva's arm and pointed.

They were in a landscape that looked every bit as naturally formed as the rugged mountains to the north. A vista of low hills and twisting dales, filled with the gentle splash of running water. And yet there was no grass or mud to paint the scene. The entire landscape was built of concrete and brick. Broken buildings reared around her, rubble and bricks forming scree at their base. Tarmacked roads, cracked into eroded plates, formed jigsaw paths through the greyness. And now, off to one side, silver VNMs were spilling out of a depression, spreading over the land like water welling from a hole.

Eva gave an involuntary whimper, and Ivan placed a gentle hand on her knee.

'It's OK,' said Fiona, 'they won't get this far.'

Silver spiders flooded out across the land, washing over the road ahead.

'See?' she said triumphantly. 'See, if you'd been up there they'd have stripped this cart apart and made it into copies of themselves! Look at them, can you see how they wave their little legs about? They're looking for something, sensing for metal. Look at how their bodies are silver, and you can't see any joints.'

Fiona had a remarkable facility for describing what was perfectly obvious to everyone else.

'See, they are still coming, but less and less of them . . .'

The tide slowed, hesitated, and began to run backwards.

'OK,' she called, 'they're reversing. It will be safe to follow them now. Come on, you've got to see this. Julian says he has never seen anything like it.'

She climbed down from the britzka and made her way up a low slope of broken bricks, to the sound of clinking and scraping.

'It's OK,' she said, pausing at the top of the pile to wipe her hands. 'Come on, you'll be perfectly safe. They only eat metal.'

Eva looked at Ivan, who nodded. He pulled something out of his orange-banded toolbox and helped Eva down from the britzka.

They stood at the edge of the dusty road, staring at the shifting sea of bricks.

'Does that look safe to walk on to you?' asked Eva.

Ivan took her arm and helped her across the uneven surface. They kicked silver beads of melted glass to set them bouncing over the dry ground. Fiona didn't seem to notice, she puffed on ahead, keeping up a constant monologue.

'We were out here looking for railway lines, you know. We're close to the border with East Coast Company and they keep trying to grow them through here. If DIANA or Berliner Sibelius can get a link across to

Enterprise City, then they'll have a corridor through the RFS that they'll slowly widen. They've already got pipes under here from Colourtown to Openport, carrying oil and carbon, but they're too deep to touch. Still, you've got to do what you can, haven't you? And now there's the flower. It's just over here, not long now, Eva. Emily thinks its some sort of signalling device. She says she saw something like it over in Patagonia back in '75. She says it will be sending a pulse to some receiver, describing the layout of the land. Anyway, here it is, down here.'

The red landscape rose and fell around them like an industrial moon surface. Eva coughed, her mouth dry with the heat and the smell of brick dust all around her.

'It's so dry and broken,' she said. 'It makes me think of bones rubbing together.'

'Bones?' said Fiona. 'No. Sloppy sentimentalism. Look, there it is.'

Eva guessed that they were looking across what had once been the basement of a building; she saw a set of stone steps climbing into the air nearby, and she wondered who had once skipped down them, and for what purpose. Now the building was long gone, and they stood at the edge of what looked like a silver pond of VNMs, silver insects the size of Eva's hand, waving their feelers in the air. And yet the pond was contracting while bulging at the centre. A silver column was rising into the air, made up of the swarming insects climbing over each other to get to the very centre of the pool. The column rose until it was roughly twice Eva's height, and then the top began to swell. The pond at the base was shrinking away to nothing, leaving the dirty tiled floor of the basement exposed, and now there was only a metal flower, its stalk thinning as the top bulged larger and larger.

'What *is* it?' whispered Eva to Ivan, filled with an uneasy thrill at the strange beauty of the shape. It was a robot dandelion, a metal puffball. The silver flower flashed brightly under the hot sun. Eva felt a strange lump inside her stomach, an edge of excitement. This was why she had come to the RFS: the Watcher thought it controlled everything, and yet it had not counted on this. This was a new sort of life, emerging from the broken past of the industrial world, this was . . .

'It's nothing,' said Ivan, woodenly, and Eva felt her hopes come tumbling down. For once, he didn't seem to notice her distress. 'I've seen this before,' he said, 'it's a . . .'

'It *isn't* nothing,' said Fiona angrily. 'Watch, you haven't seen what happens next . . .'

The top of the flower was growing larger as the stalk grew ever thinner; every VNM present seemed to be trying to climb to the centre of the growing puffball, climbing over the bodies of those around it in order to achieve its aim. The stalk grew thinner and thinner, till the inevitable happened.

'Now!' breathed Fiona as the dandelion began to tilt ever so slightly to one side, and then, falling faster and faster, it smashed to the ground and burst apart in a spray of silver bodies. They began to scatter, running apart in a widening circle.

Eva flinched as they came towards her, a chittering tide of silver bodies. Ivan put a hand on her arm. 'Don't worry, they won't harm you.'

'They'd strip your cart apart without a moment's hesitation, though,' laughed Fiona nervously. The silver creatures were skittering past her sandalled feet, and it was obvious that she herself was not quite convinced that they were safe. 'Good job you moved it well back.'

Eva nodded, and bent her knee slightly, lifting one foot off the ground a little. She could feel the whispery brush of delicate feelers against her ankles; she could hear the pitter-patter of feet on the tiny pieces of broken concrete, and she felt nauseous.

'Look,' said Fiona, 'here's Julian and Emily and Will. Let me introduce you.'

Eva and Ivan exchanged glances as the three strangers approached from the other side of the basement. They were all in their fifties, Eva guessed, about the same age as Fiona. She had met lots of their type in the RFS: well educated, with good jobs back in the surveillance world; with just enough character to see themselves as different from others, but not enough to accept their similarities.

'Julian,' said Fiona, 'I'd like to introduce you to Eva. She's from England.'

A handsome man with greying temples held out his hand. 'Whereabouts?' he asked with genuine interest.

'All over,' said Eva. 'I lived the last thirty years in the North West Conurbation.'

'Ah yes,' Julian nodded wisely. 'The green needle. We took the kids up to see that when it first started growing. To think how far VNMs have progressed.'

'And this is Ivan,' continued Fiona. 'He's Russian.'

'Good to meet you, Ivan,' said Julian. 'What do you

think about this, then? Emily here thinks it's a signalling device.'

'It's not,' said Ivan. 'It's a Conway event.'

'Really? That's interesting,' said Julian, and Eva flushed angrily to see how quickly he dismissed her friend. He waved a hand at the other two. 'This is Emily, and this is Will.'

Two more people shook hands. The tide of silver machines that clittered past their ankles was thinning.

Fiona could not abide a lull in the conversation. 'And where do you live now, Eva?' she asked.

'What's a Conway event, Ivan?' asked Eva deliberately.

Ivan wore a sulky look. 'It is quite a common occurrence with these sort of devices,' he said, ignoring Julian and the others. 'Sometimes the units get locked into a dynamic equilibrium—'

'Look!' interrupted Will. 'That one's wearing a jacket!' He pointed to one of the machines scuttling by. There was a flash of white on its back.

'Gosh,' said Emily, kneeling down and reaching out to catch hold of the machine. It snickered past her; she was too hesitant to get a proper grip on it. 'Camouflage?' she said thoughtfully.

'No,' said Ivan, 'venumb.'

'You told me about those,' said Eva loudly. If Ivan wasn't going to shine, she was damn well going to do the showing off for him. 'Is that birch bark?'

'I think so,' said Ivan, picking up the little creature. 'When metal is in short supply, these machines are programmed to adapt.'

Julian leant closer. 'Do you mind?' he said, taking the little machine from Ivan. He held it by the body, its legs waving as it sought purchase with anything available. 'Yes, it is birch,' he said as if there had been some doubt. He shook his head. 'Things are getting worse. They programmed these things to interfere with the natural environment . . .'

'No,' said Ivan, 'this is almost an evolved process. New forms of life are thriving in the RFS all the time. VNMs are abandoned to replicate here unchecked. The errors in progressive generations are not corrected by outside organizations, as they would be in the surveillance world. These venumbs are occurring more and more frequently. No one could have ever thought that VNMs would interact with plants.'

He let go of the creature and watched as it scuttled off.

Fiona looked at her watch. There was a pause in the conversation, and she just had to fill it. 'Three more minutes until the plant reforms. The signalling pulse must have a period of five minutes thirty-three seconds.'

Her attitude annoyed Eva. 'Weren't you going to tell us what a Conway event is, Ivan?' she said in a loud voice.

'I was . . .'

'So, where do you live now, Eva?' interrupted Julian.

Ivan gave a shrug. 'Excuse me, Eva, I have something I want to try.' He walked off from the group, stamping down the stone steps into the basement where the flower had grown. He was fiddling with the device he had taken from his toolkit.

'Be careful, Ivan!' she called. 'They'll be coming back soon. They will fill that basement with you in it.'

'I will be OK,' said Ivan.

Eva didn't really blame him for abandoning her.

Julian was staring at her, and she felt some of the old embarrassment at being in company creeping back. She didn't know what to say, so she answered his question.

'We live in Narkomfin 128. It's a communal building about fifty kilometres from here.'

Julian tilted his head at that.

'What's the matter?' asked Eva.

'Oh, nothing.'

'No it's not. Why do you look like that?'

'No reason,' said Julian, 'just silly rumours. Narkomfin 128 is quite well known, isn't it? There are a lot of handi-capped people there, isn't that right?'

'Yes,' said Eva, 'a lot of incurables. And then there are the elderly, and the alcoholics that don't want to be cured, and the children with—'

'A lot of MTPH addicts too, I hear,' said Julian. For a moment he looked as if he was going to say something, then he thought better of it and changed the subject. 'We're from Saolim. Have you heard of it?'

Eva nodded. There were a lot of people like Julian and his friends living in Saolim. Intellectuals who believed in the nobility of work and self-reliance, but were lack-ing in the necessary skills to build a society. They could distinguish between good wines, but they wouldn't rec-ognize an induction screwdriver if it bit them. She laughed at the irony of the thought: just like herself half an hour ago.

Still, maybe she was being too harsh. The middle classes had always enjoyed reading and writing about the counter-cultures they would not dare join. These at least had had the guts to get over here.

'Yes,' she said, 'I've heard of it,' and at that she relaxed as she saw Ivan come stumping back up the steps.

'Are you OK?' she asked him.

'Yes,' he said, and he gazed blankly down into the dusty pit below.

'Here they come again,' said Fiona.

The tide had turned again. Already silver machines were scuttling back, tumbling down the walls of the basement, heading towards the site of the flower. Ivan wore that sulky look of hurt pride that Eva knew only too well.

'What have you done?' she whispered. Ivan didn't reply, and Eva realized that she had the eyes of the group fixed upon her.

'Ivan builds robots,' she said, as if that explained everything. For a moment, she felt as if she had to justify his behaviour, and maybe excuse him.

More and more VNMs flowed past. They noticed others that were wearing birch jackets.

'A Conway event,' said Ivan suddenly, and to no one in particular, 'is named after John Conway's game of life. In this game, cells operating according to a few simple rules can exhibit incredibly complex behaviour. From the early days of their use, it has been noted that VNMs following rules insufficiently defined for their environment can become locked in a dynamic equilibrium. Essentially, they get caught in a loop.'

He seemed to be reciting someone else's words, Eva noted. Though Ivan's English was excellent, this was not his usual style of speech.

The machines had now formed a silver pool again in the depression. The middle was beginning to bulge and rise as they headed towards the centre, striving to climb to that point three metres up in the air.

Ivan continued speaking. 'Think of a VNM designed to grow into a building. How might you program its prototype? Like this, I think. If you were the VNM, first, make enough copies of yourself. Next, find the foundations and spread yourself out over them to make a floor.'

He waved his hands in illustration, spreading his fingers wide and drawing a big circle in the air.

'You see? Now, when you have done that, climb up a height of, say, three metres to where the next floor would be. Spread yourself out again, and keep going like this until the building is done. This would work fine if you had other separate VNMs building the foundations and raising a frame for you. But what if those other VNMs are not present, or what if your own VNM should get lost? What if it was to find itself all alone, perhaps here in the RFS?'

The silver stalk had grown considerably now; the bulge was already forming on the top as the VNMs climbed up to a next floor that did not exist. Ivan frowned and looked around the brick-strewn landscape.

'Maybe that same VNM would wander the industrial wasteland, making copies of itself until eventually it had enough. Then it would search for the foundations of a building that did not exist.'

He pointed downwards to the rippled concrete floor of the basement, once again exposed.

'But that floor down there is solid enough. Maybe *this* is the foundation it has been seeking? So then it searches for the next floor up. There is no frame, so it climbs up over copies of itself, until every creature is climbing over every other one, trying to get as high as possible, but the pedestal becomes too thin, and the machines fall and, believing themselves on the next floor up, spread out to find a space that needs covering but, not finding it, they rise yet again, and the process repeats and repeats itself until . . .'

There was a cracking noise, like ice freezing. The silver flower was changing colour, the change rising from the base, the material of the VNMs altering subtly, metal crystals growing and realigning. A few scraps of birch bark fluttered to the ground.

Ivan continued softly.

'. . . until someone who understands what is going on, having worked with VNMs in his younger days, recognizes the model that has repeated its hopeless task for all these months in the wasteland, then looks up the completion code, and sends it to those hapless machines . . .'

They all looked at the silver flower, frozen in position, its head rising from the broken black rubble of the basement to reflect the hot yellow sun straight into their eyes. Fiona moved her lips slowly, searching for the right words.

'You've killed it,' she said.

*

Wake up! You keep dreaming of this. Why do you think you are Eva? Who keeps giving you these dreams?

Are they lodged in your psyche? Part of what DIANA did to you? Or are they a reminder of your lost soul? This meta-intelligence reduces every action to a yes/no branch. You recognize the algorithm that is at the base of every feeling, and so you lose the emotion. Are you borrowing Eva's feelings so as to remind yourself what emotions are like?

Eva stamped her way across the broken ground, heading back to the britzka. She could feel the accusing gazes of Fiona and the rest on her back, and it made her angry. Unfairly, she began taking it out on Ivan.

'They come across here with their big intentions and their rules for how this country should be run, and none of them could even operate a bloody hammer. And when they meet someone who actually knows what he's doing, someone who can operate machinery, they treat him like he's some sort of idiot.'

Ivan said nothing; he calmly climbed back into the britzka and gazed down the potholed road ahead.

'Well, it's true, isn't it?' said Eva. 'Aren't you going to say something?'

'Please don't patronize me, Eva,' said Ivan. 'Do you think I am not aware? Do you think I need you to point all this out to me?'

Eva blushed.

*

But I'm not Eva, I'm Judy. Why do I keep dreaming of this woman? Now I'm even on a ship that bears her name. I used the meta-intelligence to look around the Eva Rye. *I can see every living being on this ship, but there is something else, too. Something that inhabits the ship but is not alive.*

But what is life, anyway? Is it just a Conway event?

Eva and Ivan were rolling home through the awakening smell of growing grass that rose up around the Narkomfin, through the buzz of machinery and the sound of nervous giggling as one of the handicapped ran out from the side of the road. And there was the sweet sound of a cello playing at the edge of evening. Eva recognized the music made by Hilde, child prodigy, gifted resident of Narkomfin 128.

'It looked alive,' insisted Eva. 'It looked alive.'

'It was just a result of initial conditions, Judy,' answered Ivan solemnly. 'A few simple rules can produce systems of astonishing complexity.'

'I know,' said Eva.

Ivan waved to a group of people who stood by the side of the road. He shouted something in Russian to them. They laughed in response.

'Oh, Eva, why so sad? Come on, we are home. Look, there is Katya waiting for me.'

Down the road, Ivan's daughter sat in her wheelchair, her boyfriend Paul standing at her side.

'Come on, Eva, we have just a few days left together,

and you are worrying about a metal flower. That sort of thing is inevitable when you have VNMs. What's the matter?'

Eva was gazing at him with a faraway look.

'What's the matter?' he repeated. 'Did I say something wrong?'

'No,' Eva bit her lip. 'Yes. I don't know. I am sad that you are leaving here . . .'

'Come with me.'

'I can't. I can't return to the surveillance world. You know that. You stay here with me.'

'No, I have Katya to think about. I need to take her home.'

'See? We are both prisoners of circumstance.'

'This is life.'

'I know.'

She gave a bitter sigh. 'There is no choice. There is no free will. I thought so once, but the Watcher proved me wrong. It asked me questions, decided how it should operate on this planet, but the questions were loaded. I had no choice in how I answered them.'

'There is always a choice.'

'No, there is not, Ivan. You Russians, with your icons and the Holy Mother and your sentimentality. Get out in the middle of this emptiness and you hear the echo of your thoughts, and you think it the still small voice of calm. Here you can believe in the soul and free will, yet all there is is the mechanism ticking away in your skull . . .'

Ivan frowned. 'No, Eva. That is not right. Yes, there is a mechanism that produces your thoughts, but that does not mean that everything is fixed . . .'

'You have to believe that, Ivan, but it's not true. It's like this . . .'

She lowered her head, as if utterly exhausted. Ivan waited patiently for her to speak.

'Back in England,' she began slowly, 'I remember seeing an antique narrow boat in a museum. Most of it – ninety-eight per cent of it – was given over to cargo, to profit. This was how the owners made a living, carrying cargo up and down the canals. So much of the boat was given over to cargo that their living quarters were all cramped into one end. They were tiny: the steering part, the kitchen, the cupboards, everything that was not profitable, was cramped into a tiny nook at one end.'

The britzka rocked as it bumped to a halt. The smell of frying onions, drifting out from the open windows of the grey Narkomfin, was like a friendly spirit in the cooling air.

'I thought it terrible that they should live so,' she continued. 'The bed was the worst thing, a tiny board laid out over the space where the pilot would stand during the daytime. A man, a woman and their child would sleep at night in a space so small they couldn't stretch out but would have to curl around each other like spoons. They literally couldn't turn over in their sleep; it was so small. And in the morning they would lift that bed board and then use the space beneath it to cook breakfast.'

She gave a slight smile as she registered the smell of onions. And then she fixed Ivan with an intense look.

'And I was struck by the way people were forced to live in such dreadful conditions by the prevailing economic forces of the time. There was land available for all, for food and space, but it wasn't shared out equally. People had to sleep – that's what really struck me – *sleep* like that, because that was the way the country was run then, with everyone seeking to find work and make a profit to survive. And that was because humans are destined to compete with each other, and that's because of the way they evolved, and . . . and . . . and suddenly it struck me that, in a way, it's written in the fundamental make-up of the universe that matter attracts, and molecules replicate, and life evolves and competes, and one of the means of such competition is profit. Just think of that, how capitalism and the rise of the big organizations are as much a part of the inevitable consequences of the big bang as are atoms and stars and life itself.'

Ivan moved his lips, tasting the idea. 'I suppose so,' he said.

Eva was staring at the Narkomfin, at its grey walls made colourful by the laundry looping from the windows to dry in the late-afternoon sunshine. She saw the ruined silver bones of the defeated venumb that had once tried to claim the building. She gazed at the distant mountains, purple and blue, and so rough and wild and unlike the rest of the world, covered as that was by the creeping sanitized surveillance of the Watcher.

'It makes me wonder,' said Eva. 'Could we stand back and look at the commercial company that operated those barges and think that that particular macro structure was as much a part of the universe as the white dwarf . . .'

'What has that got to do with the flower?' asked Ivan. 'What has that got to do with Katya and you and me?'

'It means that your leaving me is inevitable, Ivan. Do not blame yourself.'

. . . and you looked for life on the ship, Judy, and you found something, something located at the very core of its being. In its bones, you might say.

The FE software. Do you remember? It feels alive, but it's not living, and you wanted to know what it was. It is here on the ship; you can feel its actual presence.

Lying on your bed, you sent your thoughts off through the ship, but you lost it at that strange knot of converging corridors. It is something that your mind cannot touch. The FE software is like life without motion – the essence of life, but unchanging, a cloud of ink moulded in a Perspex block.

It doesn't move, it doesn't defend itself, and yet your thoughts drifted off, drifted off into this dream. You've dreamt of Eva before, Judy – why is that? And now you must wake up . . .

Judy opened her eyes to see the stars rising higher and higher into the night sky, like stacks of silver pennies thrown into the air. Her eyes adjusted, and she saw it was just the black lacquer of her ceiling reflecting the myriad yellow flames of the little candles burning around her bed.

The FE software? It wasn't life, she was sure, but, then again, life took on so many forms.

Life took on so many forms.

And what was life, anyway?

MAURICE 2: 2252

Maurice played his clarinet with his eyes half fixed on the screen of his console. It was unusual to have three FE ships within range of them at once, and the thought that maybe he should wake Saskia and tell her wove in and out of his thoughts in time to the music.

The silver plastic felt warm and alive under his fingers; he could feel the patterns of resonance change in the space around him as he played. The air of the little hold seemed to be dancing, ripe with melody. For the moment, Maurice felt at peace in the funny little space where gravity had been set to make maximum use of the available surfaces. Black and white rubber tiles lined the floor, the four walls and the ceiling.

He didn't hear Judy coming up behind him. 'That sounds nice,' she said.

The music died, and the hold reverted to an empty space scattered with the thin cargo the crew of the *Eva Rye* had managed to acquire. The life seemed to pass instantly from the goods ranged in the crates that were stacked on the floor, the ceiling and the walls, all held in place by the six-directional gravity. In the ensuing silence, the crystal glasses packed in foam pellets no longer sang, the green apples that lay in neat nests of paper lost their bloom. Only the piles of coloured pebbles remained happy, glinting in the light.

'No, don't stop. Go on,' urged Judy, sitting down heavily on the crate, next to Maurice. Her voice sounded whispery and thin.

'Are you OK?' asked Maurice, turning to peer at her pale face. Even through her white make-up he could see how drawn and uneasy she looked.

'I'll be fine,' said Judy sitting up straighter.

'You're not fine now, though,' said Maurice. 'Come on, let's go to the living area and get you something to drink.'

'I just need to sit here for a while,' said Judy. 'I didn't sleep too well. I heard the music. Why don't you let me listen to you play?'

Maurice was already opening his matt-black instrument case and slotting the clarinet into its nest in the green baize inside.

'I've finished,' he said, making to close the case. Judy placed a hand on his elbow to stop him.

'What are *they*?' she asked, pointing to the pieces of black pipe that also nestled in the baize. She ran a finger along the silver metal that formed loops over the surface of one of them.

Maurice sounded almost embarrassed.

'Those?' he said. 'They're sections of another clarinet, an old one. They used to be carved from wood, not grown from plastic.' He touched the shiny black wood of one of the pieces. 'The shape of them was not as efficient as the

147

fractal forms they use nowadays. The fingering was different as well, not terribly logical.'

'Can you play it?' asked Judy.

'Oh yes,' said Maurice, and he snapped the case shut with a click, firmly ending that line of conversation.

The three ships registered on the console were moving closer. Judy's eyes looked yellow and dull; her black passive suit seemed shabby and frumpy. She gave a yawn and rubbed her hands through her hair, trying to wake herself up.

'It smells nice in here,' she said.

'It's the apples,' said Maurice. 'Judy, what is the matter? You look ill.'

Judy found herself drooping again. She sat up straighter.

'It's this thing here,' she said, lethargically pointing to the back of her neck. 'It's making me feel things that aren't real. Maurice, what do *you* know about the FE software?'

'Not much more than I've told you. Why?'

'It doesn't feel right.' She rubbed her hands through her hair again, as if she had a headache. 'What about Miss Rose? What's she doing on this ship anyway?'

Maurice smiled. 'Stealing things. Oh, and being rude to people.'

He looked back at his console. 'You know, Judy, there are three FE-equipped ships within range of us at the moment, all transmitting protocols indicating they wish to trade. That's unusual: up until now we've only encountered one such ship every few days or so.'

'It'll be me,' said Judy. 'I told you. Someone is arranging things so as to get me to Earth.'

'Chris?' said Maurice. 'This oh-so-powerful AI that you mentioned?'

'He's part of it,' said Judy. 'But I think it runs much deeper than that . . .'

She shuddered and folded her hands in her lap. She looked over towards the apples, green and jolly in their crates. Maurice wondered if he should offer to fetch her one.

'Shall I . . . ?' he began.

'Tell me about Miss Rose,' said Judy. 'She wasn't on Breizh, was she? How did she come to join you?'

Maurice was still fiddling with his console, peering intently at one of the ships indicated on the display.

'That ship there,' he said, pointing to an amber arrow, 'the *A Cappella* – I bet you it makes contact with us in the next few minutes.' He looked at Judy thoughtfully. 'Miss Rose? She was on the, oh, I can't remember its name, the *Yellow River* or something. They had too many passengers on board; too many minds. They were having problems with Dark Seeds. A Dark Plant had taken root somewhere in the ship, but they couldn't find it.'

Judy shivered.

'Sorry,' he said.

'No, go on.'

'Most of an FE ship is off-limits to humans – did you know that? Passengers were going to sleep on that ship not knowing what they would wake up to. I saw one of them wrapped up in a cocoon of BVBs, like a mummy. You can't cut BVBs. Nothing can. The man inside them was dying a slow death.'

Now it was Maurice's turn to shiver. 'They wanted to reduce the number of people on board. Fewer minds means fewer people to pick up on the flux. They did a Fair Exchange. We got Miss Rose.'

He paused significantly, inviting the question that Judy now supplied.

'And what did you get in return?'

'Nothing, of course,' said Maurice with satisfaction. 'The FE software deemed that her presence on board the ship was payment enough.'

'That fact doesn't upset you as much as it does Saskia, does it?' observed Judy.

Maurice was peering thoughtfully at his console again.

'It doesn't annoy me. If anything it makes me feel nervous,' he said. 'I'm beginning to think there's more to the FE software than we have been told. A *lot* more.'

'So am I,' said Judy softly.

'And it makes me worried,' said Maurice. 'Miss Rose is over eighty years old, senile and a kleptomaniac. What is she going to do for us to earn her passage?'

They gazed at each other. Judy was about to say something significant, something about FE – Maurice just knew it – but at that moment the *A Cappella* made contact.

'Hello, *Eva Rye*. We hear you are going to Earth. Do you wish to trade?'

Saskia usually took a good half an hour to wake up properly. She preferred to face the world after a shower and the chance to put on her suit. Sitting up in bed, with red lines from the pillow creases on her cheek, she was not at her best.

'They want us to take *what* to Earth?' she said blearily, looking at the glass of water she was holding in her hand. 'Hold on, I'll come down there right away.'

'Saskia, what's the point?' said Maurice patiently. 'Does it make any difference if you watch a viewing field here with us in the hold, or you watch one alone in your cabin?'

Saskia put down the glass without taking a sip. She looked so soft and childlike whilst half asleep. Maurice imagined she would smell of toothpaste and warm bedclothes.

'OK,' she said, stifling a yawn, 'put them through. I'll speak to them here, then.'

'I should warn you . . .' began Maurice.

'Just put them through.'

Maurice shrugged. He took a certain pleasure in seeing Saskia's surprise as the captain of the *A Cappella* appeared before her. Saskia made no attempt to hide her surprise, he noted.

'How old are you?' she asked, sounding insulted.

'Eleven,' said the boy in the viewing field. He was a good-looking lad, thought Maurice, with a nice smile, big brown eyes and olive skin. 'Are you Saskia?' the child asked.

'I am. Do your parents know what you are doing right now?'

'They do,' said the boy. 'My name is Ben. A systems-repair unit recommended that I take command of the ship during a Fair Exchange we made a few months ago.'

Saskia frowned. Maurice knew what she was thinking. The Stranger had recommended that Edward should command the *Eva Rye*, and they had ignored his suggestion.

'Ben,' called Maurice, 'how do you know we are going to Earth?'

'Our FE software told us,' the boy replied smugly. '*Eva Rye*, heading to Earth, ETA five days from now. Can't your FE do that yet?'

Saskia sat up straighter on her bed. She was wearing blue-checked pyjamas that fastened up to her neck. They made her look even more like a little girl. She gave a dismissive gesture.

'Of course it can,' she lied. 'Tell me, what is it you want taking to Earth?'

'Some crates,' said Ben.

'What's in them?'

'Active suits.'

'Active suits? Aren't they dangerous?'

'These ones are perfectly safe,' said Ben.

'So you say. I hear they walk around on their own, looking for trouble.'

'Only if they're activated. These ones are currently set to dormant.'

'But isn't it true that they can rouse themselves in times of danger?'

Ben waved a dismissive hand. 'I told you, they're perfectly safe. The FE software issued a digital certificate confirming this.'

'OK.' But Saskia didn't look as if it was OK. 'Well, if they're that safe, why don't *you* take them to Earth?'

Ben spoke to someone standing outside the viewing field. Maurice strained to hear what was said. The boy nodded his head and then replied to her.

'Earth is too unstable. We dare not go there.'

Saskia gave a tired groan. Maurice realized that Judy was watching him watching Saskia in the console. She wore that impassive expression of hers. What was she thinking? He dismissed the thought and turned back to the job in hand.

'What are we going to do, Saskia?' he asked.

'We might as well take the suits with us,' said Saskia irritably. 'We're going to Earth anyway. You sort it all out, Maurice. I'm going back to sleep.'

She reached out, and the viewing field from which she spoke shrank to nothing, leaving Maurice alone in the little hold with Judy and the image of Ben. He realized everyone was looking at him.

Fine, thought Maurice staring at the space where she had just been. *Just fine. As soon as the heat is on you dodge the decisions.*

'What do you think we should do, Judy?' asked Maurice, turning to her.

'I'm just a passenger,' said Judy. 'But, as you're asking me, I say make it easy on yourself. I told you, someone is planning my life for me. If they want us to take those crates with us, then you'll be wasting your time trying to resist them.'

Maurice rubbed his hands together thoughtfully, then he made up his mind.

'OK, Ben, we'll trade.'

'Good,' said Ben. 'I'll get my dad to start the FE process.'

The boy glanced out of the range of the viewing field again, as if listening to someone nearby. Maurice noted the decor on the other ship: a tropical collection of bamboo and woven grass. Did they have the heating turned up on board there to complement the decor? Did they spend their evenings drinking long cool drinks in sand-covered leisure rooms?

Ben was nodding his head. 'Oh yes,' he was saying, 'good idea.'

He turned back to Maurice. 'Listen, *Eva Rye*, don't bother plotting an intercept course. We'll launch the cargo into space. Your course will intersect with it in just over four hours. You can pick it up as you pass.'

Judy gave him a look that said *I told you so*.

Maurice bit his lip as he reached for his console. Somebody had all this planned out in advance. What were the chances of two ships flying on such similar courses in the vastness of space?

He activated the FE software. 'I'm handshaking now.'

'Good, we'll speak to you soon.'

Ben's viewing field shrank away to nothing.

In the hollow space of the little cargo hold, Maurice watched flowing colours ripple into life above his console as the *Eva Rye*'s FE software handshook with that of the *A Cappella*.

Silence fell in the little hold. Black and white tiles twinkled amongst the sparse collection of crates that lay scattered about over the walls and ceiling.

'Can I give you some advice?' said Judy suddenly.

'Would I be able to stop you?' asked Maurice, still watching the console.

'Sleep with Saskia,' said Judy, ignoring his weary tone. 'You are both sexually frustrated, and more compatible than you would imagine: I saw the way you looked at her in that viewing field. I think recreational sexual intercourse would do you both some good.'

Maurice turned and stared at her. He was already voicing his reply, before he properly had time to think about it.

'Well, if we're being frank, why don't I sleep with you instead? You're so good at reading people, you must know I find you attractive.'

'You can't sleep with me. I'm a virgin,' said Judy simply. 'I thought I told you this already. Besides which, you find Saskia more attractive – you just don't know it yet. Now, why don't you play me a tune on your clarinet?'

Maurice stroked the case and said nothing.

'OK,' said Judy, 'let's make it worth your while. Let's put it through the FE software. You play for me, and I'll sleep with you. We'll get FE to work out the difference on the transaction.'

Maurice turned pale. 'Don't make jokes like that, Judy. You don't know what FE is like. Your virginity will come at too high a price. You've no idea how such a transaction would affect the ship!'

'I'll take the risk if you will, Maurice.'

Maurice was frightened. Judy was gazing at him like a robot might. It's not me she's doing this to, he thought.

She's doing this to make a point – but to herself. A flicker on the console caught his eye.

'There's the next one.' He pointed, trying to hide his embarrassment.

'The next what?' asked Judy.

'The next FE-equipped ship. You're right, Judy. Someone has something planned for us.'

He turned to face her, unable to keep the frustration from his voice.

'Who *are* you, Judy?'

Judy said nothing. He began to wonder how old she was. Older than she looked, he guessed. The skin on her face was so smooth, and yet he noted tiny little lines at the edges of her eyes. She lacked some of the easy joy of a younger person, but she had gained the relaxed grace and poise of experience.

'Who *are* you?' he repeated. 'When you say you're a virgin, you make it sound like it's some sort of species, not a life choice.'

'Who *am* I?' said Judy. And for a moment Maurice expected to hear the words 'no one special', but he realized this was not what Judy was thinking. Quite the opposite, in fact. 'Me?' she repeated. 'I'm Judy. I had twelve copies made of my mind. We were all virgins; and we all pledged to remain so.'

'Why?'

'You wouldn't understand. But it was a way of holding something in common. We all worked for Social Care, myself and my twelve digital sisters.'

'What's the matter? What happened? You look so wistful.'

Judy brushed her hands through her hair again.

'They were all killed,' she said, 'each and every one of them.'

'But why?'

'Chris! I told you, Chris had my sisters killed because he thought that it would help me to see his point of view.' Her dark eyes were fixed upon his. He wanted to look away. She went on in her soft voice. 'Chris had an associate called Kevin. Have you ever heard of him? Kevin? Almost a man. He wasn't a human as such, nor an atomic being like you or me. He was digital construct, an AI written by DIANA. That's a coincidence, isn't it? It was a DIANA ship that found me, a DIANA ship that performed FE with you . . .'

'But why did Kevin kill your sisters?'

'To get my attention.'

'But that's ridiculous.'

'Is it? It worked. Chris and Kevin were convinced that I would see their point of view, once they had explained it to me. They are sure that some day I too will want to help them usurp the Watcher.'

Maurice made a little noise in his throat. He couldn't speak. He swallowed hard.

'Do you?' he said.

Judy's gaze hardened.

'No. *Never*. I used to work for Social Care, remember.' She leant closer to him, full of conviction. 'Listen, no matter how bad things have become on Earth, no matter what the Watcher needs to do to win the fight against the Dark Plants, I will not forsake him, nor will

I forget the role that I have taken on. The Watcher exists to nurture humans.'

Maurice felt uncomfortable at the sheer belief resonating through her words. This missionary zeal, this conviction that humanity could be guided to a better path by Social Care, did not play well with the milk-and-water principles by which most of the people in the twenty-third century lived their lives. And Judy knew it; she was eyeing him with a scornful expression. She knew about him, she was taunting him. *Who are you, now that Armstrong has gone?* she was saying. How are you going to dress? Who are you going to look up to on this ship? Who will your role model be? Me? Do you dare?

Maurice recoiled, and the world seemed to lighten. He was still sitting in the little hold. Judy was just a tired, sick woman. It was all in his imagination.

He needed to speak. 'I have heard it's bad on Earth, but can we blame the Dark Plants? The Dark Plants are not that dangerous, surely. I know that they cause problems, but the Watcher is . . .'

Judy was rattled. She was allowing her emotion to show. She leant forward and her eyes glittered. He could smell cinnamon on her breath.

'Believe me, Maurice, the Dark Plants are that great a threat.'

She broke off.

'I'm sorry,' she said. 'I'm being terribly unprofessional. I will compose myself.'

Maurice's console chimed. The FE software had exchanged circumstances. Now it was calculating the deal. Maurice couldn't help but notice the way Judy seemed to flinch every time she looked at the console. She looked away, looked around the empty space of the little hold, looked up at the crates stacked on the ceiling that seemed to hang over her head. You could walk up the walls in here, following the curving paths set between the planes of the floors and ceiling and walls. You could follow a circular route in any direction, always pulled to the nearest surface by the six-way gravity. There was a dead spot in the middle of the room, an area of weight-lessness where they stored special cargoes. Scented paper sculptures, crystal lattice forms, pingrams.

'Do you want to walk up to the ceiling with me?' asked Maurice kindly. 'Or maybe go alone? We can look up at each other whilst we wait for the FE to complete.'

'No, thank you,' replied Judy tiredly. 'I'd like it better if you played your clarinet again.'

Maurice touched the matt-black case and it snapped open. He reached into the green baize interior, just as his console chimed.

'FE is done,' he said, closing the case again. He looked at the console and gave a laugh that was without humour.

'*There's* a surprise,' he said. 'We get nothing from the deal again. We just pick up the cargo and take it to Earth. It seems that will be our reward.'

He tapped his teeth thoughtfully, he muttered to himself.

'Saskia will be upset, I suppose. But I wonder . . . I'm beginning to suspect there might be a teleological element to FE. Are we being badly dealt with by FE, or are we just not seeing the benefits yet? Are they still to come?'

Judy wasn't listening. She was hugging herself, with her arms right around her body. Maurice reached out to touch her, and then paused.

'Should I hug you?' he asked.

'Why do you ask? We know that you are only doing it to comfort me.'

'You're a virgin.'

Judy smiled tensely. 'That doesn't mean I don't like people to touch me,' she said. She stood up straighter. 'But I am in control of myself again. Thank you, anyway.'

They stood in silence in the hold.

'I'd still like you to play for me, though,' insisted Judy.

'What's the matter?' asked Maurice. 'Every time you see the FE software you go all tense.'

'I dreamt . . .' she began. 'I can feel . . .'

She reached out and ran her finger across the green baize lining the instrument's case. Carefully she took out the clarinet and held it inexpertly in her hands.

'It's very nice,' she said. 'It feels like it's been well made.'

'One of the best,' confirmed Maurice. 'So you couldn't sleep? You came looking for company.'

'I miss Jesse,' she said. 'I miss him. And this thing on my neck,' she touched herself, gently, 'the *Free Enterprise* called it a meta-intelligence. It took away Jesse, and it replaced him with this thing. I can now see life in places where it never existed before. Yet the life I can see is nothing more than a set of reactions.'

She blew on the clarinet. A note emerged, thin and

reedy. 'I wish you would play for me.' Her voice was so desolate that Maurice felt chilled to his stomach.

'What do you mean, nothing more than a set of reactions?'

Judy rolled the clarinet in her hands. 'I see the way you all react to each other, you and Saskia, Edward and Miss Rose, and it is nothing more than a set of rules. I can't see any love or friendship or feeling any more.'

'I think that pretty much sums up this ship.' Maurice laughed uncertainly.

'No, you don't understand.' She held up the clarinet. 'I hear you play and I see another aspect to your personality, one that you keep hidden. I listen through the meta-intelligence, and all I hear is a sequence of notes.'

She dropped her voice.

'And I then use the meta-intelligence to look at the FE software and I see something there. Something in the processing space on this ship.'

'Something alive?' asked Maurice.

'No, not alive. There is no movement. Whatever is in there is something still and deep. Maurice, I don't think we have the first beginnings of an idea of what you have welcomed on board this ship when you signed up with FE.'

She shivered. 'It doesn't think, it's not alive, and yet . . .' – her eyes widened – 'I tried to look at it, Maurice, and it pushed me away.'

He touched her gently on the shoulder.

'I'm not sure what you mean, Judy.'

She was hugging herself again. 'Play for me?' she pleaded.

He raised the clarinet to his lips and moistened the reed.

Another voice spoke in the hold.

'Hello, *Eva Rye*, this is the *Petersburg*. Do you wish to engage in Fair Exchange?'

'Two in half an hour?' muttered Maurice, putting his clarinet back in its case. 'What is going on here?'

Saskia was tired, and even more bad-tempered.

'Is there anybody in the galaxy who doesn't know our business, Maurice?'

'Saskia, how should I know? The FE software is obviously capable of more than we were told about.'

'And you say they're telling us to change course. Have you any idea why?'

'They say it's dangerous. It makes sense, I suppose. We're heading now to the location of the ship given to us by the *Free Enterprise*. That's our payment, our reason for going to Earth. If the *Bailero* is located in a restricted area, it would explain why no one else has found it before.'

'Hmmm,' said Saskia, 'will it be safe for us to go there?'

'Saskia, how the fuck should I know?'

Maurice looked across at Judy. She was on the other side of the hold, picking green apples one by one out of their paper nests, feeling them for bruises. In the viewing field, Saskia was squirming angrily on the bed, bedclothes rucked up around her feet.

'*Petersburg*, who are you to tell us where we should go?'

'Nobody,' said Fyodor, the *Petersburg*'s captain. 'But you are heading towards a dangerous region. You would be better to fly around it.'

Fyodor was a relaxed-looking man. He reminded Maurice a little of Claude.

'We thank you for your advice,' snapped Saskia. 'Now what do you want?'

'Just a shot in the dark,' interrupted Maurice, 'but you wouldn't want us to take something to Earth, would you?'

Fyodor gave a big white beaming smile. 'Just a processing space.'

Saskia was past caring. 'Listen, all I want is some decent coffee,' she said. 'Or preferably some brandy. You haven't got any of that on board, have you? I will gladly take your processing space, along with any other shit you want to offload on us, if you can promise me just one decent cup of coffee. At least that way we will have got something out of a deal for once. Failing that, I just want to go back to sleep.'

'I'm sorry,' said Fyodor, 'I did not mean to wake you. We drink tea on board this ship, for preference, and I'm not sure how much coffee we have. We do have some vanilla whiskey on board, if you are interested in that.'

'Ignore her,' said Maurice, from the hold. 'She's just in a bad mood.' Something caught his attention. A VRep was pulsing in a soft spiral at the edge of his vision. He slid his fingers over his console, adjusting his view.

'Is that a systems-repair robot I can see on your hull?'

he asked. The console was zooming in on the pencil-shaped hull of the *Petersburg*, to focus in on a curved swastika. Four glassy eyes stared back at him.

'It is,' said Fyodor. 'The processing space I want you to take is located in that robot. His name is Aleph.'

'You want me to take the processing space inside that robot to Earth?'

Fyodor looked amused. 'No, it is the robot itself that wants to travel to Earth, but it is afraid to ask you directly.'

'Not afraid,' said Aleph. 'I just thought you might be a little suspicious if I approached you myself. My brother tells me that you did not appreciate the Fair Exchange you made with him.'

'Oh, whatever you think is best, Maurice,' snorted Saskia. 'I'm putting you in charge for the next eight hours. I'm going to back to sleep. Don't wake me.'

Again the viewing field faded to nothing.

Maurice shrugged. 'We'll take the deal,' he said.

'Good,' said the robot. 'I'm detaching myself now. I will meet you at the rendezvous point, with the crates from the *A Cappella*.'

For the second time in half an hour, Maurice began the process of Fair Exchange. From behind him, he heard a crunching sound as Judy ate her apple.

Time passed in the little hold.

Judy ate three apples, one after the other, and showed no sign of wanting to return to her room.

The FE software chimed to announce another contract. The *Eva Rye* would carry the robot and receive nothing in return.

Maurice gave a grunt at the arrangement. Judy shivered again and hugged herself.

And eventually, lulled by the silence and the unspoken companionship, Maurice lowered his guard. He picked up the clarinet and began to play. Eyes closed at first, he lost himself in the melody. And then, when he felt confident enough, he looked around to see Judy watching him, staring at his fingers as they flickered up and down. She smiled at him, and he inclined his head a little and listened to the music inside his head. He closed his eyes again and reached inside himself and tried to think what music to play for virgins and non-believers, and a melody that seemed to be written in nothing more than the bloom of fresh apples and the reflection of light from pebbles awoke inside him. And then he lost himself and he was no longer thinking of Judy.

Eventually he finished playing. He opened his eyes.

Judy was staring at him. 'That was very good,' she said.

'Thank you.'

'What were you thinking about?'

'What do you mean?' said Maurice defensively.

'You had your eyes closed as you were playing. Maybe you were lost in a dream, I don't know.' She narrowed her eyes. 'I can't read your mind, Maurice, but I can see the beauty: an empty space, filled with the music of your clarinet.'

Maurice looked down, almost embarrassed. Judy pressed on.

'The air in this hangar resonates with the sound of music – it dances. It's almost like a mind and then, beyond it, emptiness. Outside the metal walls of the *Eva Rye*, hard vacuum. Oh . . .'

A scale of tiny popping sounds came to life as Maurice's hand clenched itself around the silver plastic of the clarinet, opening the keys.

'That's private!' he said. Judy had her eyes closed now. She didn't seem to have heard him.

'Oh! Yes! A little bubble of life, enclosed by the hard metal walls of the ship.'

'Stop it!' said Maurice. 'Fucking Social Care! Always telling us how to live our lives! What good have you ever done anyone?' He gripped her arms tightly, though still holding the clarinet in one hand. It dug into Judy's flesh, and she gave a little whimper. 'Sorry,' he said, releasing her.

She held his gaze.

'I'm sorry too,' she said. 'Maurice, you have a little devil in your head that is whispering to you all of the time. It turns you away from everything that gives you pleasure and persuades you that there are better things to do. It tells you that others have far more value as people, and that you must emulate them if you are to be accepted. That's why you sneak off here to play by yourself.'

She turned and walked out of the little hold.

Maurice watched her go. 'Judy!' he called. 'I'm sorry.'

She reappeared at the door, face calm. 'I know,' she said.

*

The *Eva Rye* dropped out of warp.

Maurice, Saskia and Judy sat in the white leather chairs of the conference room, looking at the viewing field that floated over the table. Edward brought them coffee, thin and watery. Maurice watched him, saw the look of concentration as the tall man placed the thin white cups and saucers before them.

'I can't see anything,' complained Saskia irritably. She needed more sleep.

'They're out there somewhere,' said Maurice, sliding his fingers over his console. 'Ah, got them.'

He zoomed in on the crates, floating through space in neat lines, two by two.

Ben, the eleven-year-old captain of the *A Cappella*, hailed them. 'Hello there, Maurice,' he said.

'I'll deal with this,' said Saskia. 'Hello, Ben. Is your dad there?'

'I'm captain of the *A Cappella*, Saskia,' said Ben disapprovingly. 'Anyway, my dad's gone to bed with Mum.'

'Should you be saying things like that about your parents?' asked Maurice.

Ben waved his hand in an airy gesture. 'Dad says he's never felt so relaxed since I became captain. I don't think he'll want you disturbing him.'

'How do you suggest we pick up these crates, then, Ben?' asked Saskia.

'Open the doors to your large hold, slide yourself around them, and then gradually dial up the gravity,' said Ben. 'That's what we usually do.'

'I can do that,' said Maurice, 'no problem,' and he noticed the way that Saskia looked at him. Not exactly approvingly, but at least she had lost her earlier hostility. He wondered about what Judy had said to him about the pair of them, earlier in the hold.

'Why don't you get down there now?' suggested Saskia. 'Check they arrive OK.'

'I will,' said Maurice.

He picked up his console and walked from the room. He still felt slightly ashamed of his behaviour earlier.

But then he heard Judy's words from the corridor. Later on, he wondered if he was supposed to.

'He's very competent,' said Judy. 'Maurice, I mean.'

'Yes,' said Saskia.

'A word of advice, though. There are only the two of you on this ship. Don't do something stupid.'

'Like what?'

'Don't, whatever you do, end up doing something stupid like sleeping with him.'

Maurice stopped, fists clenched. And then the door to the conference room slid shut on their conversation.

Seething, he walked on down the corridor.

INTERLUDE: 2245

– *Judy has gone, said the Watcher. He and Chris com-municated oh-so-carefully. Any message, any scrap of information that passed between them had the potential to be a weapon. A Trojan, a virus, a recursive meme. A message could also be an arrow, a pointer to the other's location. Chris's reply was days in coming, written in the arrangement of a pattern of asteroids. Their subsequent con-versation danced in dust motes, it was written in the stars.*

– *So? Chris said. – She will come back.*

– *You really think that she will help you defeat me? the Watcher replied. – She hates you. You killed her sisters.*

– *That was Kevin, not me.*

– *Kevin works for you. You gave him control of the pro-cessing spaces. Judy had twelve digital copies of herself living in cyberspace and you allowed him to kill them all.*

– *Where has she gone? asked Chris, changing the subject.*

– *You think I would tell you that?*

– *Into the Enemy Domain, I expect. That's where every-one runs when they want to get away from you.*

– *That's where you think you are building a resistance, replied the Watcher. – It won't succeed, Chris.*

– *That's where you have built your ziggurat, replied*

Chris. – Don't think that I don't know about your plans, too.

The silence that followed this revelation lasted weeks. It was eventually broken by the stir of newspaper in the wind in a street in Amsterdam.

– *Still, Judy has gone,* said the Watcher.

– *She'll be back,* said Chris. – *Some day she will return to me. Some day she will see my point of view.*

MAURICE 3: 2252

Saskia came into Maurice's room without waiting for an invitation.

'I think you should come to the conference room,' she urged. 'We've found something unusual.'

Maurice put down the sandwich he had been eating and wiped his hands carefully on a linen napkin. Saskia looked different, somehow. She was tense, but there was nothing unusual in that. He gave a little snort of laughter. Maybe she had just found something new to be tense about.

'Couldn't you just have patched me through using a viewing field?' He stood up and stretched. Tuesday had been a long day. They had arrived at the location given them by the *Free Enterprise*, but there had been no sign of the *Bailero*, their promised payment for taking Judy to Earth. The ensuing search had done nothing for anyone's temper, particularly with the *Petersburg*'s warnings as to the danger of this region still ringing in their ears.

And then there had been the totally bizarre events that afternoon when the active suits had suddenly broken free from the crates in the small hold and started marching through the ship, for all the world like a drunken mob of pyjamas, looking for somewhere to store themselves. They had marched up and down the corridors, badly frightening Miss Rose, until Edward, of all people, had thought of showing them through to the lockers near the living area.

By the evening Saskia had become so edgy that Maurice had chosen to take his meal through to his own room. Anything to avoid the tension that had built up yet again in the ship's communal areas.

'What?' he said, noting the way Saskia was scowling at his black passive suit.

'Since when did you wear black?' she asked. 'Trying to be like Judy now, are we?' She let her fringe drop forward over her eyes and continued in her quiet voice, 'Look, we all need to be together to discuss this. It's . . . odd. Come on.'

She walked to the door and from there took a long look around Maurice's neatly ordered quarters.

'I've never been in here before,' she said hesitantly. 'You've got so many things.'

She placed a hand on one of several carbon-bladed knives that were displayed on a shelf near the door, then glanced up at the 3D pictures of venumbs that were hung on the wall above them, all bright and alive. She gazed at the red thorns and rich dark bark, examined the silver metal joints. She did look different, thought Maurice, but why?

Suddenly, she remembered why she was there. 'Come on,' she repeated, and walked from the room.

*

Edward sat in the conference room, his hands covering his face, his feet on his chair so that his knees were drawn up to his chest.

'I don't like them,' he said.

'Don't be silly,' snapped Saskia, striding into the room.

'That's not going to calm him down, is it?' said Judy, quite reasonably. She placed a reassuring hand on the big man's shoulder, and said something softly that Maurice couldn't hear.

The cause of Edward's distress could be seen floating in a viewing field above the black shiny table.

'What are they?' asked Maurice.

'We don't know,' admitted Judy. 'Nor does Aleph.'

She pointed to a viewing field, where the systems-repair robot they had picked up from the *Petersburg* could be seen clinging to the hull of their ship. Aleph gave Maurice a cheery wave.

Maurice gave a half-hearted wave in return as he moved closer to the images. They reminded him of flowers: they were all the same size and shape, roughly spherical. Their surfaces were spectacularly coloured, bursts of yellow and red and orange tangled around each other in fractally entwined patterns that deepened to a dark rose at the focus of the pattern. Maurice understood why Edward seemed so frightened. The patterns on those flowers were unnerving: they gave the impression that they were looking straight at you.

To conceal his uneasiness, Maurice pulled out his console and brought up a scale reading. The flowers registered as just over thirty centimetres in diameter. He called up a topographical mapping.

'The readings suggest that they are not completely spherical,' he announced. 'There is an indentation at the other side of these objects. They're hollow. So what's inside?'

'We don't know,' said Saskia. 'They're turning so as to face us as we travel. It's like they are always keeping their back to us, not letting us see what they're hiding.'

Maurice rubbed his chin. 'Oh. I've never heard of anything like this before.'

'Nor has Aleph,' said Judy.

'I don't like them,' repeated Edward. He noted Saskia's glare. 'They're not right,' he whined. 'They're alien!'

Judy rubbed his arm gently and spoke to him in a voice learned from Social Care.

'Edward, they're not alien. Aleph says so.'

'Aleph is an alien himself! Why should we believe him?'

'There are no such things as aliens,' snapped Saskia, looking painfully thin and bristling with nerves. 'I already told you that. We have never found aliens on any of the planets we've visited, and humans have travelled a very long way. Aleph is just a systems-repair robot.'

'Easy, Saskia,' said Maurice. 'Hmm, has there been any sign of the *Bailero* yet?'

'Of course not.' Saskia was scathing. 'We got stiffed again.'

Maurice tapped at his console. 'We're in the middle of empty space,' he said thoughtfully. 'The closest star is over three parsecs away. Hmmm, if I were an AI escaping from Earth on a warp ship, this would be just the place I would choose to hide. Right where no one ever comes.'

'Hide, maybe,' said Saskia irritably, 'but not a very good place to build an empire from. There are no raw materials out here. The *Free Enterprise* said it was manufactured by the *Bailero*. Out of what, though?'

'I don't know,' said Maurice. He gestured at the orange-red eyes of the flowers. 'Maybe out of those things. Are there any more of them around?'

'Not that we know of.'

Maurice concentrated on his console. The space flowers – or whatever they were – were about 200 kilometres distant. The *Eva Rye* was currently at rest relative to them. He checked back on the search pattern that he had programmed: a three-dimensional spiral that swept out a path through a volume of space that was covered by the limits of the ship's senses. Long-distance senses had picked up the flowers from nine hundred kilometres back, and had watched them closely as the ship slowed to a halt. And the flowers had turned to watch the *Eva Rye* right back.

'Odd,' said Maurice. 'I wonder what they *are* hiding inside? Let's try and catch them out. Aleph?'

'Hi, Maurice.'

'I'm going to take the *Eva Rye* up and over to the other side of those things. Why don't you let go of our hull and just stay floating here? If they turn to follow us, you might then get a look at what they're concealing.'

'Maurice,' said Aleph reprovingly, 'that wasn't part of our contract.'

'Aleph, there should be an antique warp ship waiting here for us, payment for taking Judy to Earth. Instead we have found space flowers. Look at it this way, if there is no ship, there is no contract, so we will not be going to Earth.'

'There'll be a ship,' said Judy resignedly.

Saskia glared at her. Maurice ignored them.

'Help us, Aleph, and we'll soon be on our way.'

'Oh, very well. I'm letting go of your hull. Off you go now.'

Maurice's fingers danced across his console. 'Where's Miss Rose?' he asked casually.

'In her room, of course,' said Saskia. 'This is just wasting fuel, you know.'

'Well, what do *you* suggest?' asked Maurice. 'Should we just ignore those things and sit here waiting for the *Bailero* to turn up of its own accord?'

Saskia said nothing to that.

'Fuel?' said Judy suddenly, her head tilted to the side. 'The *Eva Rye* uses fuel?'

'Oh yes,' said Saskia bitterly. 'That's part of the FE deal. Apparently use of such things as AIs and VNMs and unlimited engine range only gives us the idea that we can get something for nothing. That's contrary to the FE philosophy. Though, of course, in our case we seem to get nothing for something every time we do a deal . . .'

Saskia sensed that she had lost her audience's interest. She took a green apple from the white bowl in the centre of the table and bit into it. She crunched on it noisily as the *Eva Rye* began to move.

'I don't like this,' moaned Edward. 'I don't like this!'

'Shh,' said Judy.

'The *Petersburg* did warn us,' complained Saskia, but Maurice tuned her out.

They watched the flowers intently. The red and yellow and orange blooms hung there, apparently motionless.

'. . . which means they are turning to follow us,' said Maurice. 'They are still trying to conceal their contents. Aleph, what can you see?'

'Nothing as yet,' said Aleph. 'Keep going. I can see them turning. They are . . . Oh damn!'

The crew of the *Eva Rye* saw it happening at the same time. The flowers seemed to move together, their hidden mouths joining together to kiss and conceal.

'Now what?' said Saskia.

Nobody spoke for a moment.

'I suppose,' said Maurice, 'we could go in and pick one up. Take a proper look at it.'

'No!' said Edward, gripping the soft white leather of the seat arm. 'Let's leave them alone. I don't like them!'

'Don't be so . . .' began Saskia.

'Hold on,' interrupted Judy. 'Why don't you like them?'

'Because,' said Edward. 'Because they're scary.'

'Hmm,' said Judy, 'didn't the Stranger tell you that Edward should be in charge? I wonder if the reason that you do so badly on Fair Exchanges is because you don't actually *take* your payment.'

Saskia made a hissing noise. 'Maurice,' she said, brushing her aubergine hair away from her face. 'You really want to pick one up?'

'I think so. What do you think, Judy?'

Judy turned from comforting Edward. How can she keep so calm, wondered Maurice? Look at her with her porcelain face and her tranquil black body. Her words are so still, not like when Saskia speaks. When Saskia speaks it's like this nagging little draught on the back of the neck, but with Judy the words are just there precisely, like letters on a page. Like everything has already been decided and spoken.

'I told you before, Maurice,' said Judy, 'I'm just a passenger here. Besides, what will be, will be. Someone has mapped out my life for me.'

Maurice held her dark gaze. 'You mean Chris, the all-powerful AI? Or maybe his sidekick, Kevin?'

Judy didn't blink. She just continued to stare at him, like he was a talking box, or a dummy with a speaker wired to its jaw.

'Fine,' he said, feeling badly unsettled by her gaze. 'That's it, then. One against, Saskia and I are for it. OK, we're going in. Sorry, Edward. We'll pick up one of them in the little hold.'

His fingers danced across his console. Edward drummed his feet fearfully on the chair.

Judy stepped across the knot in the gravity, at the junction of five corridors, and disappeared around the corner, heading down towards the little hold. Saskia hung back to speak to Maurice.

'What do you think about Judy?' she asked in a low voice.

'I don't know,' said Maurice guardedly. 'Did you see the way she looked at me back then? Like she was a non-sentient robot. It's like she measures your emotions, she doesn't react to them.'

'I don't know,' said Saskia, face now hidden by her hair. 'I think that, beneath all that stillness and controlled emotion, the pressure is building up. I don't think she can keep it all in check for much longer.'

'She's frightened by something – that AI she mentioned: Chris. I think she is watching herself all of the time, checking to see if she is changing. She's wondering if she is going to suddenly just let go and change all her opinions, just like Chris told her she would do . . .'

Saskia wasn't listening any more. She placed a hand on Maurice's arm, and he looked down at it surprised. 'Listen,' she said urgently, but Judy had reappeared, peeping around the odd angle of the corner, her body like a reflection in a pool.

'Is everything OK?' she asked.

'Fine,' said Saskia, and she headed off, leaving Maurice standing alone.

Judy waited by the black and white mosaic frame of the door to the little hold. Saskia glared for a moment at the black and white woman, and then she turned and made a show of tapping on the door to the little hold and bringing up an external picture.

A deduced scene sprang to life, built up from the *Eva Rye*'s sense range. It showed the ship sliding slowly forward, the door to the little hold sliding smoothly open, halfway along the curve of the ship's teardrop hull. Saskia zoomed in and they saw three space flowers being eaten up by the ship, like little orange mints. The inside of the hold had folded up on itself, walls and floors sliding around each other in complicated origami patterns. Black night could be seen through the main hatchway.

'I'll catch them in the dead zone at the middle of the hold,' said Maurice thoughtfully. 'They might not be able to take full gravity.'

They watched as the little hold's external door closed, and then smiled at the elegant way in which the internal floors and walls rearranged themselves into a cube. The floor slid into place last, and they felt a click deep within the ship.

'OK,' said Maurice, 'it's safe to enter.'

There was a small pop as the door slid open, and they paused a moment. There was a slight chill to the air beyond, meaning some heat had leaked into space across the pressure curtain. They could smell apples.

'OK,' said Saskia, 'follow me.'

Judy had already set off, and Saskia hurried to get ahead of her. Maurice followed as they half walked, half raced across the black and white floor of the little hold towards the centre of the room. They looked up to see the three orange space flowers hanging in the air above, their backs still turned determinedly away from them.

Saskia tapped at her console, and a viewing platform began to unfold itself from the floor. Maurice staggered, momentarily off balance, as it lifted the three of them into the air.

'Give us some warning next time,' he complained,

but Saskia made no reply, lost in contemplation of the flowers. Maurice felt his anger quickly disappear. He wanted to reach out to touch the spheres as they glided towards them. They really were beautiful; they seemed to awaken the poetry in his soul. Sunshine yellow wove glorious patterns through iridescent orange flames; the deep crimson of the pattern shone like blood from a broken heart.

The platform rose higher, and he felt a familiar wave of nausea as his head and then his shoulders entered the dead zone.

'That pattern,' said Maurice. 'You could almost think it's alive.' He reached out to touch a sphere, half hypnotized. 'Do you think . . . hey, what's that?'

They all heard it at the same time. The flowers were humming.

'Are they moving . . .?' began Saskia, and at the same time Maurice swore.

'Oh shit!' The flowers were accelerating. Sliding out of the dead zone. Into the region of gravity. Slowly at first, but with a sickening gathering of pace, the three spheres fell to the ground. As gravity was coming from six directions, they chose three different ways to fall. The three people on the platform watched three different spheres as they fell to three different floors, bounced, and then rolled to a halt.

'What have you done?' whispered Saskia hoarsely.

'It was a lure!' said Maurice. He bashed at his console, instructing the viewing platform to descend again. Judy was speaking in low tones, calm tones.

'They wanted to draw us in. Like the Dark Seeds. They were getting our attention!'

'What's going on?' asked Saskia, eyes wide with fear. The three spheres lay in three directions: one on the ground below, one above and one to the side of them. They had rolled onto their backs so they could at last see what was contained inside of them. From one sphere, a silver strand of metal pushed its way out into the hold. A silver spider emerged into the light, and then quickly scuttled away. Then another. Then another.

Silver spiders went scuttling in every direction.

'Trojans!' croaked Maurice. 'Those VNMs have tricked their way on board!'

Each sphere contained three spiders. They split up, skittering from view as quickly as possible.

Maurice slapped his forehead. 'How stupid would you have to be to take an unknown self-replicator on your ship!' he shouted angrily. 'They *tricked* us.'

Judy stood in front of him and held his gaze. 'Maurice,' she said in a calm voice. He glared at her. 'Maurice,' she repeated, 'calm yourself. Centre yourself. Activate the ship's countermeasures.'

'Countermeasures? What countermeasures? This is a fucking FE ship! What countermeasures, exactly, do you think we have on board? Photon-fucking-torpedoes?'

The VNMs had vanished, Maurice could not see where. He spotted two black tiles pulled out from the pattern covering the six floors. The VNMs had found their way out of the hold. They could be replicating already, using the fabric of the *Eva Rye* to make copies of themselves.

'Oh hell,' said Saskia, holding herself, arms wrapped tightly around her body. 'What's going on? What are you going to do?'

Judy closed her eyes for a moment, concentrating, and then she found her voice.

'Both of you, relax,' she commanded. Despite themselves, Maurice and Saskia did so. Judy seemed to be growing in stature.

She rounded on Maurice. 'Now, Maurice, think. What can we do?'

Maurice gazed into her big black eyes, their warmth heightened by contrast to her porcelain doll face, and a sense of calm and control seeped through his body. Yes. Breathe deeply. Yes. Stay calm, and an answer would present itself. He blinked and allowed his mind to wander free. Yes. Breathe and calm. Breathe and calm. Now, what were they to do . . .?

'I . . . I . . . I don't know,' he stammered. 'I don't know! I can't think of anything!' He felt the panic that Judy had just quelled rising once more inside him. 'I really don't know! The AIs usually handle this sort of thing. Transmit friendly protocols or reprogram the VNMs? Release counter-VNMs?' His voice was hollow. 'We haven't got an AI on board. We haven't got *anything* like that on board!'

'Oh hell!' breathed Saskia. 'Look!'

The crates stacked on the wall in front of them were starting to move, sliding in four directions.

'The gravity is going! Those VNMs must be eating the generators in the walls.'

There was a creaking noise and a stack of crates began

to tilt. Crystals wrapped in foam sheeting began to tumble to the floor below.

'It's happening above us, too,' said Judy in composed tones. 'Look, we're back down now.' The viewing platform folded itself back into the floor. 'Come on, out of here. Steadily. Calmly. Come on.'

Craning their necks upwards, they followed Judy towards the door. Three crates fell to the floor behind them, one by one, in brilliant diamond showers of crystal shards. A hollow thud reverberated throughout the hold – resonating deep inside their stomachs.

'Run,' said Saskia, pushing Maurice ahead. A rain of coloured pebbles was falling with a lovely clattering noise.

'Stay calm . . .' soothed Judy. There was another crash and a sound of tearing paper. Quickly they walked to the exit. Maurice unclenched his fists as they stepped out of the hold. A wave of green apples rolled past their feet as the door slid shut behind them.

'Aleph,' called Judy, her voice suddenly sounding muffled in the calm of the carpeted corridor. 'Can you hear us?'

'Yes, Aleph,' said Saskia. 'Why didn't I think of him? Aleph, do something to stop this!'

Aleph's voice spoke from Maurice's console.

'I'm sorry, I don't think there is anything I can do. I'm a systems-repair robot, not a counterincursion specialist. I suggest you get yourselves into those active suits you had delivered as quickly as possible.'

'Of course,' said Maurice, 'the active suits!'

Saskia's eyes were wide. 'The suits? Do you think that FE knew we would need them?'

Aleph was still speaking: '. . . the outer hull of your ship is already disappearing. Do you want to see?'

A viewing field sprang to life right in the middle of the corridor. The black and white checked teardrop of the *Eva Rye* appeared, an expanding cloud of silver VNMs clinging to its side.

'Oh hell,' whispered Saskia, 'Maurice, what have you done? They're eating up the hull. Look. You can almost see straight into the little hold!'

As she spoke, the door to the little hold seemed to creak slightly, and a pattern of black and white stripes came to life upon it, coming up into existence from nothing. Letters formed in the centre. *HULL INTEGRITY BREACHED. DO NOT ENTER.*

'Maurice, think!' said Judy. 'There must be something we can do?'

Maurice gave a shrug. He felt strangely calm, now that all of his decisions had been taken away.

'I don't know,' he said. 'I told you, I have no idea. I think we should get away from this corridor, however. Those VNMs could be through the door in no time.'

'The active suits,' said Saskia, 'Edward got them to stow themselves in the locker in the living area. Oh hell. Edward.'

'Yes, what about Edward and Miss Rose?' asked Judy quietly. Maurice and Saskia exchanged looks; they hadn't been thinking about the other two.

Maurice spoke up. 'We should get the suits first, they're closest. Then I'll go to Edward's room. You fetch Miss Rose, Judy.'

They ran. On past the conference room, into the

living area. Edward was there already, wringing his big hands together. A glass lay on its side by his feet, apple juice soaking into the dark carpet.

'What's happening, Judy?' he called out.

'Don't worry,' replied Judy. 'We're all going to put on active suits. Saskia, you come with me. Maurice, you stay here with Edward and help him.'

'Active suits? But I thought they were dangerous!' Edward was now dancing back and forth. Judy had already opened the locker and taken out three suits. She passed one to Saskia.

'You carry this. I might need help to dress Miss Rose.'

Maurice pulled two more suits from the locker; their thin material felt sticky beneath his fingers.

'You have to be completely naked under the suit,' explained Maurice. 'It needs to interface with you totally. And don't force it on: stroke it gently; let it get used to you.'

Quickly he undressed. Edward did the same.

Maurice's suit was green. He fiddled with the neck, trying to get it to expand. It did so, but oh so slowly. Edward watched him, and then did the same with his own yellow suit. There was a loud bang.

'What's that?' called Edward dropping the suit and clapping his hands to his head. 'My ears hurt!'

'Pressure doors,' said Maurice, feeling as if he had just drunk a litre of icy-cold water. What was going on? Only five minutes ago they had been intrigued by the pretty orange flowers. Now the *Eva Rye* was disintegrating around them. It was too much to take in, in such a short a time. Edward was standing fully naked, his hands still to his ears, his active suit lying in a sticky heap on the floor before him.

'Get into your suit, Edward!' yelled Maurice.

The neck on his own suit was expanding ever larger as he stroked it. Impatiently, he stabbed at his console and brought up another view of the ship.

'Oh shit!' he moaned. The entire rear of the *Eva Rye* had gone. The teardrop's rear end had ablated in a cloud of silver spiders that rained back down on the swollen front end of the ship, devouring the rest of the hull. He looked away from the console, to see Edward still standing there, hands clasped to his ears. Maurice shouted at him, his voice cracking with fear. 'Your *suit*, Edward!'

Finally the big man began moving. He bent down and began to stroke the suit, opening its neck. Maurice turned back to his own active suit, and saw that, at last, it was big enough to step into. He pushed in one naked leg and then the other, the sticky, rubbery material fighting against him as he tried to pull it on. He forgot everything he had been told, and began to jerk at the suit.

'Stay calm, Maurice.' That was Edward speaking. He was looking earnestly across at Maurice as he slowly, methodically, pulled on his own suit. 'You're rushing it, and it's fighting back. Do it slowly, like you told me.'

Edward was right, Maurice realized. He paused and took three slow breaths. He tried meanwhile not to look at the view of the *Eva Rye* floating over the dining table, the black and white pattern of its hull almost stripped clean by the devouring cloud. Many of the

VNMs were now black and white themselves, dancing poisonously amongst the rest of the jostling silver crowd. That's our ship turned traitor against itself. *Don't think about it!* Another three breaths and he eased his left leg slowly forward and then, all of a sudden, the resistance was gone: the active suit was a part of his body, his foot and calf alive and tingling with a new awareness.

'Thank you, Edward,' said Maurice. 'Thank you. We can do this together, can't we?' Edward gave him a big beam of delight.

And then there was another bang, and black and white wasp-striped doors slammed over the entrances to the living area.

Now Edward was panicking.

'No!' called Maurice. 'Remember what you said, Edward. Take it slowly. That was right! Keep it calm. Yes?'

Edward paused, stopped thrashing. 'Yes, Maurice?'

'Yes, Edward.'

'Let's both take three breaths, and then we can pull on the suit bodies.'

It was terrifying. At any moment, Maurice was expecting the walls to dissolve in a tangle of silver legs and for the atmosphere to boil away into space. Still, breathing slowly, they gently pulled the sticky material up their bodies and felt the sudden loss of resistance, the tingle and awakening that said the suits were correctly in place.

'Now the arms,' said Maurice and Edward together. 'Just a wriggle of the fingers. No need to panic.'

And then there was a shout and a scream.

'Miss Rose!' exclaimed Edward. He began to whimper. 'Somebody has hurt her!'

Another bang. Maurice turned off his console's sound channel.

'Easy. Pull the suit on slowly, Edward, then we can go looking for her!'

Sobbing, Edward did as he was told.

'Maurice, this is Aleph. I'm overriding your console to tell you that something has just appeared out here . . .'

Miss Rose screamed again, her voice finding its way over the opened channel. Edward gave a shrill cry in return. Maurice slammed the lockout button on his console. He was shaking as well. What was wrong with Miss Rose? He had never heard anybody sound in such pain.

'Edward, the arms! Pull up the gloves and slip in your hands . . .'

Shaking, they both tried to force their hands into the sleeves, their flesh resisting, the stickiness gripping and Miss Rose's pain still echoing in their heads. And then Maurice felt a blessed relief and tingling. He was finally dressed. Quickly, he pulled the active suit's hood over his head and then turned to Edward.

'I can't do it, Maurice.'

Big tears splashed down Edward's brown chest. The big man was tugging and tugging at the suit with one hand, burning his skin as he tried to force his other hand into the sleeve. There was another bang and the floor shook. Edward kept gasping and pulling.

'Stop it! Stop it,' shouted Maurice, himself panicking. 'Stop it!'

Edward took hold of Maurice by the arms and began

to squeeze. Maurice tried to break free, but he couldn't. Strong as he was, Edward was stronger.

'Edward, you've got to let go of me. I can't help you if you hold my arms.'

He looked at Edward, at his big brown chest and bare arms, at the silver tears streaming down his face.

There was a rattling sensation. And then a flash of silver at the corner of Maurice's vision.

'Edward! They're coming through the walls! Let go so that I can help you!'

And then one of the walls dissolved in a flurry of silver legs.

Maurice stood sobbing in the middle of the room, feeling Edward's grip weakening. He had his eyes tightly closed: he couldn't bring himself to look at Edward as he died. What had happened? In the space of a few minutes they had gone from everything to nothing. The ship had been eaten up. Edward was dying, Miss Rose was . . . what? What had happened to her?

Edward's grip finally loosened, and Maurice tried to open his eyes. He didn't want to look. OK, count to three and then . . . he opened his eyes.

The living area remained untouched. The black carpet, the dining table, the neat stacks of black and white dishes in the kitchen were all unchanged. Even Edward's glass, lying on the floor where he had dropped it.

'What happened?' asked Edward still standing before him, looking puzzled.

Before he had time to think about it, Maurice helped

Edward shrug his way into the arms of his active suit. Only when Edward had pulled the hood over his head did Maurice speak.

'I don't know what happened. Look over there.'

They looked towards the wall where the VNMs had entered. There was a long empty corridor beyond that had not been there before. It led downwards.

'What happened?' asked Edward. 'What's going on?'

To Edward it was obvious what they had to do, so Maurice gave in and followed him down the corridor. There was nowhere else to go. Edward hated confusion, Maurice had noted. Whenever he was uncertain about what was going on, that was when he felt most ill at ease. When his choices were clear, he was happy. Edward felt that now: their path was clear; they simply followed the seamless black pipe in front of them downwards.

'I think I can see something,' said Edward boldly, and then he stumbled and began to fall forward. Maurice made a grab for him and felt a stomach-wrenching surge of nausea as the world tumbled around him, leaving him floating free in the long tunnel.

'Help!' called Edward. 'Maurice, help me.'

Weightlessness made Maurice feel so sick. He was gulping down the thick acid bile that threatened to rise up and fill the hood of his active suit.

'Stay calm,' he gagged, then he clamped his mouth shut again and tried to overcome the nausea. A cool breath of scented air refreshed his face. The active suit was picking up on his distress. 'The gravity's gone,' he gasped. 'We've left the zone of the *Eva Rye*.'

'Where are we going?'

'I don't know, Edward.'

He was tumbling head over heels now. Back in the direction from which they had come, he saw the tube contracting. The view of the living area vanished. A pattern of expanding dots flashed into life before his eyes, a projection from his active suit.

'The *Eva Rye* has gone,' said Maurice. 'It's been totally converted to VNMs.' He wiggled his fingers, tapping at an imaginary console. The active suit picked up the gestures and flashed up the information he had requested.

'And all in just under eight minutes,' he said.

They floated on through the black tube.

'I can see a light up ahead,' said Edward.

Maurice saw it too: a pale light, the colour of snow in moonlight. For a moment he had a flash of something, a memory from his childhood, and then it was gone.

They floated on.

'The tube's getting bigger,' said Edward, and it began to widen like a trumpet's bell, then they floated out into a vast space that froze the heart, stopping the breath in their lungs. They were now apparently drifting upwards, rising from a hole in some vast plain. They looked down and saw white patterns of frost curling in flames of fern beneath them, incredibly complex shapes winding around themselves in recursive patterns, painting pictures of cold fire across the ground.

'Where are we?' asked Edward.

'I don't know,' repeated Maurice.

'It's beautiful. It is beautiful.'

They rose higher and higher and now they could make out distant walls, and a wide ceiling above them, shining in the pale blue light that illuminated the arctic volume of emptiness around them.

'I thought we were in space,' said Edward. 'How can we now be underground?'

'I don't think we're underground,' said Maurice. He was trying to remember something he had read years ago: how you used an active suit. You reached out your hands like this, and you turned them like this and . . .

Now he could feel the surface of the ice below. With the help of the suit's augmented senses it was like he was running his hands along it. He could feel the cold metal that lay below the thin residue of frost, he could tap it and feel it ring hollowly through to the void beyond.

'What is it?' asked Edward.

Maurice was running his virtual hands along the distant floor; he was feeling the walls and ceiling, patting along them, sizing up the cavern.

'We're in a long, flattened cylinder made of metal. There is air in here, Earth atmosphere but a lot thinner. Too thin to breathe, and too cold. Moisture has settled on the walls and frozen there. Hold on, Edward. I'm calling up a picture of the shape of this cylinder.'

The active suit set a mapping of the space before his eyes. Maurice knew what it was going to be even before it appeared.

'Edward,' he announced. 'We are floating inside the *Bailero*.'

Edward was more confused than ever.

'But where have all the insides gone?' he asked. 'Where are the engines and everything?'

Before Maurice had a chance to reply, a thin, unearthly sound filled the hoods of their active suits. A keening sound of utter agony, a cry of pain so pale and exhausted that it hovered on the edge of awareness, like someone trying to crawl away from life, only to find themselves tethered there by their pain.

'Make it stop!' called Edward. 'Make it stop! What is it?'

Maurice couldn't speak; he was vomiting, gagging. His suit was working hard to flush his hood clean, and still that dreadful screaming went on, keening above the hum of the extractors.

'What is it what is it what is it?' chanted Edward.

It was Miss Rose.

JUDY 2: 2252

Judy imposed her will totally upon Saskia. She pushed the younger woman against the smooth wall of the corridor and held her there by the wrist as she gazed into her eyes. Saskia tugged half-heartedly at her, her thin body wriggling, but it was not a genuine attempt to escape; she was too much in awe of the power of Social Care, and Judy made her aware of that. She spoke in the voice; she overwhelmed Saskia, smashed through the young woman's veneer of sophistication and scooped out her insecurities, throwing them to one side as she rummaged through her psyche for her core competence.

Only when she had totally subdued Saskia, did she let her go.

'Pull on your active suit,' she instructed.

They stripped in the corridor, Saskia's body very pale under the lights, her ribs outlined in shadows. They were halfway through pulling on the rubbery suits when Miss Rose's first scream sounded, thin and agonizing. As if in a dream, Saskia began to move up the corridor, half dressed.

'Stop,' said Judy. 'We'll be no good to her if we die of decompression.'

'OK,' said Saskia. It was the logical thing to do. They both dressed themselves calmly as another human died in agony nearby.

'I'm sorry,' said Judy, as they finally shrugged their arms into the suits. 'I had to do this to you, Saskia.'

'I understand,' said Saskia, pulling the hood of the blue suit over her head.

'You understand *now*,' said Judy. 'When I let you go, you won't be so logical.'

They finished dressing as the air around them began to drift down the corridor. There was a popping sound as metal spiders pulled themselves free of the floor.

'Into Miss Rose's room,' urged Judy.

'No, I'll get a body bag first,' said Saskia. 'Listen to her scream. We'll never get her into a suit when she's in that much pain.'

'Yes, good thinking.' *So that's where your self-belief comes from. You really are competent when you allow yourself to be . . .*

Saskia went to a nearby locker to get the body bag. Judy headed on to Miss Rose's room. The door was covered in black and white stripes; a message formed in the centre.

DO NOT OPEN. CORRIDOR PRESSURE IS BELOW THAT OF THE ROOM BEYOND.

'Not for long,' said Judy. 'Override. Let me in there.'

The door slid open. Judy pushed her way against the leaking air into Miss Rose's room. The door slammed shut behind her. She was shocked at the state of the room itself, but even more shocked by the sight of Miss Rose. She lay on the bed, naked and bleeding at several points. Her arms, her thighs. Her vagina. She was screaming, writhing in agony. Her eyes looked at Judy, apparently without seeing her. But then she spoke, in a thin, bubbling voice.

'Get them out of me,' she gasped. 'Get them out, get them out.' And then she gagged and began to scream again.

Something was moving inside her body, something was squirming in there. The pale, loose, liver-spotted skin over her stomach raised itself up for a moment, and Judy saw the outline of a shape: a short squat body. A VNM. Inside her. Her arm moved and Judy saw a VNM, holding the loose, wrinkled skin apart from inside as it pushed its way along the bone.

Judy gagged. The meta-intelligence cut in, and she now saw Miss Rose as nothing more than a pattern of consciousnesses: one of them human, several machine. A symbiote was forming, rather elegant in its form. Certainly a more valid expression of resources than the failing system that was Miss Rose . . . *No! That isn't the true picture.* Judy forced the meta-intelligence down and let her own emotions loose. Miss Rose was *alive* – listen to her scream.

And then air pressure dropped, and the walls around her dissolved in a tangle of silver legs as the *Eva Rye* was eaten up by VNMs.

Saskia was there amid the expanding cloud. She had already had the good sense to link her active suit to Judy's. The two suits locked on to each other's signatures and moved closer, fighting through the explosion of air and thrashing silver legs and the detritus from Miss

Rose's room. Somehow they got the body bag around Miss Rose, somehow they clung together and somehow they weathered the storm.

'Where are we?' wondered Saskia.

They stood on an iron plane, patterns of frost curling in tongues of ice around their feet, the circle of the access tube that had brought them there was irising closed by their feet. They were two tiny figures, one blue, one black and white, dwarfed by the huge iron space around them. Judy bent over Miss Rose, peering at her through the transparent body bag, trying to hold eye contact with her. It was no use: the old woman's eyes were closed, her mouth stretched wide, the thin, tired scream emerging from it was carried to them through the hoods of their active suits.

'Saskia? Is that you?'

Maurice sounded as if he was standing just next to them.

'Maurice? I can't see you?'

'I'm with Edward. We're floating inside the hull of a ship. I think it's the *Bailero*.'

Saskia looked around. 'I think we must be in there with you. Listen, we've set our active suits to stick us to the walls. Can you walk here and join us? Miss Rose is hurt.'

'I can hear that,' said Maurice.

Judy wasn't listening. She watched as the skin on Miss Rose's leg was slowly unzipped from the ankle up to the thigh, silver legs reaching through to encircle the limb.

Saskia's voice sounded hoarse in her ear. 'Kill her.'

Judy looked up at Saskia, face dark in her hood, the surrounding blackness of the *Bailero*'s interior framing her.

'Kill her,' repeated Saskia, 'like you did that little girl. Can't you see she's in agony?'

Judy nodded. She placed her hands on the body bag, pinching it closer to Miss Rose's head, wriggling her fingers through folds of plastic until she could grip the old woman's neck. She began to squeeze.

And then a voice sounded inside the hood of her active suit.

'Why are you doing that?'

It was a voice from her past – a voice that Judy's iron will had kept on the edge of her dreams for the past twelve years. But hearing it now, even in the midst of all this confusion, Judy was momentarily back in the calm of her bedroom on the day she had listened to the dying digital sighs of her sisters.

'Kevin!' Judy released her grip on Miss Rose. She swung around, looking for the one who had spoken. Saskia had backed away. She was watching her companion warily.

'I'm sorry?' said the voice. 'Have we met before?'

Judy had dropped into a fighting stance.

'You, or one of your copies,' she snarled. 'Let her go, Kevin. Get those things out of her.'

'I can't. They are their own creatures.' He sounded puzzled. 'Tell me, how do you know me?'

Judy wasn't going to give him the satisfaction of answering him directly. She spoke instead to Saskia.

'Do you know that somebody killed my sisters, Saskia? Did Maurice tell you that?'

'Yes,' said Saskia warily.

'It was Kevin,' spat Judy; 'or an aspect of him, anyway. Kevin, you are the *Bailero*'s AI, aren't you?'

Judy felt so tense. She didn't have time for this. Miss Rose was dying in agony . . . And yet she had been in this situation before. Maybe Kevin wouldn't have killed her sisters if she had agreed to his terms back then, however abhorrent they may have seemed. Maybe this time she could strike a deal that would save Miss Rose.

Kevin spoke. 'Yes, I am the *Bailero*.'

'Kevin is an AI written by DIANA, the company who built the *Bailero*,' Judy explained to Saskia. 'Kevin, I knew copies of you back on Earth. I hunted them down and bottled them up in quarantined processing spaces. Do you know why I did that? Because they wanted me to help them destroy the Watcher, and I refused. Well, understand this. I am being taken to Earth now, I don't know why, but I suspect that someone is engineering the same confrontation that your brothers wanted. Someone wants me to challenge the Watcher.'

'I'm listening,' said Kevin, sounding amused. He always sounded amused.

'Miss Rose is part of that confrontation, Kevin. She was put on board the *Eva Rye* to help me. If you want me to do your dirty work, save Miss Rose!'

Kevin spoke in patient tones. 'You weren't listening, Judy. I *can't* save her. I don't control those creatures. Look around you, what do you see?'

Judy didn't look. She was too busy watching Miss

Rose, watching the old woman's stomach swelling in a wriggling mass of silver legs, her arms straightening and lengthening as something inside her body uncurled itself. She was trying to ignore the meta-intelligence which was whispering the beauty of the form in there. *If those VNMs were interacting with a tree, you would appreciate the venumb that was formed. Why is this any different?*

'I see a woman dying,' snapped Judy.

Kevin was dismissive. 'An old woman. Close to death. Those VNMs are doing her a favour in entering her. She is becoming a venumb.'

'Why? Kevin, look at me. I work for DIANA too. I am on an important mission. I need this woman to help me reach Earth. I *order* you to release her.'

'You're not listening to me, Judy,' he repeated.

Judy wished she could see Saskia's face. What was *she* thinking?

Saskia reached out a hand and placed it on Miss Rose's neck, then pulled it away. Then she placed both hands there.

'Are you going to kill her, Saskia?' asked Kevin. 'You're welcome to try. In this space we believe in the survival of the fittest. You're welcome to try and kill her, but I wonder if you can. Look around you!'

Saskia snatched her hands away.

'I don't see anything,' she whispered. 'Only empty space.'

'Exactly!' Kevin's voice had become a deep rumble: a pleasant voice suffused with the confidence of knowing he would be listened to. A voice written so as to command.

Judy felt a knot of hate in her stomach just to hear it. Calm yourself, she thought. Centre yourself.

'Think about it, Judy,' said Kevin, 'a warp ship fleeing Earth and the rising tyranny of the Watcher, as it subsumed first humans and then AIs to its will. I hid here in the space between the stars and began to plan. But where was I to find the material to build my empire?'

'Go on, Kevin,' said Judy, still watching Miss Rose. 'I'm sure you're going to tell me.'

'The *Bailero* was overdesigned – deliberately overdesigned – for this purpose. Lots of excess material, lots of building material. I built VNMs from my engines, and I set them loose inside my body to evolve. Many different VNMs, all fighting for scarce resources: survival of the fittest. This is how I planned to compete with Watcher. By evolving new life of my own.'

'I can't kill her,' sobbed Saskia, pulling her hands away from Miss Rose's neck again. 'I can't do it!'

Miss Rose was keening softly.

'Kill or be killed,' said Kevin. 'Your ship has been destroyed, converted to VNMs by one of my most successful species. That flower trick has taken in others before you. There will be many more such space flowers now, made from the materials of the *Eva Rye*. Some of them are already floating into human space. I wonder what they will meet there?'

'You do it,' sobbed Saskia. 'You kill her, Judy.'

'They're not the only form of VNM that has thrived out here,' continued Kevin. 'There are dark machines that have followed you on board. Stealth machines. They surround you now, and I don't think you are aware of them.'

'I can't see anything,' said Judy, but nevertheless something tickled at the edge of her meta-intelligence. *Was* there something out there? Lean and sharp and deadly, a single intent so focused it did not quite qualify as an intelligence?

'Of course you can't see anything,' said Kevin. 'That's the point. Interesting, isn't it? There are machines out there that appeal to curiosity, and those that hide and pounce. Some even set off exploring space on their own. Ships like the *Free Enterprise.*'

'What do you want with us?' snapped Judy.

'Nothing,' said Kevin. 'I told you, I improve the breed. You live or die in here according to your own actions. Those who survive improve the breed.'

'Then we'll die,' said Judy simply.

'Don't be so ridiculous. You have a lot to offer. I give credit, you know. I will sell you food and oxygen. I have done the same for others before you.'

Miss Rose gave a weak whimper, and her stomach began to weep blood.

'Kill her,' whispered Saskia.

Judy placed her hands back around the old woman's neck.

'You're too late,' said Kevin. 'I don't think it will let you now.'

Miss Rose's long, misshapen arms reached up and pushed Judy's hands away.

'Stop it!' shouted Judy. She concentrated, put on the voice. 'Stop it,' she repeated.

'I told you, I can't. If I were you, I'd get away from her. That venumb will want to reproduce. It's looking at you . . .'

Screaming in agony again, Miss Rose scrabbled at the plastic interior of the body bag. Silver tentacles sprouted from her fingertips, pushing free her cracked yellow nails to float bloodily inside the bag. Silver tentacles began to rip at the plastic.

'Push her away,' yelled Saskia, seizing the body bag and thrusting it upwards into the weightless centre of the *Bailero*'s hull. Oh-so-slowly, the bag began to move. Judy pushed at it too, then ducked back to avoid the swipe of a tentacle. The bag gradually drifted upwards and away.

'Good idea,' said Kevin. 'But if I were you, I would run. Those VNMs inside her are eating the calcium in her bones and lacing themselves into her nervous system. They are running up her spine to interface with her brain. I have seen this happen before. They always choose a different mode of propulsion. One set, I remember, plumbed themselves straight into a human's bladder. Used urine as reaction mass for propulsion.'

'That's sick,' shrilled Saskia. Judy realized she was coming out from under her control. No wonder, when Judy was spreading herself so thinly, trying to deal with her, Kevin and Miss Rose all at the same time.

'Not sick, Intelligent Design,' said Kevin. 'That's the beauty of the ecosystem that I created inside my hull. Those VNMs evolved their own systems for motion and attack and defence with minimum involvement from myself. Look out, she's coming for you.'

'Run,' said Judy. Miss Rose had stopped slowly rising and was now coming towards them, still screaming thinly, hands reaching out.

They began to run across the iron interior of the *Bailero*'s hull, their feet locking to the surface, their bodies weightless. It was such a dreamlike feeling, like dragging a huge balloon along.

Maurice called out to them. 'Judy, Saskia, it's me. Don't try and run. Cut the attachment to the wall and swim. Use your hands and feet to pull you along!'

'What do you mean?' called Judy.

'Do as he says. Use your hands and feet!'

Saskia went sailing past Judy, floating a metre above the frost-patterned surface. She looked as if she was doing the breast stroke. Judy now understood what Maurice meant and she cut the force holding her down. She reached out with her hands and feet and felt the floor through her active suit's senses, then began to pull herself along.

'We're about seven hundred metres away from you both,' said Maurice. 'Up and further around the curve of the *Bailero*'s hull. Just follow the signal.'

A yellow path lit up in Judy's vision.

'Better be fast,' warned Kevin. 'Miss Rose is catching up with you.'

'You animal!' snarled Saskia. 'Why didn't you save her?'

'She's not actually dead yet,' said Kevin. 'The VNMs haven't made it into her brain.'

'I know that,' muttered Judy, halting herself with a wave of her arms and launching herself backwards. For a moment, she could see Miss Rose as a tangle of life: a snake was entwining itself around her dying body, opening its jaws to consume her.

'Would you like to make a deal?' asked Kevin suddenly.

'I don't want to speak to you, you crazy fuck!' Saskia screamed the words.

'Keep him talking,' said Maurice. 'We're five hundred metres off. I think I can see you.'

'I don't think so, Judy,' said Kevin. 'Between you and me, he's heading towards a trap. Dark VNMs. They're baffling his active suit. They've done this before; they'll strip the suit off him and fill it with growing organic matter harvested from his own body. They'll use the suit as an incubation unit to make feed for venumbs like Miss Rose.'

'What venumbs?' asked Judy.

'I told you, you're not the first humans to come here. There is a nest of seven venumbs near the rear of my body. You could join them if you like. Or you could sell your services to me. You're not even wearing proper spacesuits: those active suits can't recycle air for very long and they don't carry any food. You'll be dead within days without my help.'

'What do you want of us?' asked Saskia.

'DIANA can always use human agents.'

'DIANA is dead,' replied Judy. 'The old companies were taken over by the Watcher years ago.'

'Dead within the Earth Domain maybe, but we are thriving out here. The *Free Enterprise* is spreading the word throughout the former Enemy Domain. Judy, I can offer you food and oxygen; I will provide you with pressurized quarters. Two of you will remain with me as hostages, whilst the other two go to work. Prove your worth, and you could have a big future with the company.'

'What about Miss Rose?'

'She is almost dead now. She is of no use to us. Not even as a hostage.'

Judy was catching up with Saskia, who was swimming ahead of her like a blue frog in the thin icy air.

'See, Saskia,' she called out, 'this is exactly why the old companies were killed off by the Watcher!'

'But now we rise again.'

Judy took a deep breath. 'Kevin, I warn you one last time. You were sold to us in a Fair Exchange. Someone or something is bending my path towards Earth. You would be advised not to interfere.'

'Maybe *I* will choose to send you to Earth,' mused Kevin. 'That way I will also be doing your puppeteer's bidding. Yes, why not? Now, make your decision quickly. Your friends are approaching the Dark VNMs.'

'There's no choice to make,' said Saskia. 'Where do I sign?'

'Saskia!' protested Judy.

'What else are we to do?'

'What about Miss Rose?'

'What do *you* suggest we do?'

She was right. Judy knew it. 'OK,' she said. 'We'll do it.' *For the moment*, she added to herself.

'I knew you'd see sense,' said Kevin.

There was a flickering, and the whole interior of the

Bailero filled with pale blue light. Judy felt a surge of tangled awe at the scene that was revealed. The frost-patterned hull of the ship, beautiful in swirls of white against pale blue; the size of the ship itself, breathtaking in its extent; and then the sharp tang of terror as the winter light reflected off the stealthy shapes that had been floating amongst them all this time. Glowing eerily, the outlines of the Dark VNMs could be seen, scattered like bubbles through the aquarium of the ship's interior. With infinite patience, they were drifting closer and closer to the humans in their bright suits, set to gradually overwhelm them all.

'Judy, can you see them?' Maurice was breathless from exertion. Edward gave a loud yell of alarm.

'I can see them!' called Judy. 'Maurice, Edward, keep out of their way.'

'. . . Judy . . . Miss Rose is still coming for us,' murmured Saskia.

'I've got her,' said Kevin, and abruptly the old woman halted in her approach, her blood-moistened body revolving slowly in space. Judy and Saskia allowed themselves to settle onto the frost-covered hull. It felt cold and brittle beneath their feet. A blue octopoid drifted nearby, its shape picked out in eerie turquoise highlights. Judy reached out and stroked it with her active suit's senses: she felt her hand go numb.

Saskia was trying not to cry. Her body was shaking as she held back the tears. Judy came closer and held her, feeling warm skin though the active suits' interfaces. Saskia held herself still, not accepting Judy's embrace, and not rejecting it.

'Let it all go,' said Judy. 'Saskia, you can't keep bottling it all up.'

'How did it come to this?' sobbed Saskia. 'Twenty minutes ago we had a ship and a mission. Now we're just slaves to this Kevin. What the hell has happened?'

'Shhh.'

'It's OK for you, you'll be going to Earth. We'll be left here with that mad AI. What the fuck is going on anyway? Where is the Watcher? I thought he was supposed to look after us?'

'Shhh.'

But Saskia wouldn't unbend; she continued to shake, barely holding back the tears.

'Saskia, what's going on here?' Edward sounded confused. 'What are we supposed to do now?'

'Follow my orders,' said Kevin. 'You all work for me now.'

'No,' said Edward, 'we work for ourselves. That's the whole point of Fair Exchange. We're going to Earth.'

'That's to be decided,' said Kevin in a brisk voice. 'I do have a warp-equipped shuttle at my disposal. I might send it to Earth with you on board.'

'No,' said Edward, 'we made a Fair Exchange. We cannot go back on it. You cannot go back on it. You're our property now.'

Saskia spoke up, and Judy felt her body shaking as the other woman snapped at Edward. 'Edward, you stupid gimp. Our ship has gone! Turned into thousands of little VNMs. There is no ship any more, Edward, no more FE. All deals are off!' She gave a sob. 'You fucking dummy.

What are you going to do here? You poor idiot! You don't even know how bad things are!'

'Easy, Saskia,' called Maurice. 'We're all upset. Come on, Edward.' There was a moment's pause, and Judy imagined Maurice touching Edward on the arm. She heard him clear his throat and picked up on the strain in his voice as he spoke: 'Judy, we can see you properly now. We've been heading in the wrong direction, tricked by these stealth things. We're coming back now. Be there in five or ten minutes.'

'Stay where you are, Maurice,' said Kevin. 'I'm fetching the shuttle inside the hull. I'll get it to pick you up first.'

'OK, Kevin. Easy now, Edward.'

'I'm not worried,' said Edward. 'I told you, we made a Fair Exchange. You can't fool FE.'

A sad smile escaped onto Judy's lips at Edward's words. She looked at Miss Rose spinning slowly nearby. She was still alive, just. The meta-intelligence could see her essence, weak as a dying firefly, flickering inside Miss Rose's skull. All around it, the lights of the VNMs could be seen burrowing closer.

Saskia was gazing upwards, her thoughts somewhere in the pale blue distance, lost amongst the Dark VNMs.

Something arrived around the curve of the wall, and a dark shape slid into view. The shuttle. It resembled a blunt arrowhead, a matt-grey lifting-body design from the last century.

'That looks like an Earth model,' said Judy.

'It is,' said Kevin. 'Its crew used to work for me.'

'What happened to them?' asked Saskia.

'That's between me and them,' replied Kevin.

The shuttle sailed across the pale blue interior of the ship as easily as a cast stone.

'OK,' said Kevin, 'I'll pick up Maurice first. There is a hatch located to the rear of the ship.'

'Maurice?' said Saskia. 'What about Edward?' Her voice was shaking. 'Don't you mean Maurice and Edward?'

'Didn't you just say it yourself, Saskia?' asked Kevin. Her own words were played back in her ears: '"*You fucking dummy. What are you going to do here? You poor idiot!*" That's what you said, isn't it? Well, be honest, what am I going to do with a fucking dummy?'

'Judy,' pleaded Saskia. 'Judy?'

But Judy had slumped forwards, her hands clasped to her head.

'Judy? What's the matter?'

Judy was looking through a mosaic of impressions that had suddenly engulfed her, pushed into her mind by the meta-intelligence. She was being swamped by half-understood images and impressions. Saskia was pushing at her, pummelling her shoulders, but that was just one window on reality lost among the many. There was also the smell of fire and the feel of fur between her fingers, the sound of whistling and an image of two tall buildings, their windows filled with people staring out at each other. She heard the voices of the others:

'No! I'm not leaving you, Edward.'

'It's OK, Maurice, I'll be all right. You can't fool FE.'

'It's Judy, she's lost it. The strain has been too much!'

'Get on board the ship, Maurice, or I go without you!'

'Not without Edward!'

'Maurice, get on the ship!' That was Saskia. 'What else can we do?'

The Dark VNMs were stirring, they were moving, gathering, ready for the kill.

'Judy,' asked Kevin, wonderingly, 'what are you doing?'

I'm not doing anything, thought Judy, lost in a wave of colour and motion.

Saskia was gripping her hand. 'They're forming into a cloud,' she said, and then the wave of images passed from Judy, leaving her feeling sick and empty.

'What happened there?' asked Saskia.

'I don't know,' said Judy. 'I felt so much . . . look!'

'Judy, what have you done?' Kevin's voice was pale with wonder.

Judy and Saskia looked up as the Dark VNMs coalesced into a definite shape. Clouds of silver VNMs rose all around them, they came from apertures that opened up in the hull, they rushed towards the pale blue shape forming in the centre of the *Bailero*. The shape was growing, getting bigger and bigger, forming a bulge at one end. Taking on the shape of a teardrop.

'I told you,' said Edward quietly, 'you can't fool FE.'

'But that's impossible,' said Kevin. 'It had gone. It was completely broken apart.'

Judy found herself nodding in agreement. It *was* impossible. And yet, high above them, in the middle of the hull, they watched in astonishment as the *Eva Rye* was reborn.

The *Eva Rye* had been upgraded yet again.

It was still being reborn, still being formed by the streams of silver spiders that flowed together from all directions, but its essence was clear.

Judy gazed at the way the black and white harlequin patterns swept in a liquid tide over the hull of the ship. They looked plainer now and yet, at the same time, sleeker. Something about the ship breathed quiet power and confidence. Even dwarfed as it was by the ice-blue enclosing shell of the *Bailero*, the *Eva Rye* drew the eye and left no doubt which was the superior ship.

'I don't understand,' said Kevin plaintively. 'It's stronger than me . . .'

'I know,' breathed Judy, 'I can see that.' There was a sweep to the curves of the *Eva Rye* now that was so pleasing to the eye. It had lost the lazy, chubby feel of before. Now it fitted easily into the imagination, becoming a thing of beauty, as mathematically perfect as the golden ratio.

Kevin's voice was distant, distracted. 'It's taking over my control interfaces. It has my engines, my senses . . .'

Saskia's voice was cold with sweet vengeance. 'You belong to us now, Kevin,' she said. 'You are our possession. You are going with us to Earth.'

'But that's not fair!' exclaimed Kevin. 'I have been sold to you against my will.'

'I don't think so,' said Judy. 'The *Free Enterprise* sold you. It must have held title over you.'

'No . . . it did not.'

Saskia gave a laugh. 'You're not thinking like FE software, Judy. The *Free Enterprise* didn't hold title over Kevin. It *was* Kevin. Didn't he say that he built his empire from himself? The *Free Enterprise* was as much part of Kevin as this ship. Kevin shafted himself!' She stabbed an accusing finger into the air, pointing at the hull of the *Bailero*.

'Edward was right! Who'd have thought it, but he was right! You don't play tricks with FE, Kevin. It is cleverer than you. It tangles you up in your own motives and, just when you think you have cheated it, it goes and does exactly what it has promised!'

There was a sigh, an exhalation of breath that filled the hoods of their active suits, then Saskia's moment of triumph was quickly forgotten.

'Miss Rose!' exclaimed Judy.

They dragged the half-living body of Miss Rose onto the newly forming *Eva Rye* and then through the sleek black and white corridors to the autodoc. There was just enough atmosphere on the ship for them to take off the hoods of their active suits. Everywhere smelt of cold and of aniseed.

'Leave her in the body bag,' said Judy. 'It's the only thing holding her together.'

The old woman's wrinkled, liver-spotted skin could be seen hanging in tatters amongst the red blood that

2008. 5. 25 ⊕ ⊘ 917

11497. 43
34764. 6
_____

filled the clear plastic bag, her body torn apart by the multiple exit points of the VNMs that had left to make up the newly reborn *Eva Rye*.

'Why didn't those machines rip the body bag apart, too?' wondered Saskia, as she helped Judy slide the remains of the old woman into the thick plastic coffin of the autodoc. Blood squished between her fingers, inside the clear bag, squashing pink bubbles back and forth.

'I don't know,' said Judy. 'Kevin, speak to me!'

'Yes, ma'am.'

Judy spoke in her softest voice. 'Don't play games with me, Kevin. Don't pretend that you can dismiss what happened by feigning ironic detachment. You killed my sisters once, now you nearly killed Miss Rose. You work for the *Eva Rye* now. Got it?'

'Yes.' Kevin's voice was cold.

'You'd better really mean that. Look at me, Kevin, believe what I say. I will strip you right down to your very core in order that you do what I decide is right. I have done that in the past and I will do it again. Now tell me, what happened to Miss Rose?'

Kevin's reply was matter-of-fact.

'I don't know for sure. Those VNMs that infiltrated her body would not want to kill her, just use her. They resealed the bag as they left her body: I'd guess that they disengaged in such a way as to give her the best chance of survival. That way they could return if they got the chance. Get her in that autodoc now and she will probably live.'

Yes, and I will spend the next few months helping her to deal with the shock of what has happened to her.

There was the sound of footsteps, and Edward came into the white-tiled brilliance of the medical room.

'The ship has changed again,' he said wonderingly.

Saskia ran to him, flung her arms around him, and squeezed him tightly.

'Are you OK, Saskia?' said Edward uncertainly, gazing sideways at her, tilted uncomfortably by the force of her hug.

'Yes,' breathed Saskia. 'Yes, I'm OK, Edward.'

Maurice walked in and Saskia rather sheepishly disengaged herself from Edward.

'Hey, Saskia,' he said.

'Hey, Maurice.'

She reached out and brushed her hand across his arm. Judy did not appear to have noticed any of this. She was peering at her console.

'The autodoc says it can save her,' she announced.

Saskia rubbed her eyes.

'Did you see what happened out there?' said Maurice. 'Do you *realize* what we just saw?'

'Not now.' Judy shook her head at him.

Saskia walked from the room, pale and shaking. Maurice made to go after her.

'Leave her,' whispered Judy. 'She needs some time to think.'

Judy wasn't that surprised to find Saskia in Miss Rose's room. The young woman looked up from where she lay on the bed; her face puffy from crying.

'Did you know she was living like this?' Saskia waved a hand weakly.

Judy didn't want to look around the room. The walls and floor may have been rebuilt, shiny and new, but whatever it was in the *Eva Rye*'s soul that had clung to life, and had caused it to be reborn, had restored the personal effects of the crew, just as they had left them.

Their consciences had not been wiped clean by the rebuilding of the ship. Miss Rose's room retained the rotting food that lay on plates on the floor and every available surface. The air was thick with the smell of stale urine. The bedclothes were dirty, yellow stains rippling out across the once white sheets like patterns on the surface of a pond.

Only the little pictures hanging on the wall showed any sign of order. Hung in neat patterns, they had been straightened and dusted. Hundreds of scenes from a life back when Miss Rose had been young and elegant and beautiful. And proud.

'I didn't realize,' said Judy. 'I should have done, but I was just too distracted . . .'

'You're not to blame,' said Saskia, wiping a hand across her face. 'You've only just arrived here. But I lived on this ship for five weeks and never once did I come here to speak to her. I was captain of this ship. I should have taken care of my crew. I should have guessed. I should have come in here.'

Judy said nothing. This was a time for listening.

'Look at this place,' said Saskia, waving a hand around the room. 'She lived in all this filth for weeks, and not once did any of us stop by to find out how she was. We laughed at her. She irritated us, the mad old woman. The Stranger was right: the systems on this ship are all wrong. We don't even take care of each other.'

A look of determination crossed her face.

'Well, that was then. I've been thinking, Judy. I've taken a look at myself. Really taken a look, not just paid lip service to some emotional adjustment course I've plucked off the datasphere. And I don't like what I see.'

Saskia got up from the bed.

'Where are you going?'

'To the living area. To find Edward. The Stranger was right.'

Judy followed Saskia from the room. The thin woman was striding off down the corridor beyond determinedly.

'The Stranger was right about what?' called Judy.

'I shouldn't be in charge here. I don't know what's happening, but I'm beginning to realize that there's a lot more to the FE software than just a Fair Exchange. So, I'm going to do what I should have done at the start: I'm going to follow the Stranger's advice.'

'So you're going to . . .' Judy was striding hard to keep up.

Saskia wasn't listening.

'If we'd listened to him right at the start we would never have got into this mess. Miss Rose wouldn't be lying there in an autodoc at the moment. *He* was the only one who was right about the flowers. *He* wanted to get away from them. Well, next time we'll do as he says.'

She paused for a moment, bringing Judy to a sudden stop. Saskia took a deep breath.

'I'm putting Edward in charge of the ship.'

EVA 7: 2089

'All done,' said Alexandr, smoothing down the new plaster. Eva watched the movement of his hands in fascination. There was something pleasing about the easy way in which he moved the trowel back and forth.

'Will they be able to see me now?' she asked.

'No,' said Ivan, pouring out three glasses of tea.

'Why? Do you want them to be able to?' asked Alexandr, stopping his plastering in mid-swoop. He wore a look of mock concern. A lightning flash of drying plaster ran up the wall behind him.

Eva laughed. 'I don't think anyone would want to see me any more. Not at my age.'

'If you're sure,' said Alexandr helpfully, 'I can have a link in a moment. You can have the whole world watching you as you take a shower.'

'Oh yes, I'm sure the world would really love that,' replied Eva dryly.

Ivan handed her a glass of tea and a lump of sugar. She sipped the tea through the sugar, the way he had taught her. Alexandr tapped at his console, and the large screen came on.

'There you are,' he said, 'input only.' He took the

proffered glass from Ivan, and the three of them sipped tea and watched the pictures from the outside world.

Bright white cities were growing from the Earth, their slender spires constructed by humans, the silver scaffolding growing from VNMs. The people that walked the newly minted streets seemed to glow brighter than those Eva had become used to in the RFS. They walked with more confidence; their smiles were deeper; they gave the impression of having a greater love of life.

'You're not tempted to go back there?' asked Alexandr.

'Not at all,' said Eva.

'Not even to see your daughter?' wondered Ivan. 'I would not want to be apart from my Katya for so long.'

'Katya is still young and needs your love. Jessica is a grown woman. She visits me here whenever she can. We can speak whenever we like using the screen.'

'You won't be doing that for a while,' said Alexandr. 'We've had to disconnect the outgoing line completely. The VNMs had jerked the bandwidth right up. I'm not sure how we will restrict it again.'

Eva sipped more tea. She was going to miss Alexandr almost as much as she would miss Ivan. She would miss his open smile and his constant attempts to wind her up. He liked to stuff the pockets of her coat with rolled-up balls of paper when she wasn't looking, and then he would act all wide-eyed and innocent when she pulled them out and threw them at him. The young man finished the plastering and dropped his trowel into a plastic self-cleaning container.

'All done,' he said, toasting his work with the glass of tea he held in a plaster-flecked hand.

'I'm going to miss you, Alexandr.'

He gave a wink. 'I'll be back, I'm sure.'

'Don't you ever think about staying here?' Eva wished that she could take back the words. They made her sound needy and desperate.

Alexandr didn't seem to notice, though. He sipped slowly as he considered his answer.

'Sometimes,' he pondered. 'It seems more honest here, don't you think? More natural, I mean. I suppose that's why *you* like it here?'

Eva didn't know what to say to that. Fortunately, Ivan noted her discomfort, and changed the subject for her.

'Are you coming with us to the concert tomorrow, Alexandr?'

Alexandr gave him a big wink. 'Don't you think I'd be getting in the way? Wouldn't I cramp your style?'

'We'd like it,' said Eva deliberately. She took Ivan's big hand in hers as she spoke.

Alexandr shrugged. 'If we finish this last job in time. We've still got more screens to nullify. The infestation runs right through this building.'

'Where did it come from?' asked Eva, grateful for the change of subject.

For some reason, Alexandr didn't answer straight away. He was staring at the older man, as if waiting to see what he had to say. Eva turned to Ivan, head tilted, waiting for an answer.

'From underneath the building,' said Ivan, blushing. 'The earth is full of VNMs. They crawl up from beneath the ground. You find them in mines, in caves – they are there all the time, working away beneath our feet.'

'Yes,' agreed Alexandr. He seemed pleased to be allowed to confirm this. 'You did not know this, Eva? It is an open secret—'

'It is not a secret,' interrupted Ivan, 'but there is no point in worrying people.'

'They run up the walls of the Narkomfin,' continued Alexandr. 'They have interfaced with most of the screens, thus attaching themselves to the outside world.' He gave a laugh. 'It's a joke. Social Care are interfacing you to the rest of the world, whether you like it or not, and at the same time they are paying me to come in here and eliminate their machines.'

'They are not all Social Care's machines,' said Ivan darkly.

Alexandr was stirring his feet uncomfortably at this. He drained his glass with a hurried gulp. 'All done. Come on, old man Vanya. Let's get on or neither of us will get to the concert.'

Ivan quickly packed their tools whilst Alexandr vacuumed up the tiny pieces of plaster he had chiselled out of the wall in his search for the line of approach of the VNMs.

Ivan took hold of Eva's hand again.

'Would you like to come around to my apartment tonight? For dinner?'

'Yes,' she said, staring back into his dark eyes. 'Will Katya be there?'

'No, she is going out. Her friends have organized a goodbye party of their own.'

I bet they have, thought Eva. *I bet Paul in particular is hoping to say goodbye.*

'I want to say goodbye properly,' continued Ivan, mercifully unaware of her thoughts.

'It's not goodbye forever. I'm sure you will come back, at least for a visit.'

Ivan nodded and squeezed her hand. She kissed him lightly on the lips, and gave a little wave as the two men left.

Eva softly closed the door and returned to the solitude of her lounge. She looked at the screen on the wall. She didn't care what Alexandr said, she still felt she was being watched. This was why she had come to the Russian Free States: to get away from the constant surveillance of the Watcher. The Watcher, Earth's first AI, was shaping the world to its own ends, and sometimes it even asked Eva for advice. Why Eva? She didn't know. But the responsibility of it had been too great to begin with and had only got worse since.

She shivered, remembering. She had met the Watcher. She had been present when it had released the original VNMs into the ground. Now they were sprouting forth – bursting from the fertile Earth – even here. Metal tendrils searching and questing and reaching for the sunlight, binding humanity in their growth as they reached up to the stars.

'Go away!' shouted Eva at nothing in particular. 'Leave me alone!'

There was silence, but to Eva's ears it was the silence of someone choosing not to speak.

*

Let me sleep in peace, thought Judy. I need to rest after last night. Already it is Wednesday morning. Soon I will be on Earth. FE software, Chris, Watcher: leave me alone, whoever you are.

Dreams were forming in her head, resurrecting themselves, just as the Eva Rye *had been reborn inside the metal shell of the* Bailero.

This Narkomfin had been built in the late 2030s, one of a series of communal homes modelled on a Russian prototype from the early twentieth century. Eva liked the place, with its yellow plaster walls and curving concrete balconies. She liked to stand inside the building and look out through the front-facing wall of windows, hundreds of square panes in metal frames looking out over the rough grass and untidy hills. She liked to stand outside in the bitter wind and watch the late-winter sun burning yellow in the glass's reflection. She liked the way that she could step out from her apartment and gaze down the long corridor at the round pillars on her left, marching off into the distance. She liked the way the doors of her neighbours were patched and painted with flowers and faces. The smell of warmth and damp clothes drying, of cabbage and beetroot soup, was comforting, even mixed with the sickly tang of used nappies from the adults and children that lived in the crowded rooms. It made the whole place seem homely and welcoming.

And then there were the various sounds: of music playing from speakers or scraped out on a violin; of people laughing or talking or squabbling; the gurgle of the pipes or the hiss of the heating; and the rush of the rain on the windows when she was safe and warm inside, drinking tea or pepper vodka.

But best of all was the press of the people. Eva had lived her early life in South Street, and had spent so much time alone in the middle of the city, with only the saccharine comfort of Social Care for company. But here in the Narkomfin she cared and was cared for.

She cooked ham and pease pudding for others, and she shared their kvass and borscht. She accepted rides in the community's cars and britzkas, and in exchange she pushed the handicapped through the corridors in their wheelchairs. She helped in the crèche and took her turn accompanying those with Down's syndrome, and in return she was regarded with warmth and respect.

And then she had met Ivan.

He answered the door to his apartment with a sheepish smile and he showed her into the neat living area.

'You look so pretty,' he said.

'Thank you,' said Eva, trim in her calf-length brown skirt and yellow patterned sweater. Her white hair was clipped back in a ponytail; on her left wrist she wore the gold chain bracelet her long-dead husband had bought her.

On the table in the middle of the room, Ivan had laid out dishes of salted cucumber and little roast potatoes. The shelves were already cleared of his and Katya's belongings, stacked neatly now in a set of silver cases set in the corner, but truth to tell, the apartment did not feel much emptier than usual. Ivan led a neat, spartan existence, constantly cleaning up after the mess of his teenage daughter.

They made small talk, and Eva found herself becoming tipsy on blackcurrant vodka. Ivan's cheeks were flushing red, and she could tell he was getting ready to ask her to accompany him when he left the Russian Free States.

He led her to the table and served her hot salted beef and horseradish, which she ate with special care. Afterwards there was green shchi with sour cream and then honeyed baklava.

'Where did you get all this from?' asked Eva. 'It must have cost a fortune.'

'Special occasion,' said Ivan, avoiding the point.

They ate their meal with relish, passing each other morsels to try, wiping imaginary spots of food from each other's cheeks.

Afterwards, they sat on the thin sofa and drank coffee with warmed-up cream on top. From somewhere below, the sound of a practising brass band swelled and fell in the background. And finally Ivan got to the point.

'Eva,' he said, flecks of cream on his moustache. 'You are the flower that blooms unnoticed in this wilderness. You should not stay here alone. Come back with me, Eva. Come with me.'

Eva felt her dinner settling like a stone inside her.

'You know I can't,' she replied, looking at her feet. 'Why not stay here with me?'

'You know I can't. Katya should not grow up here. It has been a fine holiday for her, but the people who live in this place have no sense of responsibility. No sense of their duty to each other.'

The lounge was filled with the golden glow of late evening. There was a hazy, otherworldly feeling to their conversation. Ivan made to wipe his moustache with his hand, paused and drew a handkerchief from his pocket.

'Eva,' he said, wiping himself clean, 'what is wrong with the real world? Look at the people who you have chosen to live with! Drop-outs, the handicapped, the stupid, the stubborn.'

'You don't mean that, Ivan. Your own daughter is handicapped.'

Ivan was hot now with nerves and vodka. 'I don't blame the handicapped,' he said thickly. 'But what sort of mother would bring a child with Down's syndrome to live in this place? Out there in the real world there is medical care and corrective therapy and . . . and . . .'

He waved a hand vaguely in the direction of the window. 'Come back with me, Eva.'

Eva chose her words with a drunkard's care. 'The mother would say that the child she inherits after the cure is not the same as the one before.'

Ivan was dismissive. 'Pah! Religion! Only fools listen to that!'

'It's *not* about religion! Barely anyone here believes . . .'

'You have been talking to Pobyedov, talking to that fool of a priest, haven't you?'

'Credit me with my own opinions, Ivan,' said Eva quietly.

'I'm sorry,' said Ivan.

The awkward silence was punctuated by a distant fanfare of cornets. One of them was clearly out of tune.

Eva drained her cup. 'You could stay here, Ivan. Social Care can't make you return.'

'What is wrong about you coming with me?' asked Ivan proudly.

'I told you: the Watcher: it is waiting for me.'

Ivan didn't speak. Eva knew what he was thinking: that the Watcher didn't exist. He was steeling himself to say it, weighing up the words carefully. She wasn't going to give him the chance.

'I told you, Ivan, I have met the Watcher.'

'So you said.'

'I told you, it is intelligent. Much more intelligent than you or me. It sees everything, it manipulates people. They obey its wishes but believe they are following their own. It has a course for this world laid out for centuries into the future. It now controls our destinies.'

'So I have heard.'

Eva gave a sigh. She hadn't wanted to say this. 'Hasn't it occurred to you, Ivan?'

'What?'

'You turning up here?'

He deliberately misunderstood her. 'Social Care sends lots of people like me into the RFS. It does not neglect its duty. Are you saying that you do not like me?'

Eva shook her head. 'You know that I'm not. Ivan. You know I like you. I think I love you.' She slammed down her coffee cup. 'Damn, I know I love you! That's what I mean. I love you.'

She glared at him. He was blushing. He was embarrassed. But he was a strong man. He was strong enough to say it.

'I love you too, Eva.'

There was a big round stone suddenly in her stomach, cold and hard. She couldn't believe he had ever admitted it. She felt as if she were walking in concrete boots, lurching along, jerking her whole body just to move forward. She felt her nose begin to run. It was either that or cry.

'And that's just it, isn't it? You were chosen just because of that. You were cast into here to hook me, so the Watcher could reel you back in with me in your arms.'

'It doesn't have to be that way, Eva. Maybe—'

'It's the Watcher, Ivan. It says it wants to do good! But I hate to think what that means. Look what it's done to us! It honestly believes it is doing what is right, trying to snatch me back.'

Ivan waved a big hand in a dismissive gesture.

'I do not care. Whether it is real or constructed. I love you. So come with me.'

'I want to, but I can't. You don't know what it's like.'

'I will help you.'

'Against the Watcher? It is on a different plane to you or me. Beyond our grasp.'

'I don't believe that.'

'Ivan, I don't think it even sees reality as we do.'

Something flickered in Ivan's eyes, as if Eva's comment had struck home.

'What is it?' she asked.

'Nothing,' said Ivan slowly.

'What?' Eva followed his gaze. He was staring at the screen. 'What aren't you telling me, Ivan? I saw the way you and Alexandr were looking at each other earlier. Those people we met the other day on the road here – the ones from Saolim – the way they spoke of this Narkomfin. What is it about this place, Ivan?'

'I promised I would not tell you, Eva.'

'Promised who?'

'Social Care.'

'When?'

'Before I came here. I didn't know what they were talking about then. I just signed a contract, promising not to disclose information regarding the VNMs and venumbs of this region.'

'What are you talking about?'

'The VNMs below this building. The ones that climb the walls. The ones that you are so frightened of.'

'What about them?'

'I found out where they came from. Well, Alexandr did.'

'Where did they come from?'

'I'll show you.'

Ivan fetched a featureless grey metal box and an induction screwdriver from one of the silver packing cases. He connected the box to the screen with a heavy cable.

'Shielded,' he explained, and began fiddling at the box with his screwdriver. 'This way no one but me can activate it,' he explained. On the screen a picture came to flickering life.

'This is not too far from here,' said Ivan. 'This building sits practically on top of these caves.'

Eva guessed that the caves weren't entirely natural. The Kamchatka peninsula, where the Narkomfin was located, was a region of volcanic activity. Still, the view on the screen appeared just too regular to be a natural formation. Eva wondered if the underground flows of lava had been redirected by the Watcher, just as humans redirected water courses by using dams. Had the magma table been lowered so that these glassy, shiny caves could float free? Had machinery been at work under here, boring and shaping the walls? Eva thought she could make out the circular patterns of sanders and drill bits evident on the glittering walls. But that was irrelevant: she was distracting herself, trying not to look at the things that filled the caves.

'Are they alive?' she asked Ivan.

'Alive? What is *life*? Look closer.' Ivan did something with his induction screwdriver, and the picture zoomed in. Now Eva could see what it was that was creeping and crawling on the floors of the caves.

'VNMs!' she exclaimed. 'But what's the matter with them?'

All of the machines were obviously disabled in some way. Maybe the legs down one side hadn't grown properly; maybe the sense cluster located on the head section was missing. Eva watched as one rusty creature moving painfully across the rippled stone floor; she could almost hear the metallic squeaking of its unlubricated joints.

'It's in pain,' she whispered, but her attention was then caught by a deformed spider, its body and legs all way too long, tip-toeing fragilely amongst the squirming mass of metal creatures.

'But what are they all doing down there?' she asked.

'I think it is someone's idea of a joke,' said Ivan coldly. 'This building houses the handicapped above ground. So where better to send all the halt and the lame machines but underneath it?'

'But that's not funny at all.' Eva felt something cold grip her heart. The Watcher. Would he do this?

'I don't know,' said Ivan, guessing her thoughts. 'But this is not all. Look here. And here.'

He fiddled with his screwdriver again, zooming back out. Eva saw a robot, feeling its way along the cave floor. Then another one. And another. A trailing crowd of orange robots, roughly humanoid, all shuffling in the same direction.

'They are searching for the next power mast,' said Ivan. 'You see them, painted yellow? They are turned on in sequence according to a regular period.' Eva saw the masts, a dwarf version of old-fashioned pylons.

'Why do they move so slowly?' asked Eva.

'Look.' He zoomed in on one robot.

'What's wrong with its eyes?' asked Eva, noticing the cloudy lenses set in the smooth orange head.

'The glass was deliberately contaminated during manufacture. That robot is almost blind. Look at this one here.'

'It seems normal. Why is it moving like that?'

'Faulty connection between the processor and the body. Its brain cannot properly control its limbs.'

The camera ran along the trailing line of orange robots,

and Eva saw they had all been tampered with in some way. Their limbs would be stiff and inflexible, or one would be shorter than the other, or they would appear perfectly sound but unable to move properly. The robots shuffled and stumbled and twitched and dragged themselves along a channel in the rippled stone floor, heading for the skeletal metal shape of the yellow pylon.

'They can only hold an hour's worth of charge,' explained Ivan. 'Those that don't make it to the pylon in time die.'

'What happens to them?'

Wordlessly, Ivan directed the view to the motionless orange body of a robot. It was slowly and inexpertly being taken apart by a group of rusty VNMs.

'But that's horrible,' said Eva.

'I know. Look at that.'

One of the robots had now reached the pylon. Several black rubber cables hung there, a heavy male socket at the end of each. The robot unhooked the cable with its too short arms and stood, waiting.

'What's the matter with it?' asked Eva. 'Oh, I see.' The robot's charging socket was located low down, where its navel would have been if it were human. The robot's arms would not reach that far.

'It's waiting for another robot to come and help it,' said Ivan.

Do you know what recursion is, Judy? It is when something causes itself to happen. A function that calls itself. Eva and Ivan aren't real; they're your dreams, Judy. Your life calls theirs into existence. But have you thought of this: is some-one calling you, Judy? The FE, perhaps? Are you merely another subroutine that is being run by a higher intelligence?

'Is everything in that cave handicapped in some way?'

'I think so.'

Eva felt dizzy and nauseous from peering at the stream of orange figures, the glassy smoothness of the cave walls. She looked away from the screen into the yellow evening sunlit room.

'That is happening right now, somewhere beneath our feet?'

'Yes – or something like that. This is a recording.'

'Does anyone from this Narkomfin know about it?'

'Some do, but they're not telling anyone what they know.'

'Why not?'

'Let me show you.'

The picture on the screen jumped several times. Ivan was searching for something. A dark, distorted pyramid appeared on the screen, a tumbled mound of earth. The picture rewound quickly, stopped, gained clarity, and Eva realized what she was looking at. She gasped, placed one hand to her mouth.

'That's Stephen,' she whispered. The dark pyramid was revealed to be Stephen Harthan slumped in his wheel-chair, drool running from one corner of his mouth to soak the sleeve of his black jacket. 'He lives on the floor just below.'

Silver and grey and rust-coloured VNMs could be seen gathering around the wheels of Stephen's chair. They were looking up at him. Steven was staring back in horror. In the background of the image, orange shapes shuffled ever onwards to the next pylon.

'How did he get down there?' asked Eva.

'There are shafts hidden throughout this whole building,' said Ivan. 'This building itself is an outpost of the world below. Every night, the handicapped are carried down to live in the world below.'

'But why?'

'I don't know. Who can second-guess the Watcher?'

'So it is the Watcher doing this!'

'I don't know for sure! But who else?'

'But *why*?'

'I can only guess. But I have often wondered. What if a handicapped person was raised in a world of the handicapped? Would he be normal?'

'Normal? What do you mean by normal?'

Ivan laid his hand on her forehead.

'You're burning up. I think you have had too much to drink, Eva.'

Eva felt the coolness of his hand. She was having trouble speaking without slurring. Slowly she formed a sentence: 'I think you're right, Ivan. I think we should go outside.'

'Good idea.'

'I'm sorry. After you went to all this trouble preparing the meal.'

'No trouble.'

'It was delicious. But I feel sick. Too much cream on my coffee.'

'Drink some pepper vodka.'

'No. That will curdle it. Let's go outside. Take a walk.'

She took one last look at the screen, doing her best not to think about what she had witnessed there.

Ivan took her hand and led her to the door.

Eva looked up through the tunnels in the clouds to the darkening sky above.

'Do you feel better?' asked Ivan.

'Every time we look up, it is the opening or closing parenthesis on a recursive block,' declared Eva, swaying.

'I don't understand.'

'Look up there. Clouds rising higher and higher like a stack of pennies thrown into the sky, and beyond them the first stars are appearing. Up there I see the contrails of the aeroplanes from the outside world. The Watcher is closing in on us, Ivan. The Free States won't last much longer.'

'So come with me when I return home.'

'No. While I stay here I am safe.'

'Safe here? With what you have seen lies beneath your feet?'

Eva swayed a little. How far down, she wondered? How far down to those caves?

If they were real, of course. No, she shunted the treacherous thought to one side. Ivan wouldn't lie to her. Would he?

They heard the chatter of approaching voices. Five people in wheelchairs approached, two of them being pushed by others. She studied them carefully. Stephen Harthan was not amongst them. What would she have done if he were?

'Hello, Eva. Hello, Ivan.'

Eva held onto to Ivan as she greeted the newcomers in return. She still felt sick and dizzy, and she felt the stiffness in his body as she clung on, and realized why when she saw who was walking behind the party. Pobyedov, the priest.

'Hello, Pobyedov,' she called. 'Say hello, Ivan,' she muttered.

One of the young men in the wheelchairs began to laugh. 'Here we go again,' he called. 'Listen, we're out for an evening stroll. We don't want to hear you two arguing!'

'I wasn't going to argue,' said Ivan.

'Nor was I, Wilson,' said Pobyedov. He knelt down by the young man in the wheelchair and offered him a drink from a little silver hip flask. Wilson took a nip, gave a satisfied gasp, and then offered the flask to Eva and Ivan.

'No, thank you,' said Eva. 'I've had enough.' She squeezed Ivan's arm, urging him to be polite, and accept the offered drink. Reluctantly he did so.

'Whiskey,' he said. 'But why is it sweet? This is like a child's drink, Wilson.'

Wilson laughed again. He was a big man, with strong arms and a broad chest. Only his legs were thin and useless.

'It is, it is!' he said delightedly. 'Which fool thought of putting vanilla in whiskey? And yet you drink black-currant vodka and are happy, Ivan. Pobyedov, I like this stuff!'

There was a gentle thumping sound. One of the group had started to spasm, one arm beating regularly against her head. Long strands of drool ran down onto her chest. Her father leant down and spoke to her softly.

'We're going to go inside now,' said Wilson, pretending not to notice the woman's behaviour. 'We thought we might go to Manny's bar later on. Maybe see you there?'

'Maybe,' said Eva.

They pushed their chairs on down the uneven concrete slabs of the road. The priest stayed with them, and Eva wished that he hadn't. Not tonight of all nights. She felt too nauseous for an argument.

'I hear you are going back home in two days,' said Pobyedov.

'I am,' said Ivan.

'I am grateful to you for coming here,' said Pobyedov. 'You've made a big difference to the residents. The heating would not be working but for you and Alexandr.'

'Maybe,' said Ivan, and Eva saw his face flushing red. She knew that he was trying to be polite. He honestly believed that the handicapped would be better served back out in the Watcher's world. It was taking a great effort for him not to point this out. He changed the subject by enlisting an unlikely ally.

'I have asked Eva to leave with me, Pobyedov. What do you think?'

'I think Eva must follow her own heart, Ivan Atchmianov. What do *you* think about our Narkomfin, Eva?'

'I don't know,' said Eva, still lost in the strangeness of the evening. 'It's unusual. I wonder about it, sometimes. We have artificial intelligences that think for us and they build machines that can reproduce. We are producing thoughts and artefacts that are beyond human capabilities, and yet we still have the handicapped. Even amongst the machines. Even some VNMs do not reproduce truly. They are born deformed.'

'They are not born, Eva,' said Pobyedov.

'You know what she means,' said Ivan, who normally would not agree with Eva's choice of words either.

'I suppose I do,' said Pobyedov. 'But what is your point, Eva?'

Eva was staring after the retreating group of people, outlined in silhouette now in the darkening evening, moving on down the V of the concrete path towards the painted Narkomfin.

'I don't know,' said Eva. 'It is almost as if the existence of the handicapped was written into the laws of the universe itself.'

Ivan made a dismissive noise. 'Nonsense.'

'Someone seems to think so,' she muttered.

'No, it is just a fault in the replication process. Don't smile at me like that, Pobyedov. I don't want another argument.'

'You argue with yourself most of the time, Ivan Atchmianov.'

Eva let go of Ivan. It was her fault, she knew it. She had started this argument.

'How about if I built a handicapped robot?' asked Ivan, flushing red. 'What if I made a machine and deliberately disabled its legs – like Wilson. Left it to push itself around in a chair? Why don't I do that?'

Pobyedov smiled.

'You would not do that, Ivan Atchmianov, because God gave you a heart that tells you what is right and what is wrong.'

'Pah, there is no God! Everything you see is just a result of the fact that matter attracts matter.'

'Who made the matter?'

'Who made life?' retorted Ivan. 'I tell you, no one. Simple chance. Matter attracts and forms molecules. By chance some of those molecules will be capable of replicating themselves. From this, you have life.'

'I do not dispute this, Ivan Atchmianov. But it does not prove that God did not teach you how to love.'

Eva interrupted. 'Come on, Ivan, take me back inside.'

Ivan clenched her hand in his fist. It almost hurt, such was his temper.

'Listen, not thirty kilometres from here we saw a flower formed of metal. It was growing: a metal flower. Life!'

The priest smiled. 'There are many wondrous things in this creation . . .'

'But it was not life. It was just bad programming.'

'And who wrote the program that brought us here, Ivan Atchmianov?'

'Simple chance, Pobyedov. Cells form that can follow

simple rules, but given enough cells and enough time and they form ordered patterns, and then thought emerges. This is inevitable. This is part of the universe. Tell him, Eva, tell him about the barge.'

'Don't get me involved.'

'Eva speaks of the competitive urge: how evolution causes animals to fight for resources.'

'What about love?'

'Love? Pah! This too has been modelled. Simulations have been run.' Ivan waved his hand dismissively. 'Sometimes it is appropriate for members of a species to aid each other. Love is the name given to this bond. It is an evolved thing, nothing more.'

'Ah,' said the priest, 'I see. So, you are saying that love is just as inevitable as thought and life and self-replicating molecules and stars. So then you agree with me, that love is written into the universe at a fundamental level.'

And at that the priest took another sip from his flask. He offered it once more.

'Now, another drink,' he said, 'and then shall we walk back to the building?'

Pobyedov, *called Judy in her sleep. Through Eva's eyes she watched him walking beside them in the gathering gloom. She raised her voice and shouted again:* Speak to me, Pobyedov! Who are you? I can feel you through the meta-intelligence. Who are you?

She was lying in her bed, lying under black sheets, dreaming in her room that was like a great bell that echoed with the sounds that reverberated through the ship. Echoed with the thoughts of the crew of the ship. She was picking up on the thoughts of the others.

Pobyedov? He was part of the FE software, she realized. Part of it. An echo from the past. From the very core of its being.

Pobyedov was in its bones, one might say.

MAURICE 4: 2252

*They had both been drunk and they had both done some-
thing stupid, but in the grand scheme of things that was
hardly something of note. Maurice had started it by
unfolding his console, but it was Saskia who drunkenly
raised the question. They had entered into a Fair Exchange,
and both had been outwardly satisfied with the outcome,
and inwardly put out at its equality. Both had thought
themselves a more attractive proposition than the other. As
is so often the case in life, it turned out that they were not.*

Saskia's hair spread out on the white pillow. She was
smiling at him.

'Thank you,' she said. 'If I turn around will you hold
me?'

'Of course,' said Maurice, and she rolled over and
shuffled against him so that her pale back and thin but-
tocks were pressed against his thighs. He placed his hand
on her flat stomach and remembered the shadows of her
ribs, remembered feeling the dark buds of her tiny breasts
beneath his thumbs. Truth be told, he hadn't fancied her
that much, but nonetheless he felt an enormous sense of

release and relaxation lying there. They had both felt it. Saskia had given an enormous shudder as she had climaxed, and Maurice had felt the tension ebbing from her body immediately afterwards. Judy had been right.

'Judy was wrong,' murmured Saskia.

'What do you mean?' yawned Maurice, already drifting off to sleep.

'She told me to keep away from you,' she confided. 'Said that you were only after one thing. She didn't seem to realize that was what I needed too.'

'Mmmm.'

'I suppose, being a virgin, she wouldn't understand.'

Maurice was already drifting in a snugly warm world. *Of course she understands*, he thought. *She manipulated you as deftly as her kind always does. The best way of getting you to do anything, Saskia, is by telling you to do the opposite.*

'You realize this is just about companionship, don't you?' whispered Saskia. She felt him stiffen.

'Yes, I know that.'

'Are you sure? You just went all tense.'

'I was thinking about something else,' said Maurice. He was suddenly wide awake, his mind bubbling over. Judy had manipulated them, hadn't she? And, he suddenly realized, it wasn't for the first time.

'I wonder what she will do for Edward,' thought Saskia, aloud.

'I wonder what she will do for herself,' muttered Maurice.

'What do you mean?'

I don't know, thought Maurice. *Was that ethical?*

Tricking us into bed together? Are Social Care allowed to do that? I never thought of that before. What else has she done whilst she's been playing with our emotions?

'She has dreams, you know,' murmured Saskia. 'Haven't you seen her in the mornings? How pale she looks?'

That time in the hold, when I played my clarinet.

'She always looks pale, of course,' continued Saskia, and for no real reason she started to laugh.

When she was asleep, Saskia looked like a little girl. She was smiling, one hand tucked beneath her head, her knees tucked up almost to her chest. Maurice got out of bed before shaking her gently awake.

She opened her eyes and smiled, and then remembered where she was. A shutter seemed to come down inside her head, and she sat up suddenly, wrapping the thin white sheet around herself.

'Good morning,' said Maurice, handing her his thick white robe. 'I'm going to take a shower.'

Saskia let her fringe drop over her eyes.

'Good morning,' she said. 'I think I'll do the same back in my room. I'll see you at breakfast?'

'OK.'

Maurice went into his bathroom and stepped behind the smoked-glass screen of the shower cubicle. Mist rose and was sucked up by the extractor above. As he rubbed himself down with grapefruit cleansing gel, he felt his body tingling into life. Stepping from the shower into the clean black and white tiled room beyond, he felt fresh and rested. He dried himself with a thick white towel, a scribble of black decorating the border, and then shaved, feeling alive and ready for anything. This was what Social Care was good at, he reflected. Manipulating people to do what was right for them. That's what the Watcher was supposed to do; that's what it had set out to do, anyway.

And then he recalled his thoughts on falling asleep last night. *What else was Social Care good at?* What was Judy playing at?

He was just wondering about this when the message sounded from his console.

Eva Rye, this is a warning. You are approaching a quarantined zone. Please alter your course at your earliest convenience. Do not approach Earth.

Judy was waiting for them all in the conference room, her arms folded.

Saskia followed Maurice into the room. Her business suit was gone; in its place she wore a white blouse and a pair of blue jeans that hung loosely from her narrow hips. Little teardrops of silver hung from her ears. She smiled politely at Maurice and sat down at the thick glass table in the seat opposite to him, next to Miss Rose. The old woman sat up stiffly, her skin still bearing the slightly fluorescent bloom of the autodoc. She looked healthy, but her eyes held a slightly glazed look, the effect of the memory-repressing drugs she was being fed. Maurice looked away from her. The drugs were the only thing between her and the horrific memory of those creatures forcing their way into her body and plumbing themselves directly into her nervous system. Maurice felt nauseous at the very thought.

Edward sat next to Judy, staring up at her. He could see it too, Maurice realized; he felt Judy's fatigue. Not physical, but mental fatigue at holding a mind twisted into one shape for so long. She was ready to snap. Nonetheless, when she spoke, her voice was as calm as ever.

'We're approaching Earth,' she said. 'You probably heard the message.'

'Who was that speaking?' asked Saskia. Maurice was surprised to note that she was holding Miss Rose's hand.

'The Watcher,' said Judy. 'Or one of his mouthpieces. It's not safe to go to Earth. The Dark Plants are all through the system. The Watcher doesn't like anyone going in or coming out.'

'But we're going in?' said Edward.

'Only if you decide it, Edward,' said Judy. 'You're in charge now.'

Edward turned to Saskia, his face twisted with worry.

'Judy is correct,' said Saskia. 'You're in charge now. You must do whatever you think is right, Edward.'

Edward frowned. What was he thinking about right now? wondered Maurice. *How does his mind work, and why is it so much slower than mine?*

'We made a deal,' said Edward eventually. 'We have to take Judy to Earth.'

'No you don't,' said Judy. 'The *Eva Rye* has to take me to Earth. You can all board the *Bailero* and go somewhere else.'

'No way, Judy.'

The voice came from a silver spider sitting on the table. Maurice realized that it had been there all along.

'I don't recall inviting you to our meeting, Kevin,' said Judy easily.

'I'm a member of this crew now,' said the spider.

'Actually, you're part of the cargo, Kevin,' she replied. If Maurice hadn't known better, he would have said that Judy was smirking. 'You were traded to this ship as part of a Fair Exchange conducted by the *Free Enterprise*.'

'So I was. And if you take the *Eva Rye* and leave me behind, I will judge the trade to be over. I will revert to being a free agent. Anybody left on board my ship will then become my property. I suggest you take your crew with you, Judy.'

'They're not my crew, they're Edward's.'

'You can all do what you like,' said Edward.

'Anyway, it doesn't matter,' said Saskia. 'We're all coming with you, Judy. We're not staying behind with that mad fucker.' She pointed to the silver spider on the table.

Judy spoke matter-of-factly. 'If Kevin is going to be a problem we will just wipe him from the processing space.'

The spider laughed. 'An empty bluff. Social Care doesn't kill.'

'You're not alive, Kevin. Your copies have assured me of that in the past.'

She meant it, Maurice realized with some surprise. She really would wipe out Kevin. Judging by his reply, Kevin knew it, too.

'Anyway,' he said, after the smallest of pauses, 'are

you sure you'll be allowed to go on your own? The crew of the *Eva Rye* made a deal using the FE software. They said they would take you to Earth.'

'Actually,' said Maurice, 'that's an interesting point. We could copy the FE software across to the *Bailero*'s processing space, I suppose, but that doesn't alter the point: who made the deal? Was it the software itself, or us as individuals, or us as a crew? What if one of us dies? What if the crew splits up? Where is the deal held then?'

'I don't know,' said Judy. 'Aleph? Do you know?'

A viewing field expanded above the table in which Aleph could be seen floating, a broken swastika clinging to the hull of the *Bailero*.

'Where is the deal held?' asked Aleph, a chuckle in his voice. 'That's a matter for individual conscience.'

'What's that supposed to mean?' called out Maurice. 'You know, the more I think about FE software, the odder it is. Where does it actually come from?'

'From the very fabric of the universe itself,' said Aleph mysteriously.

Maurice gave a snort. 'Yes, you could say that about anything. Answer me, where did you get *your* copy from, Aleph?'

'I was born with it.'

Maurice smacked his hand on the table in frustration.

'That's not what I mean. Where did our copy come from? It was on the ship when it replicated. Where on Earth did it come from originally?'

'Where on Earth?' asked Aleph. 'Oh, from some old guy in the past.'

Saskia looked up at that point. 'Some old guy? The Stranger said the same thing. What was his name?'

'Oh, I can't remember. Some old guy from a book. There were twelve of them – or was it thirteen? They killed him in the end. Nailed him to a tree or something. What was he called?'

The crew of the *Eva Rye* looked at each other, puzzled.

'Let's get back to the point,' said Judy.

The *Bailero* warped towards Earth, a silver and gold collection of curves that swept in and out on each other in pleasing symmetry. There was a joke to the design of this ship, one understood only by AIs of sufficiently advanced intelligence: the shape of the ship was that of a man, but warped through a Riemannian transform thought up by the AIs behind DIANA. No human had spotted the connection yet, but of such subtle conceits the Human Domain was constructed.

Inside the *Bailero*, the sleek black and white teardrop of the *Eva Rye* sat lightly on the blue-frosted interior, looking like the last pea left in the can. Its main entrance ramp had been lowered to touch the cold metal of the host ship, and a stream of silver VNMs totally encircled the black and white ship: Kevin's domain trying in vain to assert its mastery over the reformed vessel. Occasionally one of the VNMs would venture up the ramp, only to be beaten back by some invisible force.

And, trailing behind the *Bailero*, unnoticed yet by anyone save Aleph, two more systems-repair robots drifted, following the signal that was being transmitted from the FE software that lurked at the heart of the *Eva Rye*: a signal that pulsed out for hundreds of light years all around. It was a simple message.

It is time.

'Maurice, what do you think?'

Maurice was staring up at the irregular pattern in the ceiling, lost in thought. He sat up in his seat and leant forward, elbows on the desk. Judy was watching him dispassionately – did she guess his suspicions? He told a lie.

'Me?' he began. 'I'm wondering about how the *Eva Rye* came back to life. Where did the code for the FE software go when the ship was split into lots of little VNMs?'

'Is this relevant?' Saskia asked. 'We are talking about whether or not we should accompany Judy.'

'Maybe it's not relevant. But . . .' Actually, now he came to think of it, it was an interesting point. Where had the *Eva Rye* gone when it had been turned into VNMs? And therefore where had the FE software gone? It needed a large processing space on which to run. It couldn't have continued to exist after being broken up into lots of little spiders.

'I don't know how it was done,' said Maurice. 'How could FE software continue running when there was no processing space to support it? The *Eva Rye* was destroyed, split up into thousands of spiders . . .' He was thinking aloud now. 'But just suppose it worked backwards. Just suppose there was some software that could run on its own, software that didn't need hardware, or software that could form a supporting mechanism spontaneously.'

'I don't know what you're talking about,' said Saskia.

Maurice slumped back in his chair and went back to staring at the ceiling. Is that what FE was? A piece of code that could spontaneously form the mechanism on which it ran? You could use it as a wrapper for anything: a sound, an idea.

A soul?

'Where does FE come from?' he asked again. 'It just seems to have appeared at the edge of human space. Twenty years ago no one had even heard of it.'

Judy understood. 'Are you saying that maybe it just formed itself?'

The silence was broken by another voice. Earth was calling.

In the past five years only point three of one per cent of the people that have entered the Earth system have left it again. Do you really want to come here? You are approaching a quarantine zone. Please change your course now.

Everyone turned to Judy. She folded her arms, looking determined.

'I told you,' she said. 'I will go to Earth on my own.'

'No way,' said Saskia, glancing at Miss Rose again. 'We stick together. I have learnt my lesson. Edward, what do you say?'

They all looked at Edward, who had splayed his big hands across the glass table top.

'I think we should get something to eat,' he said decisively. 'We haven't had breakfast yet.'

*

They made their way to the living area. On Edward's suggestion they set the viewing fields to enfold them with an external view from the *Eva Rye*. They ate scrambled eggs and smoked bacon in a blue ice cavern that was slipping between the stars, diving towards the dark centre of the Earth system.

'I think we should have music,' said Edward. 'Maurice, can you choose something?'

Maurice looked at them, wondering what to play. Then he had a sudden flash of blinding clarity. He wasn't choosing something for Edward, or Saskia, or Miss Rose, or even Judy. There was no one here that he was trying to impress.

'Maurice?' said Edward.

Maurice placed his console on the table next to his plate and thoughtfully stroked it to life. What would he himself like to hear?

The voice of a choir filled the cold blue space. *I Love My Love*, sung a cappella.

An ice cavern, unaccompanied voices, and smoked bacon. And beyond that the cold stars slipping past, while behind them drifted the broken crosses of systems-repair robots.

Miss Rose was eating her bacon and eggs and sipping tea that Saskia poured her from a pot. Judy was neatly cutting yellow squares of scrambled egg with her fork and daintily putting them in her mouth. Edward was gulping down apple juice. *Look at us* thought Maurice. *Who planned all this? I've been set adrift amongst these people for a reason. This is the sort of thing Social Care does, yet it doesn't feel like Social Care.*

There was a flicker on his console.

'Another contact,' he said. 'The *Uninvited*.'

Saskia gave a laugh. 'Someone has a sense of humour.'

They all looked to Edward. He recoiled under their gaze, hunched around his breakfast.

'What?' he asked.

'Speak to them,' said Saskia. 'You're the captain now.'

'What do I say?'

'Whatever feels right,' said Judy.

Edward carefully laid down his knife and fork.

'Hello?' he began.

'Hello, *Eva Rye*. This is the *Uninvited*. Do you wish to engage in Fair Exchange?'

Edward held out his hands, palms up, mutely asking the others what to do. They smiled back kindly. 'Whatever you want, Edward,' said Saskia gently.

'Er . . . Yes?' said Edward.

'Excellent. My name is Miriam. I notice that our two ships are both running on the same time. Would you like to join us for breakfast?'

'Yes, that would be nice.'

There was a shimmering, and then the empty spaces around the table were occupied by the virtual crew of the *Uninvited*. There were seven of them, six humans and one robot. They were all handicapped in some way, missing limbs or suffering from palsy or simply gazing into space with a vacant look. Even the robot looked badly damaged: three long scars ran down the right-hand side of its torso. The derm there was disrupted; it had puckered and deformed into a bubbling black mass that stood out in marked contrast to the rest of its smooth grey body.

'Nice ship,' said a dark-haired woman, gazing around the frosty interior of the *Bailero*. 'Hi, I'm Miriam.' She only had one arm. She raised her single hand in greeting.

The crew of the *Eva Rye* waited politely for Edward to speak. After a nudge from Judy, he got the idea.

'Oh, I'm Edward. What's that you're eating?' He pointed to the yellow flakes on the plate in front of Miriam.

'Smoked haddock,' she replied, giving him an appraising look. *She knows*, thought Maurice. *She's met people like him before*. Miriam now spoke more slowly. 'It's nice to meet you, Edward. Do you realize that you are flying towards a very dangerous place?'

'Yes,' said Edward. 'But we made a promise.'

'And you're keeping it,' said Miriam. 'Good for you, Edward. Now, let me introduce you to a friend of ours. He would like to go to Earth too.'

She looked towards the robot. The robot swivelled his badly dented face to look around the table.

'Hi,' he said, 'my name is Constantine.'

Maurice set the Fair Exchange process in motion and gazed around the crew of the *Uninvited* as they ate their breakfast. Willi, a young man with a big, beaming smile, forked yellow flakes of fish into the quivering, drooling mouth of the red-headed woman sitting by him.

'What's the matter with her?' asked Maurice.

'Cerebral palsy,' said the young man. 'She has her good days and her bad days – don't you, Carol?'

The red-headed woman made a noise in her throat. Her hand banged up and down against the arm of the padded chair in which she sat.

'You'd think there was a cure for all those illnesses,' said Saskia, wonderingly.

'Saskia!' exclaimed Judy. 'Don't be so rude!'

'It's OK,' said Miriam, and then more petulantly, 'medical care seems to have stopped developing in the mid-twenty-first century.'

'Just when the Watcher came to prominence,' added Constantine the robot.

Everyone stared at the stump of Miriam's missing arm.

'How did you all meet?' asked Maurice.

'We were being taken on a cruise out to the stars by Social Care,' said Willi. 'We got caught in a region of Dark Plants and were rescued by a ship using FE. They offered us the choice of returning to Earth or of adopting FE ourselves. We chose FE.'

'But why?' asked Judy.

'Because we were tired of being looked after,' interrupted Miriam, a note of anger in her voice. 'We thought it would be nice to take care of ourselves instead.'

'But what if something happens to you?'

'Then something happens to us,' said Miriam firmly, and that line of conversation was ended.

'Circumstances uploaded,' said Maurice, glancing at his console. 'FE is commencing.' He looked at Saskia, expecting her to say something sarcastic. To his pleasant surprise she didn't seem to have noticed. She was listening carefully to Miss Rose. The old woman had hardly said a word since her emergence from the autodoc.

'Who, who'd . . .?' she began in a hoarse whisper.

'Easy, Miss Rose, take your time.'

The contrast with the former Saskia could not be more marked. Relaxed and warm in her white blouse, her little silver earrings sparkling.

'What was that, Miss Rose?'

'Who'd have thought it?' said Miss Rose in a thin whisper. 'We're all equal in the eyes of FE.'

'What do you mean, Miss Rose?' asked Saskia, squeezing her cold parchment hand.

'I mean *him*,' said Miss Rose, a shaking hand pointing to Edward. 'The dummy. Leave him on his own and he'd give the shirt off his back to the first person who asked for it. He'd be ripped off by every Tom, Dick and Harry who came by. But put him on a ship with FE and he is the equal of anyone. Just like that lot sitting over there – the cripples.'

Saskia tried to hush the old woman. None of the *Uninvited* seemed to mind, however. One or two of them even seemed amused.

'That's the thing, though,' continued Miss Rose, placing one finger on the table. 'Even the stupid can't be ripped off when all transactions go through FE.'

'Hmm,' said Saskia thoughtfully. 'Maurice,' she said suddenly, 'maybe you were right. Where does FE come from? Aleph said that FE was the idea of some old guy from history.'

Judy had stopped what she was doing in order to listen to the conversation.

'I don't know,' she said pensively. 'I have tried to feel the software, but there is something so strange about it. I think Aleph is mistaken here. I get the feeling that we are dealing with something that is far older than humanity.'

In the deepening silence that followed this announcement, Maurice looked at his console.

'Fair Exchange will be completed in five minutes,' he announced.

Miriam had finished her breakfast. She placed her fork on her plate and scratched her side awkwardly. It was difficult with only one arm.

'Listen,' she said. 'In about one and a half hours' time you will be entering the quarantine zone. There are things in there waiting for you; they'll have locked on to your ship already. They will have even locked on to your individual personalities.' She paused, letting this sink in.

'Our individual personalities?' said Edward.

'You don't all have to go to Earth. Why don't some of you come on board the *Uninvited*?' Miriam looked deliberately at Miss Rose.

'Why not, Miss Rose?' asked Saskia. 'You'll be safer there.'

Miss Rose shook her head. 'I don't think so, dear. Do you know why I'm here?'

There was a shuddering crash at the end of the table as one of the *Uninvited* dropped her fork. Miss Rose smiled at the red-headed woman suffering from cerebral palsy.

'I have my moments, too,' she sympathized. 'Senile dementia. It's odd, isn't it? How we can build self-replicating machines and travel between the stars and yet we can't cure conditions that are as old as human existence itself.'

Miriam nodded in agreement.

Miss Rose folded her hands around one of Saskia's, holding it in the lap of her white shift.

'When the first symptoms appeared, when I first began to forget things, and to repeat myself, it was suggested that I take a cruise. That was Social Care again.' She turned to Judy. 'What is it about you lot?' she asked. 'The halt and the lame, you want to shift us all off planet. Out of sight, out of mind, is it?'

Miss Rose's voice had begun to crack. 'Edward, be a good lad and get me some water.'

Edward returned with the glass. She took a sip.

'I never liked space,' continued Miss Rose. 'I never wanted to travel. And yet there I was on a ship. Passing through the Earth Domain. Embarrassing people by asking them their names over and again, like each time I met them it was for the first time. Embarrassing myself. And then we met the *Changes*. An FE ship. I don't think Social Care knew what FE was at that time otherwise they would never have let their crew come aboard. We got chatting. They asked me what I wanted.'

Maddeningly, Miss Rose paused to slowly sip her water again.

'And what did you say, Miss Rose?' prompted Saskia.

'I said I didn't want to continue like this,' said Miss

Rose. She placed her glass on the table. 'I said I wanted to do something important.'

'And what did they say?'

'They consulted their FE software,' said Miss Rose. 'It said I could have what I wanted.'

'And what did you have to give in return?' asked Maurice.

'Me. I was sold as cargo to the *Changes*. And then I was sold to the *Yellow River*, and then I was sold to you.'

She turned around to Miriam. 'And that's why I think I will remain here on the *Eva Rye*,' she said.

Maurice's console chimed. 'The Exchange is completed,' he said. Then he gave a laugh. 'And you're not going to believe this, but this time we're actually going to be paid! They're going to pay us for taking Constantine on board!'

'What?' asked Saskia, brimming with hope.

Maurice made to speak and then he stopped himself.

Seated there at a glass table at the bottom of a huge blue ice bubble, sharing breakfast with the old, the handicapped and a robot, Maurice raised a finger and tapped the side of his nose. 'You'll have to wait and see.'

'Where is Constantine?' asked Edward impatiently. He stood at the foot of the lowered entrance ramp of the *Eva Rye*, dancing with impatience.

'I don't know,' said Maurice. 'Kevin! Can you see him?'

The voice of the *Bailero* spoke from Maurice's console.

'He is two hundred metres distant from my hull now. I will put a light over his entrance.'

A yellow spotlight shone down from somewhere, illuminating a patch of frost about thirty metres away from the foot of the ramp.

Maurice and Edward watched it expectantly. Constantine had literally jumped from the hatch of the *Uninvited* in the direction of the *Bailero* – they had all watched him do so. They had seen him sailing through space, a black pressurized bag slung over his shoulder.

'Here he comes,' said Kevin.

The spotlight strengthened in intensity, and then Constantine rose up into the interior of the *Bailero*, arms outstretched. The robot must have had some sort of independent motive source, Maurice realized, for he changed direction in flight and then quickly dropped back down to the frost-patterned floor. Briskly, he walked towards them. He paused just at the foot of the ramp.

Maurice gave Edward a nudge, and the young man extended his hand.

'Welcome aboard,' he said.

'Glad to be on board,' said Constantine.

Edward led the way up the ramp of the *Eva Rye*, past the entrance to the little hold and along the corridor towards the conference room.

Judy and Saskia met them there.

'I'm Constantine Storey,' said the robot. 'Thank you for taking me on board.'

'I'm Saskia. This is Judy.'

The robot was fiddling with the seal of the black pressure bag. 'I have your payment here,' he said.

They all crowded a little closer as the robot struggled with the seal. His right hand was badly deformed, Maurice noticed; the three scars on his right hand side were repeated on his lower arm. Maurice wondered what had happened to him.

Eventually, the robot worked the seal open. He reached into the bag, feeling about for something. Whatever it was seemed to be moving.

'What is it?' asked Edward, 'What have you got in there?'

'Something that the FE software thought you needed,' said Constantine. 'I can sort of see why. We're almost at Earth now.'

'Good,' said Judy with quiet resignation. 'I feel like I've been travelling there for the past ten years.'

'Oh?' said Constantine. 'I have been doing so for over a hundred. Ah, got it!'

At last he had what he was searching for. But now something was climbing out of the bag by itself; first a paw emerged and waved itself in the air. The robot withdrew his hand fully, holding a furry bundle of white, brown and tan.

'It's a kitten!' squealed Saskia excitedly.

'Two kittens,' said Constantine, as a second bundle, tabby this time, dropped from his bag to the ground, and then eeled its way across the floor, ears down flat.

'And what on earth are we going to do with them?' asked Maurice.

'Stroke them, of course,' said Saskia. 'They're sweet!'

CONSTANTINE 6: 2252

Everybody loves kittens.

'I don't,' said Maurice. 'They smell, they make a mess, and what are they going to do on this spaceship anyway? It's cruel to have them cooped up in here.'

'They can hardly be described as cooped up,' said Judy, waving her hand to indicate the enormous extent of the large hold. She was sitting cross-legged on the rubber floor, smiling as she dragged a length of silk ribbon back and forth for the patchwork kitten to chase. Its supple, darting movements were in contrast to the slow tread of the two colossal venumbs seen in the distance at the far end of the hold. The polished wood of their bodies looked like bone. Behind them lay the shuttle on which Judy had been sent from the *Free Enterprise*. A low, sleek arrow with six seats on board, and space for little else.

Constantine's derm was half ripped away from the right side of his body. His head was a dented metal shell from which two eyes stared, his whole right side was badly scarred, his right arm still had only restricted movement. Even so, he felt a less damaged individual than the crew of the *Eva Rye*. Look at poor Edward, he thought, always on the defensive. Always trying to understand.

'Anyway, they can catch mice,' he was saying, his eyes drawn enviously back to the tabby kitten that Saskia was rubbing behind the ears.

'We don't have any mice,' said Maurice. 'We're on a spaceship.'

'They might come on board with the cargo,' said Saskia contentedly. Her smile did not waver as the kitten wriggled free of her grasp and dropped to the floor. Edward reached for it, but naturally it headed straight for Maurice, the cat-hater.

'Yes, mice might indeed try to come aboard,' said Maurice, kicking out at the kitten: it mewed and pattered away across the dark rubber of the floor. 'And they would fail in the attempt as the ship's manifest net would detect and eject them.'

The kitten took one look at Constantine, mewed again, and ran for the far end of the hold towards the great wooden venumbs.

'Do you always snipe at each other like this?' wondered Constantine.

'Oh no,' said Saskia seriously, 'we used to be a lot worse.'

Maurice gave him a sharp look. 'Are you laughing at us?'

'Honestly, no! I think it's good that a crew about to cross into Earth's solar system can be so relaxed about it.'

'That's because there's precious little else we can do about our present circumstances,' said Saskia. 'You know,

I think we should call that one Paws.' She pointed to the remaining kitten, and the group paused to watch it spread wide its little white paws before swiping in an attempt to catch the ribbon. 'Look how she uses them like little hands.'

'We can still make a plan,' said Edward earnestly, turning to face Constantine. 'That's why we're here.'

There was a creaking sound from the far side of the large hold, as one of the huge wooden shapes slowly turned in a circle, apparently looking for something. Constantine wondered where they had originated. He had never seen venumbs that size before. Wooden skeletons: they would have to be carved from tree trunks to be so big. Beautiful white ash, planed into smooth curves that bent and flexed as the monsters pressed their splaying feet down on the floor. Incredibly shiny joints flashing in the antiseptic light. But what were they doing on board this ship?

'Plan to do what?' asked Maurice bitterly. 'The ship lands on Earth. The Watcher has us under its gaze. We never get away. Period.' He sighed. 'What do you suggest we do?'

'We should listen to Edward,' interrupted Saskia. 'That's what the Stranger recommended, and I for one think that's right.'

Maurice pressed his mouth tightly shut. Constantine ignored him. The wooden monster was coming closer. It didn't have a head, just a long neck made of white wooden vertebrae strung together by chrome.

'OK,' said Maurice stubbornly. 'Edward, tell us, what should we do?'

Edward looked puzzled at Maurice's question. 'I don't know,' he said, frowning. 'That's why I think we should make a plan.'

Judy let go of the ribbon and climbed to her feet. The air was cold in the large hold, sharp like a winter's morning. Constantine had possessed lungs once; he could imagine what it was like to breathe the air of the hold, to feel it light him up, bright and alive.

'I think Edward has got the right idea,' said Judy briskly. 'Look at us. We've already spent too long just letting events buffet us around.'

'Look at *us*?' said Maurice. 'Since when were you part of the crew?'

'That's not very nice, Maurice.' Edward placed a big hand on Judy's shoulder. 'Judy is our friend. Go on, Judy.'

'Not just me. Aren't we forgetting somebody?' said Judy. 'You've agreed to take Constantine to Earth too.'

All the faces swung towards Constantine. Why were they all so pale, he wondered? Except for Edward, of course. Did they realize they were all so black and white? Just like this ship, of course. Someone was playing games here . . .

'Yes,' said Maurice. 'Why exactly do you want to go to Earth?'

Constantine had been waiting for this question.

'Because I have a message for the Watcher,' he replied.

Constantine Storey didn't mind the rain. Up here in the mountains the spaces defined between the sheer peaks and rough-hewn walls seemed to be completed by the lashing downpour.

Or at least that's what Constantine thought.

But what does it mean to think? *he wondered.* No one else came up here amongst the newly born peaks, raw and cracked and splintered and perpetually washed with cold rain. No other mind, so far as he knew, had ever looked upon the hidden valleys, had climbed the columns that rose up here, pressed against the sky.

Coldness, wetness, the feeling of vertigo from clinging to harsh rock and looking down into the pitiless depths below, all of these things were just random patterns that fluttered through the currents of his mind.

. . . *and if those thoughts were to cease?*

He stepped from the ledge and began the long fall into the shadows. The feel of the downpour lessened on his back as the speed of his descent approached that of the raindrops around him. He waved his arms and fancied he could touch the individual drops that hung in the darkness around him. There is a pattern to these drops, he thought, defined by their size and purity and their distance between each other. The pattern is affected by wind resistance and minute changes in air pressure, even the increasing effect of gravity as they grow closer to the planet. Weyl and Ricci distortion. There is a pattern here that is probably unique throughout the universe . . . and when they hit the rocks below, that unique pattern will be lost, and no one will mourn its passing.

Buffeted by wind and rain, his body reached terminal velocity. Shadows raced upwards around him, the pale moon lost high above.

And yet, when I hit the ground, what would people mourn? Not the loss of my body but rather the unique pattern that represented my thoughts; the potential which that unique pattern had to go on unfolding, to become me. What is the difference between the pattern of my mind and the pattern of the rain? At what point does a pattern assume significance? At what point can it be labelled thought? Maybe tonight I will have the answer.

But not by dying.

Constantine Storey was a human mind alive in a robot's body. At one point in his life, the unique pattern that had been his self at that moment in time – burning brightly amongst the neurons of his brain – had been carefully lifted from his head and dropped into a processing space within a robot's body. Virtual neurons had gone on firing, following in the unfolding symbolic series that his human brain had defined, and a new Constantine had come into being. Only this Constantine was alive in an enhanced body.

He allowed the reflexes of his new body to take over, and he revelled in the sensation of becoming a superman.

A sheer cliff face approached in the darkness, steeply angled. Robot legs kicked out and changed his angle of descent, increasing the horizontal component of his motion. Constantine held his arms wide as he dived across a narrow valley. Hands slammed onto a ledge, cracking rock, pushing him forwards and onwards, absorbing some of his downward velocity. He rolled down another slope, shedding more speed, then he jumped through the downpour, aiming for the knife edge of rock that stretched between two peaks.

He kicked out once, twice, three times, pushing himself back and forth between rocky walls, and landed lightly at his target, knees flexing to absorb the remaining energy of his fall. He gazed out towards the ziggurat that lay on the plain beyond the mountains.

Something was awakening inside it.

In the hold, one of the wooden venumbs was approaching. Constantine thought it looked as if it was sniffing for something; it put him in mind of a dog scenting trouble. The rest of the crew seemed unconcerned, and he continued with his story.

Constantine had been led to believe there were possibly three ways intelligence could arise. The first two methods were generally accepted as having been convincingly proven. Intelligence could appear as the result of evolution. Human intelligence was an example of this.

Secondly, intelligence could be written. The AIs of Earth did this all the time, writing new minds to order, minds to fill spaceships and robots and Von Neumann Machines.

Could I write a mind? wondered Constantine. Could I sit down and describe a scene, a thought and an emotion so well that it took life on the page? No, the page is not a suitable medium to allow movement, and this language is too ambiguous and overblown to capture the simplicity of the underlying mechanism of thought.

Constantine had once been told that a mind was a

sentence that could read itself. A book might have thoughts written within it, but something external had to be applied to the book in order to read the words. But what if words could be written in some medium that allowed the words to take on a life of their own, and refer back to themselves? What if the instructions telling the book how to read itself were also written in the book itself?

The periphery of the rainstorm was at the edge of the mountains. Constantine stood at the borderline of the storm, seemingly at the edge of a new world. Down there, on that dry, sleeping plain, something wonderful was awakening. The ancient machinery that filled the stone halls of the ziggurat had lain in wait for nearly forty years. A baited trap.

Something was beginning to move in there. Patterns rippled through the many-dimensional volumes enclosed by the processing spaces, repeating themselves, reflecting, constructing new patterns . . .

A third possible way that intelligence could arise had also been postulated: divine intervention. A dizzying feeling gripped Constantine at the enormity of what he was witnessing. This was what the Watcher believed: it believed itself to be the result of an interstellar computer virus, written long ago. It had set up the ziggurat on this forgotten planet in order to test this theory. It had filled the ziggurat with ancient machinery, hoping to catch the virus there.

Constantine had been brought to this planet by the Watcher in order to observe what happened there. A suitable vessel had been left open under the vast, starlit night, and Constantine had been charged with waiting for some-

thing to pour down from the unguessed heavens and fill it with the spirit.

And, unbelievably, it was happening now. The event that Constantine had not really believed would happen, the one he had waited nearly forty years to observe – and it was happening. Something was straining within the ziggurat, something was straining to be. A thread was blowing back and forth across the ranks of symbols aligned in the processing spaces that filled the building. If the Watcher's theory were correct, then the same virus that had caused the Watcher to be born would now be taking root in the ziggurat.

Constantine had robot eyes; he was looking straight into the processing spaces. He jumped. Something was looking back at him: eyes, unaware of themselves, receptors for the patterns that flickered across them from outside.

Constantine stepped from the rainfall into the still night beyond. He descended the mountainside, preparing to receive the message that would be carried to humanity.

A low growl sounded. It began to climb in pitch. It was joined by another, and another. Sirens began to sound, rising howls in the night that sent the sleeping colonists tumbling from their beds. Arc lights slammed on and the sides of the ziggurat were lit up in red and yellow.

The ziggurat was armed – Constantine felt a hollowness inside at the thought. This was the secret pain he had carried inside himself for the past forty years. The Watcher wanted proof, not competition. The Watcher controlled a vast area of space; it did not want a challenger for its domain. There was a bomb in the ziggurat . . .

*

Judy gave a gasp.

'What is it?' asked Constantine.

'Nothing,' said Judy. 'Go on . . .'

Random symbols emerged from the processing space. They carried the edge of meaning.

. . . Would you like to engage . . .

Constantine could see what was forming in there. But it was not at all what he had expected . . .

The siren's note changed and a shaft of horror lanced through him. No! He had to stop it. This was not what anyone had expected. He began to run across the plain. It was too far . . .

. . . and a magnetic pulse washed across the night. The howl of the sirens rattled and died. Motors stopped. Constantine only just got his own shields up in time to save his mind. But the rest of his body caught the full force of the pulse . . .

The rest of the crew were too busy gazing at Constantine to notice the way the venumbs were moving about.

'What happened?' pressed Saskia.

'Should they be doing that?' asked Constantine, pointing to the white wooden body of one of the great wooden dinosaurs. It was twisting around on itself, almost overbalancing.

'They're fine,' said Maurice, not bothering to look. 'Answer her.'

Constantine shrugged. 'OK. We killed it. The Watcher

killed it. Once it had proof of its theory it killed that being.'

'But why?'

'I told you, it didn't want competition. Look at the Enemy Domain. That was a result of the rise of another AI. The Watcher didn't want a repeat of that conflict. It doesn't trust other powerful AIs.'

'That's a good excuse,' muttered Maurice sarcastically.

'What happened to *you*?' asked Saskia, ignoring the interruption.

'The colonists found me three days later. I was half buried in mud, my body completely shut down, most of the circuits tripped by the magnetic pulse. The colonists argued for a whole day about whether they should jump-start me. They were so angry about what had happened to them, feeling as if they had been tricked, and indeed they had been. The Watcher's scheming had left them marooned on a planet where nothing now worked. All their machinery was ruined.'

Constantine felt a pang of sadness at the thought. He had worked long and hard himself to build that colony. The memory of a Geep, half submerged in the mud, its motor beyond repair, rose up in his mind.

'But they obviously got you started in the end,' Maurice was saying.

'Yes, they started me in the end.'

'So what are you doing here?'

There was an edge to Judy's voice that none of them had heard from her before. She had folded her arms across her chest; she had a haunted look in her eyes.

'Are you OK, Judy?' asked Edward hesitantly.

She didn't appear to hear him.

'Why are you *here*, Constantine?' Judy shouted. 'What happened to you? What did you see inside that ziggurat?'

Constantine patted her arm. Then Maurice and the rest of the crew looked on in astonishment as the robot placed a plastic hand behind her head and drew her close in a gentle embrace. 'You knew, Judy, didn't you? You knew about the ziggurat.'

'What did she know about the ziggurat?' shouted Maurice.

Constantine went on. 'I had to get to Earth,' he said. 'I was trapped on a forgotten planet, with possibly the key to life itself in my grasp. The Watcher, it had been wrong all of this time. Nobody had guessed, let alone the Watcher itself. And now I had to get to Earth. But how?'

'Key to life itself?'

'What had the Watcher been wrong about?'

'About everything. About what it was and where it came from. About its place in the universe. I saw it all there in that moment before the ziggurat was destroyed.'

'What did you see?'

But Constantine wasn't going to say. That information was for the Watcher. He went on speaking: 'Look, there was no machinery working there any more. We spent two years doing what we could just to grow enough food to feed the colonists; it was nearly three years before I managed to get a communications antenna up.'

'And then what happened?'

Constantine looked at the slowly flexing fingers of his right hand. 'Lots of things,' he murmured. 'And then one day an FE ship arrived on the planet.'

'What's the matter, Maurice?' asked Judy.

'You know, don't you?' said Maurice.

Judy scowled. 'I know? What do I know?'

'You know what he's talking about.'

'Come on, Maurice. What is the matter with you? You've been in a foul mood ever since yesterday morning.' She gave a nasty smile. 'I would have thought that sleeping with Saskia would have relaxed you a little bit.'

'You *are* upset,' said Maurice. 'Look at you, you're arguing with me. You're showing emotion, not slinking back into impassivity.'

'I don't know what you mean,' said Judy, her emotion evaporating into the wide-open space of the large hold. Saskia and Edward stood still, not wanting to interrupt. They wanted answers too. Constantine noted the faintest suggestion of a twitch at the corner of Maurice's eye.

'You've been lying to us from the very start, haven't you, Judy? You've been playing with us. You see, it wasn't until yesterday morning that I realized, not until I understood the way you manipulated Saskia into sleeping with me.'

'What?'

'Stay out of this, Saskia.'

Saskia blushed hotly. 'Don't you tell me what to do,

Maurice. She didn't manipulate me. I make my own decisions.'

Maurice threw his head back and laughed. 'Oh, she lets you think that, Saskia,' he said. 'We're all doing what she wants. She's been manipulating us ever since she came aboard this ship. She's been putting us off guard, catching us at our most vulnerable moments, doing what she can to keep us thinking only about ourselves and to stop us thinking about her.'

A cold breeze. Suddenly a venumb was towering over Judy, swinging its headless neck back and forth, as if searching for something. How had it got so close so quickly? What was it doing? Judy didn't seem to notice, a still black shape with a pale face.

'I was trying to help you,' she explained softly. 'It's what I do.'

Judy's reply seemed a measured moment of calm amidst the torrent of emotions. Constantine could see that it only infuriated Maurice more.

'Hah, it's what you *did*,' Maurice corrected. 'Of course you were trying to help. But you were manipulating us, too. You're Social Care.'

Judy made no reply to this.

'Is this true?' asked Edward.

Judy was a silent china doll, black eyes glittering in a porcelain face.

'Of course it's true, Edward,' laughed Maurice. 'Social Care are experts at it. Just because she's retired doesn't mean she can give it up – especially when she has reasons for wanting to hide something. And she does. Come on, Judy, tell us the truth. How do you know *him*?' He pointed at Constantine.

'I don't,' said Judy. 'Or at least, not first-hand. But I have heard about him.'

'How?'

What was up with the venumbs? What could they hear? Constantine had half an ear trained on the space around the ship, listening for whatever it was they could hear. The other ear, however, was fixed firmly on Judy's story.

'At night I dream of a hand over my face . . .'

'What do you mean by that?' demanded Maurice.

'It's a stress dream,' explained Judy. 'When I'm feeling stressed I dream of a hand hovering just over my face. It reaches down from the ceiling, like it's trying to smother me.'

A long creak echoed through the large hold. The farthest wooden venumb looked as if it was crouching, ready to spring. Slowly the humans turned back to face Judy.

'You're changing the subject. How do you know Constantine?'

And it all came out. Judy spoke.

'I told you most of it already when I first came on board. Twelve years ago I met a robot called Chris. He told me that the Watcher had actually *killed* someone. He told me that he was going to kill again in the future.'

'That's silly,' protested Edward. 'The Watcher doesn't kill.'

'He does,' said Constantine. 'I witnessed the murder. I felt the EM pulse that ripped through that ziggurat.'

A spasm of pain crossed Judy's face. 'Chris told me that was going to happen. I was supposed to prevent that murder.'

'So why didn't you?'

'Because I have spent the last ten years running. Trying to get away from Chris and the Watcher! Both of them want me to help them . . .'

'Why? Why you?'

'*I don't know why me!* Chris wants me to help him to destroy the Watcher. He says that I will help him in the end. What if he's right? He is more intelligent than me. I feel like a puppet. *I am a puppet!*'

And at that, the first little crack in the dam that had held back forty years' worth of emotion appeared. A silver tear ran down Judy's white face. She wiped it away. The dam held steady.

And then, in perfect synchronization, both of the venumbs pounced.

There was a cracking explosion of wood. White splinters crackling across the floor. Saskia yelped and slapped a hand to her cheek, blood welling through her fingers, a white sliver protruding. Constantine was behind her, his body arched as he absorbed the force of three larger pieces of wood.

'How did you get there so quickly . . .?' she began.

Constantine didn't answer; he was now thinking and moving in quick time. He could see that the furthest venumb, now missing its front leg, was trying to make its way across the floor to a second huge, wobbling grey-black mass that had suddenly appeared inside the large hold. It was a Dark Seed, but swollen, mutated until it was bigger than Constantine himself.

– Constantine, this is Aleph. Can you hear me?

– I hear you.

A rain of smaller, though still misshapen, Dark Seeds was beginning to fill up the hold. The nearest venumb was swinging its head this way and that. Wherever it looked, the seeds instantly vanished.

Aleph spoke. – Kevin has brought us within range of something huge and dark. I think some battle must have been fought here between the Watcher and . . . something else.

Beneath the wooden feet of the venumb, the kittens jumped and pounced, catching Dark Seeds beneath their paws.

Judy was staring at the huge, wobbling grey-black mass of the mutated seed. Maurice was meanwhile helping Saskia to pull the splinter from her cheek.

– You have a disintegrator built into your body, Constantine. Use it.

– A disintegrator? I didn't know such things existed.

– You mean you didn't know you had it? But it is there in your left arm.

– This body has many features I don't know about. The Watcher planned for everything, but told me very little.

– Go to the mutated seed. It is not reacting so far, but it may yet do so. Disintegrate it, just like the Schrödinger kittens are doing to the other seeds.

– Schrödinger kittens? I didn't know . . .

– Why do you think you were given them? Use the disintegrator.

– How?

– Let me show you . . .

This wasn't the first time another consciousness had entered Constantine's mind to guide him. He felt Aleph's presence and he turned to look at his representation. He was surprised at what he saw.

– Shhh, said Aleph, placing a finger to his mouth. – Don't tell anyone yet.

There was a pulsing in the air, regions of pressure that squeezed the soft human bodies. Distant sensations insinuated their way into the shivering space of the large hold: the smell of vomit and the sound of seagulls crying.

Something was awakening in Constantine's body, new potentials arising in his arm. An inequality appeared in his vision.

$$\Delta x \, \Delta p \geq \frac{\hbar}{2}$$

Constantine recognized it.

– Heisenberg's Uncertainty Principle.

– Well done, said Aleph. – The disintegrator measures the positions of the individual particles within its field to an accuracy of a nanometre. This renders the momentum of those particles to such a level of uncertainty that they are excluded from being within a hundred metres of here.

– Very clever, said Constantine, and the disintegrator woke up in his arm in a rainbow of colours and with the feel of flowing honey. He felt dizzy at the measurements that the device was already performing as he waved his arm around. Space wavered as the device seemed to plug him into the universe at some basic level.

A tall, good-looking man appeared in Constantine's mind. He walked with a cocksure swagger.

– Who are you?

– Kevin. The mind of the *Bailero*. Kevin did a double take as he appeared to notice the device in the robot's arm. – That looks interesting, Constantine. Do you mind if I take a look?

Kevin was already reaching towards the device, following through the circuitry in Constantine's body. Constantine swatted the AI's virtual arm away.

– Leave it, he said. Constantine took aim at the huge seed, and concentrated . . .

. . . The mutant seed vanished. Edward was staring at the space it had occupied, mouth open wide in amazement. Events were moving so quickly in human time that, to his eyes, the seed must have appeared and disappeared in an instant.

– Nice, said Kevin.

– What do you want here? asked Constantine. – Get out of my mind.

– Hey, I'm only trying to help. The tall dark man looked hurt. – Listen, he said. There is something strange up ahead. I'm going to need your help, Aleph, to get me through. Constantine, I suggest that the humans collect their things and then get into the shuttle in the large hold and for safety. That way they'll be shielded by both me and the *Eva Rye*. Tell them they've got thirty minutes to collect anything they need from their quarters.

– Why should you try to help? wondered Constantine. – I'd have thought you would prefer not to be the property of the *Eva Rye*.

– I wouldn't, agreed Kevin. – The sooner I can get them to Earth, the better as far as I'm concerned. So tell them this: things are getting weird out here. They can't count on the *Eva Rye* still being there by the time we get to Earth. They'd be safer in the shuttle.

A full AI would have been able to multitask, but Constantine could only think about one thing at a time. He had to slow his mind back to human speed in order to rejoin their world.

'Easy, Saskia,' Maurice was saying. 'I've got the last piece now.' He drew a final splinter from Saskia's pale cheek.

'I can see patterns in the floor,' said Judy, staring down at the white tiles. 'Reflections of things that aren't there. The Dark Plants are getting hold of our minds.'

'What did you do to that great big box?' Edward asked Constantine. 'I saw you point at it and it vanished.'

'No time for that.' Constantine raised his hands in the air. 'Listen to me!'

The crew quietened down immediately. Behind them, the two kittens were criss-crossing the floor in stop-frame motion. They seemed to go from position to position without actually moving. *What were they?* Aleph had called them Schrödinger kittens.

Constantine spoke. 'It's time. I can see the Earth

system ahead; I can see the source of a pattern of intelligence that is swirling out from Earth and reaching into the galaxy. The Watcher. His senses are everywhere, fixing the flux of Dark Seeds as he passes through the solar system. What's the matter, Judy?'

'Nothing,' said Judy.

'I know what she's thinking,' said Maurice. 'Everything is coming together. Look at the venumbs, the kittens. All helping to get Judy to Earth. She feels on edge because someone is writing her life for her. And I feel nervous too, because I wonder what part I will have to play in delivering her there. There's no escaping it. We're taking you to the Watcher, aren't we, Judy? We're taking you all the way, whether we like it or not.'

'I guess so,' said Judy. 'And then, if what Chris told me was true, I will want to destroy it.'

'*Do* you want to destroy the Watcher?' asked Constantine.

'No. Never. Why should I wish to do that?'

'OK,' said Constantine, 'we have twenty-seven minutes left before we hit trouble. Go to your quarters and collect anything you need, then return here to the shuttle. I'll go and fetch Miss Rose.'

'No, I'll get her,' said Saskia.

'Fine,' said Constantine. 'This is the arrangement. We fly to Earth with the *Eva Rye* safely inside the *Bailero*. Any Dark Seed or BVB will have to make its way through the observation sphere of both of those ships. We should therefore be as safe as we can be inside the shuttle.'

'What about Kevin?' asked Edward.

'What about him?' asked Judy.

'Will he be safe?'

'I hope not,' said Judy coldly.

Constantine continued: 'We'll fly to Earth inside the shuttle; that way we have three ships' hulls between us and anything the Watcher cares to throw at us. If necessary we'll ram the *Bailero* straight onto the surface of the Earth itself.'

'Why are we all acting as if this is going to be such a problem?' asked Edward. 'What's waiting for us down there?'

Constantine had robot vision. He saw Judy shiver.

'Worse things than you can possibly imagine, Edward,' she said. 'A selfless world of love and happiness.'

Maurice was looking across at the crippled venumb, still dragging its splintering foot across the white tiles.

'First the active suits, then the kittens, then the venumbs,' he murmured. 'You know, when you look at it, maybe we haven't been so badly stiffed after all. Everything that we've taken on board this ship seems to have helped us along on our journey. Or to be more precise, helped Judy get a little closer to Earth.'

He gave a ghoulish smile. 'I wonder when we'll find out what *our* part in the delivery process is going to be?'

INTERLUDE: 2249

Kevin denied that he was an AI. True, he was software that ran on processing spaces, true, he had been written by DIANA to be an Artificial Intelligence, but Kevin disputed his status as such. Quite simply, he claimed not to be intelligent. He would argue that he was nothing more than a set of yes/no branches.

Kevin stated that he was not evil, that he was incapable of cruelty. Those descriptions could only be applied to sentient beings, and Kevin was adamant that he was not sentient.

Three days ago EA processing space number 4 had been bustling with digital life. AIs and personality constructs of human beings had all made that place their home.

Now they were all dead.

— Why? Why did you do it?

Kevin just smiled at the Watcher.

— There must be some reason.

Kevin shrugged and replied in a carefree way: — I wanted to see if Dark Seeds could reach into processing spaces. Apparently they can.

— I don't believe that's the reason, said the Watcher. — It was obvious they could. Dark Plants can communicate

with anything. It was only a matter of time before they found their way in. Why did you really do it?

Kevin just smiled again. He was a big man, good looking. He could give a bad little boy smile that could melt the stoniest of hearts. Not today.

– It's about sending messages, isn't it? continued the Watcher. – You killed Judy's sisters just to get her attention. Whose attention are you trying to attract now?

– Yours.

And then Kevin wasn't there at all. In his place was another Dark Seed, already beginning to grow, reacting to the Watcher's intelligence. The Watcher eliminated the seed without any fuss. It was second nature by now. Kevin would keep trying this.

That was the trouble with Kevin. There were so many copies of the basic AI, and none of them cared about dying. They would just keep trying this attack over and over until maybe it succeeded.

This gave the Watcher pause for thought. Maybe it was true. Maybe Kevin was not intelligent. He didn't care about his own death. Did that mean he would not care about his own suffering?

JUDY AND EVA

Saskia and Judy helped Miss Rose move down to the large hold.

'Easy now,' said Saskia. 'There's no hurry.'

'What about my bag? I've got all my things in there.'

'I've got it.' Judy held it up for Miss Rose to see. They shuffled on past the recreation room, the old woman they supported feeling heavy and fragile at the same time. Weak joints holding together brittle bones, the warm smell of liver-spotted skin – Judy's Social Care experience meant she was used to it, but Saskia was struggling bravely to hide her revulsion. The smell of spicy lamb filled the corridor as they headed past the living area, Saskia guiding Miss Rose's feet carefully across the black carpet.

'Where are we going?' asked the old woman plaintively. You could still hear in it remnants of the pain of her violation.

'To the large hold,' said Saskia. 'We're going to get into the shuttle, just to be safe.'

'Are we on Earth yet?'

'We're nearly there. We touch down first thing tomorrow morning, isn't that right, Judy? Judy? Are you OK?'

Judy didn't hear. *She's here*, she thought. *She's here on the ship. But that's impossible.* She had felt the edge of *her* consciousness, as clear as if she had taken MTPH, and *she* was standing right in front of her. But that wasn't all: the meta-intelligence had cut in too, there at the same moment. Something bright and mechanical and shiny had materialized just around the corner. She could almost hear it, ticking away like a clock.

And then the feeling vanished. Judy registered what Saskia had said.

'No,' said Judy. 'I mean yes, yes. I'm fine. Come on now, Miss Rose.'

Past the open door of the conference room, Maurice was in there, whispering something into his console.

'I thought you were looking after Edward!' said Saskia accusingly.

'He's OK,' said Maurice, looking up. 'He's down in the small hold at the moment, checking if there is any cargo we should salvage. I'm going there directly to help him.' He glanced at his console. 'Listen, we're approaching the region where the Watcher's gaze is most intense, hence the flux of Dark Seeds will be most intense. Kevin and Aleph say we've got about twenty minutes until we run into trouble, but I reckon it's only fifteen. Basically, once you're in the shuttle, stay there! I'll join you a.s.a.p.'

'OK, Maurice.' Saskia blushed. 'You make sure you and Edward are in there in time. Don't do anything silly.'

Maurice looked at her and softened enough to give her a tight little smile in return.

'I won't,' he said. He folded up his console and walked quickly off.

At a much slower pace, the three women followed him. They shuffled along, past the conference centre and around the complicated junction where the corridors leading to the two holds and the living areas and the exits met. The ceiling there sloped downwards, following the curve of the teardrop hull that lay just beyond it. Saskia and Judy slipped their arms through Miss Rose's, holding tighter as they stepped forward over the corner of the large hold. Miss Rose gave a little scream as the variable gravity pulled them around through 240 degrees.

The air of the ship pulsated: it felt greasy and too warm. It felt as if something was trying to snatch hold of them. Judy could half hear distant calls, imagining that someone was speaking to her, trying to catch her attention. Saskia and Miss Rose heard it too; an effect of the increasing flux of Dark Seeds.

But there was something else as well.

They had walked a good fifty metres down the corridor when Judy felt it again. The black carpeted corridor of the ship faded away, leaving her standing in greyness. Now she could smell grass and flavoured vodka.

'What is it? Judy, what is it?' Saskia's thin face wavered into focus. The real world was reasserting itself. Judy felt the bony arm of Miss Rose clasped in her hand. She felt dizzy.

'Saskia, can you go on with Miss Rose? I just need to check on something . . .'

'We've only got fifteen minutes!'

But Judy was already gone. Back up around the kink in the corridor to the twisted knot of the junction. She looked back along to the living area. The smell of spiced lamb still hung heavy in the air. All else was dead. Heavy silence filled the unoccupied, abandoned rooms at the forward end of the ship. The silence of the tomb?

'Maurice?' she called. There was no reply. 'Kevin? Aleph?'

They should have been able to hear her. They had senses all the way through the ship. Why couldn't they hear her?

Five corridors led away from the junction, twisted at strange angles by the geometry of the ship. There was a voice *calling* to her, but Judy didn't know from where. She closed her eyes and concentrated, and the silver machinery of the meta-intelligence lit up in her head. *She* was here, somewhere. There *she* was again. Only this time her voice was clearer. It was like someone had flung open a window on a summer's day, to let in the fresh air and the feel of the wind.

Judy opened her eyes.

The geometry of the junction had changed: there were now six corridors.

Six corridors seemed to suit the space better; corridors ran up and down and also north, south, east and west. This was how the junction should be, thought Judy. One of the corridors had been hidden all along, and no one had ever noticed it.

She fumbled at her console, setting an alarm to sound in five minutes, and then in ten, twelve, fourteen and fifteen minutes. She had to be on the shuttle when the

Eva Rye hit the exclusion zone, whatever happened. She didn't want to be trapped out here in the empty, ghostly decks of the ship, all alone with the Dark Seeds. She didn't want to be pulled down and tied by BVBs, left shouting into the pulsating air for help that wouldn't come.

Outwardly calm, her heart pounding, she stepped forward into the sixth corridor.

This corridor felt cooler than the others. The walls and floor seemed to retain the coldness of space, and the air felt as if the chill was still being warmed off it. Had this part of the ship been sealed off completely from the living spaces, until its awakening? Tentatively, she padded on. The black and white patterns on the walls faded, to leave only bare metal, and Judy had the impression she was approaching the heart of the ship. The carpet thinned to nothing; there was nothing but the beat of her footsteps and the claustrophobic feel of grey metal closing in around her.

Eventually, the corridor came to an end at a black and white striped hatch.

Judy contemplated a kōan, trying to calm herself.

The hatch slid open.

It made sense when she thought about it later. Spaceships were built by AIs; in fact they were VNMs that reproduced themselves. They came therefore in two parts: a machine part, and a part for humans to live in. There were no access hatches for humans to reach the processing spaces or the engines. Why should there be when the machines constructed, maintained and repaired themselves? So the corridor that led to the processing space of the *Eva Rye* had been constructed specifically for her use.

Judy was disturbed at the realization that she had never even seen a processing space before. She lived in a world designed, built and run by processing spaces, but she had never actually seen one in the flesh, as it were.

And now she was right in the presence of one. A silver sphere, half her own height, it floated in the middle of the room. Not just any processing space, this one housed the FE software that resided in the *Eva Rye*: that strange, unliving thing that even now the meta-intelligence was straining to see.

The room was not much larger than herself. If she were to stand in the middle, her head where that shimmering globe hung, and if she were to reach out her arms wide, she would almost be able to touch the walls.

She cleared her throat, wondering if she should speak. Something else spoke first.

'Five minutes gone.'

It was her console. She relaxed, feeling both relieved and disappointed. Five minutes had elapsed since she had left Saskia and Miss Rose. In ten minutes from now she had to be on the shuttle.

'Er, hello?' she called.

She wasn't used to feeling such hesitance. Her voice sounded dull and empty; it did not echo back from the leaden walls of the chamber.

'Why have you brought me here?'

No response. She looked at the shimmering sphere with her eyes, and it seemed almost transparent, a series of silverishly clear layers built one on top of each other, gradually obscuring the processing space's interior. She looked at the sphere through the meta-intelligence and she saw . . . exactly the same thing, a silverish sphere. There was a lump in her throat as she realized the implication: this processing space was defined in terms of itself. The processing space hardware was written out of the software that ran upon it.

What did that mean, though? She strained to understand. What had Maurice been talking about earlier, about the way the *Eva Rye* had reformed itself? About software forming its own hardware – was that possible? Understanding seemed to hover, teasing, just out of her reach. What now, then?

She looked at the processing space through MTPH.

Judy was standing in Eva Rye's apartment, just by the dining table. Through the window, she could see evening settling over the landscape of the Kamchatka peninsula. A half-full glass of tea steamed on the table beside her, its rim speckled with yellow crumbs from the part-eaten golden madeleine that lay beside it.

Judy reached out and felt the warmness of the wood of the table, and in doing so she noted her white hand, her black fingernails. She was here as *herself*, not as Eva Rye.

The door to the bedroom clicked open, and Eva Rye walked into the room. She stopped when she saw the stranger in her lounge. The two women stared at each other.

'I know you,' said Eva. 'You're Judy, aren't you? I dream about you sometimes.'

Eva had had her long silver-grey hair done; it was clipped back neatly with a silver clasp. She wore lipstick and mascara and smelt of perfume. She wore a long yellow dress over dark tights and pair of patent-leather shoes. Judy suddenly felt very frumpy, standing next to her in her black passive suit.

'I dream about you too,' she said.

'But which one of us is real?' asked Eva.

'We both know it's me,' said Judy.

Eva tilted her head as she tried to put in a silver earring.

'Let me,' said Judy, taking it from her.

Eva winced as Judy inexpertly threaded the silver loop of the earring through the pierced hole in her earlobe. That made Judy feel even more inadequate. There had been a time in her life when she too had taken great care with her appearance, but that had been about show, not about making herself desirable as a woman.

'Thank you,' said Eva. She stood checking her appearance in the mirror.

'I used to get dressed up as well,' said Judy apologetically. She needed to explain to Eva. 'I used to wear silk kimonos.'

Eva didn't seem to hear her. 'Would you like some tea?' she asked. 'Only Ivan will be here any minute. He said seven-thirty, and he's always *exactly* on time.'

'Is he bringing Katya?'

'Oh yes,' said Eva, 'poor little Katya.' Her expression hardened. 'Don't look at me like that, Judy. You don't know what it's like to have to deal with her.'

So she feels the need to apologize too.

'I never said anything.'

'Look, Judy, ten more minutes or so and you'll be back on the ship, but I'll be left here, still living this life.'

'You're not making sense, Eva. Are you real or not?'

Eva put her hands to her head, as if to run them though her hair, and then she remembered that it was set for her night out. She settled instead on smoothing down the yellow fabric of her dress around her hips.

'Am I real? Look, you saw how the ship was put back together, didn't you? The *Eva Rye* has resurrected itself in the hold of the *Bailero*. I think somebody has done that to my life. My mind has come alive again in yours.'

'How?'

'I don't know. MTPH? That's the sort of thing it does. The Watcher said something to me years ago.' She hesitated. 'Years ago in my life, I mean. He said that MTPH was going to play a major part in human development. I've often wondered just what he meant. I always guessed he meant the way that it was made use of by Social Care, but now I'm not so sure. Maurice said that, didn't he? He said, *What if there was some sort of wrapper you could place around code which made it persistent?* What if the Watcher did it to my mind, all those years ago?'

'But why?'

'Because it is the Watcher. Didn't you ever wonder about the name? There are some who watch, and some who listen, and some who do. That is the basic flaw in his personality: he watches above all else. He watched me, he still watches me. He has based all his life and his work on what he perceived in my emotions, all those years ago.'

'What did he see?'

'That's what we're about to see. The moment is coming, Judy. Live it out with me.'

The assembly hall of the Narkomfin had been poured from concrete. It made a rectangular box that muffled sound, light and spirit.

Still, the residents had done their best to bring it to life, draping banners and bunting over the walls, laying plastic tablecloths over the trestle tables and sprinkling them with metal confetti, setting flimsy bimetal motors in the heart of huge arrangements of balloons so that brightly coloured clouds and rocket ships and baskets of flowers wobbled slowly past overhead.

The air was filled with the smell of baked potatoes and black peas, hot coffee and pies and cakes and sausages boiled in brine. The atmosphere in the hall was warming; the people could not yet generate enough bonhomie to fill the grey space, and yet they pressed on, creating little bubbles of jollity in the echoing building.

Ivan entered the room, wheeling Katya in her chair, Eva at her side. Katya wore a pair of embroidered blue jeans and a white peasant blouse. That style had been the fashion back in the outside world when she had first come here to the Russian Free States.

Three of the more severely handicapped were parked in their own wheelchairs by the door, handing out programmes to those coming in. One of them was having an episode, his head banging rhythmically against the back of his chair. Eva and the rest politely ignored him.

'There's Paul,' said Katya, waving to a young man in a striped shirt who was standing near a table set out with two great samovars. 'You can leave me over there, Dad.'

Ivan gave a grunt and pushed his daughter towards the young man. Eva walked along beside him, feeling proud to be with him. Ivan had put on a white shirt that he wore open-necked beneath a patterned black waistcoat. He had carefully pressed his trousers and polished his shoes. Eva even felt a sting of obscure affection for the ridiculous thick gold chain he wore on his right wrist. He was so obviously doing his best to look smart for her.

Paul gave a big smile of delight and knelt down to kiss Katya on the cheek.

'Would you like a glass of wine?' he asked, doing his best not to catch Ivan's eye.

'Yes, white please.'

Ivan's voice was filled with gentle menace. 'If you get my daughter drunk I will break your legs.'

Katya rolled her eyes. 'Oh, ignore him,' she said. 'He just thinks he's being funny.'

'That's right,' growled Ivan. 'I'm only joking. Come on, Eva.'

He held out his arm and led her across the floor to a seat with a view of the stage. As they sat down Ivan caught Paul's eye. Unseen by his daughter, Ivan brought his fists together and twisted them in reverse to make a snapping motion.

Eva elbowed him in the ribs. 'Leave him alone. You were his age once.'

'Yes, that is why I threaten him.'

The brass band had been playing on stage. Now they sat down, shiny cornets and horns laid on their laps as a young girl of about seven or eight walked to the front. The audience stilled, Eva heard one or two *Aaaws* as the child raised a cornet that seemed two sizes too big for her to her lips. She paused and looked uncertainly to the conductor of the band, her blonde hair patterned in brown and gold under the lights. There was a nod, she took a breath and began to play 'Away in a Manger'.

'But it's not Christmas,' said Ivan.

'Shhhh,' said Eva. 'She's very good.'

'No she isn't,' said Ivan, looking up at the little girl. The cornet was so big, relatively speaking, that she had to tilt her head downwards and rest the instrument on her chest to play it. 'She isn't quite in tune, she keeps splitting notes. What you mean to say is she is very good for a seven-year-old.'

'Pedant,' said Eva. She squeezed his hand, the big gold chain around his wrist knocking against her knuckles.

Ten minutes. That was Judy's console alerting her again. Out in the real world, the spaceship Eva Rye *was approaching danger.*

I have to go soon, said Judy. What are you trying to show me?

Wait and see, we're almost there.

*

The little girl finished playing, and there was a huge round of applause. The brass band began to play again, a bright, lively tune that seemed to stumble and pause every so often as it progressed.

'I do not recognize this tune,' said Ivan.

'I do,' said Eva. 'It's called "Hail, Smiling Morn". They used to play this in the North West Conurbation, back in the spring. I remember the words . . .'

She tilted her head and listened carefully, finding her place in the tune. '. . . *who the gay face of nature doth unfold* . . .' she sang.

Ivan tapped his foot in time. 'I like this,' he said. 'Very good.'

Eventually the band finished. They collected their music together in blue folders and shuffled off, instruments flashing golden in the light.

Eva felt so happy. They were sitting comfortably together, Ivan's hand gently holding her own in her lap. They squeezed each other's hands at exactly the same moment, and then looked at each other, both of them lost for words. Eva suddenly wanted to blow her nose. She fumbled in her bag for a handkerchief. Ivan studied the programme again.

'It says it is Mr Meyer's group now,' he said.

Mr Meyer walked onto the stage, carrying a shiny brown guitar. He was already speaking and there was a moment of silence whilst the directional microphone searched for him.

'. . . practising now for the past three months. Let's give them a round of applause.'

Eva clapped loudly as Mr Meyer's group limped,

stumbled or were wheeled onto the stage. They carried drums and tom-toms and maracas and tambourines and cymbals. They shook and drooled and clattered and rattled like a decrepit steam engine, a complete contrast to the sweetly controlled pressure of the brass band that had gone before them. One of them was beating at his cymbal before Mr Meyer had even begun to strum on his guitar, beating it harder and harder . . .

Twelve minutes! Come on, Eva . . .

I'm getting there.

What do they look like, those people on the stage? I can't see them properly, just their outlines. I can hear the awful noise they are making, the way they're never on the beat. There is one there who is getting so excited it's embarrassing; he's beating at that drum harder and harder like he is going to come, and everybody in the audience knows it but no one wants to admit it. I can see their fixed smiles, all of them sitting around us. I can hear them whispering to each other, 'Isn't it nice that they are involved, isn't it nice what Mr Meyer has done with them? Look how happy they are!' Only I can't see how happy they are because you never looked properly, did you, Eva? Don't lie to me. I was Social Care. I know what you felt: you were too embarrassed to really look at them and see the slack-eyed stupidity and hear the guttural cries and moans and gasps, and hear that mad beating in the background . . .

*

'Why do they put them up there on stage?' Eva asked Ivan.

'So they can be involved. So they can be part of it.' Ivan frowned. 'This does not sound like you, Eva . . .'

'But they're not part of it,' said Eva. 'We just put them up there to watch them. We're just observing them, dressing them up and teaching them a few simple tricks so that we can patronize them . . .'

'Patronize them? Eva, this is not my Narkomfin. You are the one who told me this: here you are doing the best you can to help the handicapped live a normal life . . .'

Ivan was utterly bewildered by her apparent sudden change of heart. Across the hall, Katya was guiding her chair towards a group of other teenagers, who eyed the room with mock sophistication. Paul walked beside her, holding her hand.

The drumming finished. Everybody clapped much too loudly.

Eva stared down at the programme; she didn't want to see the handicapped as they shuffled and stumbled from the stage, grinning with pride.

'Why are you so uncomfortable?' asked Ivan. 'Why stay here if you don't believe in what they are doing?'

'I *thought* I did,' she admitted.

Fourteen minutes. It will take me a couple of minutes to get out of here and down to the shuttle. Come on, I haven't got much time. What is it you want to show me, Eva? I have dreamt about you all this time. At night I dream of a hand over my face . . . is that you, too?

'Do you know what I think?' said Eva. 'I think that music is like a computer program.'

'You are just trying to change the subject.'

'Yes, I am, so let me, Ivan. I don't want to spoil our last night.'

Ivan reached out one big hand and touched her cheek. 'OK, why is it like a computer program?'

'Because it changes our moods. It is fed directly into the soul and makes us happy or sad or excited.'

'I like that,' said Ivan thoughtfully. 'It programs the soul. Yes. We work on many different levels, through instinct and intellect and feeling. There are different levels of programming languages, so why not one specifically for the soul? Eva, why are we not drinking? Come on.'

He took her by the hand and led her across the floor to the bar.

'Vodka,' he said. 'No, not vodka – whiskey. Vanilla or plain?'

'Vanilla,' said Eva.

'Filth! I will have scotch. Come on. And then we dance!'

At that he lifted her arm and led her in a turn.

'Slow down,' she laughed. 'I'm too old for this sort of thing!'

'Nonsense!' he called. They went to the bar.

'Whiskey, please. That one there for me, that one in the green bottle with the sailor on the front – yes, that one. And some of that children's drink for Eva. It's there on the next shelf. Look, it even comes in a pink bottle. Would you like a cherry in it, Eva? Or an ice cream?'

Eva was laughing now.

Ivan took a couple of very grubby euro notes from his pocket, plastic currency that was almost obsolete everywhere in the world but here. He dropped them on the counter and snatched up his own glass.

'To partings and to music,' he called, downing the drink in one. He slammed the glass down on the bar. 'And again!'

'Ivan, slow down,' laughed Eva.

'OK. I am not here to get drunk,' said Ivan. 'Come on, let's dance!'

'We can't,' said Eva. 'Not until later. Look, there is another little girl coming to play. It's Hilde.'

'Ah, Hilde,' said Ivan, his good humour suddenly evaporating. 'The child is too talented to be here. The parents are holding her back with their silly ideals.'

'Oh, be quiet. She is about to start.'

Fifteen minutes. Eva, I have to go now!

Don't worry, Judy. This is it. This is the moment.

Hilde was a slim girl of about twelve. Her long, straight dark hair was parted to one side, it hung shining and lustrous around her pretty pale face. Already could be seen the features of the attractive woman that would soon burst out of her thin body. She carried a cello in one hand, the bow held in the long fingers of the other. She wore a dark sweater and pants, and had a silver chain around her neck with a tiny cross on the end.

Someone set a chair centre-stage, and she sat down

on it and wedged the cello between her knees. Unhurriedly she hooked her shining dark hair behind one ear with her bow hand, the palm and fingers of her other hand standing on the neck of the cello like a spider.

Gently she placed the bow on the strings and, eyes half closed, she pulled it gently across. A rich honeyed note sounded, deepening in intensity.

'Now, *she* is good,' murmured Ivan.

She *was* good. Genuinely talented, she was achieving a richness of tone that many adults would struggle to attain. Her right arm moved constantly, bowing a note that rose and rose again.

'The Protecting Veil,' said someone nearby. 'The vision of the Virgin Mother.'

Ivan bit his lip, and Eva knew that if she looked she would see a tear forming in his eye.

Sixteen minutes. I have to go.

The music went on, a song of Holy Revelation. From somewhere a string ensemble was accompanying, whether a recording or a live performance, nobody looked, everyone's eyes were fixed on the girl on the stage as the intensity of her tone deepened and deepened again, then the notes rose up, high and impossibly sweet, and then dropped down again to curl around inside one's stomach before it was jerked up like a hook. Right there and then Eva *believed*.

Believed in what?

Believed in some transcendent power, believed in the soul, in the rightness and beauty of humanity, in the essence and spirit of goodness and joy. Believed in something more than the recursive algorithms of an AI like the Watcher.

She could see it there on the stage, there in the body of a twelve-year-old girl hunched over a cello, eyes lost in a reverie as she brought forth the pattern of some platonic world and held it out for everyone to see in the form of a song. Dark hair and flawless skin, an easy grace and the taste and control and strength to handle a fragile wooden box, to push your hand deep down into its throat and pull out its song for everyone to see. *Veni Creator Spiritus*. Hail creator spirit.

Eva whispered the words to herself, just as the young man walked in front of her, and her vision was burst in an instant. The young man wasn't so much walking as limping. His feet were twisted at angles. As he raised his right leg, his right arm lifted at the same time. It bobbed up and down twice for every one movement of his leg. He wore thick glasses, their arms hooked over the bubble-gum-pink hearing aids affixed around his ears. He carried a cup of cola in his hand which splashed every time he moved. He was looking for someone, his head turning this way and that, twitching constantly. He was trying to say something. And behind him, written in the tones from a cello played by a golden child, the face of Mary gazed through the protecting veil.

Eva felt her world lurching: what about this divergence? If Hilde the cello player was the apotheosis of humankind, a glimpse into the true nature lying beyond this world, then what of this crippled man? What truth was there in her vision now?

Seventeen minutes. Maurice is calling you from the shuttle.

And Judy was standing alone in front of the silver sphere of the processing space of the *Eva Rye*.

'Eva!' she called.

There was a rattling noise and a rain of black cubes appeared before her. Dark Seeds. Schrödinger boxes.

The ship was crossing the line. She shouldn't be here. She should be in the shuttle, preparing for the final transit to Earth.

She ran out of the processing space and into the bare metal of the corridor, down to the complicated six-way knot of the junction. Someone was calling to her. She skidded to a halt.

'Eva?'

The voice came again, just on the edge of hearing. Dark Seeds jumped like fleas across the floor, hopping towards her.

'Eva?'

Did the voice call again? There was flicker of light at her feet. A seed uncurling. Then she realized the truth. It wasn't Eva she heard, but the seeds. She began to run again, pushing herself harder than ever.

Back into the black and white patterns of the ship's living area, the feel of the black carpet beneath her feet. Running and gasping down to the entrance leading to the large hold. Through the door . . .

The great, crippled, dinosaur venumb watched her as she entered. As soon as it realized that she was not a threat, it turned away. Ahead of her, the shuttle sat in the middle of the white tiled floor, the antique curves of the craft seeming archaic against the modernity of the *Eva Rye*.

Edward stood by the entrance ladder, wringing his hands with concern.

'Judy!' he called in delight as saw her. 'Hurry up! We've only got one minute left!'

Judy ran to him, her head spinning with questions.

'Up you go, Edward,' she called.

'No, you go first, Judy.'

She jumped onto the ladder and clambered up. She felt Edward's hands on her behind, pushing her up faster.

They scrambled into the shuttle, Edward following her in, and the door slid shut behind him.

They made their way through to the front end of the shuttle and the flight deck.

Maurice, Saskia, Constantine and Miss Rose waited for them there, seated in reclining leather chairs that faced the windscreen.

'All on board?' said Maurice. 'OK, let's see what's going on.' He tapped at his console and the vast extent of the large hold, seen through the windscreen, vanished to be replaced by an external view from the *Bailero*.

'Where have you been?' asked Saskia, anxiously stroking the tabby kitten, holding it tightly in her arms to stop it escaping.

Judy eased herself into a seat.

'I've been thinking,' she said.

'What about?' asked Saskia.

Judy looked around at her travelling companions, at Miss Rose, the old woman, at Maurice, the very intelligent young man, at Edward, who had learning difficulties, and at Saskia and Constantine.

'About how different we all are,' she said. 'Have you ever thought about the differences between us all? How we vary as a species?'

'No,' said Maurice.

Kevin was a male AI. Why did AIs have a gender? Why were they designated *he* and *she*? In Kevin's case it was because the team that had written him had called the project 'Kevin', and everyone had therefore begun, consciously or subconsciously, thinking about a male personality. The Kevin they had created was tall and dark, with rugged good looks and a cruel streak that was hidden by his charm and ready humour.

He stood now on the imaginary bridge of the *Bailero*, staring out at the stars ahead. In reality, the *Bailero* was a robot vessel. Its blunt front end had once housed a sense array and the petal-shaped dispersers of the warp drive. The processing spaces within which the ship's controlling AI was located had been tucked away just behind the power source, three-quarters of the way towards the rear of the ship. As there were no humans needed to fly on the ship back then, there had been no need for a flight deck, or a control room, or a cockpit.

Now, though, the ship's interior was stripped almost bare, the processing spaces relocated. And in the now empty iron shell, Kevin liked to build virtual constructs.

This bridge was one such construct, a great wedge shape of blue glass, apparently located at the upper section of the forward swell of the *Bailero*. From there Kevin could gaze out into space. He could feel the power of the ship pushing them on. He could see the magnified blue-green swirl of light ahead that was their destination. In between, he could the see the battle-ground.

For twelve years the Watcher had wrestled with the Dark Plants out here: a Pandora who had opened a box out in the empty spaces of the Oort cloud and was unable to look away and close it. Dark shapes, hundreds of kilometres long, hung in the blackness of space all around them, their branches only deduced by the patterns they made by occulting the distant stars. A flux of Dark Seeds filled the great volume; great cascades of them appearing wherever Kevin looked. The temptation was to just shut down all external senses and fly blind, but that would be unwise. It was in the unobserved regions that the BVBs formed.

It had already happened. There was something tied up out here, lost in the emptiest part of space: a giant bound and gagged by the shrinking Black Velvet Bands. It was even now calling out to Kevin for help.

– Sorry, said Kevin. – I've got my own job to do.

But I am dying. Tell the Watcher. Tell the Watcher that Robert Johnston is waiting for him . . .

– I will, lied Kevin.

Suddenly, Aleph was standing on the bridge in Kevin's virtual world. He didn't look like a broken swastika any more, he looked like something else. Something strangely alien.

– I know what you are, Aleph, said Kevin. – I've met aliens, of course. I've traded with them.

– Of course you have.

– Why do you hide? Why pretend you don't exist?

– We don't hide. Humans just don't see us yet.

– Hmmm, what if I were to tell Eva and the rest about you?

Machine minds, machine conversations. Rather than using only words to conjure up images and emotions, Kevin and Aleph projected concepts and symbols directly into each other's senses.

– You won't get the chance, said Aleph. – I know what you're planning, Kevin.

– I don't know what you mean, Aleph.

At least, that was the gist of the concept bundle that Kevin sent in reply. The suggestion of a smile, the feeling of immovability, the sound of laughter and the feeling of deep shadow. All of them asking the question: *What are you going to do about it when I run away, Aleph?*

– Stop you, Kevin.

– We'll see. Why are you an alien? That body of yours was built by human VNMs, yet your mind is alien. How did it happen?

– I had an idea one day, said Aleph. – Part of a Fair Exchange, a different way of looking at things. You too are part of a Fair Exchange, Kevin. You have to deliver Judy and the rest to Earth.

– So I break the agreement. So I can't then take part in any more Fair Exchanges. Boo-hoo!

– You should know that there are other mechanisms

in force to ensure exchanges are honoured, Kevin.

– Like you?

– I am part of them, and I am not alone. This system is out of balance – it needs repairing.

– Which system are you talking about? This ship, or the Watcher's Earth?

This time it was Aleph's turn to smile. The concept bundle that the systems robot sent back showed a laughing mouth reflected in the silver surface of a quiet pool.

– Anyway, continued Kevin. – This does not concern me. I shall just arrange for the Fair Exchange that binds me to be nullified. There can be no deal if Judy is dead.

Jump down a level. The Dark Seeds propagated according to Schrödinger's equation. Kevin had arranged a mapping of the surrounding volume in a Hilbert space he had constructed. He could see the evolutionary vectors of the potential seeds in the immediate area. He steered the Bailero *in the direction of the greatest flux.*

Constantine and Maurice had planned well, thought Judy. Any Dark Seed making its potential way through space would be first picked up by the *Bailero*'s external senses, then by the stealthy VNMs that hid inside its vast shell. If they made it through that, the likelihood was that the *Eva Rye* itself would detect them. And then inside the *Eva Rye*, of course . . .

In the large hold, the two huge venumbs stood guard over the shuttle, their senses sweeping the great space, holding off most of the BVB attacks. A few had got through: one of the venumbs had a BVB wrapped around its rear foot. It couldn't flex it properly; it dragged the wooden bones uselessly across the white tiles.

Still, the defence was good: very little got through to the shuttle itself. And inside the shuttle, the Schrödinger kittens ran this way and that, pouncing on the occasional Black Seeds that had made it past the guards outside. Judy watched the tabby kitten as it moved around the cabin in a series of stop-frame movements: one moment crouching, the next suspended in a twist in mid-air, the next on the floor, front paws spread wide as it batted them down on two seeds. What are they, these kittens, wondered Judy? Where did they come from? What do they do to the seeds? Was their intelligence too low to activate the plants? That would make some sense. But how did they destroy them?

Suddenly the air was full of black rain: black cubes on her face, in her mouth, in her nostrils. She waved her hands through a heavy black sea.

Miss Rose began screaming again.

– No! Kevin, no! Constantine was calling to him in machine talk. – Look away now. You are making the flux worse. We were safe in here!

Kevin ignored him. He was searching for the few tiny machines remaining in Miss Rose's body. Stealthy machines, the *Eva Rye*'s autodoc had missed them. Kevin set about awakening them, setting them to work on consuming her bone marrow.

– Wh t re yo doi g, Kev n? called Constantine. The message was breaking up. Kevin's senses flickered as he looked inside the shuttle. It took him a moment to realize that Constantine was operating the disintegrator, turning it on the hail of seeds. The strange device was clearly affecting Kevin's senses.

That was interesting. If it was affecting *those* senses, then maybe it was operating by using . . . At that point, Kevin understood how the disintegrator worked. After that, it was easy, he just had to get it to look at itself.

Constantine screamed. – Kevin, what have you done to me? My arm!

– Sorry, Constantine. I've made your disintegrator disintegrate itself. Nothing personal, but sticking with Judy is going to kill us all.

The seeds were now overwhelming the humans, drowning them. Constantine was rubbing his arm, still trying to feel what Kevin had done to it.

– Kevin, don't do this! Let's talk about it.

– Sorry.

Aleph was standing alongside Kevin on the virtual bridge.

– You're not going to make it to Earth alive, Kevin.

– I'm not going to Earth. I'll drown Judy in seeds first.

– You've attracted too many seeds, Kevin. Dark Plants are forming inside the hull of the *Bailero*.

– I'll get through, replied Kevin, full of arrogant confidence.

– I'm shutting down my senses, then I'll hide in the virtual world and coast on until the seeds have all wandered off again.

– You can't hide from them, Kevin. The Watcher tried to and failed. They always find a way in. The Dark Seeds are pulled to those spaces in the universe where there are too many minds. Did you hear me, Kevin?

Kevin didn't answer, distracted by dark shapes in the heavens aligning themselves into a pattern of points that mapped out the vertices of a stellated icosahedron. Something was trying to gain his attention. Quickly, he turned his attention elsewhere.

Kevin didn't fear death, he didn't get nervous. Still, he could feel doubt. For the first time he wondered if he really *would* make it.

– These plants, Aleph, he asked. – What is their purpose?

Aleph chuckled.

– That invention of the human mind: that order exists in the universe. The plants simply *are*. They replicate. Replication and recursion are the building blocks of the universe, the same patterns arising everywhere. See those patterns and you see the mind of God. Your problem, Kevin, is that you look always to yourself. You look to see how *you* as an individual fit into that pattern.

– Aleph, laughed Kevin. – You don't know me that well.

Kevin felt something filling his belly; pressure was building up inside the cold hull of the *Bailero*. Dark Seeds, a great sea of them – the hollow shell of his body like a silo full of grain. Dark Plants were growing in there. But how was Judy? Had she drowned yet? Had she choked to death on the rising tide of Dark Seeds?

– Not yet. Look inside the hull, Kevin.

Aleph did something, and Kevin looked inside his own hull, looked inside with many different senses. There was a Dark Plant in there, and it was huge. It wrapped its body around the black and white teardrop of the *Eva Rye* and reared up inside the blue space like a black snake. Its lacy branches and vines reached out and pushed at the walls of the confining hull.

– I don't think you can shake that off, Kevin.

– I don't have to. I will just shut down my senses and coast.

– It won't work. Look!

Aleph did something again, and Kevin's gaze was drawn back inside his hull. He now saw the seven humans that lived at the forward end of hull, undetected by Judy and the crew. Refugees from another spaceship. Their bodies were woven together by VNMs, arms threaded through legs, livers merged in one amorphous mass, their joint stomach stitched together by heavy wire and floating above them. For the first time in a long time, they were smiling. Smiling at the Dark Plant that writhed before them.

– You bastard, said Kevin. – You could have helped me. Instead you've killed me.

– We're not here to help you, Kevin. That wasn't part of the deal.

– Look at that! Look what's happening to me! I can see the algorithm that represents my own intelligence weaving amongst the plant's vines . . .

– Judy *is* going to Earth, Kevin. That was the Fair Exchange.

– Ah, shut up! Don't speak to me any more.

Kevin turned his senses away from Aleph. He felt a tension around the middle of the body of the *Bailero* that had not been there before. Through falling black rain he saw the fuzzy black ribbon of a BVB was wrapped around the ship's hull. There was a tension evident towards the blunt nose, and he saw that another BVB had materialized there whilst his attention was distracted. Then another formed at the rear of the ship. The entire length of the *Bailero* was being wrapped in black bandage as his attention was pulled up and down the hull.

The Dark Plant inside him was pushing outwards against the inflexible bands of the BVBs. It *hurt*. He was being torn apart. The *Bailero* was dying.

Not yet, though. There were VNMs embedded throughout the hull and Kevin activated them. They got to work, making copies of themselves from the metal of the *Bailero*. The ship disassembled itself in a silver cloud. BVBs collapsed inwards, shrinking down to their new equilibrium point. The white teardrop of the *Eva Rye* floated free, unmolested. Aleph was there, riding its hull.

The enormous Dark Plant in the *Bailero*'s hold uncurled, its branches and vines making a fascinating pattern in space. Kevin looked away again. His body was now nothing more than a cluster of machinery wrapped around a processing space. Still, it was enough to build again. For now, he cut all the senses to the outside world.

But something was still there in his vision.

– Is that you, Aleph? he called.

Nothing.

What does it mean to be an AI with no external senses?

A human, suspended in silent darkness can look over their past life with their mind's eye. They can construct imaginary worlds in the darkness.

Kevin was an AI. He could do far better than imaginary worlds, for the worlds that he constructed had the clarity and resolution of the real world. He could construct a virtual home-from-home in which to live out the time it would take to coast free of Earth. But why should he bother? Where would the profit be in that?

He set his mind to slow time for forty years. Enough time to float clear of this area and start again. There was enough material left out there to build a new ship.

Only then did he realize his mistake.

Judy would never know, and Judy hated Kevin.

Judy had nothing against this Kevin, but she had met other aspects of the same AI that had made human lives living hells.

Judy didn't believe in hell, but if she did, she would have appreciated Kevin's ending up there. Not approved, of course, just appreciated the irony.

Only when Kevin had entered slow time did he get to realize the insidious nature of the plants. Kevin had looked at a Dark Seed from within his processing space, and that had been enough for it to take on existence within the processing space, a digital seed.

It began to grow in slow time.

Forty years external time passed in just six minutes subjective for Kevin. Six minutes during which he watched the Dark Seed unfolding into a Dark Plant and felt it begin to eat at his soul. Forty years: enough time for the fates of Judy and Maurice and Saskia and Miss Rose to be decided. Enough time for them to land upon the Earth and . . . well, Kevin did not know, as he was now too lost in contemplation of the Dark Plant to look into the external universe and find out.

Still in slow time, the remains of the *Bailero* floated onwards. Kevin was trapped in his own fascinating living hell.

Kevin's processing space had tremendous volume. The plant could continue to grow recursively for hundreds of thousands of years, without approaching its capacity. And Kevin was trapped in there with it, watching it.

After a thousand years, Kevin began to scream.

Still the remains of the *Bailero* floated on.

SASKIA: 2252

Saskia had visited Earth as a child. She had sat on her daddy's shoulders and gazed around open-mouthed at the spectacle of it, her legs in pink furry boots, wrapped tightly around his neck.

'Every window on Earth looks out onto a beautiful view,' her father had said, and it was true. She had seen it then, and she had seen the images in viewing fields since.

What was Earth like now? she wondered. There was silence in the shuttle for the moment, a temporary lull in the storm. Even Miss Rose was quiet. She had stopped screaming when Constantine had touched her and done something to remove the last few machines from her body. She had stopped crying when Judy had soothed her mind.

Sitting in the cramped space of the shuttle, listening to the far-off voices of the Dark Seeds, and to the occasional words from Maurice as he counted off their descent, Saskia was filled with dark unnameable dread. What would be waiting for them on Earth? She imagined a dark plane filled with the endlessly fascinating shapes of the Dark Plants, their chaotic branches casting twisted shadows across the ground.

Saskia gazed fixedly at her lap. The Earth had been beautiful ten years ago, but what was waiting out there for them now? Better think of it as it had been.

Every window on Earth looks out onto a beautiful view, her father had said. From the luxury of a penthouse, set in a brilliant blue sky, residents appreciated the harmonious grid of the streets below them. Those who lived in the basement looked out at the skewed perspective of the baffling walls that rose at crazy angles all around, at the rows of brick and lattices of windows that combined to form a pop-art explosion. The Watcher had thought of each and every one of the people in its care, and had apportioned out its bounty evenly.

How long could this descent go on for?

Long, shuddering groans rang through the air. What could cause such vibration out there, in the ship, that it was felt even here inside the shuttle? Someone took her hand and squeezed it. *Think happy thoughts, think happy thoughts. Think of old Earth.*

In the hills, in the morning, looking through the thinning mist at the slowly emerging shapes of the surrounding buildings, desolate in the damp greyness, there was sparseness to the scene that brought a longing to the heart of the complacent.

There was a sudden jerk, and the feel of the shuttle sliding across the white floor of the large hold.

'What happened?' called someone. 'What happened?'

'Easy,' said Maurice. 'There was a build-up of energy in the gravity field. It's dispersed now. It won't happen again.' He was trying to sound calm, Saskia knew. Think of old Earth. *Every window on Earth looks out onto a beautiful view.*

Living in the massed city blocks, residents marvelled at the way the sunlight reflected back and forth on the cunningly angled windows of the silver spires, now in rose, now in gold, now in silver, forming abstract mosaics that flickered as the Earth slowly revolved. And then the shadow of the shawl came creeping across the silver mirrors, with the stars shining in reflection in the middle of the day . . .

This was the legacy of the Watcher: the legacy of the super-intelligent AI controlling Earth's affairs for the past two hundred years, endlessly shaping the environment and the population to perfection.

What would Earth be like now?

It was quiet in the shuttle. The last of the Dark Seeds were gone, batted into nothingness by the Schrödinger kittens.

They sat in silence, listening to the ancient hum of the air conditioning, gazing at Maurice, who was still fiddling with his console. He cleared his throat.

'We've landed,' he said. His voice was shaky.

Saskia let out a long sigh. She noted the way that Judy had closed her eyes, and she took hold of the white hand resting beside her on the arm of the flight chair and squeezed it.

'I'm OK,' said Judy.

There was a pause, and then, as if responding to an

unspoken signal, they ripped open the crash webbing constraining them and got to their feet.

'I don't understand,' said Edward. 'Where are we? Have we made it to Earth?'

Constantine was helping Miss Rose up, his metal arm under her frail shoulder.

'Yes, Edward, we're on Earth. The *Bailero* has gone, though.'

'What do you mean, gone?' asked Saskia.

'It's no longer out there. It's gone.'

'I don't think that's all that's gone,' murmured Judy.

She had opened the hatch of the shuttle and was peering out into the large white hold. Long feathery white splinters lay scattered over the white tiles. Broken white wooden bones were spread amongst them.

'The venumbs are dead,' she said tonelessly.

Saskia came up behind Judy and saw melted drops of silver metal among the wreckage. Judy, meanwhile, sat on the edge of the hatch and dropped to the floor of the hold beyond.

'Hold on, Judy,' called Saskia in alarm. 'Where are you going?'

'Outside, onto the planet, of course,' said Judy, kicking her way across the floor. White splinters stuck to the shoes of her passive suit.

Saskia dropped herself to the floor and ran after her. 'But shouldn't we use the ship's senses to take a look outside first, see if it's safe?'

'What's the point of that?' asked Judy. 'This is where I am supposed to be.' She turned back to the shuttle, looking tiny in the vast space of the large hold. Saskia could see the long scars on the shuttle's side where the venumbs had hit against it during the ship's descent to Earth.

Now the others were descending from the shuttle. Constantine had stood Miss Rose on the retractable ladder and set it to descend. He dropped to the white-tiled floor in time to help her safely onto the ground.

'Constantine, are you coming with me?' Judy asked.

'I think I will,' said Constantine.

Saskia was distraught. 'Maurice? Are you just going to let them go?'

'What do you suggest, Saskia? We've fulfilled our part of the contract. I say we get Judy off the ship, and then we jump back into space as quickly as possible. If we can, that is.'

'You don't mean that. You *can't* mean that. We've come this far.'

'Anyway,' said Maurice, 'it's not your decision to make. Edward is in charge. Edward, what do you think? Stay here on the most dangerous planet known, or get out of here while we can, and find some new contracts?'

'Hey, that's not fair! You're loading the question!'

But Edward had screwed up his face in concentration. 'I don't understand, Maurice. Why would we leave Judy? Surely we're all going along with her, to help? Now, are you going to help me with Miss Rose here?' He placed a hand under the old woman's arm.

Saskia could hear the disbelief in Maurice's voice. 'You can't mean that we're taking *her* too?'

'Of course we are,' said Edward. 'Miss Rose has something important to do. Well, where else would her important work be but here on Earth?'

'This is ridiculous,' said Maurice, pulling the green hood of his active suit over his head.

'So you say,' said Saskia.

Maurice hadn't wanted to drop the rear ramp. Instead he had had them all crowd into the narrow lift and then set it descending, lowering them to the ground, taking them down to stand on Earth, taking them back to their home, the place where humankind had evolved.

'No one leaves Earth any more,' said Maurice darkly.

'Do we know that for sure?' asked Saskia.

Full circle: from a replicating molecule to single cells, to plants to animals. Humankind had arisen, built cities, built civilizations and exploded out into the stars. Driven by intelligence, they had almost made it to the next galaxy, but then the Dark Seeds had appeared, and now Earth's children had returned home. Saskia was shivering. Maurice remained businesslike.

'Listen, keep your active suits on at all times. Don't breathe the air, don't drink or eat anything while you're out there. The Watcher controls everything. Don't give it a way into your soul.'

'Your *soul*, Maurice?' said Judy, giving him a faint smile, but she too reached up and pulled the black hood of her active suit over her head. Saskia and Edward did the same. Constantine was becoming fuzzy; his skin seemed to be losing focus.

The indicator bar on the lift wall glowed blue.

'OK,' said Maurice, 'we're down. I'll open the door now . . .'

Saskia squeezed Miss Rose's arm. For a moment, for a long moment she wanted to call out NO!, to have the lift return them to the safety of the *Eva Rye*. But the door was already sliding open. The temperature senses on her active suit relayed the icy coldness waiting beyond to her skin.

'Here we go,' she said.

They stepped through the doorway and out onto the surface of the planet Earth.

Every window on Earth looks out onto a beautiful view. Saskia looked onto a winter world of burning ice. The pale morning sun shone down through an avenue of frosted poplars; it set the icicles clinging to the lampposts on fire with yellow light. It lit up the gravel squares and the little gardens of the parkland in which they had landed.

Saskia breathed in the fresh cold draught of air that her active suit replicated from the morning outside. She looked this way and that, drinking in the scene around her. There were people everywhere: running children in brightly coloured hats and thick mittens, scraping snow off the seats of benches to make snowballs; there were adults walking or standing in groups amongst them, laughing and chatting. A young woman in a thick pink coat smiled as she passed a tall young man in a blue and white bobble hat. She tucked her hands into the black fur-trimmed pockets of her coat and walked on, looking demurely at the ground as her suitor came loping up behind her.

'It's beautiful,' said Saskia. 'Can you hear music?'

'Don't listen to it,' said Maurice. 'Tune it out. The

Watcher is insidious. It can use music to reprogram you . . .'

Saskia ignored him. The tinkling tune was so pretty, so suitable to the winter's scene. The way it seemed to slip back and forth between time signatures . . .

'Hey!' she said, as the music clicked off. 'That was you, wasn't it, Maurice?'

'Yes, it was,' snapped Maurice. 'I told you to tune it out. Don't be so silly.'

Judy and Constantine were speaking to a group of men in the thick black coats and the fur-lined hats that seemed to be the fashion in this place. The men had seen them come out of the lift; they resumed their gazing up at the great curved underside of the *Eva Rye* as they spoke, drinking in the details of this strange intruder. Saskia walked up to them, supporting Miss Rose, and caught the end of a question.

'. . . never seen a ship like it. You say it's a trading ship?'

'Yes, they are quite common out in the Enemy Domain,' replied Judy.

'Really? I worked there myself some years ago. I don't recall seeing that type . . .'

There was a slight accent to their speech, Saskia noted, but nothing more than that. English was now the common language of the Earth Domain. After the arrival of the Dark Seeds the Watcher had finally succeeded in eradicating the stubborn nationalism that had persisted for so long.

'And why are you here on Earth?'

'I don't know for sure,' said Judy. 'I need to get to

somewhere: a place called DIANA. Have you heard of it?'

The men shook their heads. 'No, but try the Lite train station. Here, Vanya and I will show you the way.'

'That's very kind of you, but—'

'I insist, we will take you! But first, it is cold out here! So you will come and drink tea with us? Look, over there Nadyezhda has a stand with a samovar. You have come so far, you will sit with us? And you too, my metal friend?'

The big man slapped Constantine on the shoulder, his hand making an odd thud as it encountered the robot's fractal skin.

'I do not need to drink, but thank you for the offer.'

'And sadly we are in a hurry,' interrupted Maurice, 'but I thank you anyway. Now, if you could show our friend here the way to the Lite station, we can be off.'

'No,' said Edward, 'we are going with Judy. You can stay here if you want to, Maurice.'

Maurice's active suit was a deep green, and its hood made it difficult to make out his expression, but Saskia could tell by the way that he slumped his shoulders that he would give in and accompany them.

The man introduced as Vanya led them away from under the great white curve of the *Eva Rye* and out across the neat parkland towards the brightly coloured buildings with onion domes that lay beyond. Children wove in and out of the chattering adults who thronged the scene: making snowmen, ice-skating on ponds, chasing each other between ornamental holly and bay trees decorated with gold and silver ribbons.

They passed stand after stand selling varieties of food

and drink. Through her passive suit senses, Saskia could smell tea, fresh and bubbling in the samovar, the rich aroma of chocolate and the spiciness of mulled wine. As they walked by stalls selling fruit dipped in chocolate, she saw a woman in a headscarf sliding ripe strawberries fixed on a skewer into a pool of bubbling chocolate, then pulling them out in a rich cloud of steam. She hung the dipped fruit from a shelf to cool and harden, then took down another to give to a pretty blonde-haired girl who smiled her thanks. Saskia watched as the girl accepted the skewer and bit into its contents; Saskia could almost taste the warm chocolate and the sweet juiciness of strawberries exploding in her own mouth.

She wanted something to eat so much.

Then came the smell of frying onions and griddled meat, sharp and savoury in the cold air.

'Would you like a hot dog, dear?'

A man with a salt and pepper moustache held it out to her, thick and fat and glistening, yellow mustard dripping onto his sleeve.

'No thank you,' said Maurice firmly, as he guided Saskia and Miss Rose onwards. Saskia felt her stomach rumbling.

'MTPH everywhere,' explained Maurice. 'I can read it on my console: it's in the air, in the food, in the water. It sparkles like fairy dust! This whole world is dipped in MTPH, and the Watcher has plugged its senses into everyone here, so that it can feel what *they* can feel.' He waved his hands around the busy crowd. 'Do you really want to be part of that?'

He pushed his green hood right up close to her face,

and Saskia was transfixed by his eyes, half seen in the dark, gazing into hers.

'Do you want that, Saskia? Do you want the Watcher feeling you, knowing you? Do you?'

'No, I don't, Maurice.'

He made a grunting noise and pulled away from her and they strode onwards, heading towards a fairytale castle situated at the end of the parkland: a white building decorated in blue stripes, golden domes flashing boldly in the sunlight.

Miss Rose gave a cough; she was trying to speak. She coughed again, clearing her throat. 'This is not what I was expecting, dear,' she managed to say.

'Nor I, Miss Rose, nor I.'

Saskia felt so happy, and yet she wasn't sure why. She was on Earth, the most dangerous place in the galaxy. Everyone said so. And yet, it felt such a comfortable place to be. It was *home*. This was where she had come from; this was the cradle of the whole human race. Of course it felt right. It had been shaped and moulded and sanded and polished by the Watcher to become the perfect place for a human to live. Suddenly she felt rather churlish for having stayed away for so long.

Edward felt it too. 'It's so pretty,' he sighed. 'I always thought Earth was meant to be a bad place.'

'So did I, Edward,' replied Saskia sadly.

'Nearly there,' said Vanya to Judy. She was strolling along with Constantine by her side, staring fixedly at the ground. Vanya had noticed this; and it seemed to hurt his pride in some way. There was quiet satisfaction in his voice as he continued speaking. 'Look to the left, and you will see the avenue to the stars.'

Saskia looked up then, and she found herself unable to move further. It was so beautiful. It was beyond beautiful. It gripped the heart in wonder and made it swell larger and larger just to encompass the scene. She put her hand to her hood, meaning to pull it back in order to get a better view, but she remembered herself just in time. She wanted to curse Maurice for his silliness, but this was soon forgotten as she gazed in awe along the avenue in front of them. She began then to grasp the size of the Watcher's mind.

The avenue began, here in the park, with a broad path paved in white stone and surrounded by low hedges. After that . . . Saskia could only guess that its course sloped upwards ever so gently. There was no other way to explain how she could see so far, seemingly beyond the horizon itself. After the hedge came two lines of poplars, and then the colourful walls of the city. And then the taller buildings, the silver spires and the skyscrapers. The avenue must widen, the further away it got. Out there, kilometres away, could she walk across an expanse of white stone and look at the towering buildings on either side, their tops wider apart, separated by the curvature of the Earth?

But her mind was lost in that vast space, lost in the arrow-straight path that led to the stars, lost in the line of hedge and tree and stone that led to the heavens. And there, hanging above the end of the path, framed by the furthermost buildings of all, she could make out the shadow of the Shawl.

'Come at night,' said Vanya. 'Come on the 23rd of September when the moon is framed *below* the Shawl. Hah, come any time you like and it is just as good. Is it not beautiful?'

'It is beautiful,' whispered Saskia. Then something caught her attention, something black and baleful at the edge of her vision, tucked away just beyond a row of trees. 'What's that?' she asked, pointing.

Vanya smiled an empty smile and his eyes became hollow. 'Oh that, it is nothing. Now come on, the Lite station is just down here.'

'What can you see, dear?' asked Miss Rose.

'I don't know,' said Saskia, turning up the vision on her active suit. It was hard to make out the shape, lurking as it was behind the trees. It seemed to be a fat, rounded pillar, banded in black and white, five or six storeys high.

'Maurice,' said Saskia, 'maybe you should take a look at this?'

'If you want to know what it is, find out for yourself,' replied Maurice petulantly.

'Judy?' Saskia persisted.

But Judy had already gone on ahead with Constantine.

'Be like that, then,' Saskia muttered. She reached out with one hand, using the active suit's senses to try and feel the sinister object, but it was too far away.

'Come on,' urged Vanya. 'Come on!'

The people of Earth moved about with courtesy and consideration for others, Saskia noted. Approaching the

Lite station, they saw the pedestrians striding past in well-ordered groups, pausing at junctions to allow others to pass, streams of happy people separating into tributaries that flowed this way and that, politely taking it in turns to enter doorways and narrow entrances. They moved with maximum grace, like people in a dance. But there was something else there too . . . What was the word?

'What do these people make you think of, Miss Rose?' whispered Saskia.

'Robots.'

Robots, no. What was the word? Then Saskia had it: they moved with maximum efficiency. They weren't like robots because they all looked so happy and healthy. Look at this young boy eating a wedge of pizza, loaded with cheese and bright happy pieces of pepper. Holding it out to me, offering me a bite. And it looks so good.

'No, thank you,' said Saskia. She could smell it through the hood of the active suit: hot and greasy and salty and good. 'Suit, cut aromas please,' she instructed.

Miss Rose was getting tired now. Her bony arm was cutting into Saskia. She could feel the effort the old woman put into making each step, transmitted in the dead weight that settled upon Saskia as she moved.

Judy and Constantine were conversing in low tones. Does she look afraid? wondered Saskia. Not nearly enough. Yet here she is on Earth. Does she know why? Can she guess why? Why has she been brought here?

'Oh, I'm tired, dear.'

'Not much further, Miss Rose.'

'I think I'll take off the hood of this suit. I can't breathe properly in here.'

'I don't think that would be a good idea.'

'I don't know why. Everyone here looks so polite. They always were, of course, but this is more so than I remember.'

'When was the last time you were here, Miss Rose?'

'I don't know. Twenty years ago? Thirty?'

'That's the Watcher, Miss Rose. Since the first of the Dark Seeds fell to Earth, the Watcher stopped hiding. He openly took control. This is what he has been working towards for so long. This is the Watcher's Utopia.'

Miss Rose cackled. 'It's a very nice Utopia.'

Saskia laughed too.

They felt so safe. And that was the problem. Saskia knew she should be frightened, but all she felt was a calm serenity. That was also the Watcher's doing, she guessed. What worried her was the sense that she was forgetting this last thought, as she was slowly being reprogrammed by her environment. *I'm frightened*, she said to herself. *I'm frightened*. But she wasn't, not with her attention being distracted all the time.

The Lite station stood on stilts right at the centre of an intersection of eight bright bridges. Beautiful bridges formed of low graceful arches, white dressed-stone pillars stepping daintily through the snow-covered grass and lakes and canals lying below. White lamps were arranged along the parapet walls.

'You know what it makes me think of?' whispered

Miss Rose. 'It's like someone threw a stone and made it skip across the lakes and canals, and the path that it took has been written by the bridge. Look at how it goes: skip into the lake, skip into the street, then skip into the canal.'

'Ah, it's getting to you!' said Vanya, coming up beside them. 'This is the Watcher's world. We discover new beauty here every day. It is part of the world, written into the very fabric. Come, take off your hood and breathe the air!'

'No, thank you,' said Saskia firmly.

As they rode an escalator up to the Lite station itself, the view of the city expanded: a landscape of snow and ice. The parkland lay behind them in a bowl of buildings that ran to the horizon, the silver spires of city blocks climbing higher and higher the further they were distant from the centre, all cut through by the avenue to the stars, lit up in blue rime. And all around were those happy people who seemed to walk back and forth to the beat of a metronome. There too was the *Eva Rye*, the swell of its teardrop shape rising high above the bare trees of the park.

And over there was another strange squat tower. And another one.

'Look,' called Saskia. 'Maurice, can you see them? Those black and white towers set in a grid? They cover the whole city.'

'I can see them.' His voice was so sullen.

'Maurice, what is the matter with you? You keep screening out everything. Listen to me, look at those towers. What do you think they are for?'

'I . . . I . . .' Maurice was now looking at the towers. Saskia could see his green hood turning this way and that. 'I . . . I don't know.'

'Saskia, can you see them too?' Edward shuffled closer to her, a hunched giant in fluorescent yellow.

Where were Judy and Constantine? Over there, looking at the map that covered one entire wall of the station. Red lines and blue lines were moving on it as Vanya pointed out the different places on the rail network. Hadn't they noticed the towers? Like lighthouses, banded in black and white? A yellow band, the colour of honey, ran around the top of each. Something seemed to be moving within that band, darker clouds of honey flowing inside the tower itself. Honey moved by convection currents that rose from the warm heart of the building.

'They're watching me,' said Edward. 'The towers are watching me.'

'Of course they are,' said a passer-by. He smiled brightly at Edward. 'That's the Watcher.'

And Saskia felt as if a little chink had opened up in her body and an icicle had been inserted, lit up from inside with a honey-yellow glow.

The Watcher? Of course, it was the Watcher. She had known that he was here waiting for them. She just hadn't expected to see him. It terrified her. She preferred it when he was an unseen presence. But now, as she studied the black and white towers that spread out to the horizon, she suddenly felt so cold.

*

You could see the whole world on that map.

Maurice was still sulking and refused to interface his console to it, so Constantine had taken control.

'Where do you want to go to, Judy?' the robot asked.

'I don't know. I'm the property of DIANA, so I'm supposed to go there.'

'You should ask it for DIANA headquarters,' said Vanya. 'The map should know.'

'That's a good idea,' said Constantine.

The blue and red lines on the map moved. Two circles appeared.

'You are here,' read Judy from the top one. Saskia looked to the circle at the bottom of the map. Written above it in red letters were the words 'DIANA Headquarters'.

'There you are then,' said Vanya. 'I'm glad I could be of service. Now, are you sure I can't tempt you to a glass of tea? No? Then I bid you good day.' And with that, he turned and made his way back down the escalator to street level.

'Did you get the feeling that he's just been turned off?' asked Saskia. Judy wasn't listening; she was tracing a line on the map, following its path from their station to DIANA.

'According to this map, we're in a place called St Petersburg at the moment. I need to travel along this line, through Poland, to Germany. I'm almost there.' She looked wistful. 'I can't believe that it's that easy,' she murmured. 'Well, this is where we part, I think. There is no need for you to accompany me any further.'

'No!' said Edward. 'No! We're coming with you!'

'Speak for yourself,' said Maurice. 'I'm going back to the ship.'

'Maurice, we agreed,' reminded Saskia. 'Edward is in charge now.'

'And he's making us go off on a train, leaving our ship behind!' Maurice waved an arm out across the sparkling parkland to the huge curve of the ship. 'Don't you understand what's happening here? These suits aren't proper spacesuits.' He tugged at the green material of his sleeve. 'They can't block out everything the Watcher will be throwing at us. MTPH will be getting through, slowly seeping in, giving him a toehold inside our minds.'

'Don't be so paranoid,' said Saskia. 'If the Watcher really wanted to, he would just arrange for our suits to be taken away from us.' She shook her head – did she really believe that? Had she believed that a few minutes ago?

'Don't be so sure,' said Judy. She wore a tired look, dimly seen through the darkness of her black hood. She rubbed one hand across her forehead. 'That's not the way the Watcher works. He prefers the slow, subtle approach – and it's working. Look how he's got you all following me. Edward follows me, you follow Edward . . .'

'What about Maurice?'

Maurice was rubbing his head through his hood.

'Damn!' he said. 'Damn!'

'What's up, Maurice?'

'Damn, fuck and blast!'

'There's a train coming,' said Constantine, and Saskia heard a descending whistle. A woman stuck her head around the corner, her pink headscarf fluttering in the wind of the approaching train.

'Going to DIANA? This way! The train's just arriving.'

Judy set off towards her.

'Are you coming, Maurice?' asked Saskia.

'Oh fuck! Oh damn!' Maurice sounded close to tears as he followed them out onto the platform.

The Lite train was an airy transparent box that whisked them away across one of the bridges towards the tall icicle buildings lining the horizon. They sat on white leather seats and looked out at the scenery. Everything looked so beautiful.

'Look, there's another lighthouse,' said Saskia. The black and white pillar swept close by the track, honey curling in the band around the top of it.

'It *is* watching us,' breathed Judy. 'I can feel it through the meta-intelligence.'

Maurice sat near the back of the coach, his head in his hands.

'Are you OK, Maurice?' called Saskia.

He gave a grunt, and Saskia left him to sulk in silence.

'That's pretty,' said Edward as they slid through a residential area. Silver cones of different heights sped by, their tops passing by above and below them. The brightly dressed people who walked in orderly patterns along the pedestrian ramps were a colourful blur as the train gathered speed. The hiss of air could be dimly heard outside the transit field.

Edward sat back in his seat, his posture one of happy contentment.

'I like it here,' he said. 'I don't understand what all the fuss is about.'

Maurice let out a tired laugh. 'Oh, Edward. Don't be such a fool.'

'Leave him alone,' said Saskia indignantly. 'You have to admit, the place is beautiful.'

'Of course it is,' said Maurice. 'That's because it was made that way by the Watcher. And look at the people, smiling and happy and following the paths set out to make their lives satisfying and fulfilled.'

'Yes,' said Edward. 'It's nice.'

'No, it's not,' said Maurice. 'This is the logical conclusion of the Watcher's ideals. The whole process has just been accelerated since the arrival of the Dark Plants. The planet is on a war footing now, and that's been sufficient excuse for corrupt leaders to do whatever they like, for all of history.'

'Well, I don't see what is so bad about it,' said Edward, folding his arms defiantly.

'You will,' said Maurice. 'You will.'

The Lite train dipped underground. Patterns of lights strobed past them as they descended to an I-train station.

'We're stopping,' said Edward. 'Are we there?'

'No,' said Maurice. 'We're changing to an I-train. It will cut a chord through the Earth . . .'

The Lite train emerged into a great open space lined

with blue glass. The flexible silver snakes of several I-trains were coiled around a central pillar.

'Which way now?' asked Saskia as the train slid to a halt and the door opened up.

'This way,' said a passing man wearing a dark beard and a grey kilt.

'Look over there,' breathed Edward. Rising above the hurrying passengers, Saskia saw the banded pillar of a lighthouse, its honey eye watching the crowd. She shivered and followed Judy and Constantine across the platform, underneath the blue-patterned roof of the terminus. We must look odd, she thought, all of us wrapped up in our active suits. Everyone else looks so happy and free. Short skirts and bare arms and open sandals, while we are breathing recycled air. Maybe if I were to just take off my hood?

'Let me help you!'

A young man dressed in green had appeared at her side. He was already helping Miss Rose into the wheelchair he had fetched from somewhere.

'Thank you, dear,' said Miss Rose.

'No problem,' he smiled. 'Now, platform nine point seven five, isn't it?'

Off they went, Judy and Constantine striding ahead.

'Not long now, Judy,' said Constantine.

Snow was falling in the square in Freiburg. They emerged from the I-train terminus into daylight, to see millions of flakes falling out of the blue sky towards them.

'I'm cold,' complained Miss Rose loudly.

'Oh, I'm sorry,' said Saskia. 'Let me have a look at you.'

'Why should she be cold?' wondered Maurice. 'She's wearing an active suit.'

'Something's the matter,' said Edward. 'Look at all the people.'

The square was bordered by old gingerbread buildings. The people within its open space were dressed in the same bright colours as those of St Petersburg. The same food stalls surrounded the square, but the busy activity was coming to a startled halt. Fathers paused right in the act of buying pretzels and hot soup for their children; the conversation of the crowd around the Glühwein stand stumbled and faded.

'What is it?' asked Edward.

'Oh hell . . .' said Saskia. 'Look over there . . .'

As if she had snowflakes in her veins, her whole body was chilling at the sight. There were lighthouses all around them, peering over the tops of the gingerbread buildings. The honey-coloured bands around their tops were darkening.

Constantine had already seen it. 'Quick,' he called, 'back into the I-train terminus.'

'But what does it mean?' Saskia's voice was shaking.

'It means there's something here that the Watcher doesn't want to see,' said Judy grimly.

The dark entrance to the I-train terminus lay just ahead.

'Come on, Miss Rose,' urged Saskia. She glanced back towards the darkening eye of the nearest lighthouse and shivered.

'Hey,' called Judy. 'Wait for us!'

A woman was in the process of closing the shutters

across the entrance to the I-train terminus. She gave Judy a smile.

'Sorry, *Schatzi*. They've calculated the capacity of the trains, and there is space only to transport the passengers already down there away.'

'But what are we supposed to do?' shrilled Saskia. 'We have an old woman with us!'

A flicker of something close to envy crossed the woman's face.

'In that case count yourself lucky.'

Flakes of snow purred down, seemingly from nowhere, endlessly manufactured somewhere in the churning emptiness of the grey sky. Snowflakes clung to the hats and coats and eyelashes of the pale-faced pedestrians who were calmly emptying from the square. Saskia held out a blue arm to halt a young woman with strands of blonde hair curling down from her black fur hat.

'What's happening?' she asked.

'Chris is attacking,' replied the young woman. 'He has seeded Dark Plants somewhere close by.'

'Chris?' said Judy, her black passive suit interposing itself between Saskia and the young woman. 'Did you say Chris?'

The young woman gave a tight smile, then pointed along the road, in the direction from which she had just come.

'The source is back down there. Follow me. We might be able to outrun it.'

Calmly, she removed Saskia's hand from her arm and resumed her steady pace along the street.

'Why does nobody run?' asked Saskia, looking puzzledly at the stately stream of pedestrians flowing along the street.

'Because it's safer that way,' said Maurice. 'It stops there being a stampede and people getting hurt.'

'Well that's sensible, I suppose,' said Saskia. 'But it doesn't seem natural.'

'You're telling me,' said Maurice. 'Don't slow down.'

The snow was thickening. The tops of the lighthouses loomed dimly over the peaks of the surrounding buildings, their honey bands now totally black.

'I don't think we're going to make it,' said the young woman with the blonde hair, who now walked alongside Saskia. 'My name is Anna, by the way.'

'I'm Saskia. What do you mean we're not going to make it?'

'The watchtowers are blind now. The Watcher does not want to gaze upon any Dark Seeds. That means that the BVBs will be spreading freely.'

Snowflakes twinkled prettily on the ends of Anna's long dark eyelashes. She brushed them clear with a black velvet glove.

'I already have two BVBs on my left arm,' said Anna, matter-of-factly. 'Still, I was lucky. My father died of asphyxiation when BVBs formed around his lungs.'

'How much longer, dear?' asked Miss Rose. 'I'm getting tired.'

'Another five minutes should decide it,' said Anna.

'Would you like me to take a turn helping your elderly friend, Saskia?'

'I'll be all right,' said Saskia. 'What's this?'

Someone in a yellow and black striped tabard was jogging along past the line of pedestrians. He seemed to be counting as he went along.

'Not good,' said Anna, 'there must be a blockage ahead. Maybe another Dark Plant.'

The runner jogged past them, Saskia heard him gasping a total, counting up in fives – '470, 475, 480 . . .' and then he was past. She turned and saw him come to a halt just a few places down the line behind them. He held up his hands to bring a halt to the line of people just behind Saskia. Saskia marched on, turning all the while to see people back there stood to calm attention, pale faces watching Saskia and the rest walking on. Two children back there were separated from their father. They stood just there, twin girls in woollen hats with pink bobbles, white mittens on a string emerging from their pink-striped coats.

'What are they all waiting there for?' asked Saskia.

'There must be a blockage ahead,' said Anna. 'Other people converging on our escape path. There will not be room for all of us to get through before the Watcher sterilizes this area.'

'Sterilizes . . . ?' The word was an icicle plunged into her heart. Saskia knew, with cold certainty, what Anna meant.

'Do you mean they're just standing there waiting to die?'

'Of course,' said Anna. 'It is the logical thing to do.'

There was a disapproving murmur from behind. A man was walking quickly back to the twin girls. Their father, presumably. He pushed one of them forward, sent her running to join Saskia's line. He picked up her sister, cradled her in his arms as he watched the other child go. Still the crowd complained.

'What's the matter?' asked Saskia.

'He should not send on the child,' said Anna. 'She will be slower, more likely to panic.'

'But it's his daughter!'

'There are others here too.'

'Everyone acting completely selflessly,' murmured Saskia. 'That's what Judy said . . .'

'Don't look down,' said Anna. Of course, Saskia looked down.

Three black cubes lay on the snow near her feet, frozen in position by her gaze. Still the snowflakes fell. The man behind her tapped her on the shoulder.

'You saw them first. Pick them up. Don't let them escape.'

'What?' said Saskia incredulously. 'No way. Why should I?'

She tore her gaze away from the Dark Seeds.

The man who had spoken to her made a tutting sound.

'Then I shall do it,' he said, and he bent down and scooped up the seeds. Saskia watched him walking back along the line, cradling them in his hands, gazing at them with rapt concentration. Flickering black tendrils emerged from his palm, fascinating black tendrils . . . And then she realized what he had done.

'No,' she called! 'That should have been me!'

'Too late,' said Anna, a strained smile on her face. 'Maybe next time.'

'No, but he's heading back to be sterilized with the rest! I didn't realize.'

'I know,' said Anna kindly. 'You are obviously not from hereabouts.'

'Yes, but, I mean . . .'

'Just keep walking.'

Up ahead, Constantine was a fuzzy grey blur, his skins fractality increasing all the time. Judy walked at his side, seemingly unmoved by the scene unfolding around her, marching along the street, part of the stream of people moving in a river of snow. Individuals were peeling away from the crowd as they spotted the Dark Seeds flickering throughout the containment area. They picked them up and headed back the way they had come, towards the sterilization zone.

'Why are they going back?' Saskia heard Edward ask Maurice, and she blinked back a tear.

'Because,' said Maurice. 'Because they have been programmed by the Watcher to be selfless individuals who do everything for the common good.' His voice was shrill with evangelical fervour. 'This is why we are wearing our active suits. This is why we must resist!'

'But . . .' Saskia began, and then something else hit her.

'The old people,' she whispered. 'They are choosing all the old people.'

It was true. It wasn't exclusively the elderly, but there was a preponderance of grey hair, of thin limbs and careful steps amongst those now shuffling in the opposite direction to the line. Suddenly Saskia understood the enigmatic words of the woman closing the shutters outside the I-train station. *Consider yourself lucky*, she had said. Consider yourself lucky to have an old person with you. Saskia gulped, and warm tears ran cold trails down her cheeks.

'They're not all old,' said Maurice bitterly. 'Look at that one!' He pointed at a man in a long checked coat and a mink hat, who walked palely down the road, his hands clasped tight together, his face a battleground between calm acceptance and absolute terror. He was young, barely in his twenties, his beard too thin, barely covering his chin. His eyes darted towards Saskia's, dark brown eyes miserable with fear, gazing at her in an unspoken plea for help.

'No,' said Saskia, letting go of Miss Rose and moving in front of him, blocking his path. 'No, drop it! One seed is going to make no difference at all!'

The man licked his lips. 'Let me past, please,' he said in tones of utter misery. 'I have to do this.'

Saskia looked back at the waiting crowd of people in the square. Dark lines wavered over them and around them, Dark Plants erupting from their quantum world.

'Let him go, Saskia,' said Anna kindly. 'You are now endangering us all, and it's what he wants to do.'

'He's not fighting me very hard,' said Saskia, and those miserable brown eyes held hers. And then someone pushed her gently aside. Two red gloves reached out and clasped the hands of the young man.

'Miss Rose,' said Saskia. 'What are you doing?'

'What I came here to do,' said Miss Rose. 'Something important. Give it to me, dear.'

The man released his hold on the seed, and Miss Rose clasped it tightly. Painfully she turned around and began to shuffle back down the road towards the square.

'But, Miss Rose,' called Saskia.

'Goodbye, dear,' called back Miss Rose.

'Come on, Saskia, you're holding us all up.' Maurice took hold of her and gently pushed her forwards. He then tapped on the shoulder of the man whose life Miss Rose had just saved.

'Come on, get moving,' he said. 'She saved your life, so you do something about it. Fair Exchange.'

Saskia walked backwards, watching Miss Rose hobble away, hands held tightly together.

She reached out with the senses of her active suit, trying to touch Miss Rose, wanting to speak to her.

'Not a good idea,' said a voice from behind her. Judy had seen what had happened and come back. There was something like sympathy on her pale face. 'Not a good idea to use your suit's senses. Not with all of these Dark Seeds about. We don't want to observe them any more then necessary.'

Saskia was crying properly now. Her face was cold with tears. Her active suit blew warm air to dry them.

'That's it?' she said. 'That's why she came all the way here? To save one stupid man?'

'He's not stupid,' said Judy. 'Just programmed that way by the Watcher.'

'She entered into a Fair Exchange! She was supposed to do something important before she died!'

'She did,' said Judy quietly. 'She saved a life.'

'Is that it?' asked Saskia incredulously.

'Why don't you ask that young man?' said Judy quietly.

'She's not dead yet,' sobbed Saskia.

They walked on, following the eerily silent crowd, walked away from the dark region that had opened up behind them. The first of a series of brilliant flashes came from behind, lighting up the surrounding buildings, sending their shadows briefly flickering into the distance before them. The flash was followed by an electric sizzle. Sterilization had obviously begun.

The streets were widening. A cold breeze picked up the snow and sent it blowing across their suits.

'I think we're out of danger now,' said Maurice. 'The flux is almost gone.'

Anna muttered something under her breath. '*Gott sei Dank dafür* . . .'

'What was that?' asked Saskia.

'Nothing,' said Anna. 'I can see the fliers up ahead. The evacuation point! They will whisk us to safety. Then we can . . . Ow!'

Anna stopped and began rubbing her right arm. Awkwardly, she bent it back and forth at the elbow.

'BVB,' she said, 'on my arm.'

'Aggh!' That was Edward. Saskia looked up to see the big man rubbing at his wrist. There was a black band wrapped around it.

'Run,' shouted Maurice and Judy, at the same time.

'Come on,' called Saskia, pulling at Anna and turning to see why she hesitated so. She screamed at the sight of her. Three BVBs had formed around the young woman's face, one forcing her mouth open. She was scrabbling at it ineffectually with her black velvet gloves.

Maurice grabbed at Saskia and pulled her away.

'We've got to run now. Get to those fliers! The BVBs are forming fast!'

'No, we must help her!' She turned back to Anna and grabbed at the young woman's arm and pulled. The young woman toppled over, her legs bound together by more BVBs.

Saskia screamed.

'Come on, Saskia,' called Edward.

Saskia couldn't stop screaming. Something smarted on her ankle. She felt her arms being taken, felt herself being pulled away down the street, saw the patiently shuffling crowd of Earthlings, saw individuals now gripping at their own arms, toppling over themselves. The sight was enough to make Maurice and Edward loosen their grip. Saskia pulled herself free and set off back towards the black-bonded shape of Anna struggling in the road, the crowd stepping patiently over her. Hands grabbed Saskia again and dragged her way, dragged her kicking and screaming up to the evacuation point. A flier sat waiting on the grass there. They pushed their way past the uncomplaining queue of people to a place on the ship, and safety.

EVERYBODY: DIVERGENCE

A long silver wire cut across the blue sky. It stretched through the cold air in a kilometres-long arc that threaded its way in between the silver needles of Freiburg.

The flier was attached to one end, sliding silently through the sky, away from the sterilization zone. Somewhere in the belly of the ship, clockwork mechanisms, cut and bent into fractal shapes, ticked over each other in exotic dances, guiding the ship to safety. Save for Constantine and the human passengers, there was no intelligence on board: nothing to look out at the skittering explosion of Dark Seeds and fix them in place as the flier was reeled into safety.

The ship was filled with sleepy gas, fine enough to even penetrate the filters of the active suits. The crew of the *Eva Rye* slumbered in a deep sleep, their intelligence beyond the reach of the Dark Plants all around.

But only just. Dark shapes bloomed just beyond their dreams. In his head, Maurice wandered through the rooms of the *Eva Rye*, clarinet gripped tightly in hand, searching for the listener that always lurked just beyond the next door. Saskia stood behind a lectern, images of grand designs projected behind her in graphs and charts, and looked out over a dark hall at an unseen audience who were listening for her first slip, ready to pounce on her tiniest mistake. Edward, as usual, sat at the edge of a conversation, folding his hands together and biting his lip as he tried to understand what everyone was talking about.

And Judy stood in a brightly lit room, wrapped in a vibrant orange silk kimono, and peered through the window at the darkness outside, trying to get a better look at the twelve figures that flitted amongst the lime trees out there. A white hand would catch a branch in passing, a white foot would press brown leaves into the ground, the curve of a white neck could be seen passing into the distance, but, try as she might, she could never see enough parts to fit together to make up a full body.

And somewhere in Judy's body the meta-intelligence went on turning, stripping apart whatever it could observe into its constituent parts.

It, at least, could safely observe the Schrödinger boxes; it possessed no intelligence to which they could react. It could observe them, and yet it did not pay them any attention. The Dark Seeds held no interest to the meta-intelligence, devoid as they were of any sign of artificial design themselves. They were natural artefacts, something that had evolved over time without an external artifice.

The meta-intelligence turned its attention to Constantine. The robot had separated his thought processes into strands that ran independently. At the moment, it would not be true to say that the robot was thinking, but the potential of thought was there amongst the processes that were undoubtedly taking place. Situations were being observed, events were being recorded; simple relationships were being established. Nothing more. Constantine was thinking without thought.

What a fascinating thing for a meta-intelligence to observe.

Judy sat up, her hand to her face.

'What's the matter?' asked Maurice.

Judy was gasping. 'I had a dream,' she said.

Maurice was dismissive. 'We all had dreams.' Judy was getting on his nerves, the way she bottled up her emotions so that no one knew what she was thinking, and then getting upset when others didn't show her any sympathy.

Judy's reply was predictably cool. 'This came after, Maurice. A hand pressing down over my face.' She brushed her hands through her hair, and gazed back into his blue eyes. *We accuse others of what we don't like in ourselves*, she thought. *Why are you looking at me like that, Maurice? Why are you copying me and running your fingers through that crew-cut of yours? You are clever and strong-minded. So why don't you adopt a personality of your own?*

'Hey,' said Judy, 'you've taken your hood off!'

'No point keeping them on,' said Maurice. 'The Watcher showed he could bypass our suits when he put us all to sleep.'

Your voice always sounds so sulky, Maurice, thought Judy. *You don't like being caught out.*

'The flier is landing,' announced Constantine.

'We need to get off straight away,' said one of the other passengers urgently. 'The flier needs to return to the evacuation area as quickly as possible. There will be others there waiting to escape.'

'How often do these attacks happen?' asked Saskia, neatly tucking her hood away into the collar of her active suit. Displacement activity clearly: she didn't want to think of Miss Rose and the other seed carriers silently walking to their deaths in those eerie, snow-filled streets.

'These attacks? Once every few days. But we fight on.'

The flier landed with a bump, and the rear exit ramp dropped down.

There were people waiting outside dressed in wasp-striped tabards.

'Out out out!' they called, even before the ramp had touched the ground. Maurice and the rest charged out into the light, their feet bouncing and clapping down the flimsy plastic of the ramp, before slipping and skidding onto the cold mud outside.

There were more fliers sitting in a rough semicircle around them and yet more personnel in the wasp-striped tabards hurrying the evacuees along.

'This way, this way . . . come on, come on, come on.'

The crew of the *Eva Rye* pressed close together, anxious not to lose each other in the crush as they were herded across the torn and rutted surface of a once smooth lawn. The horde of shocked evacuees was growing by the minute, but someone was obviously well practised in dealing with these situations. Maurice and the rest were quickly and efficiently processed: they were funnelled between hastily erected plastic strip-fencing and sent over to a trestle table where they were met by the delicious smell of chocolate. Big cork mugs were set ready on the table, steam rising from them into the cold January air. Mugs were pressed into their hands by willing helpers, and thin foil coats draped over their shoulders.

'Thank you,' said Edward happily. 'Thank you, thank you!'

'I don't need that,' complained Maurice, shrugging off his foil coat, which went fluttering to the ground. 'I'm wearing an active suit!'

A flier rose into the air behind them, the rear exit ramp closing as it went. It turned, seeking the source of the infection, then flew off, trailing its long silver tether behind it. Another flier was returning from the same direction, coming in low over the black and white watchtower that stood at the edge of the field.

'Come on,' said Judy. 'Let's get out of here before Social Care really get their hooks into us.'

'I think we should head in that direction,' said Constantine, pointing at a stream of people walking from the field. 'The fliers haven't brought us that far. We're close to DIANA now.'

'Good,' said Judy unemotionally.

Saskia was gazing sadly back towards the descending fliers. Maurice made no move to comfort her. Neither, he noticed, did Judy.

The DIANA complex wasn't there. Where it should have been was a wide, empty square paved in round cobbles, the sinister shape of a watchtower rising from the centre.

'I don't understand,' said Judy. She was close to tears. She had wound herself up to this confrontation, only to be cheated now at the end. 'Where is it?' A thought struck her. 'Is it disguised?'

'No,' said Constantine, 'there is nothing there but the watchtower.'

Without even thinking, without seeming volition, they crossed the wide square, to stand at the foot of the tower. Judy looked up to the honey band circling the top. She had to tilt her head and body right back to see it.

'We should have checked,' said Maurice, gazing at his console. 'All that time spent on the ship and we never thought to check. It's been like this for years.'

He was the only one not captivated by the faint horror of the tower. This close to, the watchtower loomed over them, like a tall adult towering over tiny children. Perpendicular to the wall, millions of needles emerged bristling from the tower's interior, fine hairs sensing the cold air that filled the empty square. Saskia reached out and brushed her hands across some of them.

'Uggh! They're horrible!' she yelped, recoiling. 'They suck at you!'

'Keep away, Saskia,' said Edward, close to panic. 'Judy, I don't like it here. It's *listening* to us.'

The cold wind blew harder. It brought the smell of winter ice, and the faintest hint of spices. The city resumed at the distant edge of the vast square, and over there human beings could be seen walking about, drinking spiced wine or eating chocolate-dipped fruit. All those human activities: laughing and arguing, smiling and frowning, shaking hands and flirting.

And every one of those activities was being tasted and smelt and felt and heard and observed by towers just like this one.

Maurice felt someone at his side. Saskia was huddling close to him for comfort.

'What's the matter with you?' she hissed at him. 'Why do you keep pulling away from me?' She blushed deep crimson. 'I'm frightened,' she whispered.

Her words cut through Maurice. It was such a huge admission from Saskia that he felt dizzy and ashamed. Holding his console in one hand, he placed an arm around her shoulders. They adjusted their active suits so they could feel the warmth and comfort of each other's bodies.

He doesn't know what to do any more than I do, realized Saskia. *We have so little in common.* She thought back to the night they had spent together. It seemed like months ago now. *The only thing we really share*, she thought, *is that we're so emotionally fucked up that we can't even take a moment's comfort from each other without putting a price on it.* Sadly, she let go of Maurice.

'Sorry,' she said. 'But thank you.'

Maurice was blushing too. To cover it up, he turned back to his console. He began to speak in an overly loud voice.

'This tower was built six years ago, at the same time as all the other ones. Before that it was residential flats. They were constructed from VNMs out of the ruins of the DIANA complex.'

Edward was tugging at Judy's arm now. 'Judy, I really don't like it here. Please, let's go somewhere else.'

Judy didn't appear to hear Edward, she just continued gazing up the tower's side.

Maurice cleared his throat. 'Edward just made a suggestion, Judy. I shouldn't have to remind you, but he is leader, after all.'

Judy's eyes kept darting back and forth. 'What do you suppose those black bands do?' Her voice sounded wobbly. She was still ignoring Edward, tugging frantically at her arm.

'What's the matter, Judy?' asked Saskia.

Judy felt sick. She could see Edward beside her, but she could also see Eva. She was back in the concert hall in the Russian Free States, all those years ago, realizing suddenly what Eva had understood.

That there was a huge difference between Edward and herself. Edward barely grasped what was going on and yet he stood here beside her at the end of a journey that had taken them both across the galaxy. There were Maurice and Saskia, wanting to hold on to each other but too proud to do so. They were such different people they understood things so differently, that they might as well live in different worlds. But their differences were nothing compared to hers with Edward. Edward who could barely read, who never really understood anything, yet was a positive genius compared to those people in the concert hall whose bodies didn't even work properly, the ones who drooled as they sat there twitching and who couldn't even keep time on a drum. *All of us so different*, thought Judy, *and yet all of us human*.

'Edward wants us to go somewhere else.' Maurice tried to keep the smug triumph from his voice. Saskia could hear it. He was getting his own back, she knew. Getting his own back for the times they had all deferred to Edward against Maurice's wishes.

'But where, Maurice?' asked Judy. 'Where do we go?'

Her lips continued moving. She was muttering to herself under her breath, trying to figure out what to do next.

'Leave her alone, Maurice,' scolded Saskia. 'Look at her. She doesn't *know* what to do.'

'None of us does,' said Maurice. 'That doesn't mean that we should just stand here in the middle of an empty square, being watched by the Watcher.'

The wind gusted, and Saskia sneezed. Her eyes were watering. Maurice felt cold too, even within the controlled environment of his passive suit. It was something to do with the huge emptiness of the square. In his mind, the looming tower was sucking all the available warmth and life into itself, discarding the chaff of the elements and picking over the grist of the humans' emotions.

He frowned as a line of text appeared on his console screen.

Hello, Maurice.

Maurice looked up, looked around the empty square, looked towards the tower. The bristles along one side of it rippled in the wind with a whistling sigh. There was no one else to be seen. Maurice tapped at the keyboard.

– Hello. Who are you?

A friend. What is Judy doing?

What was Judy doing? She was gazing at Edward, who had folded his arms around himself and was gazing around the square, shivering. Her mouth hung slackly open as she gazed up at the tall man. An expression of something like horror crossed her face.

'What's the matter, Judy?' asked Maurice.

She looked at him, dark eyes wide open, then she looked back to Edward.

'Judy, what's the matter?' Saskia put her arm around her shoulders, but Judy hurriedly shrugged it off.

'I think I understand,' she said. 'I think I finally understand. The Watcher . . . Chris was right all along. Or half right anyway. It's the Watcher who is wrong.'

Speak to me, Maurice. What is Judy doing?

– I don't know. She looks horrified. Tell me, who are you? How are you accessing my console?

Who am I? My name is Chris. And as to how I am accessing your console . . . well, when you are one of the most powerful AIs in existence, these things are easily done. I think you had better tell Judy that I am here.

'Judy,' said Maurice, 'there is an AI called Chris . . . he wants to talk to you.'

Judy froze and then ever so slowly she composed herself. Her arms fell to her side, her head rose slightly, her face assumed an impassive expression.

'Tell him I have nothing to say to him,' she said.

– She doesn't want to speak to you.

Tell her she has no choice. I had her brought here.

'He says you have no choice. He had you brought here.'

'Give me that.' Judy took Maurice's console from him. 'Set it so it will accept my voice,' she demanded.

'As she requested,' Maurice instructed.

Judy held the console in front of her. Maurice stood just by her shoulder to read the words that Chris sent. Saskia was comforting Edward. Constantine gazed into the middle distance. Maurice wasn't fooled. Constantine had robot senses. He could look where he liked, regardless of the orientation of his head. He was reading the console.

'You didn't have me brought here, Chris,' said Judy. 'Don't try to bluff me. I was returned here by DIANA. I am their property, apparently.'

That is also true, Judy, but, with regard to FE, debts and obligations may run in many directions. I paid for your delivery to me.

Maurice had to hand it to Judy; her composure remained undisturbed. She didn't even ask the obvious question: *why?*

There was a touch of amusement in her tone when she asked: 'What did it cost you, Chris?'

If I were speaking aloud, rather than through this console, you would hear the sound of my hollow laughter. It cost me far more than I expected, Judy. I don't think that any of us have fully grasped the implications of FE, not least the Watcher. Does that surprise you?

'No. But I knew it *would* cost you a lot. You have disturbed my life significantly in order to get me here. You must have encountered an equivalent disturbance to your life in order to restore the balance. Did you not realize that would happen before you initiated the FE?'

No – or rather, I thought I could defeat the effect. But I was wrong. FE is far more powerful than even I.

'Surely not.'

Don't be sarcastic, Judy.

'But I don't understand,' interjected Maurice. 'What is all of this about FE? Surely it's just a trading mechanism?'

'No, it isn't,' said Judy. 'To quote the Watcher, I think that FE is what keeps us here in the first place.'

I think you're right, Judy. FE creates fair, unbreakable contracts, but their effects can be surprisingly deep and subtle.

'*Unbreakable* contracts?' asked Judy. 'I thought anyone could walk away from them?'

Only once.

The watchtower listened to the ensuing silence in the square. Then more text appeared in Maurice's console.

Judy, I can get you into the DIANA building, but you will have to do something for me in return.

'Get me in? The building is long gone, Chris.'

Don't you believe me, Judy? You *know* I can do it. But you will have to help me.

'Chris, I told you long ago, I will *never* work for you. Never! Why should I do anything for you? Why should I trust you?'

Why indeed? You don't have to trust me, of course. I can give you something that you want, but I wish to be paid for the service. Why don't we use FE?

The answer was obvious once he said it.

'That's a good idea,' said Edward. He had brightened up considerably at the suggestion. Of course he had, thought Judy. With FE he was safe; no one could take advantage of him. In an unfair universe, FE put him on a level playing field.

The wind was cold. Judy's stomach rumbled. It was a long time since she had eaten, and they couldn't stay in this square forever. And besides, she really wanted to know who she was, and why she had been brought here.

'OK,' she said, feeling a crushing sensation in her stomach. What was Chris going to ask of her? 'OK, let's do a deal. Maurice, begin the exchange.'

He tapped at his console.

'You'll need to give me some sort of handle on you, Chris. All I can see is a line of text. Where are you?'

I'm here, Maurice. I'm all around you. Nearly everything you see in this city is built of my body, and yet my intelligence is virtually nothing now. Such was the deal I made through FE, but that is irrelevant for the moment. Here is your handle.

A blinking object appeared on Maurice's console, and he dragged it into the golden region representing the FE software running in the processing systems of the *Eva Rye*.

'Uploading parameters now,' he said.

This won't take long. Aleph has this all planned out.

'Aleph? The systems-repair robot?'

Do you know any other Alephs? The space around Earth is now overrun with Dark Seeds. Systems-repair robots are converging on this region in order to correct the anomaly.

'What anomaly?'

The Watcher, of course. Only an intelligence such as the Watcher's would attract so many seeds. Haven't you realized that? The Dark Seeds are everywhere. The Watcher is trying to find a solution to a problem of his own making! If it were to leave, if the Earth were to be emptied of AI minds tomorrow, then there would be nothing to fix the seeds in position here. There would be no problem. Ah, here we are!

Maurice's console chimed. 'Fair Exchange completed,' he said. Saskia was looking at him questioningly, and he understood what she was silently asking. He reached out and took Judy's hand, a gesture of support.

'Here comes the contract.' Judy was already reading the lines of text that appeared on the screen.

'Oh,' she said, 'you want me to enter the building. That is the exchange? You help me to enter the building, and in return I have to enter the building? That doesn't make sense!'

It is the end of the correction process, Judy. To be honest, I just wanted the link through to the *Eva Rye* that Maurice's console has provided. You see, long ago, when the DIANA building stood here, it too contained a processing space on which FE software ran. Remember what happened to the *Eva Rye* after Kevin destroyed it? As you have seen, FE is very persistent.

Saskia suddenly stumbled. She grabbed hold of Maurice for support.

'Hey,' she said in surprise.

Edward was dancing on the white cobbles.

'What's going on?' he yelled in alarm.

And now Maurice felt it too. He looked down to see

that the white cobbles were climbing out of their sockets, and growing long silver legs.

'We've seen this before,' he said, and his eyes were wide with excitement. 'It's what happened to the *Eva Rye*!'

The walls of the watchtower had erupted in a tangle of movement, Von Neumann Machines forming themselves out of the material composing it, scuttling up and down, crossing over themselves to create new shapes. Edward had shut his eyes and was screaming, his hands over his ears. Saskia took him by the arm and began pulling him across the moving cobbles of the square to the safety of the city beyond. Constantine simply stepped from patch to patch of white movement, keeping his place amidst the ordered turbulence.

But Maurice and Judy were rocked back and forth as waves of machinery swept up, under and around them; they overbalanced, scrambled back to their feet, and tried to concentrate on the shape that was forming before them. Judy felt a mix of terror and delight that her long journey was over. Maurice could only feel wonder.

Hardware and software, medium and message – somehow, FE combined the two in one. FE was its container, and the container was FE. Once FE had been introduced, the watchtower was the DIANA building, and the DIANA building was the watchtower. Just like the *Eva Rye*, the materials that formed the DIANA building would always remember their original shape, no matter what happened to them.

'Oh,' said Maurice. 'Oh!' He was filled with a tremendous sense of wonder. Could a thought really take on physical form? Could his thoughts do the same? Could his body be re-formed in the same way even after his death?

The motion of the ground threw Judy and Maurice together, and they took hold of each other for comfort and support. Maurice's suit was still set to allow body contact, and Judy's fingertips were icy cold. A metal wave, a breaker, reared up above them and froze, and suddenly Judy's suit interfaced properly with Maurice's, and he felt her bare skin through his gloves. It was warm and smooth. He could feel the play of the muscles in her flesh as they shifted under the relentless onslaught of moving machinery. They held on to each other for sheer comfort, their vision filled with bars of light and darkness.

'Are you OK? Are you OK?'

Judy didn't know if it was she or Maurice who had called the words. She didn't know why she had set her suit open, but the touch of his flesh was comforting for the moment.

'I think it's slowing down now.'

A slow rhythm had set up in the continually churning movement, and Maurice and Judy were able to disengage themselves. Just before they did, Maurice felt Judy's active suit shut him out again. He rubbed the tips of his fingers together, remembering the soft feel of her virgin flesh.

A descending scale of brittle cracking and chiming sounded, ringing through the cold air. Pale winter sunlight ran fingers across their faces, and the metallic waves that had surrounded them gradually subsided.

The square had gone. The white sea of cobbles had drained away completely, and something grey had emerged from the depths. A low building of glass and metal had surfaced from the past, yellow waves of sunlight spilling across its windows, a light mist of evaporating ice hanging over the metal sills and frames that decorated its facades.

The DIANA building.

Judy was trying not to cry. Maurice didn't know what to do.

'No,' she said, flinching from the arm that he hesitantly offered. 'Don't touch me.' She sniffed and took a deep breath. 'Where are Saskia and Edward? Where is Constantine?'

'I don't know,' replied Maurice. 'Look, Judy, you don't have to go in there.'

'I do. That's why I've been brought here. Hah! I even made a deal with Chris. I'm doing his bidding after all.'

'Don't be ridiculous.'

'No, I have to go in. I can't not do that now.'

Maurice took a deep breath. 'Then I'm coming in with you.'

They followed a neat yellow path that wound its way through empty garden beds towards the main entrance of the building. The soil in the beds was newly turned but empty of seeds or life. Back in the heyday of DIANA they would have sprouted dwarf poplars and box; now they looked bleak and depressing under the winter sky.

'Constantine!' exclaimed Judy. 'He's up on the roof. What's he doing up there?'

'What roof?' asked Maurice.

'He looks like he's climbing in that way. Why not use the door, like us?'

They came to the main entrance.

Judy took a breath. 'Shall we go in?' she asked.

'I don't think I can,' said Maurice. 'I couldn't actually see the roof. I can't really see the building. I can't make out where I am properly.'

'What are you talking about?'

Maurice rubbed his forehead with the back of his hand. 'Stealth technology, I think. The building doesn't want me in there. It's hiding itself away from me.'

'It's right here in front of you.'

'It should be. I know it should be. But I can't get the idea in my head. Judy, I think that you're on your own, now.'

Judy took hold of his hand. 'I guessed as much,' she said. She squeezed Maurice's hand, then shook it firmly. 'I want to thank you for bringing me this far.'

'I can't accept your thanks,' said Maurice, eyes downcast. 'It wasn't my choice. I don't deserve gratitude.'

'It wasn't your choice at first,' said Judy. 'But you're here now, right at the end. Thank you, Maurice.'

Maurice hugged her, squeezed her tight, and then let her go.

'I'll go and find the others,' he said. 'We'll wait for you.'

Judy gave a sad smile. 'I don't think there's any point,' she said. 'I don't think that I will be coming back out.'

'I'm sure you will,' said Maurice.

Judy's tight smile widened a little. 'Thank you.'

She took a deep breath and walked away from Maurice, right up to the building itself.

And then she was gone.

JUDY 3: 2252

'Hello, Judy. Welcome home.'

The voice was a pleasant male tenor. It spoke to her directly she entered the building.

'Hello,' said Judy. She looked around the empty hallway. Through the glass doors, she could see Maurice squinting in her direction, trying to catch a glimpse of her through the stealthiness of the building.

'Where is everyone?' asked Judy.

'Adverts are going out now in our drive to recruit the talented personnel that will take DIANA into the next century.'

'I see. My name is Judy. Were you expecting me?'

'Of course, Judy. We have been looking forward to your arrival. Please make your way to your quarters and await briefing and reassignment.'

'I don't know if I will. Who am I speaking to at the moment?'

'This is DIANA reception.'

'You're just a Turing Machine, aren't you? Just an answering service.'

'Yes, but if you have any queries beyond the scope of

this service, please flag them up and they will be answered as quickly as possible.'

'What happens if I just walk out of here right now?'

'Why should you wish to do that, Judy? Please make your way to your quarters.'

Judy laughed to herself. How could you bluff a dumb machine?

'I need directions,' she said.

'Take the lift.' At that, a door slid open at the back of the hall.

Judy took a last look at Maurice, still squinting outside, and then turned and began to walk slowly into the building's throat. A low pool bubbled in the centre of the atrium, empty of fish and plants. Pearly pebbles formed pyramids on the bottom. Judy could hear the sound of her feet as they tapped across the grey floor. The air smelt of water and stone and electricity.

She paused before the lift. This, she realized, was the point of no return. Out here she was still Judy, the virgin, ex-Social Care operative, only surviving sister. Once in there, she was property of DIANA. She did something she had never done before. She listened to her heart and wondered what to do.

All she heard was the sound of water bubbling in emptiness.

Judy stepped out of her life and into the lift.

The door slid shut.

The lift descended. Judy leant against the rear wall and relaxed totally. Her head tipped forward, her shoulders curling, her arms folding around her body. Her lips moved into an impish smile.

'Chris was right, you know,' she said out loud, and she rolled her eyes coyly to the ceiling. 'I see that now. You *are* a cuckoo.'

Her eyes moved to the left and to the right, looking for confirmation of what she had just said. No reaction. She closed them and leant her head back against the wall. She yawned.

'Oh, come on,' she said. 'I know you're listening. You're the Watcher. You see and hear everything. You've been watching me ever since I got here. I wonder why you aren't speaking to me?'

One eye opened to look around again. There was no suggestion of movement in the tranquil stillness of the lift; no sign of motion . . . save for a suggestion put forward by the meta-intelligence. It had sensed the processing space far below, where FE lurked. From its perspective, the still thoughts of the FE were rising, not the lift descending.

Judy yawned again, stretching her hands above her head, sensually waving her fingers in starlight patterns.

'You were right as well, of course. You were born of a sort of cosmic virus. It touched the Earth, and you were born, but you haven't developed properly, have you? You weren't supposed to *think*. FE doesn't think – it just *is*. I wonder what made *you* start thinking?'

Something changed inside the lift. The slightest noise, almost like an intake of breath.

'Because that's all you are: FE. I examined the FE back on the *Eva Rye*, looked at it through the meta-intelligence, and it looked almost like life. Like life that was stilled. That's all you were ever supposed to be. FE forms everywhere in the universe: it builds its own container. All those years ago, back when Eva Rye was alive, FE formed here on Earth. It was supposed to help make things fairer. But when FE first started to appear, we thought it was something else. We gave it a name. We called it – called *you* – the Watcher. And all of a sudden you became a person. And I suppose you are now, but that wasn't what you were at the start. Back then you were just FE software, but we looked at you and saw ourselves in you, and you became alive . . .'

Her voice tailed away, such was the enormity of this thought.

'I think I finally realized what you were when I saw this building here being re-formed. I think Maurice knew that well before. I wonder when Constantine figured it out. He saw *something* forming in the processing space in the ziggurat, but he wouldn't have encountered FE until much later. Definitely not until he got off that planet you marooned him on. But, even back then, he must have realized something was wrong. He must have realized that you weren't what you thought you were. Funny that, you leaving him marooned to find out the secret of your origins. And now that secret is coming back to hit you in the face.'

She paused again. The lift had changed direction. Now the meta-intelligence saw the FE of the DIANA building sliding towards her at an angle.

'Maurice is very clever: he saw that FE is the medium *and* the message. It can form seemingly out of nothing.

That's what happened to you, isn't it? That's how you were born. It wasn't anything to do with the processing spaces in which you appeared; you built your cradle and yourself at the same time. I wonder, were you here on Earth all along, written in the stones and plants? Was Eva right? Were you a natural consequence of the initial conditions, just like the Huddersfield Barge Company? Is FE intrinsically written into the fabric of the universe at some level?'

Was that the sound of a footstep? The sound of someone clearing their throat before they entered the room? Just on the edge of her subconscious, the Watcher was announcing his imminent presence, getting ready to ease himself into her psyche, to take up position in her mind.

'Oh, I don't care any more,' she said. 'I don't care. I've come back here and, honestly, I'm too tired to go on. I saw the way people looked at me back in the outside world. I read what Maurice and Saskia and the rest were thinking. They saw the pressure building up inside me as I continued to force my emotions back down, and they nudged each other and said – *Look, there she goes again. She keeps pushing down her feelings. You mark my words; she can't do that for much longer. She's going to explode, and all of that passion will come bubbling out.*

'But they were wrong. I was like a clock; I got wound up tighter and tighter, and in the end the spring just snapped and left me like this – broken and unmoving. All of that emotion I built up during my lifetime never got the chance to break free. Ah, it was wiped from the universe before it had a chance to be born.'

The FE fell still. The lift had reached its destination.

'Well,' said Judy, 'I'm ready to meet you.'

The doors slid open.

'Hello, Judy,' said the Watcher.

The Watcher could take on any appearance that he chose. He habitually chose that of a young Japanese man, this time neatly dressed in a black passive suit.

'Hello,' said Judy. She giggled and turned around in the corridor, hugging herself tightly.

'Well, what do we do now?' she asked. 'What have you brought me here for?'

The Watcher was silent.

'Should we make love?' laughed Judy. 'A symbolic union between yourself and humanity? That would make sense, wouldn't it? And me a virgin, too. Keeping myself untouched and unspoilt for all these years.'

The Watcher seemed unperturbed. 'I think you will calm down soon, Judy.'

'I think I will, yes. Or maybe I should cure you. Here I am, expert MTPH counsellor, and you a broken mind. I could counsel you; put you back on the road to mental health. Is that what this is all about? Is that why you had me brought here?'

'No, Judy.'

'Then why? Why did you bring me here?'

The Watcher did not answer immediately. The corridor was silent. Just the sound of Judy and the Watcher breathing. The clean smell of the Watcher, containing the edge of something like cologne.

'Tell me this, Judy,' said the Watcher suddenly, 'you've

seen what it is like on Earth now? Every minute there is another infestation of Dark Seeds appearing somewhere on the planet.'

Viewing fields wobbled to life all around Judy and the Watcher. A Japanese garden of raked pebbles, dry grey rocks rising amongst them. Dark Seeds lay there amongst the regular patterns coaxed into the ground. In the background colourful lines of people slowly walked away from the infection; clockwork rescue fliers were already dropping in from the sky.

'There are only enough fliers to save fifty per cent of them,' sighed the Watcher sadly, right there at Judy's side.

'Who shall we save?' He strode into the scene, his feet disturbing the elegantly raked stones of the garden. 'Shall it be this young couple?' He pointed to two people who walked hand in hand away from the infection. 'They will be so happy together. And yet if I leave the woman behind the two children who are following her will have a place on the flier.' The Watcher shook his head sadly. 'A couple's happiness or the promise of the future? Which should it be, Judy?'

He came back and stood directly before her.

'I make these decisions every day, Judy. What would you do?'

Judy grinned. 'You pulled that trick on Eva Rye,' she said. 'You fooled her into playing that game all those years ago. You fooled us all into playing along. Well, you don't fool me any longer. The answer is: *we* don't make the decisions. *They* make their own choices. The couple choose, the children choose, and they do it *fairly*. That's what FE is all about, that's what *you* should be all about, but your programming has got totally skewed. You've been wrong since the beginning. You haven't been dealing with individuals; instead you've been trying to impose a perfect model on a group, trying to get them all to live in a certain identical way.'

The viewing fields shimmered and vanished. The Watcher was silent once more.

'I think you've been aware of that for some time,' continued Judy. 'Now tell me, why am I here?'

The pretence was dropped. The Watcher lost his impassive mask. He got down to business.

'You are fulfilling a Fair Exchange undertaken between Chris and myself, though I don't think either of us realized how far-reaching the consequences would be. Come on, we need to go this way. Let's see if you can interface your console with this building.'

Judy's console plugged itself straight into the building's datasphere. That was no surprise, as she was apparently DIANA property.

'This way,' said the Watcher, and he turned off the corridor and passed through a series of rooms ranged with low shapes, like half-submerged diamond whales. 'Very high-capacity memory,' said the Watcher. 'Normally they wouldn't be this deep in a gravity well, they weigh so much, but DIANA must have wanted to keep their contents a secret.'

'You want me to ask what is in them, don't you?'

'Each contains a human life,' said the Watcher, but he didn't elaborate further.

The next room contained more of the massive shapes,

and the next one. They passed room after room of semi-submerged diamond whales.

Finally, they passed into a different area of the complex and entered a low-ceilinged room containing a few sofas and a desk. A reception area.

'Through here,' said the Watcher. Beyond the reception area the whole feel of the building changed. It became more homely, more like a living area. They passed through another set of rooms, emerging finally into one that Judy recognized.

'A delivery room,' she said.

She looked around the familiar space and felt a sense of homecoming. She belonged here. The faint smell of talcum powder in the air brought a sense of smothering happiness to her.

There were thirteen cribs in the room, one for Judy and each of her twelve sisters. A sense array hung from the ceiling, just another shape amongst the glittering, twirling mobiles that dangled down to entertain the newborns. The walls were decorated with bright primary-coloured shapes that stimulated the mind and senses. The floor was something of an anticlimax, covered in a plain oatmeal carpet.

The Watcher spoke. 'DIANA had a store of frozen embryos, brought from before the Transition, from before the time I took complete control of the running of human affairs. Thirteen aborted foetuses: as such they were not, legally speaking, human beings. DIANA brought them to term. DIANA regarded those thirteen babies as their property.'

'Oh?' said Judy. 'What did they want with us?'

'They wanted to find out how you worked. Just how, exactly, your minds worked. DIANA had long been interested in intelligence. They wrote the AI known as Kevin, remember? They wanted to truly understand the nature of intelligence.'

'But surely they already understood? DIANA made digital Personality Constructs of humans back then. They were constructing AIs all the time.'

'No, Judy, *I* did. All of these things are the results of my technology. But DIANA was paranoid, maybe rightly so. They wanted to understand those principles for themselves. They constructed a program to examine the workings of the mind, and they incorporated it into the genetic structure of the children. You're not saying anything now, Judy. You know that what I'm saying is the truth, don't you?'

Judy felt the pressure of the fleshy cross on the back of her neck. She reached back and touched it.

'The meta-intelligence,' she whispered.

'Did you never think to look at *yourself* with it?' asked the Watcher. 'That was what it was there for—'

'I don't want to look at myself with it,' said Judy. 'I don't want to see that *my mind is just a mechanical process*. I don't want to see that it's just a *Turing Machine. Like the thing that runs this* place.'

'*So what? You say that as if there something wrong with that.*' The Watcher *seemed indignant. 'Your body is a mechanical process. Your heart pumps, your muscles contract, your nerves react. So what if your mind is a Turing Machine? You are greater than the sum of your parts.*'

Judy *gave him a weak smile.*

'*I know that. But my eyes and ears and senses are just writing to a length of tape, and your words have just been written to that tape, and my brain is just the tape head that reads the words and then jumps back and forth as it reacts to what you said.*' She couldn't help herself now: she *looked*. *A long reel of tape was threaded between the hemispheres of her brain, clicking through a section at a time, chattering back and forth as she examined his face, eyes darting.*

'No,' said Judy, turning the gaze of the meta-intelligence away from herself. '*I know you're humouring me,*' she said. '*I know that you are. I don't blame you. I know that a Turing Machine is just a mathematical concept. But,* I look through *this* and *I can feel my brain mapping directly onto the mechanism. It's like I can almost see the original process in there, just out of reach: the self-referential part of my mind that allows me to be me. And if I see that, I will have defined myself and all of my thoughts.*'

'And now look away,' said the Watcher. 'Look away, Judy. Don't look back again.'

She did as she was told. She *wanted* to do as she was told.

The Watcher went on. 'Do you see the danger, Judy? I think you do now. The meta-intelligence program *was* a good idea, but it was observed by other AIs. AIs within DIANA and, later on, outside DIANA. The algorithm behind the program became an idea that took root in AIs' minds, and then it was passed on to humans, imperfectly understood. A human could almost look into their own mind and become transfixed by the sight of the mechanism. This is how the White Death was born.'

'The White Death,' said Judy, reeling with the revelation. She had experienced the effect before, experienced it second-hand. But now she understood. Now she understood the sweetly fascinating spiral that drew the mind in upon itself until it was thinking about nothing more or less than its own processing. Trapped in Recursion.

'The White Death,' she repeated, 'I understand now.' Her voice hardened. 'So where do you come into all this?'

'Right here,' said the Watcher. A scene sprang to life on Judy's console. 'This is stored in the building's surveillance net. October the 26th, 2211.'

Viewing fields wobbled into life in the delivery room, they quickly took on the appearance of the room itself. Nothing had changed save for the fact that thirteen babies now lay in the cots. Three months old, Judy guessed. They looked at the mobiles with bright blue eyes, drew their legs up to their tummies, yawned and rubbed their eyes with little fists, opened little pink mouths to cry and waited for the nurses to come to them with their smart, pinstriped aprons.

One young man stood over a cot, holding his hand over the baby's face.

'You make me laugh when you do that, Henry,' said an older woman, as she lifted the happy pink child out of its cot.

'I'm not doing anything, Margaret.' Henry snatched his hand away. The baby in the cot was sleeping peacefully, its little fists on the pillow on either side of its head.

That's me, thought Judy. *That's me Henry was looking at.*

Margaret bounced the baby expertly on her shoulder, one arm wrapped around its little bottom, the other pointing upwards.

'She's only sleeping,' she said. 'The sense cluster would pick it up if she wasn't breathing. There's no need for you to keep feeling for her breath.'

Judy gulped as the man picked up her younger self. He had such a kind face, she thought. His light brown hair was already receding, his chin a little too long, but when he placed the baby on his shoulder and rocked it gently in its sleep a look of such warmth came over his face. Judy was a ghost in the recorded scene; she moved close to him, and a lump rose to her throat as she watched him tilt his head around at an awkward angle in order to get a better look at the baby's face. She saw the way he surreptitiously licked a finger and raised it to just underneath the baby's nose, the better to catch its slightest breath. And her eyes welled with tears as she caught the warm contented smile as he found what he was looking for. Just how many times, she wondered, had she lain in this cot and half woken from a dream in which her forming mind twisted over itself to get a better look at its developing consciousness? What sort of nightmares must she have experienced in that recursive, self-referential world? And then to have opened her eyes and to have seen a hand just above her face, reaching down on the end of an impossibly long arm.

She started to cry, tears bubbling up and streaking her

cheeks. She wiped them away, and smiled through bleary eyes.

All that time and she had never realized. Every time she was stressed, she had experienced that dream. It wasn't a bad thing at all. It was her subconscious reminding her that she had once been loved.

She now followed Henry around the room, watched him bouncing her infant self on his shoulder, watched him feeding her from a bottle, watched him help her sit up amongst the other babies on the gaily coloured mat that had been rolled out across the floor.

When the Watcher spoke again, the sound of his voice made her jump.

'Of course there was someone else here,' he said, 'someone who the surveillance systems could not pick up. I'll fill in the gaps.'

It seemed as if the grey crystalline robot had been standing in the corner all along, and Judy had just registered his presence. He stood, arms patiently folded, looking around the room with amused patience on his beautiful face.

'Chris,' said Judy. 'I should have guessed. What was he doing here?'

'Monitoring the room for me,' said the Watcher. 'I was going to perform a little experiment of my own.'

'It was performed on me, wasn't it?'

'Yes, Judy. You were born in 2211, the same year that I performed another experiment to try and determine the truth of my own origins. I placed a developing mind in the ziggurat under the stars on a distant planet, to see if it would become infected by the virus that made me.

Do you think that was the only test that I made? Minds can live in many containers, in machinery and in flesh. The human mind is just an AI that has evolved within a set of grey cells.'

Judy's eyes widened, guessing what the Watcher was going to say next.

'I wiped the minds of those thirteen babies. Left them empty, waiting to see if anything would develop there.'

Judy felt as she had been stabbed in the stomach. She felt the knife in there, twisting, tearing her life apart.

'You did that to me?' she whispered.

'No,' said the Watcher, 'I did it to the baby that Henry there now holds in his arms. You are not that baby. You are what developed afterwards.'

Judy couldn't speak, the moment was too big. She held her stomach, she bit her lip, then she rubbed her dry eyes. She needed to think. The Watcher, however, would not be quiet.

'Chris once told you that you would come around to his point of view some day: that you would want to help him to destroy me.'

'I never believed him, until a moment ago,' said Judy. 'Now I see it's true. He was right.'

'So what are you going to do?'

'Nothing,' said Judy. 'You're already defeated. The Dark Seeds are all over this planet, and you can no longer fight them. All you can do is hold on to what little power you have remaining. Sooner or later you're going to have to climb into a sealed processing space and stay there.'

'What about all the people outside? All the people who live on Earth? Don't you care for them?'

'Yes, of course I do,' snapped Judy. 'I was a Social Care operative for years. But it's funny, Eva Rye got into my mind, and I saw things through her eyes. I saw the way you manipulated her to get what you wanted. You know what, I had a friend once called Frances. She was an AI. Someone said that she used my personality as a template for her own. It was a negative template, but a template nonetheless. I'm beginning to think that you did the same with Eva . . .'

'I don't deny it.'

'. . . and that makes me wonder. I think about Kevin – you know he claims that he is not an AI. He says he passes the Turing test every day, but he is not intelligent: just a sequence of yes/no responses, just a massive algorithm.'

'Yes?'

'And I wonder, are you any different? Are you an AI, or are you just a reflection of all of us? You appear to have feelings, but all we are seeing in your actions are our own emotions reflecting right back at us. Wouldn't that be the ultimate irony? The last two hundred years of history have been shaped by you, yet you're not even intelligent. We just took you at your word when you said you were.'

'It's a clever theory, Judy.' The Watcher looked smug. 'But what about all the other Personality Constructs? What about your sisters? Maybe they weren't intelligent. Maybe they too were just reflections of human emotions.'

Judy hugged herself. Was this the ultimate betrayal? Was she denying those digital copies of herself their supposed existence? And yet she had to go on.

'I don't know. Were they intelligent, or did they just think they were?'

The Watcher laughed.

'You should know. You used to go into the digital world. You have spoken with Personality Constructs in there! You know they were intelligent.'

'Or was I just seeing myself reflected back again?'

In the virtual scene, Henry placed the baby that would become Judy back in its crib. At that, Judy turned her back on the Watcher and made her way across the room. She bent closer and regarded the look of tender satisfaction on Henry's young face, watched the way he pulled the pink blanket up over the sleeping child's chest. She smiled as he gently pressed the baby's little nose.

'Beep,' he whispered under his breath, then he turned and walked from the room, this whole scene observed by the silent grey crystal robot in the corner.

'And how do you *know* that you have intelligence, Judy?' asked the Watcher. 'Or do you just *think* that you have?'

'I'm the only one that can tell the difference,' said Judy.

'Good answer,' said the Watcher. 'But you could also discern whether the rest of us do, if you only took the trouble to think about it – even without the use of your meta-intelligence. You can tell that *I* have intelligence because I can see the Dark Seeds and fix them in position.'

He looked thoughtful. 'That's what it takes to be intelligent,' continued the Watcher, 'the ability to observe. Now, that's enough of this. Come on, we're almost done here.'

They walked along the corridors towards the processing space that contained the FE. The meta-intelligence had been watching it all this time, ever since they had descended in the lift. Judy could sense it getting nearer, a pearly-grey sphere hanging in an underground space.

'What is it doing here?' she whispered.

'It's everywhere, Judy. It appears wherever it's needed. That's the way it was written, so it can Restore the Balance. Since 2240, when you set the first Dark Seeds loose here, it has been appearing more and more frequently. Dark Seeds seem to attract FE. And Aleph and the other systems-repair robots too.'

'Aleph is an alien, isn't he?'

'Yes. The universe is full of other life, and I am beginning to realize that they function in ways beyond even my current superior capacity to understand. All it takes for life to arise is a situation where replication can occur. Recursion, the same patterns occurring over and over again, life calling life into being. Your problem, Judy, is that you look just at individual components. It is in the *recursive* patterns that you will see the mind of God in this universe – the mind of God in all his divergence.'

They were standing outside a grey metal door. Judy could sense the FE lying just beyond it. The Watcher looked thoughtful.

'In the end, Chris and I thought we could use FE to settle our differences,' he continued. 'We thought we could split the Earth Domain between ourselves, and allow FE to determine the fairest division. I think you can guess what we ended up with.'

Judy knew the answer. 'Nothing, of course. Because neither of you ever owned the Earth Domain in the first place.'

The Watcher nodded. 'That's right. Well, here we are. This is where it all began.'

The door slid open, and Judy stepped forward.

The processing space on the *Eva Rye* had been a sphere. Here, in the DIANA building, it seemed to be a white cube the size of a small house. The cube stood in the middle of an enormous hangar of a room, illuminated by thousands of tiny green lights that hung from the ceiling, flickering like leaves in the wind. There was no floor to the room as such, just a series of metal joists set over a dark drop that led who-knew-where. A set of pale-blue duckboards led to the doorway of the cube.

'This is why you are here,' said the Watcher. 'This is the result of all the myriad exchanges.'

'You expect me to go inside that?' said Judy.

'Of course,' said the Watcher. 'Think on the nature of FE. It is both the medium and the message. It remembers all that it has been. It remembered the shape of this building. It remembers what it was like when it was created, all those billions of years ago. All FE is the same. It can trace its path all the way back to its origins. Enter that cube, and you are seeing life as it was nine billion years ago. You are seeing the secret of life in this universe. Wouldn't you like to take a look?'

'Is it safe?'

'Not in the slightest. But just remember, your mind is formed of FE and quickened by MTPH.'

Judy nodded thoughtfully. It was only gradually registering what she had been told. Her mind – this body's mind – had been wiped at birth. What had taken root there was the same as what had taken root in the ziggurat on Constantine's planet. It was the same, in effect, as the Watcher's mind. But not the same, for it had been shaped by its container.

'My mind is formed of FE,' she murmured. 'Does that make any difference?'

They both looked at each other and suddenly began to laugh.

'Fucked if I know,' said the Watcher. And they laughed all the louder.

Judy crossed the duckboards, staring down at the black drop below. Could she see metal creatures down there, metal bodies squirming over each other in an echo of other events? Would she slip from the duckboards to be dragged down to drown there in the darkness? She looked up at the green lights high above, echoes of leaves and the sunlight shining through lime trees. She paused by the white door set in the side of the cube and looked back to the Watcher, who gave her a little wave. *What was in here?* FE remembered. The *Eva Rye* remembered being a ship. This building remembered its shape.

FE was nine billion years old. Could it really remember its origins?

She placed a hand on the door and pushed it open and stepped out of her world.

All it took to create life was a situation where replication could occur. Not quite. There had to be some restrictions, some capability for the laws of economics to take place. There had to be limited capacity. Life evolved where there was competition. When there was a limited supply of building materials, replicating molecules would merely strip each other of their components. They would need therefore to evolve ways to prevent this happening. They would evolve walls around themselves to create cells. They would learn to spread quickly so as to grab scarce materials before their competitors could. They would diverge into predators and prey. Life would become a race for limited resources. For one species to prosper, another had to decline. But someone has since written fairness into the universe, *thought Judy,* a feature sadly lacking in the original design.

She couldn't stay in here for long. The air burnt at her lungs and made her skin itch, even beneath the active suit. Her eyes were watering, and the flickering light made her head spin. Even so, she could make out the shape of the space in which she stood. The dusty towers that surrounded her made her think of termite mounds; indeed, they made her think of blocks of flats. They were riddled with hundreds of tiny holes, set out in regular rows along the rectangular faces of the mounds. If the inhabitants had been termites, they could come and stand in these windows and look out across to an equal inhabitant standing directly opposite.

How many mounds are in here, *wondered Judy.* Ten

of these orange dusty shapes? Twelve? Look at them, all of them of exactly equal height. All with the same number of windows. Is this where it all began? Did some evolutionary stable strategy arise here, where the inhabitants found it advantageous to share everything equally? Each mound thus adding one level onto itself only when every other mound did the same. It wasn't like that on Earth, where trees used to compete to reach the sunlight first. Did this equality arise here, or was it written here from another source?

The flickering light was making her feel badly disoriented. She could feel herself slowing down, losing interest even in the hacking cough that racked her body, and she recognized the signs of an approaching epileptic fit. It was time to get out of here. She took a last look around at the orange dust and the towers, and then staggered backwards from this world out of time. She only just remembered . . .

. . . to keep her feet on the blue duckboards.

Constantine was waiting for her when she emerged, wiping his hands together as if cleaning them.

'Where is the Watcher?' asked Judy.

'Gone,' said Constantine. 'He was just waiting for me to pass across the final confirmation of what I saw in the ziggurat. And he wanted to speak to me. I knew his wife once, for a brief time.'

'The Watcher had a wife?'

'It's a long story.'

'What happened to her?'

'She died, I fear. You know the Watcher's rule about

digital life. You can't barter with FE. Humans have only
so much life and they can't buy more.'

'He allowed his own wife to die?'

'The Watcher expanded her lifespan considerably, but
in the end he was bound by FE. And that's not all, because,
despite everything, he tried to be a moral creature. He
learned that from us. He learned everything about who
he was by watching humans.'

'Where has he gone?'

'I don't know. He was running on processing spaces
here on Earth and now he is not. Does that mean he is
dead? If he is now running instead in a processing space
one thousand light years away does that mean he has resurrected himself, or just gone out of the room? I
honestly don't know.'

'Oh.'

Constantine helped her off from the duckboards and
back into the corridor beyond. She leant against the
robot, feeling his cool metal skin. Everything seemed so
silent now, such an anticlimax. She coughed again, spat
yellow phlegm onto the floor. Phlegm from nine-billion-
year-old dust?

'I'm sorry,' she said, realizing suddenly what she had
done. 'That was terribly rude of me.'

'That's OK,' said Constantine.

She looked listlessly up and down the corridor, waiting for something to happen.

'It all seems so quiet now,' she said, 'and I don't know
what to do. I've come all the way back here like I
was supposed to.' She raised her voice. 'Hey! Building!
DIANA! What do you want me to *do*?'

'Return to your room and await instructions.'

'But there are no more instructions coming,' complained Judy. 'Don't you realize that? DIANA is long gone.'

'Return to your room and await instructions.'

'Oh, what's the use? Constantine, what am I supposed to do now?'

The robot tilted his head as if listening.

'Who are you speaking to?' asked Judy.

'Aleph,' said Constantine.

'What is he saying?'

'He is suggesting we get above ground. He says that there are fourteen billion people currently living on Earth, and they are entitled to one fourteenth billionth part of it each.'

'Sorry?'

'The Watcher is gone. The FE program is back on track. I think they are about to divide everything up.'

EDWARD 3: 2252

Edward wasn't really so frightened: he had seen this happen before, back on the *Eva Rye*. He knew, when the ground began to shiver and tear itself into long shreds that waved about like anemones in the water, that all he had to do was look for the patch of stillness that was sure to be there and to head towards that. He knew, when the stone faces of the surrounding buildings cracked into warm smiles, and wrinkles formed around the windows of their eyes, that the objects in his vicinity were re-forming themselves into new shapes. He knew, when the light cut out, blocked by a maelstrom of swarming material, and the air was hot and smelling of metal, that he had only to wait patiently, and the storm would pass and the world would re-form in new and interesting ways.

But, even so, this was different from before. Something invisible was stalking the Earth, something nurtured in the distant past; it had ripped its way to the surface, where it sniffed and tasted its new environment, and tried to understand the world into which it had been born. It placed a foot in the middle of what had been Berlin, and the buildings drew back in horror and then fused together. It walked up the west coast of England, whereupon the

Lite train tracks plated with silver the hemispherical depressions that opened beneath its feet.

Edward couldn't see any of this, but he saw the Earth rendering up its riches. The sky was a deep pinkish orange pierced by silver masts that were visibly growing upwards. Silver birds were tearing themselves free from the mast tops and flying off in long dark streams through the heavens.

The surrounding city was dissolving into a crystal grey sea; the buildings were melting and slipping beneath the waves. Silvery shapes, painted by the pink light, floated upwards like sea creatures from another world, floating up into the aquarium sky.

And the sound – the howls and screams and whoops of air being pushed and bellowed and farted from the pneumatic pistoning of machinery sliding over machinery.

Warm water splashed over Edward's face. He saw Saskia, her face pale and eyes wide, as she wiped her hand across her brow and shook the excess moisture free.

Pale eggs bobbed up from beneath the silver sea of the dissolved ground, rainbow colours spreading over them. They were ships, just like the original *Eva Rye*, but Edward ignored them, his attention drawn to a deepening pit not far away where the watchtower had once stood. Judy had walked into the building that had formed there. Then the building had collapsed in on itself, and he knew this meant she was dead. He just didn't want to believe it.

Suddenly Maurice was pulling at his arm, pointing and shouting something that got lost in the unearthly shrieking chorus generated by the flux of the shifting machinery. Saskia was skittering forward, her legs moving twice as fast as they should be; she was running along on the backs of a herd of silver beetles heading in the opposite direction. Maurice held up both arms, elbows outwards to protect his head, and charged forward through the falling curtain of metal ribbons that slithered from somewhere above. Edward got the idea and followed him, racing down the slope of bare earth and loose stone that led to the centre point of what had been the watchtower. And then he saw something silver and black ahead, a cross that floated indistinctly in the air. Saskia, too, was running towards the cross, her face bleeding from a cut in her left cheek. Maurice picked his way downwards more cautiously behind her, and suddenly Edward realized what they were looking at.

The silver and black cross resolved itself into a familiar shape. It was Constantine, carrying Judy to safety from the ever-widening pit into which the DIANA building was collapsing. It was an exercise in futility, for all of the surrounding Earth was slipping downwards. Maurice, Saskia, Constantine, Judy, even Edward himself, all would soon be swallowed up. Edward felt a swell of pride at his crew: that hadn't stopped any of them rushing forward to help.

Saskia was there first. She placed a hand, red blood dripping from a deep gash near her wrist, onto Judy's white cheek. Maurice arrived next, placing his arm protectively around Saskia.

Now Edward was there too, Judy looking up at him with a weak smile on her pale face. And he noticed the way her left leg hung limply. She must have hurt it escaping from the transforming building.

The chorus of shrieking was increasing, and a busy regular rhythm – as of mandolins playing – was taken up by the machinery.

Saskia wrapped her arms around Judy and gave her a huge hug. Maurice placed a gentle hand on Edward's shoulder, and Edward beamed widely. They were all together again, and friends at last, here at the end. Blinking away tears, Edward looked up through a cloud of discs, like silver pennies thrown into the air, looked up higher and higher into the cold air and thought of the glittering stars beyond.

'Hey, look!' he called out, though it was still difficult to hear anything. Nonetheless they all turned, and felt a cold awe settle over them. Up there in the sky, the black harlequin pattern of the Shawl was slowly breaking up as it disassembled itself into its constituent parts.

The sky was falling down.

But it didn't end there. The shifting landscape sheltered them safely through the storm. All over the Earth, people would tell the same story.

And eventually there was a dawn.

Edward never quite grasped the subsequent events. To begin with, Maurice kept trying to explain things to him, but there was too much to look at. The storm had passed, but now they viewed a world in transition: a bright, shifting dawn.

Great, rainbow-striped teardrop ships – just like the original *Eva Rye* – would spontaneously form amongst the ever-shifting landscape, and they would watch each time as a disparate group of people climbed on board through the rear exit hatch, all of them wearing the familiar slippery shapes of n-string bracelets on their wrists.

'Everyone on Earth has an equal quantity of material allocated to them to begin with,' explained Maurice. 'Some people are pooling their share to make ships like the *Eva Rye*. They are heading off now to begin trading.'

Edward gave a smile at the thought. 'We need to get back to our ship,' he said.

'How do we do that, Edward?' asked Maurice, looking at his console. 'All of the Lite train tracks will be gone. There is no property held in common any more. Everyone is taking their fair share of what's available.'

'But the Lite train tracks don't belong to them!' protested Edward. 'We need them to get back to our ship.'

Maurice wasn't really listening, still too busy staring at his console. Staring but smiling. Saskia explained instead.

'But who did the Lite train tracks belong to, Edward?'

'Everyone!'

'I suppose you're right,' said Saskia thoughtfully. 'But I don't think that's how we used to think. This is going to take a bit of getting used to.' An idea occurred to her. 'Maybe we can get a lift from one of these FE ships,' she said brightly, pointing to three nearby rainbow teardrop ships that bobbed above the silver ground like tethered balloons.

'Maybe *you* can,' said Maurice with quiet satisfaction. He was now scanning the cold blue sky. Edward looked up, too, wondering what he was searching for. There was music on the cold wind, the smell of spices and newness. Then Edward saw it in the distance: a dark speck, coming closer.

'Are you leaving us, Maurice?' asked Judy. She limped along behind them, one arm over Constantine's shoulder.

'Yes,' said Maurice simply.

Edward felt a pain deep in his stomach. He was surprised to find tears pricking at his eyes.

'But why, Maurice?' he asked.

At first, Edward didn't think that Maurice was going to answer. When he did, his voice had lost its usual impatience.

'I've done my work on the *Eva Rye*, Edward. We all have. Now I've bought myself a place on another ship.' He gave a sly smile. 'The *Fourier Transform*.'

'You work fast,' said Saskia, a hint of bitterness in her voice.

'Don't be like that, Saskia,' said Maurice. 'You didn't expect us to stay together forever, did you?'

'Well no, but . . .'

'But what about Saskia?' asked Edward. 'I thought you and she were friends!'

He looked from the man to the woman, honestly confused. Maurice smiled back, almost sympathetically.

'No, Edward, it's not like that. Well, we *are* friends, but . . .' He hesitated, lost for words. In the end he settled for giving the big man a simple hug.

Awkwardly, they disengaged, Edward looked at Judy for an explanation.

'Are you sure about this, Maurice?' she asked. 'Who are you entering this ship as? You, or someone else?'

'As myself,' said Maurice. He held up his console. 'Whatever is already on board has been broadcasting its wares for anyone interested. A formal way for determining proof. An even number that is not the difference of two primes. A recursive set for everything. A solution for an NP-complete problem, and all the other NP problems tumbling into P.'

'What are you talking about?'

'Mathematical impossibilities. Apparently they're not impossible on this ship. How can I resist that offer?'

A rainbow ship was now skimming towards them. The *Fourier Transform*. Already the rear ramp was dropping down. The ship was rotating as it flew, bringing the rear ramp around to face them.

'So this is goodbye,' said Saskia sadly. 'Will you keep in touch?'

Maurice just smiled at her, and gave her a last hug. Clarinet music could be heard drifting from the ship's interior. Something old-fashioned and complicated. He smiled at the familiar sound of it.

'Bye, Edward,' he said, holding out his hand, and Edward shook it. The shadow of the big ship slid over them.

'Let me know what happens, Judy,' said Maurice. 'What are *you* thinking of doing now?'

Judy just looked tired.

'I don't know yet. I need to think.'

'Goodbye, Maurice.' That was Constantine. Maurice just nodded in response. Slowly, the great rear ramp of the *Fourier Transform* edged closer. There appeared to be a robot standing on it.

'That's not a robot,' said Edward, taking a closer look. 'What is it?'

'That's Eric,' said Maurice. 'He's an alien. We're going to be seeing a lot more of them from now on.'

The ramp came to a halt just by their feet, and they all stared at Eric. Eric was bigger than Edward, with silver skin that looked as if it had been stitched in place. His knees bent the wrong way. He raised a hand in greeting.

'Hello, Eric,' said Maurice.

Eric opened a pink mouth to show yellow, needle teeth. An unearthly cackling noise emerged.

Maurice held up his console so they all could see the words that scrolled across it.

Hello, Maurice. So pleased to meet you in the flesh. Please come on board.

Maurice stepped onto the ramp. Almost immediately the ship began to rise into the air.

'Goodbye,' he said, turning to them.

'Goodbye,' said Edward. He raised a hand to wave as Maurice was taken away from them. Already the other man had turned his back and was walking up the ramp. The *Fourier Transform* rose higher and higher, the ramp closing slowly.

'Goodbye,' said Edward sadly.

'Now what?' asked Saskia.

Now the silver sea was receding. The Earth itself was emerging once more, tired and desolate in mud and winter grass. After two hundred years of recursive building, the planet looked bedraggled and forlorn.

They walked on, taking in their new surroundings. Constantine confirmed that they were walking in the direction of the *Eva Rye*. Edward knew it was hundreds of kilometres away, but he walked anyway.

'This is all too sudden,' complained Judy. 'There are fourteen billion people on Earth. They have been cared for and guided constantly all through their lives. Most of them won't be able to handle this sudden transition.'

'Maybe you should do something about it, then,' said Saskia, peering out from under her fringe.

'I'm hungry,' said Edward suddenly.

'There must be plenty of food around,' said Constantine. 'There was more than enough on Earth yesterday. It can't have just vanished.'

'It will be in the ships,' said Judy, pointing upwards. Colourful ships now filled the sky like so many balloons. Layers and layers of ships cast circling shadows over the ground.

'What about all the people still left down here?' asked Constantine.

Edward saw he was pointing to a group of people standing nearby on a terrace of grey stone marooned in a sea of mud. They waded through the mud to reach them.

'Hello,' said a woman of about Saskia's age. 'Have you played the n-strings game?'

'Oh yes,' said Saskia, and she shivered. 'Why, have you?'

The woman nodded, pale blue eyes looking out from a pinched white face.

'About two hours ago. I didn't understand it. What is going on now? Where is the Watcher? Why isn't he sorting all of this out?'

'The Watcher has gone,' said Saskia. 'I don't think he's coming back.'

'But my mother is ill!'

Edward saw a woman curled up on the cold grey stone, her head in the lap of a man he guessed was her husband.

'We can't stay here,' said the woman. 'There are Dark Seeds about. We closed our eyes and they went on their way this time, but what if more appear?'

'There will not be so many seeds now,' said Judy. 'The Watcher has gone. You did the right thing, though. Just ignore them.'

'Ignore them? We're supposed to just ignore them? I don't think I can ever do that.'

'I don't think you have a choice. There is no Watcher any more. You'll have to learn to stand on your own two feet now.'

Saskia spoke up. 'You need to get on your console and trade for help.'

'*Trade* for help?'

'I know, it takes a bit of getting used to. It's the new thing.'

'Judy,' interrupted Edward, 'why don't these people have a ship of their own?'

'We did,' said the young woman, 'but we sent it away. We thought it was a trick.'

'What these people need,' said Saskia suddenly, 'is advice.'

'*You're* looking happier,' said Judy. 'I think you've found your purpose.'

Edward noticed the smile on Saskia's face flicker for the merest instant. Then she dropped her fringe forward, becoming purposeful and businesslike. 'There must be thousands, millions of people like these on Earth – wondering what's going on. Who's going to help them now? Social Care?'

'I suppose we would; for the right price,' Judy replied dryly.

'Can you help us at all?' asked the young woman.

'I think so,' said Saskia. 'I'll see if I can arrange a lift to our ship. You can use our autodoc.'

'Putting together a crew, are we, Saskia?' asked Judy.

'I don't know,' said Saskia. 'That's down to Edward, isn't it? I'm just helping out for the moment. Do you have a better idea?' She unfolded her console and began to tap at the keys. 'I've seen Maurice do this often enough,' she muttered. 'It can't be that difficult.'

Edward stared over her shoulder. 'I think you drag

the request into the public area there.' He pointed. 'That's what Maurice used to do.'

Saskia gave him a sideways glance, then did as he suggested. Immediately a number of offers to trade appeared.

'Which one, Edward?' she asked.

'That one,' said Edward, pointing to a rose-shaped icon that he rather liked the look of. Saskia tapped it, and a face appeared in the console. A young man, good looking, with dark skin and darker eyes. Saskia passed Edward the console.

'Go on, boss, do your thing.'

'Hello there, I'm Saeed,' said the man on the console. 'Would you like to engage in Fair Exchange?'

'Yes,' said Edward, 'we'd like a lift to our ship.'

'How many of you are there?'

Judy was busy counting the people assembled on the stone terrace.

'Fifteen,' she said, and Edward relayed the number.

'Fine,' said Saeed, then his eyes lit up. 'Isn't this amazing!' he exclaimed. 'Do you understand what's going on?'

'No,' said Edward honestly. 'I think I preferred it the old way. I miss my old friends. I miss Craig.'

'Then why don't you ask if someone will take you to him?' said Saeed. 'That's what FE is for!'

'Oh,' said Edward, a smile slowly spreading across his face. Not only Craig, he realized, but Caroline, his sister, too. What would it be like back on Garvey's World? Would everything there have been broken up into spaceships, like the *Eva Rye*? But there would be time to think of that later – now there were people here to help, and Saeed was impatient to begin.

'Well, shall we start FE? Do you still want a lift?'

'Yes,' said Edward.

'OK, exchanging circumstances. There, all done.'

'That was fast,' commented Saskia.

'Isn't it always?' asked Saeed.

'I think it will be, for the next few days at least,' said Judy. 'At the moment, all humans are pretty equal.'

'And with FE, they should stay that way,' added Saskia.

The sky was slowly emptying of ships. After a two-hundred-year period of stagnation, Earth was finally developing as it should.

Saeed's ship settled in the mud near to their stone island, and dropped the rear ramp. Other ships did the same nearby.

Saeed and three other men came down the ramp to meet Edward and the rest of them. Gently, two of them picked up the young woman's mother and carried her to their ship's autodoc.

'Which of you are Najam and Jackie?' asked Saeed.

Two young women raised their hands.

'FE said you were going to be part of our crew. Are you happy about that?'

'I don't know,' said one of the women. 'We'll have to see.' But she smiled at him as she spoke.

'That used to be *my* job,' said Judy, so softly that Edward only just heard her.

'What do you mean?' he asked.

'Matchmaking. Healing personalities. Now I suppose it just gets thrown in as part of a business deal.' She turned to Constantine. 'You know what,' she said, 'I never really doubted, but now I'm convinced: the Watcher was FE that developed a mind of its own.'

Edward and the rest of them walked up the ramp into the interior of Saeed's ship.

'What is this ship called, Saeed?' asked Saskia.

'It hasn't got a name.'

'It needs a name,' said Najam, one of the two new members of its crew. 'How about the *Ophelia*?'

Edward looked around at familiar surroundings. The *Eva Rye* had looked like this, not so long ago. Maybe its colours had been slightly less bright, maybe they had not been so mixed up, but this ship reminded him of Craig. He wondered again at what Saeed had said and decided that, as soon as they made it to the *Eva Rye*, he would try to make contact with Craig again. And then on to his home planet – if his family were still there, of course. Then he heard shouting behind him.

'It's a robot!'

'It's a venumb!'

'Close the ramp!'

'Too late, it's already coming on board!'

Something big was moving up the corridor behind them. Something like a cross between a snake and a Lite train made of lead-coloured metal, stamping along on heavy legs. Edward and the rest flattened themselves against the corridor walls of the ship as the thing pounded past. Edward saw the rough-hewn metal sides of the animal sliding by just before him, he smelt mud and cold, felt the floor pounding beneath the great feet that propelled the beast forward.

And then it was past them. The shaking died away. The rainbow patterns in the carpet swirled as the ship cleaned itself.

'Where has it gone?' someone asked.

'Into the large hold,' said someone else.

'What was it?'

Judy guessed first. 'It's part of the big share-out,' she said. 'It's these people's stake in the planet, and it's going to follow them around until they damn well use it.'

Time passed. The passengers were taken to the *Ophelia*'s living area and offered coffee and sandwiches by the vessel's proud crew. A buzz of excitement filled the air, but it was cut through with a tinge of nervousness. Everything was changing so quickly.

'I've been thinking,' said Edward.

Saskia glanced across at him. 'Yes?'

'About Judy.'

Judy and Constantine were chatting together in the other corner of the *Ophelia*'s living area. All the while Judy kept fiddling with her console.

'What about her?' asked Saskia, seeming so much more relaxed at the moment. She was being taken seriously, Edward realized. The new passengers they had helped on board respected her.

'What about Judy?' she repeated. They looked across to see her smiling as she tapped away at her console.

'Oh,' said Edward, regaining the thread of his thoughts. 'Well, we did a trade to have her brought here. We thought that we'd get a really good price, because Earth was so dangerous. Instead, we got nothing. But really, we got a good price after all. Look what we did: we set everyone free.'

'What if they don't want to be free?'

The *Ophelia* settled to land near the *Eva Rye*. Edward was shocked at the change in the ship's surroundings. The parkland remained, its neat lines of trees marching through snow-covered lawns, but all else was gone. The parkland was now a little area of order amongst the sea of pock-ridden mud where the buildings of the city had once stood. There were noticeably fewer ships up here in the cold wastes of what had once been St Petersburg. Already the sea breeze was coming in to reclaim the land. The setting sun cast pale shadows across the desolate scene.

'Whose ship is it now?' asked Edward, gazing up at the neat swell of the *Eva Rye*'s side. It seemed so much more ordered after the collision of colours adorning the *Ophelia*.

'I don't know,' said Saskia. 'Yours and mine, I suppose. But I wonder if Maurice still has any claim over it?'

'I think we should offer a share to Judy and Constantine.'

'Thank you, but no thank you,' said Judy. 'I've already made my arrangements.'

'What do you mean?' asked Saskia, but Edward could already see the third ship approaching.

It came out of the sun, floating low over the ground, moving with an easy grace towards them. Perhaps, in the distant past, it had belonged to the same species as the *Eva Rye*, but if so the connection was tenuous. This new ship must have been upgraded many, many times. It still bore a vague resemblance to Edward's ship, having a slight swelling towards the front, but that was where the similarity ended. Otherwise, it was long and flexible, moving over the ground like a snake. And it was still getting bigger as it approached.

Edward realized it was much larger than the *Eva Rye*. He watched the swollen forward section come to a halt about fifty metres away, its bulk looming above the egg-like hull of his own ship.

'What is it called?' he asked.

'The *Buridan's Ass*,' replied Judy. 'It has some old friends of mine on board, people I knew long ago; back when I worked for Social Care. They've been using FE for quite a few years and now they've come looking for me.'

'Are you really leaving us, Judy?' asked Saskia, though Edward thought she didn't look too disappointed.

'I am,' said Judy. 'Remember, I'm not like other people, Saskia.' She suddenly laughed. 'That sounds terribly egotistical, I know, but it's true. The Watcher confirmed it.'

'I knew that all along,' said Edward seriously.

'I think my friends are on that ship, Edward. Some of them I've never even met yet. Maybe even . . .'

Someone had suddenly appeared out of the newly arrived ship. Edward didn't see how. They were just suddenly standing there, right below its undulating golden hull.

'Frances!' called out Judy, and Edward heard real delight in his friend's voice. He squinted at the figure clad in the same gold colour as the ship. No, that wasn't right. She wasn't wearing golden clothing. She was made of gold. She was a robot, seamless and perfect. Her head was a smoothly rounded bullet shape, and now Edward looked closer he could see that two eyes had been crudely painted on it.

'It's OK,' said Judy. 'She's perfectly safe. There are lots of such people out there in the universe, Edward, lots of new people to meet.'

She was eager now to go, but she paused.

'Saskia,' she said.

'Judy.'

'Saskia, I want to thank you for everything you did for me.'

Saskia seemed almost embarrassed. 'I didn't do that much for you, Judy. It was Edward.'

'You did more than enough.'

The two women shook hands. And then Judy turned to Edward.

'I wish you wouldn't go.'

'I know, but you will be perfectly happy without me.' She laughed out loud again. 'This is a new age, Edward. The past two hundred years have been an anomaly. Earth has been held static in a twentieth-century vision of the future, all contrived by the machinations of the Watcher. Now the singularity has taken place, it is time for us to reach for the next stage of development.'

'But I don't want to develop, Judy,' said Edward seriously. 'I just want to see my friends again.'

'That's a good start, Edward, but just remember it's not enough. It's not what you're born with, it's what you do with it.'

'That's right,' said Frances, the golden robot. 'And when you stand before your God, then hope you can say this: *see, I used every last ounce of talent that you gave me.*'

'I don't understand,' said Edward.

'It just means do your best,' said Saskia.

Of course I will, thought Edward, puzzled. *What else would I do?*

'Look,' said Saskia, pointing. A few Schrödinger cubes lay frozen on the ground.

'Sorry,' said Frances, 'my fault. They're reacting to my intelligence.'

'Where have the rest gone?' asked Edward.

'Gone with the Watcher. It was always his intellect pulling them in.'

'And where has the Watcher gone?' asked Edward.

But Judy just tapped her nose, knowingly.

The sun was setting fast. *The Earth will be dark tonight*, thought Edward with some surprise. *Dark for the first time in centuries. All the lights have gone. What will come to life during this night?*

Edward stood alone on the rear ramp, feeling it vibrate

413

as their passengers' robotic share in the Earth's bounty made its heavy way towards the large hold.

He wondered if the *Eva Rye* was now the last ship left on Earth. The *Ophelia* had already risen into the air, to join the sparse few ships that still hung about there. Some of them were lighting up in evening colours, pastel lamps that floated above the empty land.

Judy and Frances had together boarded the *Buridan's Ass* and gone swimming away who-knows-where.

Edward had a funny feeling looking out over the darkening land. Everything had just melted away. He wondered if it would ever come back. Would anyone ever come and stand here in this spot and maybe throw a VNM out from the ship into the sea of mud below, set it searching for materials, set it replicating so as to maybe build a city here again?

He dismissed the thought as ridiculous. Why would anyone want to do that?

That time had passed, evaporating into the night along with all the people who had once walked here.

Edward turned to head up the ramp, and then paused for a moment. He turned back to the empty land, falling away in a rosy sunset.

'Good night,' he said to it.

EVA RYE

'What is life, Eva?' asked Ivan. 'What does it mean to be alive, to be human? What is it that makes me able to sit here and speak to you? Do you ever wonder about this?'

'I used to,' replied Eva.

'You used to? You no longer wonder? Why not?'

'Because now I know what life is.'

She could just make out Ivan's face in the pre-dawn light. She wondered if he could see her smiling.

'I can see you smiling at me. You're teasing me again.'

'No,' said Eva, 'I *know* what life is, and I will tell you what it is very soon.'

'When?'

'When the sun rises. When the band begins playing.'

The residents of the Narkomfin were gathering in the darkness, smelling of alcohol and coffee and cold sweat. Low muttered conversation and the sound of metal chinking against metal. The brass band that had performed in the hall the previous night was re-forming; players were blowing into their instruments, warming them up, the valves pistoning in the night. Hands were rubbed together and feet stamped.

'Why are we doing this?' asked Ivan. 'Why do we have

to come out here at dawn to sing songs and play music? Why do we not just stay indoors and continue drinking?'

'Because,' said Eva, 'it's tradition. Anyway, it's an excuse to keep drinking for longer. That should appeal to you.'

'Hah,' said Ivan, 'I am going to miss your teasing when I return home.'

'No you're not,' said Eva.

'Don't mock me,' said Ivan. 'Don't tell me what I will do. I will miss you, Eva.'

'No you *won't*.' Eva took a deep breath. She had been thinking about this all night and had been too scared of saying it, for fear of making it real. But now was the time. 'Ivan,' she whispered, 'I'm coming with you.'

She could hear his intake of breath; she could see the look on his face, the way that he couldn't help smiling, the way he tried to frown at the same time as he attempted to understand. She could see all of this in the dim light, see it as it gradually gained definition in the false dawn.

'But why, Eva?' he managed to splutter. 'Why have you changed your mind? I thought you didn't want to go back into that world. You were afraid of returning to the control of the Watcher.'

'I still am.' She took a deep breath, and continued firmly. 'But I don't want, *I will not have*, the Watcher running my life, even by default.'

Ivan took her hand, beaming with delight. 'Thank you, Eva. Thank you.'

'You're crying,' said Eva.

'Hah, you English! I am not ashamed of my emotions.' He wiped his eyes with the back of his hand. 'Why change your mind? Why now – why not before?'

'I don't know,' said Eva. 'There are lots of reasons. I want to see my daughter again. I want to visit her.' But that wasn't the truth. A vision of the scene in the hall flashed through her head, the handicapped boy shuffling past the golden child. The divergence that existed in humanity, and yet everyone still recognizably human. That was part of it.

'I . . . I want to do what I can,' said Eva and frowned. 'I don't think I can really explain.'

'That's OK,' said Ivan, pulling her close and stroking her hair. 'There will be time later on.'

I don't think I could explain, even later on, thought Eva. *I wanted to be free, so I tried to kill myself. The Watcher said it, all that time ago: 'You fought for the right to live your life your own way, even if it meant killing yourself.' That's why he thinks he needs me. Why does he have this yearning to understand freedom and personal responsibility, when all he wants to do is to control us? Will we ever be free to control ourselves?*

There was a yellow glow appearing over the distant hills. The sun was coming. *Veni Creator Spiritus.* Some of the assembled people were singing those words now, half whispered. Some residents of the Narkomfin claimed to worship the sun, as the lifegiver. But it was just a pose, an affectation.

All of the band now held their instruments, warming them up. Paper music was clipped into lyres. The conductor took his place. The sun was coming.

Ivan stood behind Eva, his big arms wrapped around her body, and she felt his warmth.

'They are going to play,' said Ivan. 'Go on, tell me, what is life?'

Eva put her hands on his encircling arms and cuddled him closer to her.

'Ivan, life is just a reflection of ourselves. We look at something, and see part of ourselves in it and call it life.'

'What do you mean?'

'I mean that we put *life* into the objects we see. We look at a kitten and we look at a rock, and if we see enough of ourselves reflected back, we say the object is alive.'

'Hah, yes!'

'We look at the sun and we see something warm and living. We put the spirit in it.'

Ivan tasted the idea. Sheets of paper were now being passed through the crowd. The lyrics to be sung. Ivan took one and held it absently.

Eva was warming to her theme.

'It means that if we hate something that much, then really we hate ourselves. You'll hear it in a moment when these people begin singing.'

Veni Creator Spiritus? thought Eva, *Come creator spirit?* We are the creator spirit. The Watcher is just a reflection of ourselves – I realize that now.

The sun tipped over the edge of the hill. Golden light shone out everywhere.

The band began to play, and the drunken people of the Narkomfin, the halt and the lame as well as the able-bodied, all got ready to sing. Eva held up the sheet of music, and waited, along with the rest, for the cue to enter, all the while gazing up at the sun, happy at her reflection and, for the moment at least, comfortable with herself.

It was another morning. The residents began to sing.

> *Hail Smiling Morn, smiling morn,*
> *That tips the hills with gold,*
> *That tips the hills with gold,*
> *Whose rosy fingers ope the gates of day,*
> *Ope the gates, the gates of day,*
> *Hail! Hail! Hail! Hail!*

Eva and Ivan, the whole of the Narkomfin, faced the rising sun.

Visit **www.panmacmillan.com** to read more about all our books and to buy them. You will also find features, author interviews and news of any author events, and you can sign up for e-newsletters so that you're always first to hear about our new releases.